ROYAL COURT

What Reviewers Say About Jenny Frame's Work

Unexpected

"[Jenny Frame] has this beautiful way of writing a phenomenally hot scene while incorporating the love and tenderness between the couple."—*Les Rêveur*

"If you enjoy contemporary romances, Unexpected is a great choice. The character work is excellent, the plotting and pacing are well done, and it's a just a sweet, warm read. …Definitely pick this book up when you're looking for your next comfort read, because it's sure to put a smile on your face by the time you get to that happy ending."—*Curve*

Royal Rebel

"Frame's stories are easy to follow and really engaging. She stands head and shoulders above a number of the romance authors and it's easy to see why she is quickly making a name for herself in lesfic romance."—*The Lesbian Review*

Courting the Countess

"I loved loved loved this book. I didn't expect to get so involved in the story but I couldn't help but fall in love with Annie and Harry. …The love scenes were beautifully written and very sexy. I found the whole book romantic and ultimately joyful and I had a lump in my throat on more than one occasion. A wonderful book that certainly stirred my emotions…"—*KittyKat Book Reviews*

"*Courting The Countess* has an historical feel in a present day world, a thought provoking tale filled with raw emotions throughout. [Frame] has a magical way of pulling you in, making you feel every emotion her characters experience."—*Lunar Rainbow Reviewz*

"I didn't want to put the book down and I didn't. Harry and Annie are two amazingly written characters that bring life to the pages as they find love and adventures in Harry's home. This is a great read, and you will enjoy it immensely if you give it a try!"—*Fantastic Book Reviews*

A Royal Romance

"*A Royal Romance* was a guilty pleasure read for me. It was just fun to see the relationship develop between George and Bea, to see George's life as queen and Bea's as a commoner. It was also refreshing to see that both of their families were encouraging, even when Bea doubted that things could work between them because of their class differences. …*A Royal Romance* left me wanting a sequel, and romances don't usually do that to me."—*Leeanna.ME Mostly a Book Blog*

Charming the Vicar

"The sex scenes were some of the sexiest, most intimate and quite frankly, sensual I have read in a while. Jenny Frame had me hooked and I re-read a few scenes because I felt like I needed to experience the intense intimacy between Finn and Bridget again. The devotion they showed to one another during these sex scenes but also in the intimate moments was gripping and for lack of a better word, carnal."—*Les Rêveur*

The sexual chemistry between [Finn and Bridge] is unbelievably hot. It is sexy, lustful and with more than a hint of kink. Bridge has an overpowering effect on Finn as her long-hidden sexuality comes to the fore. The scenes between them are highly erotic—and not just the sex scenes. The tension is ramped up so well that I felt the characters would explode if they did not get relief! …An excellent book set in the most wonderful village—a place I hope to return to very soon!"
—*Kitty Kat's Book Review Blog*

Heart of the Pack

"A really well written love story that incidentally involves changers as well as humans."—*Inked Rainbow Reads*

Hunger for You

"[Byron and Amelia] are guaranteed to get the reader all hot and bothered. Jenny Frame writes brilliant love scenes in all of her books and makes me believe the characters crave each other."—*Kitty Kat's Book Review Blog*

"I loved this book. Paranormal stuff like vampires and werewolves are my go-to sins. This book had literally everything I needed: chemistry between the leads, hot love scenes (phew), drama, angst, romance (oh my, the romance) and strong supporting characters."
—*The Reading Doc*

Visit us at www.boldstrokesbooks.com

By the Author

The Royal Romance Stories

A Royal Romance

Royal Rebel

Royal Court

Heart Of The Pack

Courting The Countess

Dapper

Unexpected

Charming The Vicar

Hunger For you

Soul Of The Pack

ROYAL COURT

by

Jenny Frame

2019

ROYAL COURT

ISBN 13: 978-1-63555-290-4

This Trade Paperback Original Is Published By
Bold Strokes Books, Inc.
P.O. Box 249
Valley Falls, NY 12185

First Edition: January 2019

Credits
Editor: Ruth Sternglantz
Production Design: Susan Ramundo
Cover Design By Sheri (hindsightgraphics@gmail.com)

Acknowledgments

Thanks to Rad, Sandy, and all the BSB team for all their tireless work in getting our books out there. Huge thanks to Ruth Sternglantz for her hard work in helping me make my book the best it can be.

As always, thanks to my family for their continuing support and encouragement.

To the two loves of my life, Lou and Barney—you make life a loving, exciting adventure. Thank you for loving me.

xx

Dedication

To Robyn and Amy—with love and kisses.
The two best nieces an aunty could have.

xx

PROLOGUE

The rain bounced off the tarmac of the Royal Marines command parade ground. The clouds were dark grey, almost black, and matched the ache in Captain Quincy's heart and soul.

The parade sergeant barked out orders to the assembled marines and navy personnel, to salute the parade commander who was at a covered podium in front of them.

"Today we are here to honour a Royal Marine who exemplifies all that we hold dear. Ingenuity, determination, loyalty, and courage."

The rain dripped off Quincy's peaked cap, down her face, and felt like the tears she could not shed herself. She rigidly kept to attention, the commander's words not even penetrating her mind. She shot a quick look to her mother, Vice Admiral Ophelia Quincy, seated beside the podium. Ophelia sat as rigidly as Quincy stood, her eyes staring impassively forward.

Quincy prayed that this would be over quickly so she could get back to her quarters. She never liked the limelight, and this ceremony for her was the last thing she wanted.

The commander was awarding her the Victoria Cross, the country's highest award for bravery in combat. Normally it would be given to the recipient by the Queen in a lavish ceremony at Buckingham Palace, but due to the secret nature of her unit's operation, it was to be kept in-house.

A roll of thunder clapped and Quincy gasped in fear. She could hear the screams of her men, the smell of smoke and burning flesh, and then an intense burning heat all over her body.

Only the shouts of the parade sergeant broke Quincy from her memories. She tried to get ahold of her breathing. Now was not the time to feel. It was never the time to feel.

She was called forward, and her mother, the admiral, was given the honour of presenting her medal.

As Ophelia reached forward and pinned the medal to her uniform, she looked into her mother's eyes and saw no warmth there. The admiral, as she and other family members called her, was not the motherly type but had brought her up to the best of her abilities, as if she'd been training a new recruit on deck.

Quincy suspected the admiral was proud of her winning the Victoria Cross, though, because it somehow vindicated the training she had given Quincy growing up.

"Well done, Captain," the admiral said.

"Thank you, ma'am." Quincy saluted and returned to her position on the parade ground.

The ceremony over, all of her men and fellow officers came up to her, patted her on the back, and gave their congratulations—all except one man, Lieutenant Rodwell. He met her eyes and scowled at her with bitterness and anger.

Rodwell had been on the very mission for which she was being honoured, and the only one to get back home with not a scratch. When she looked at him, she saw the faces of the men that died, and the screaming pain of her friend and second in command, Jacob.

She watched him spit on the ground and walk back to the barracks. How she would handle seeing him every day, knowing what he did, she had no idea.

The officers and special guests retreated to a reception in the officers' mess. Everyone was in groups chatting, drinking tea, laughing, and joking, none of them knowing of the darkness that tormented Quincy. She took her tea and walked over to the window alone.

"Congratulations, Captain," said a voice from behind her. It was the admiral. "The family are very proud of you." She shook her hand.

"Thank you, ma'am. It's a great honour," Quincy replied flatly.

"And how are you recovering from your injuries?"

Quincy gulped hard and closed her eyes briefly. "Very well, ma'am."

The admiral leaned in to give her the barest of kisses on the cheek and whispered, "Never show them any hurt, any emotion. Keep control, Addie."

The admiral rarely used her first name, Adelaide. Her words only added to the crushing weight Quincy felt. The weight of her pain, her fear, her terror, her shame and guilt were screaming to get out.

Her mother had taught her from an early age that if she wanted men not to see her gender, then she must show no emotion. Emotions would define her and keep her from the sort of advancement her mother had achieved. *Never show your feelings. Feelings label you as weak, Addie.*

"Of course, ma'am. If you'll excuse me."

Quincy walked out of the reception and pulled off her new medal, then stuffed it in her pocket.

She headed to her room. All of the corridors and offices were quiet as everyone was at the reception, but as she walked down the corridor, she heard scuffling and shouts from one of the marines' rooms.

Quincy started to run when she heard a woman shouting. Her heart began to pound, and panic flooded her body. She could hear the screams of her men in her head, but she wasn't in a burning warehouse, taking out a munitions store. She was in Britain at her base.

She found the room where the shouts were coming from, burst in, and found Rodwell holding one of the younger female officers down on the bed. Her shirt was ripped open and her trousers pushed down around her hips. Quincy acted on pure instinct. She pulled Rodwell from the officer and restrained him, with his hands behind his back.

The young woman was crying and shaking, her clothes ripped. Quincy shouted to the young marine, "Go and get help. I've got him."

"Get off me, you fucking arsehole!" Rodwell shouted.

Quincy slammed him up against the wall, her bottled up anger and fear so near the surface. "You're going nowhere but a prison cell, Rodwell. You might have managed to talk your way out of your court martial when we got back from our mission, but not this. You wanted to feel powerful, did you? Attacking an innocent young recruit? You're a coward, Rodwell."

"And you're such a fucking hero, aren't you, Quincy? You're nothing. You've had your career handed to you on a plate, because you're a fucking Quincy."

Quincy turned him around and placed an arm across his throat. "I have worked for everything I've achieved in the marines."

She and Rodwell had graduated from officer school at the same time, but Quincy had risen up the ladder more quickly and Rodwell had gotten bitter as the years had gone on.

"I hate you, Quincy, and can't wait for the day someone smashes that fucking silver spoon out of your mouth."

Quincy said nothing. Her hands were starting to tremble. All she could hear were the screams of her men when she looked in Rodwell's eyes.

Rodwell must have seen the anger in her usually stoic expression because he said, "How's Jacob? I heard he was burned so bad that he should have been put down."

"Don't you ever speak about Jacob, you coward."

Rodwell grinned. "Must be hard for his wife, without a proper man in her life. When you go and visit her, tell her if she gets lonely, I'll gladly come around and fuck her."

Quincy saw red and felt a mist of rage descend. She pulled back and punched him repeatedly until he fell. Every ounce of fear, pain, and anger was released from her unrestrained.

She punched until she felt herself being pulled and restrained by the Royal Marine Police. Her breathing was heavy, and the mist started to clear. She had left Rodwell beaten and bloody, but as she was being dragged away, he grinned at her.

Captain Quincy looked at her dress uniform, hanging pressed in her suit carrier. When she zipped up the bag, her life in the marines would be over. She walked over to her wardrobe mirror and checked that her grey tie was still sitting smartly. She would have to get used to this new look of grey suit and tie.

The television on the wall caught her eye. She had left the news on as she got ready. Her friend Queen Georgina's new baby girl was to be christened today at the Royal Chapel in St. James's Palace. Quincy was so happy that George had found such love with Queen Beatrice and was now enjoying a family.

Quincy couldn't imagine living with such happiness or feeling that much love. *I don't feel.*

She walked over to her bed and sat to watch for a few minutes. Since Princess Edwina, the new heir to the throne, was born, the world and the media had gone wild. Quincy thought it was quite comforting to know a woman would be head of state for the next few generations.

"Computer, volume up four."

The cameras were trained on the front door of the chapel.

The Queen's car has now arrived, and we await the first look at six-month-old Princess Edwina Abigail Georgina. She will be wearing a christening gown that dates back to Queen Victoria, the commentator said.

The protection officers got out and opened the car door. Queen Georgina walked around to the other side, helped Queen Beatrice out, and then lifted Princess Edwina out of her car seat. There were cheers and shouts and the flash of cameras going off.

Quincy took note of all the protection officers and their positions. There were a lot more than usual as Queen Rozala of Denbourg and her consort were attending the family christening too.

Beatrice took Edwina from George, which allowed her to shake hands with the religious leaders gathered there.

The commentator continued: *As you can see there is a representative of every major religion here today, to take part in this solemn ceremony. This tradition was first introduced by Queen Georgina's great-grandfather, as a way to bring together all parts of the British community. The royal family are very keen to promote togetherness and discourage division.*

In the next cars are the Dowager Queen Adrianna, Queen Sophia, and Prince Theodore.

Quincy smiled as she watched Prince Theo help his mother and grandmother. He was a great personality, and so different from his sister, George. She always enjoyed his company when they played polo together.

Queen Adrianna and Queen Sophia cooed and fussed over Edwina while Theo embraced his sister.

In the next three cars are Princess Edwina's godparents—the Queen's cousin Queen Rozala of Denbourg and Crown Consort Lennox, followed by her cousins Lady Victoria and Lord Maximilian Buckingham, and Queen Beatrice's friends—

Quincy tuned out the television commentary. Her eyes were glued to Queen Rozala, as she exuberantly embraced George. Then George and Bea greeted her partner, Crown Consort Lennox, who came behind her.

The attack that had made Rozala queen of Denbourg had changed Quincy's life as well. She could still hear her commanding officer's voice saying, *Denbourg has been attacked. The King and Crown Prince have been assassinated by the criminal Thea Brandt's people. We are joining with Denbourg special forces and neutralizing her organization. You will be taking your unit to take out one of their weapons stores. Prepare your team.*

Quincy's heart began to thud, and she flinched as she heard the explosions, the shouts and screams.

She tried to take deep breaths, as she had taught herself, to try and regain control. If she was truthful with herself, it wasn't that she didn't feel, but that she couldn't allow herself to feel. If she did allow herself for one second, she would be lost.

"TV off."

The noises started to quieten, but she looked down at her hands and saw a tremor there. She stood quickly and went back to her bags.

Her phone rang and she said to the computer, "Answer call."

"Quincy?"

It was the admiral. She stood straighter and more stiffly. "Yes, ma'am."

"Are you packed and ready to go?"

Quincy looked over at the bags on her bed. It wasn't much to have accrued from a life in the marines.

"Yes, ma'am. I'm reporting to the close protection unit at Royal Military Police headquarters for training this afternoon," Quincy said.

"Good. How long will you be there?"

"Six months, ma'am. Queen Beatrice's protection officer is leaving for a new post then."

There was a short silence, then Admiral Quincy said, "I want you to listen to me carefully, Quincy. You have been given a lifeline after you besmirched your previously unblemished record. Do not let emotion rule you again—that is, if you wish to live up to the family name."

Despite having rescued a young woman, her attack on Lieutenant Rodwell had been excessive, to say the least. She should have been court-martialled and possibly discharged from the marines, but because she'd stopped a sexual assault and had recently won a medal for gallantry, and because of who her mother was, the command hierarchy were reluctant to discipline her out of the service.

But Quincy's operational effectiveness was questioned, despite managing to pass a psychological assessment. The solution came when, at George's request, her commanding officer asked if she would consider retraining as a close protection officer for Queen Beatrice.

Quincy's court martial was quietly shelved, and a new life awaited her, while Rodwell was given a prison sentence for his attack on the young woman and discharged from the marines.

"Yes, ma'am. I will never let this happen again." Quincy's walls were up and she wasn't letting anything through again.

"It's such a great honour to serve Her Majesty. Make me proud, Captain."

Quincy walked over to her uniform bag and zipped it up. "I will, Admiral."

CHAPTER ONE

Six months later

"If only I was Bea's size..." Holly Weaver picked up a box of shoes from the rows and rows in Queen Beatrice's walk-in wardrobe. If you loved fashion, then Bea's dressing room in Windsor Castle was like a designer shop that held all the major fashion brands. Bea was always happy to share clothes and jewellery with her friends, but Holly wished more than anything they shared a shoe size—she'd be in shoe heaven in this dressing room.

After a successful career as a hair and make-up person in the TV and movie industry, Holly had been delighted to be asked by Bea to join her staff as her Royal Dresser. In her new role, she got to travel the world with Queen Georgina and Queen Beatrice, shop for the most beautiful designer clothes, and take care of her close friend personally. Another member of their close circle of friends, Lali Ramesh, was Bea's private secretary and travelled everywhere with her. Greta, the final member, was a wife and full-time mum to her three kids, but Bea always made the effort to include her in as many of their social occasions as possible—like tonight.

Holly heard a car door and walked over to the window holding the shoes in her hand. She saw Greta and her partner Riley getting out of their car. Their group of friends had been close since university but had become even tighter since Bea married Queen Georgina.

When Bea's life changed overnight, the group pulled together to help and made sure she was supported, and her privacy protected, which made nights like tonight important. George and Bea were hosting a Friday night dinner and drinks evening. It kept Bea's friendships strong as they spent so much time travelling all over the world.

Since Bea had given birth to the new heir to the throne, Princess Edwina, the world had gone royal baby crazy. Bea's mum and dad now lived in a beautiful cottage on the Windsor estate, which meant Bea could see her parents whenever she wanted, and her mother could help her with the new princess. Between her friends and her parents, Bea had a bubble of support around her, a royal court, to make things just a bit easier. And Holly was proud to be part of that bubble.

Holly sighed. She wouldn't be going to tonight's get together. Of course she was invited, and not that she had anywhere else to go, but she was sick of feeling awkward as the only single one in the group.

She walked over to the dress hanging on the clothes rail and placed the shoes below. Not that any of her friends ever made her feel uncomfortable, in fact they badgered her to join them all the time, and she had, but sometimes it was just too much. She was the last single one. Bea had George, and Lali had been chased and finally caught by Captain Cameron, Queen Georgina's personal dresser and close protection officer.

Lali had been dating Cammy for a while, but at Christmas, Cammy proposed. Lali said yes and they were planning a late summer wedding. It was strange—Holly never felt any need or want to have a partner when Greta or Bea got married, but since Lali had gotten engaged, she had sensed something was missing in her life, and felt loneliness for the first time. Even when she was in a club full of people, she was alone.

Holly shook off her melancholy thoughts. All of Bea's clothes were laid out for church on Sunday, and it was time to get out of here.

Holly locked the door to the dressing room and hurried along the corridors of the ancient castle. She skipped downstairs and approached the drawing room. She'd promised she'd have a drink with her friends before she went.

Sam, one of the footmen on the door, smiled warmly at her.

"Evening Sam, how are you?"

Sam blushed, as he often did around her. He was sweet and had a little bit of a crush on her, she was sure.

"Great, thanks, Ms. Holly." He opened the door wide and she found her friends enjoying a pre-dinner drink.

"Here she is," Lali said.

George took a glass of champagne from one of the footmen holding a tray of drinks and brought it over to her. Holly curtseyed, then took the drink and George's offered arm as she escorted her over to the rest of the group.

"Are you sure you can't stay for dinner, Holls?" Bea said.

"Sorry, I already promised to meet someone at that new club I told you about." Holly felt terrible lying.

Greta moved a few paces to her and said, "Just be careful and get a taxi home. I always worry about you. There's lots of bad people out there."

"Listen to Mother," Lali joked.

Holly smiled. They each had their role in their group of friends. Greta was the mother of the group, Lali the organizer, Bea the single-minded, determined one, the glue that kept the group together, despite their very different lives and personalities, and lastly herself, the fun one. Holly, the life and soul of the party, who kept them young and stopped them taking themselves too seriously.

"Don't worry about me. I'll be okay." Holly sipped her drink.

Greta put her hand on Holly's shoulder. "If you're ever stuck, just call me and I'll send Riley to get you."

Riley pulled Greta to her and smiled. "Anytime, Holls."

It was always nice to see how much in love and passionate Greta and Riley still were. Greta had met Riley at university, and all these years later, they still adored each other.

As she looked around the room, Holly felt a twinge of jealousy that she didn't have someone to look at her the way her friends and their partners looked at each other. She gazed over at George and Bea, and just seeing them together, their connection, the way George looked at Bea, was unquestionable devotion. It was only Holly who hadn't been that lucky, not that she hadn't searched. She had searched a lot, but no one made her feel what her friends had.

Holly could only remember one experience approaching what she saw in her friends' smiles, and it was something that was constantly in her thoughts these days, after years of trying to forget it.

Bea and Lali came over to join Holly and Greta, leaving George, Cammy, and Riley talking amongst themselves.

"So, Holls," Bea said. "Who's the man of the moment?"

Holly looked down at her glass. "There isn't one."

"There hasn't been anyone for months," Greta said. "You're the last single one. You have to let us live vicariously through your exciting life."

"I don't have time for dating now," Holly said.

Lali stage-whispered, "Maybe her crush on Story St. John has ruined her for all the nice guys out there."

Holly rolled her eyes. "Stop with the crush thing."

Greta joined in, suggesting, "Or maybe dashing polo players fill her head and make her heart pitter-patter."

Holly had a little-, well, maybe a big-girl crush on action hero film star Story St. John, and her films were usually a part of the girls' night they held every month. Her crush wasn't a shock to her, as she had always been attracted to women, as well as men, but her friends didn't know that about her. It was something that she didn't want to talk about or think about again. But for the past year, her attraction to women was so hard not to think about. She couldn't help thinking that maybe it was a woman she was meant to love.

After all, how could she explain the feeling in her heart, the excitement in her soul when she looked at women like Story St. John, or the feeling she'd experienced at the polo match last year. Holly had mistaken one of the tall strapping polo players for a man, until Cammy informed her that *he* was a *she*. Their former military friend, Captain Quincy.

She'd tried to forget the way she'd felt when Captain Quincy had pulled off her polo helmet. She'd revealed an utterly gorgeous butch woman, with the most beautiful eyes and chiselled cheekbones, that made Holly's stomach flip and other parts ache.

Holly had avoided Quincy that day. She'd excused herself, and went to chat up one of the eager men there. For so long, she'd sought out men who simply wanted sex. Because while she could enjoy sex, she didn't want to give away her heart. Not again. She'd given away her heart a long time ago to a woman, and had her heart broken to pieces. Never again.

"Holls?" she heard Lali say and forced a smile on her face.

"Yeah?"

"Do you think maybe—"

"No. Don't even say it," Holly said with a tinge of sharpness in her voice.

Lali, Greta, and Bea looked at each other.

"Sorry, girls. I'm just a bit tired," Holly said.

She was rescued from the awkwardness when Sam came into the room and bowed. "Your Majesties. Nanny Baker is asking if you could come up to the nursery. Princess Edwina is a little distressed, and Nanny thinks she might have a fever."

Bea looked at George and said, "I knew something was wrong this afternoon."

George put her glass down. "Would you excuse us?"

As George and Bea left the room, Holly said to her friends. "I better get going too."

Little did her friends know that she was going home to watch a Story St. John film and eat her way through a tub of ice cream.

Quincy sat beside the hospital bed of her friend, Lieutenant Jacob Goldman. She had been here for the last hour, sitting quietly by his bed while he slept. The volume in the room might have been quiet, apart from the occasional beep of a machine, but her head was anything but.

Jacob was covered head to foot in white dressings, with only a portion of his face untouched by the explosion and flames that had ravaged his body. Jacob and his wife Helen had been good friends since officer training school—well, as good friends as Quincy could ever have. They understood her limitations and never pushed her into social situations she couldn't cope with.

The guilt and anger that she hadn't been able to get to her friend in time to save him ravaged Quincy even more when she visited him here. She asked herself the same question she did every time she saw and heard the pain he was in. *Why could it not have been me instead?*

Jacob had a wife, children, a life, while Quincy had nothing to lose. Life was just not fair.

She looked at her watch and thought she'd better be leaving soon. Just as she was about to stand, Jacob's raspy voice said, "I know what you're thinking."

Quincy didn't even realize he was awake. "What was I thinking?"

"What you always do, what I would think if I was in your shoes, torturing myself for what I could have done differently," Jacob said.

Quincy cleared her throat nervously. He could always tell what she was thinking.

"I have to report to Buckingham Palace shortly. I just wanted to say goodbye," Quincy said.

"The big American tour, eh?"

She knew Jacob didn't mean it this way, but Quincy hated that she would be off living and experiencing the world while he was stuck here in agony.

"Yes, I'll call Helen and make sure you're behaving for the nurses," Quincy said.

Jacob started to laugh, then began to cough instead. Quincy jumped up and gave him a sip of water.

"It's a great honour to be serving the Queen," Jacob said.

"It is," Quincy replied.

Jacob looked straight into her eyes and said, "Promise me one thing, Quin. Live a life, have some fun. I know you hide yourself away, but you've only got one life, and you never know when it will be taken away."

Quincy nodded, but she didn't know if she really meant it. How could she live a life when Jacob couldn't?

"Promise me, Quin," Jacob repeated.

She smiled and said, "I promise."

Quincy said her goodbyes and walked out of the hospital room. She found Helen waiting there. Quincy couldn't imagine a better wife than Helen. No matter what they'd been through, she always remained positive and kept Jacob going.

"You said your goodbyes, then?" Helen said.

"Yes, I'll call you when I get to the States," Quincy said.

Helen leaned in and kissed her cheek. "I know what Jacob asked of you. I also know how hard it is for you to socialize at the best of times—the admiral has left her mark on you, now even more so. But I want you to promise me too, Quin. You have to grab for life, and love, and hold on. Promise me?"

Quincy gave her a forced smile. "Promise."

She reached into her suit jacket pocket and brought out her Victoria Cross. "Give this to Jacob, will you. He is braver than I could ever be."

Quincy was led along the corridor of Buckingham Palace by a footman. She followed him downstairs, and as she did the walls and decor became less ornate. She guessed this was the staff area of the palace.

The downstairs corridors and rooms were busy with people coming and going, the noise of chatter, and shouts of instructions. This was truly the palace engine room, the place that made everything run smoothly.

The footman stopped. "It's just in here, Captain."

"Thank you." Quincy knocked and heard someone tell her to come in.

She opened the door and found herself in a state of the art operations room, nothing like the historic, antique palace outside this room. There was a huge conference table surrounded by desks, with what appeared to be the latest in security equipment and computer interfaces.

Around the conference table sat a team of plain-clothes men and women and, at the head, Inspector Lang, whom she had already met.

"Quincy, come in and take a seat," Inspector Lang said.

"Thank you, sir."

Quincy joined the five protection officers at the table, all but one of whom had their eyes glued to her. One woman at the end of the table didn't even look her way. She was dressed smartly in a blouse and tailored slacks and had her hair pulled back into a tight ponytail.

Inspector Lang stood and said, "Everyone, this is Captain Quincy. She joins us after a distinguished career in the Royal Marines and has trained for the past six months with the Royal Military Police before joining us." He turned to Quincy. "Quincy, these are the more senior officers in the squad, except Captain Cameron—she is assisting the Queen at the moment, but I believe you already know her?"

"Yes, sir."

She heard the woman at the end mutter under her breath, "Yeah, you're very well protected."

"Sorry, Garrett?" Inspector Lang said.

The woman she now knew as Garrett gave him a smile. "Nothing, sir."

Lang narrowed his eyes and continued, "This is Boothby, and Jones." He pointed to two sharp-suited men who politely nodded their heads. "And this is a recent recruit, Veronica Clayton." He pointed to a young woman sitting a few chairs away. "She will be working under your command for the Queen Consort and the princess. The Queen and I felt you needed another pair of eyes with a toddler running around."

The Queen had asked Quincy to help train a younger member of the team, with an eye to the future when Princess Edwina would need her own guard.

Clayton gave her the warmest welcome in the room, smiling and walking around the table to shake her hand. "Nice to meet you, ma'am. It's an honour to work with a VC," Clayton said.

Garrett sighed audibly, but Quincy froze at the mention of her Victoria Cross. She wished no one knew about it. It symbolized her failure as a leader, and shame slithered around her gut.

"Good to meet you, Clayton."

Lang said, "Clayton, why don't you take Captain Quincy along to the Queen's private apartments? We leave for the airport in an hour. We can go over the itinerary on the plane."

"Yes, sir," Clayton said.

Quincy stood to attention before nodding to Lang and walking out the door. As soon as they were out of earshot, Clayton said, "I'm really excited to work with you, ma'am."

Clayton was so much younger than the rest of the team. A good thing if she was to fit in with the princess in years to come. Clay had warm black skin, short shaved hair at the back and sides, and tight brown-tinged curls on top. Unlike the other members of the team who could be mistaken for bankers in their suits and tailored clothes, Clayton wore a much more fashionable blue suit, with an open-necked white shirt and studs in her earlobes.

"Not everyone on the team seems to be," Quincy said.

Clayton glanced at her and raised an eyebrow. "You mean Garrett? Don't worry about her. She's hardly said two words to me since I started my assignment here."

"So what's her problem?" Quincy asked.

Clayton smiled. "Your job. She thought it was hers since your predecessor handed in her notice."

Great. Jealousy and disappointment. From Quincy's experience, that was exactly what a good team didn't need.

Just then the sound of a child's laughter came from behind them. They both stopped and turned to see what was going on, and Quincy saw a woman with Princess Edwina in her arms, and a honey-coloured dog walking beside them. Princess Edwina had a Rupert Bear in her arms and was hugging it tightly.

The woman's thick reddish-brown hair was obscuring her face, until she looked up, smiling at them both.

It was *her*. The woman from the polo match, whom her security files had identified as Holly Weaver. She got the same strange sensation looking into her eyes as she had that day when she pulled off her polo helmet. An excitement in her chest and a shortness of breath.

Holly held her gaze silently for a few seconds before giving Clayton a smile. "Morning, Clay."

"Morning, Holly, and good morning Princess Edwina, and Rex." Clayton waved.

Holly moved Princess Edwina around to hold her in her arms. "Say hi to Clay, Teddy."

The one year-old smiled, and waved vigorously. "Hi."

It was the first time Quincy had seen Princess Edwina up close, but she was so like George with that dark brown hair and blue eyes.

"Who's your friend, Clay?" Holly asked.

"This is Captain Quincy, Queen Beatrice's new protection officer."

Quincy was sure Holly was giving her a forced smile. "Another captain? We are well stocked up with captains, then. If you'll excuse me, I'll get Teddy back to her mummy."

"Walk, Holl," Princess Edwina said.

Holly put her down and took her Rupert Bear from her. Princess Edwina toddled back along the corridor, one hand in Holly's and the other on the back of Rex.

"See you, Holly," Clayton said.

Holly picked up her pace and soon she disappeared the way she'd come.

Clayton let out a long breath. "Gorgeous, isn't she? She's exactly the kind of woman I'll be looking for someday. And that hair...don't you just want to run your hands through—"

Clayton stopped midsentence when Quincy gave her a pointed look. "I don't think that's appropriate while we are working, Clayton." Obviously things were very lax here.

"Sorry, ma'am," Clayton said quickly.

"I know that Queen Beatrice has probably fostered this easy-going attitude, with good intentions, but we must be professional."

"Got it, Captain. Yes, she does. Her Majesty is so nice, and everyone on staff is a little bit in love with Queen Beatrice."

"I can imagine. Just remember she and her personal staff deserve respect," Quincy said.

"Yes, ma'am. I'll take you to her now."

George sat at her desk, going through her paperwork as quickly as possible, so she could spend a quiet evening with Bea and Teddy before the madness of their royal tour ensued. Her dogs, Shadow and Baxter, lay on the rug beside her.

She gazed at the moving picture of Bea and Teddy in a silver photo frame. She wondered for the millionth time how she could have been so lucky. In those dark days after her father died, George never could have imagined such happiness was around the corner.

Bea had fallen into her life and become not only the perfect wife, but also the perfect consort. The country adored her as she did, and Bea was making the role of consort her own, bringing her skills as a former charity director to organize and design targeted campaigns, in conjunction with the other members of the family, to put important social issues on the national and world agendas. She worked so hard, George found it difficult to keep up.

Only last week Bea and Theo were campaigning together for a child bereavement charity. Her brother Theo had really knuckled down to his role as prince, and they were a powerful threesome in support of lots of causes.

Then there was her little princess, Edwina. They had started to call her Teddy, not long after she came home from hospital. Although Edwina was a fine strong name for a future Queen, it was quite serious for a little girl. Not only was Teddy short for Edwina, but seeing how close she was to her teddy, Rupert Bear, George started to call her that and it stuck.

George prayed that Teddy's namesake, her father Edward, was proud of the family she had made. Nothing made her happier, and every day she felt so blessed.

George signed one of the documents from Number Ten and placed it in the last red box of the morning. She lifted the final file out and saw it was some amendments to her speech for the first stop in their North American tour, Toronto.

This tour was going to be so exhausting for Bea and Teddy—that was the only thing that worried her. When Prime Minister Bo Dixon and her team were putting together this tour, they seemed to forget that they were a family and not robots, although George had managed to negotiate a number of solo engagements for herself, while Bea and Teddy would stay behind and rest.

George felt like Bo Dixon used her and Bea as Britain's own diplomatic corps. Anywhere Bo needed support in the world, or to mend fences with unfriendly countries or their leaders, she would deploy them like an army. It was their role to be Britain's goodwill ambassadors, but to her mind, Bo was cynical about it. The moment after the United States elected their first African American woman commander-in-chief, Bo began organizing this tour. She wanted Britain to be the first to visit President Virginia Watson.

New trade and manufacturing deals were up for grabs, and it was George's job to make sure the US felt a strong bond of friendship with the UK.

George was interrupted by a knocking at her office door. A footman walked in and said, "Captain Quincy to see you, ma'am."

George smiled and stood. "Yes, of course. Bring her in."

Quincy came in, bowed her head at the door, then walked forward when George extended her hand. Quincy bowed again when she arrived in front of her, then shook her hand.

"Good to see you, Quincy."

"Good to see you, Your Majesty. You asked to see me?" Quincy said.

"Yes, let's sit down." George indicated the couch at the window.

The dogs jumped up and wagged their tails excitedly. Quincy patted them as she passed.

"Calm down, you two," George said.

"They are still very excitable then, ma'am," Quincy said. She had met the Queen's dogs many times at polo and horse events. They were always bouncing and following close behind her.

"You could say that," George said as she sat.

Quincy followed suit and patted Baxter the boxer's head. Shadow had already gone to lie down.

"What about Rex, ma'am? I know he was very close to King Edward," Quincy asked.

George crossed her legs and smiled. "He's Queen Beatrice's dog now. He adores her, although Teddy runs her pretty close. Rex has been stuck to her like glue from the start. Never lets her wander too far and guards her from all foes," George joked.

Quincy smiled, but she felt a tightness in her chest. How was she going to cope in this close kind of family environment? She just wasn't equipped for it.

"So how are you doing, Quincy? Are you well recovered?" George asked.

"Quite recovered, ma'am." What a liar she was. She had a scarred body and a scarred heart and soul. She would never recover.

George narrowed her eyes. "Really? You know you can speak to me or Cammy anytime, in the strictest of confidence."

"I know that, and I am quite well and ready to serve, ma'am." She didn't even talk to her mother. She would never talk—it was her burden to carry this pain inside of her.

George patted her on the shoulder. "It's George in private, remember? And the admiral? Is she well?"

"Yes, she is." Quincy would never know what her mother was feeling. Feeling was weakness to her.

"Well that's the ticket then, isn't it? I hope you will enjoy working with us, Quincy."

"It's an honour, George. I promise, Queen Beatrice will always be safe with me."

"I know that, Quincy. That's why I asked for you. I trust you implicitly. Bea is my life, and her safety and Teddy's safety are my top priority."

"I promise you, I would die to protect her, ma'am."

Never again would she let her friends down. Never again.

CHAPTER TWO

Beatrice smiled broadly when she saw George walking through the plane with their daughter hanging by her ankles, giggling, but still managing to hold on to her Rupert Bear.

They had been in the air for only twenty minutes, and Teddy was restless already. Luckily, their private plane was big enough for her to toddle around and use up energy under the supervision of her other mum.

Bea was sitting in the lounge area of the plane that had comfortable upholstered seats, a coffee table, and a drinks fridge. The back of the plane featured an office and private bedroom, while the front of the plane had seats and tables where the staff generally did their work and planning.

"George, you'll make her sick," Bea said.

George turned Teddy the right way around. "Not at all. You're quite all right, aren't you, Teddy?"

"Uh-huh," Teddy said, "'orsey, please?"

George gave her a big kiss and said, "In a little while, Teddy bear. Mum has to go and practise her speech."

Bea held out her arms. "Come to Mummy." George handed her over and gave Bea a lingering kiss. "Don't kiss me like that when you have a speech to practise, and I have your daughter in my arms."

George grinned, apparently pleased she still had the capacity to excite her wife with the merest kiss.

George leaned over and whispered, "Do you remember how we used to spend our time on these long-haul flights before?"

Bea remembered. Despite the speeches to be rehearsing, and the red boxes to be done, they'd always found time for each other and some fun in the plane's private bedroom.

"I remember only too well, Bully. That was before we became responsible and had a baby. Now we have neither the time nor the energy."

"Oh, I've always got energy for you, Mrs. Buckingham."

Right on cue Teddy said, "Juice, Mummy."

"You see?" Bea said.

George smiled and reached into the fridge for a bottle of Teddy's favourite juice. "I wouldn't have it any other way."

Bea sighed contentedly. "Me either. Now go and play with your papers. The people of Canada are waiting to be stunned by your speech," Bea joked.

George raised her eyebrow and said, "They might be out of luck since our beloved prime minister wrote it."

Bea chuckled. George had said that with huge dose of sarcasm. Bo Dixon's popularity had plummeted with the public ever since she'd invited President Loka of Vospya to the UK, despite his appalling civil rights record. The only thing in Bo's favour was a really weak and unelectable opposition.

"Well, do your best," Bea said.

"I'll try." George kissed both Teddy and her on their foreheads and made her way to her office.

As soon as George walked away, Holly slipped in to sit beside them.

"Hi, Holls."

"Hi. Your outfit is steam pressed, and good to go," Holly said.

"The blue dress?" Bea said.

"Yes, and Teddy's to match," Holly said.

"Thanks, Holls. I don't know what I'd do without you. I never pictured myself being a clothes horse, and yet here I am."

Holly sat back and smiled. "It's easy to pick things out when you're dressing someone with your figure."

"Hardly, Holls. It's taken hard work to shift the baby weight after this little one right here."

Holly laughed. She absolutely loved her job, having worked as a make-up artist in the TV and film industry, where generally she didn't get much of a chance to be creative, because she was always working to someone else's vision. Now she was working for her best friend, and she had the complete control of Bea's wardrobe, and the responsibility to cater exactly for each public event she attended.

Holly knew Bea's likes and dislikes, and without any budget concerns, she could really go to town and express herself. It wasn't always easy. This North American tour had taken six months to plan. Once the destinations and activities were decided upon, it was her job to plan, source, and buy an entire wardrobe. It had been stressful at times, but they got everything done.

Bea went to settle Teddy down for a nap, and Holly flagged down one of the airplane staff and ordered coffee for them both. While she waited, Holly looked over to the other seats where Lali and Captain Cameron were supposedly going over the plans for the visit, but Holly smiled when she saw their hands clasped together.

They were so perfect for each other. Bea had told her that Cammy had been a bit of a lady's woman in her past, but that had all ended when she clapped eyes on Lali Ramesh.

Would she ever be that lucky?

Holly then shifted her gaze to the seats behind Lali, and to her surprise found Captain Quincy's eyes already on her, the captain's face set in what she thought was a scowl. When Holly had found out the dishy polo player was joining the staff as Bea's protection officer, she had been both excited and scared. Excited because she couldn't wait to find out if Quincy lived up to her good looks, and scared because—just like with Story St. John—Quincy reminded her how much she was attracted to women, and that she was denying a whole part of herself that was screaming to get out. Because she didn't ever want to have her heart broken again.

Since her first love broke her heart, she had sought out flings with men who didn't want an emotional connection. That suited her and had given her the reputation as a man-eater.

But Holly needn't have worried and shouldn't have judged a book by its cover. So far Captain Quincy had been as dull as dishwater.

She stood guarding Bea like a statue, never breaking into a smile, and only speaking to bark orders to those staff around her.

Even though Quincy screamed butch lesbian, everything else about her was straight and boring. Plain grey suit, slightly darker grey tie, white shirt. Her short dark hair, simply combed to the side. There was nothing about Quincy that showed any sort of individuality.

Holly longed to go over there and ruffle up her hair and maybe give her a red tie, something to liven up the ordered grey appearance.

Quincy had ignored Holly, and she supposed that suited her, but the cold stares and scowls were annoying.

She looked right at Quincy and said pointedly, "Can I help you?"

Quincy looked back down to her computer pad quickly and never replied.

"What am I? Invisible?" Holly said.

"Who's invisible?" Bea said sitting back down.

"Nothing. Teddy go down okay?" Holly asked.

Their coffee was delivered, and Bea took a sip and sighed. "Yes, all the excitement has gotten to her. I left Nanny Baker with her."

"I think Nanny Baker will want to join Teddy in a nap. It's all too much excitement for her too."

Bea laughed. "I know. I promised her that as soon as we come back from this trip I'll hire a new nanny." When she was a young woman, Nanny Baker had looked after George and Theo, and when Bea was reluctant to choose from the candidates offered for Teddy, George had persuaded her own nanny to come out of retirement. However, the pace of royal life and Teddy's energy were a little too much for the older lady. "I hate having to have a nanny in the first place, but I know we can't take Teddy everywhere."

Holly saw the guilt in Bea's face every time she had to leave her daughter, and it made her more determined to keep things fun for them both.

"This trip is going to be such hard work," Bea said. "I don't want Teddy to feel the stress of manically going from one venue to another, and I don't want her to be pushed aside."

"Don't worry, Your Maj. I promised I'd organize some fun stuff for the personal days you had scheduled into the trip, and if you and George want some space, I'll take Teddy out."

"Thanks, Holls. I don't know what I'd do without you and Lali. I need my own support system inside this royal bubble. Do you know, some of the older royal courtiers wanted Teddy and me to travel separately from George?"

"Why?" Holly asked.

Bea scowled. "Some outdated nonsense about the monarch and the heir to the throne travelling together. If the plane goes down, so does the heir."

"That's bloody morbid, and hardly likely these days," Holly replied.

"I know," Bea said. "George and I soon shot that idea in flames. We're a family and we travel together."

"I doubt you were that polite," Holly said. She was well aware Bea had little tolerance from the stiff older courtiers who still populated the palace staff.

"You know me too well. George was diplomatic, but I said, not bloody likely!"

Holly laughed.

❖

Captain Quincy cursed herself for being caught looking over. She was reviewing the files on all the royal court staff that she would be working with. She lingered on Ms. Holly Weaver's file, and she just had to compare the picture to the real thing.

She was interested by the woman, who was obviously intelligent, who had studied psychology at university, then after graduation went on to study hair and make-up. It was a strange career move, and one that interested Quincy.

While she gazed at the photo in the security file on the computer pad, Quincy found herself tracing the contours of Holly's face with her pen. Holly had delicate, almost elfin features, yet had plump, full lips. She was beautiful, and as Clayton had pointed out, her thick, layered shoulder-length reddish-brown hair made you want to run your fingers through it.

Despite her delicate features, there was something very wild about Ms. Weaver. She was bohemian in appearance, and she didn't fit in with the very proper royal staff. Today she was dressed in tight, ripped designer jeans, a black and white striped top, and black heels.

Ms. Weaver's jewellery said as much about her as her clothes. She wore a cluster of beaded bracelets on her wrists, large black triangle earrings, and many rings—mostly small silver ones, and one with a large aquamarine stone.

Nothing in Ms. Weaver followed a pattern, and to someone whose life and whole being was ordered and governed by rules, that was in equal measures terrifying, aggravating, and intriguing.

In Quincy's very short time at Buckingham Palace, Ms. Weaver's voice and laughter had been the loudest. She obviously lived life to the fullest. It was funny—women never usually left such a lasting impression on her, but she had never forgotten Holly from the polo match, more than a year ago, or the man she had left with. Quincy remembered the sense of disappointment she'd felt—not that she would have ever done anything about her initial attraction. That wasn't something she could do.

Quincy looked up when Holly squealed with excitement at something Queen Beatrice had said.

"You're kidding? Story St. John is going to be there?" Holly said.

Quincy couldn't help but eavesdrop.

"Uh-huh," Queen Beatrice said. "I've made sure you got an invite."

Holly jumped up and hugged the Queen. "Thank you so much."

Story St. John? Quincy had no idea about popular culture and quickly typed the name into her computer pad. Hundreds of links and pictures appeared.

She clicked on one that said, *Who is action hero film star Story St. John dating now?*

Quincy was surprised when a whole host of women's pictures popped up.

Ms. Weaver was excited about meeting a lesbian film star. Was she just excited to meet a film star, or had she misread Ms. Weaver's choice of partners? Was she interested in women?

A part of Quincy felt a thrill at that thought, but she immediately chastised herself. Getting excited meant running the risk of losing control, and that could never, ever happen again. She remembered the shame on her mother's face when she'd called her after the incident with Lieutenant Rodwell.

Her thoughts were interrupted by Clayton. "Ma'am, Inspector Lang would like to see us in the meeting room in ten minutes."

"Thank you," Quincy said.

As Clayton walked away, Captain Cameron sat down beside her. "Quincy? How are you finding things?"

Quincy chose her words carefully. "It's quite different from regimental life, but I'm sure I'll adjust."

Cammy laughed. "Aye, I know what you mean. Everyone knows their place in a regiment and follows instructions and rules to the letter. In this job you have to be more flexible, and remember it's a family, with all the problems of family life."

Quincy smiled at her friend. "I can see it takes patience."

Cammy crossed her legs and chuckled. "I don't have as many problems. Queen Georgina is like you and me. Military, follows rules, sticks to the schedule like clockwork, but Queen Beatrice is a little less…conventional, shall we say. She doesn't like to do things the way they have always been done, and schedules can change at the drop of a hat. So be prepared to think on your feet, improvise, and go with the flow."

"Go with the flow?" Quincy said.

There couldn't be a concept that was more alien to Quincy than that. She liked to know what was going to happen, when it was going to happen, and plan for it a month in advance.

Cammy laughed. "Don't worry. You'll adjust."

Quincy nodded in agreement, even though she didn't think she could. She looked up to where Queen Beatrice and Holly were sitting, and saw that Lali Ramesh had joined them, and was equally as excited about this meeting with the film star. How strange.

She turned back to Cammy and said, "Congratulations on your engagement, by the way. I couldn't believe it when I heard Captain Cameron was engaged, but seeing your beautiful fiancée, I can see why."

Cammy looked over at Lali and got a silly grin on her face. "She is beautiful, isn't she? I never thought I'd ever want just one woman forever, but when I saw Lali, I didn't want anyone else."

"Good for you, Cammy. You deserve to be happy," Quincy said.

"It wasn't easy, believe me. Lali is very careful. She doesn't jump into things, and it took a lot of persuasion on my part just to get one date with her, but it was so worth it. Your turn next, eh?"

Quincy said nothing. That was something she would never have. Never mind marriage—who'd want to date someone who couldn't dare express emotion?

Cammy smacked her on the shoulder, and said, "We'd better get to Lang's meeting."

❖

All the members of the protection squad filled the meeting room aboard the plane. The higher ranking officers—Captain Cameron, Quincy, Garrett, Boothby, and Jones—sat around the table, while Clayton and the rest of the protection team stood behind them.

Inspector Lang stood in front of a large computer screen, detailing their arrival in Toronto.

"The principals will be met by Canadian officials, then escorted to a meeting with the Canadian Prime Minister, where Her Majesty will make a speech. We then make our way to the hotel…"

Quincy didn't need to listen to her commanding officer. She already knew every part of the plans, every inch of the route, and every potential area of security risk. As long as Queen Beatrice kept to the schedule, and the plan, there shouldn't be any problems. That was what worried her.

Inspector Lang finished the meeting and the officers started to file out. Sergeant Garrett passed behind her and stopped.

"A huge responsibility isn't it, Captain," Garrett said.

Quincy noticed that Garrett always used her rank instead of calling her *ma'am*. Her rank obviously bothered Garrett's ego.

"Of course. It's a responsibility I relish," Quincy said firmly.

Garrett leaned over and whispered in her ear, "Let's hope you don't crack up under the weight of the responsibility."

Garrett walked away with a smug look on her face, and Quincy felt a sense of panic. What did Garrett know about her?

"Ma'am?" Clayton stood beside her.

Quincy shook away those feelings of disquiet and stood. "Yes, Clayton?"

"Any last instructions before we land, ma'am?"

Clayton looked uptight. She was forgetting this was Clayton's first big tour, and it was Quincy's job to keep those under her command calm and focused.

She put a comforting hand on Clayton's shoulder. "Just keep focused on your principal, Princess Edwina. I don't envisage that she will be away from either of her mothers' arms, but you never know. Remember it's my job to keep eyes on Queen Beatrice, so don't be distracted."

"Yes, ma'am," Clayton said nervously.

Quincy smiled at her and said, "You'll do exceptionally well. I have faith in you Clay." Clayton stood a little straighter then and smiled.

"I won't let you down, ma'am."

CHAPTER THREE

After the royal family landed, Holly went straight to the hotel with the luggage, while Lali and Cammy accompanied the two Queens on their first engagement.

Holly rushed about frantically, trying to organize the royal luggage. Before they'd left, Holly had designated certain trunks to hold clothes for certain times during the trip, and this overnight in Toronto was meant to be the easiest—one day's worth of clothes, then off to the United States. But now that she was invited to the film event with Story St. John, she had her own outfit to work out too.

She directed the hotel staff with the bags, unpacked Teddy's overnight bag and some toys, then set out Bea's ballgown.

At each hotel on the tour, a whole floor of rooms had been booked out to give the royal party privacy, and so security could be maintained. The close personal staff and heads of security all had rooms on the floor, plus a lounge area to socialize. Holly and Captain Cameron each had a room to house, clean, and prepare the clothes the royal couple would need. Holly stood in Bea's dressing room using her hand steamer to get rid of all the creases the dress had picked up during its travels. The TV on the wall was playing the twenty-four-hour news, and George, Bea, and Princess Edwina's visit was the main story.

It occurred to Holly that the public would never know how much preparation went into these visits. They saw George and Bea, but behind them was a little private community, the royal court making everything work.

She looked up to the screen and watched the royal family making their way through the crowds. The reception they were getting was bigger and louder than any film star's. There was screaming and shouting, and she could see it was a little overwhelming for Teddy, who clung to her mummy tightly.

Her gaze was drawn to the tall figures of Quincy and Clay following discreetly behind.

Quincy had the same impassive look upon her face when she was working as she'd had on the plane. Did she ever smile?

She jumped when someone got a little too close and made a grab for Teddy. As quick as a flash Quincy was in front of Bea, pushing back the overeager person.

Bea appeared rattled for a few seconds, then handed Teddy to George who'd come striding over. From that point on, George walked with her arm around her wife and held Teddy protectively in her other arm, until they went into the government building.

Holly was impressed with the speed of Quincy's reactions. She might not be the friendliest, but at least Quincy was good at her job.

Holly finished steaming the dress and everything was set. All she had to worry about now was her own dress, and the fact that she didn't bring anything approaching the glamour of what Bea would be wearing.

Oh well, as long as she made Her Maj look good. Holly chuckled to herself.

Sometime later, she heard voices and lots of pairs of feet outside in the hallway. Holly peeped out and only caught the backs of George and Bea going into their room. She saw Inspector Lang say something to Quincy and pat her on the back. Once he walked away, and Quincy was all alone in the corridor, Holly saw Quincy's hand tremor.

Quincy took a deep breath, squeezed her hand into a fist, and walked off.

That was strange. What made the unshakable Captain Quincy shake?

Quincy was glad of the two hours' break she had before evening duty. This afternoon's walkabout had disturbed her. Dinner was served in the lounge for the personal staff but she couldn't stomach it, so she headed back to her room to get showered and changed before the evening engagement.

She let the intense heat of the shower beat down on the back of her neck as she braced herself against the shower wall. Today's events played on repeat in her mind, over and over again. Queen Beatrice walked along the line of the crowd, Princess Edwina in her arms. The crowd was enchanted by the little girl who had mastered the important royal skill of smiling and waving already.

Quincy had been constantly scanning the crowd, looking for anyone unusual, anyone who didn't fit, but everything looked normal. The crowd began to lean further and further over the barriers making Quincy more and more nervous. She had just told Clayton to stay alert when out of the corner of her eye she saw a young man rummage around in his backpack. She'd moved just as he launched forward to grab for Princess Edwina, with something in his other hand.

She'd shouted, "Weapon!" then restrained him, while the other officers moved Queen Beatrice away. That was when she and the others saw there was no weapon, only a soft toy the young man had brought to give to the princess.

As the police took him to the side, Garrett walked past and said, "Jumped the gun a little there, didn't we? I heard you had a hair trigger, Quincy."

Had she overreacted? Inspector Lang and Queen Georgina had congratulated her for acting quickly, but when she'd arrived back at the hotel and passed the lounge area, she heard Garrett and a group of officers laughing about the dangerous soft toy.

When Quincy shut her eyes, the memory of the officers' laughter changed to the roar and explosion of bombs, and the heat of the shower turned to flames, burning all over her body.

She opened her eyes quickly and shut off the water. She leaned her head against the shower wall, gasping for air. She heard her mother's words echo around in her mind.

Never show your fear or emotions if you wish to be taken seriously, Quincy.

One gulp and her emotions were swallowed deep down, stored in some dark space inside of her, never to be let out. She walked over to the dinner suit she had laid out for tonight and began to dress.

This evening was a formal black-tie affair, so the guards had to be dressed accordingly. Quincy pulled on her black suit trousers, then walked over to the mirror to put on her white shirt and bow tie. She slipped on the shirt and, as she was buttoning it up, stared at the scars that ran from below her waist, up her torso to just below her neck.

Quincy hated these scars. They were a symbol of her failure, how she hadn't saved the men under her command. Deep down she believed she deserved every one of those scars.

She heard a knock at her door, so she quickly buttoned up her shirt but left her bow tie hanging. When she opened the door, she found Clayton standing there, similarly dressed.

"I need help." Clayton held up the tie.

Quincy smiled and ushered her in. "You're having problems?"

"When the inspector said we'd be handed out evening wear, I thought there would at least be a ready-made bow tie. A police constable from Brixton isn't trained on wearing black tie."

Quincy held her by the shoulders. "Stand still." She began to make up the bow tie. She had a couple of inches on Clayton, but Clayton was a lot broader and more muscular, as if she worked out. Quincy was glad to have some muscle on her side.

"What gives you the impression I'm well trained in black tie?" Quincy asked.

"You're posh, ma'am. Your accent, you went to the same boarding school as Queen Georgina, and your mum's some big deal in the navy."

"How did you know that?" Quincy asked.

Clayton's smile faded as if she regretted saying that, and she looked everywhere but at Quincy's eyes. "I just overheard Garrett talking."

Quincy's stomach dropped. Garrett had been checking up on her. Quincy sighed while looping the tie together.

"I suppose I'm all the gossip after today's events," Quincy said.

"Garrett might be my superior, ma'am, but she's a bloody arsehole. I didn't listen to her stupid gossip. Inspector Lang, Her Majesty—they all think you did the exact right thing, ma'am. That guy could have had anything on him."

"But he didn't," Quincy said. She was really doubting her judgment.

"*I* should have been more alert. I should have seen the guy rummaging in his backpack. Princess Edwina is my principal, ma'am," Clayton said.

"You did fine. The man was no threat, and everything else will come with experience. Don't worry. How did you find yourself in the royal protection squad?"

"I just joined the police, ma'am, and applied to join the firearms division. My superiors were more than happy with my test results, and my commanding officer put me forward for the role."

Quincy smiled. "Good shot, are you, Clay?"

The biggest grin appeared on Clayton's face. "I can shoot the wings off a fly."

Quincy finished with her tie and patted her on the shoulder. "Well, I'm glad to have you by my side. Go and look in the mirror."

Clayton walked over to the mirror and checked her tie, and then her hair, before smiling broadly. "I think it suits me. What do you think, ma'am?"

She thought the young protection officer looked handsome, with her warm black skin set against the snow-white shirt and classic dinner suit. "You look fantastic. Very dashing."

"If only the girls thought so," Clayton said.

Quincy smiled. She was sure Clayton wouldn't have any problem attracting women, just maybe not the confidence to realize what she had to offer.

Clayton turned around and said, "I heard Story St. John is going to be at the event tonight. Everyone's been talking about how Story is Holly's big crush."

"But Ms. Weaver is straight, though, isn't she?" Quincy said.

"Labels don't matter when you find someone who sets your heart on fire," Clayton said with a wink.

She'd forgotten that Clayton was a generation younger than her, a generation to whom strict categories did not matter. "I suppose you're right. What's this Story like, Clay?"

Clayton grinned. "She's got everything. Money, good looks, charm, can get any woman she wants—she's the envy of every lesbian

I know. She even tried to flirt with Queen Beatrice the last time the Queen came to the environmental summit in New York."

Quincy felt a strange sensation in her stomach. Like it had been tied in a knot. "Let's hope that Story St. John is everything Ms. Weaver wants her to be," Quincy lied.

George leaned over into Princess Edwina's cot and gave her a kiss. "Have sweet dreams, little Teddy bear."

Teddy was sound asleep, her arms wrapped around Bea's Rupert Bear. It had belonged to Bea's deceased sister and never left Teddy's side.

The nursery room door opened and Bea came in with her ballgown on. "Is she asleep?" Bea whispered.

"Sound asleep, and as adorable as ever," George said.

Bea leaned in and stroked Teddy's forehead. "I hate to leave her, Georgie. She'll be all grown up before we know it."

"She's happy, safe, and warm here, my darling. Tomorrow we're travelling to Washington, but then we have a family day. Tonight she won't even realize we're away." George took her wife's hand and kissed it. "You're ready awfully early, Mrs. Buckingham. I usually have to hurry you along."

"Holls got me ready early, so she could get ready for tonight. She's so excited."

George sighed. "I can't imagine what is so exciting about that annoyingly smarmy actor."

Bea play hit George's shoulder. "Stop pouting. It's all about Holly tonight. It's a dream come true for her to meet Story."

"I thought Holly went for men," George said.

Bea leaned her head on George, who put her arms around Bea in turn. "Not quite. She's always had crushes on women. She thinks that we haven't noticed, but I know she's never been in love with any of the men she meets. I think one day the right woman might make her fall in love."

"You don't mean Story St. John," George said with disdain.

"Oh no. I don't think Story is the one-woman kind of girl," Bea said. Teddy kicked her covers off and turned onto her side. "She's definitely your daughter, George. You always wake up with no covers."

Bea pulled the blankets back over Teddy.

"Only because you steal them away from me," George joked.

Bea sighed contentedly as she gazed at her daughter. "It's amazing to think our little girl will be Queen one day. A little girl that can't sleep without her bear—a Queen."

"She'll grow up to be good and kind just like you, Bea. She'll be a perfect Queen," George said.

"I hope she gets your height, Georgie. I wouldn't wish my small stature on anyone," Bea joked.

"I love your height, my little smout."

CHAPTER FOUR

Holly literally skipped down the hall of the hotel. She was going to meet Story St. John, and she couldn't wait. She hoped she would fit in amongst all the rich and famous.

There was only one dress she'd brought that would fit the evening-dress brief—a short black velvet dress with sequins around the neck and long sheer sleeves.

Bea had told her that she would be travelling in the car following them, and she went along to the Queens' room, singing one of the latest popular love songs as she went. She spotted Clayton and Quincy standing guard by the door in dinner suits. As she got closer she smiled and said, "Don't you two look dashing and handsome."

Holly got a look and a smile from Clayton, but Quincy continued staring forward.

"Thanks, Holly. Captain Quincy helped me with the bow tie thing. You look beautiful, by the way."

Even though Clayton was speaking to her, Holly's gaze stayed on Quincy. She was intrigued by the woman. She was a statue.

"Thanks, Clayton. Good evening to you, Quincy," Holly said, forcing Quincy to respond.

"Good evening, Ms. Weaver," Quincy replied but didn't look at her.

This aggravated her no end. She walked up to Quincy and said, "Listen, Quin. You could at least have the decency to look at me. What's your problem?"

Quincy barely moved a muscle but lowered her eyes to look at Holly and repeated, "Good evening."

Holly wasn't going to waste any more time on her special night trying to get an ignorant upper-class twit to talk.

"Does she ever say more than two words, Clay?" Holly said. Clayton looked up at her commanding officer nervously, not sure what to say, so Holly rescued her. "I can't wait to go tonight and see all those film stars. Do you think there'll be dancing?" Holly grasped Clayton's hands and twirled and danced with her.

Clayton laughed. "You'll be the prettiest one there, Holly."

Holly stopped dead and said in a breathy voice, "Do you think Story will speak to me? I think I might faint on the spot."

"If she has eyes in her head, she'll think you're beautiful," Clayton said.

Holly gave Quincy a quick wink, but she still looked forward impassively. Was she angered or appalled by her? She couldn't tell.

Holly turned around when she heard laughter and footsteps from the other end of the corridor. It was Captain Cameron and Lali, holding hands and walking towards them.

Holly had a few moments of envy that her friend had someone to love and appreciate her, but then all she was concerned with was Lali's dress.

As they got closer Holly said, "Lali you look absolutely gorgeous."

"I told you," Cammy said to Lali, then kissed her hand and went to talk to Clayton and Quincy.

"So are you ready to meet your crush? You look wonderful, by the way," Lali said.

"Thanks, but Story won't even look my way," Holly said.

Lali gave her a knowing smile. "Oh, I don't know."

Just as Holly was about to ask what she meant by that, the Queens came out of their room looking, well, regal. Bea was wearing a fabulous silver ballgown with a tiara and the most sumptuous diamond jewellery.

Bea said, "Right, girls. Let's go and wow the stars."

❖

Quincy prowled the perimeter of the black-tie event, never straying far from her principal, Queen Beatrice. It was a charity dinner hosted jointly by the Canadian and UK film industries, to raise money for an arts scholarship fund. She watched as the working-class girl from London charmed and wowed film stars, directors, and producers.

Beatrice had a natural star quality that left the film stars awed, which was not a normal state of affairs. Queen Georgina had chosen well.

She had known George from school, although George was a couple of years above her. And thanks to the Quincy family's position, she had mixed with her at horse events and the many polo events in the year.

They were then thrown together when Quincy's regiment was stationed aboard George's Royal Navy ship. It was then that she'd met Captain Cameron. It amazed Quincy that Queen Georgina managed to pluck up the courage to talk to Beatrice, never mind romance her. George was like her—during shore leave they would both stay aboard ship, or at most visit the educational tourist sights. Captain Cameron on the other hand eagerly sampled the sights, sounds, drink, and women of each local culture.

When she'd heard the rumours about the Queen's romance, Quincy was surprised but delighted for her, and then when she finally met Queen Beatrice, she could quite understand why George fell for her.

When she wasn't focused on Queen Beatrice, there was one other direction Quincy's eyes flitted tonight, and that was towards Holly. Despite Holly Weaver's annoyingly irreverent attitude and flagrant disregard for rules, Quincy couldn't help but admire her beauty. Holly's black dress was simple but beautiful. Amongst all the glitzy ballgowns and bling on show, she was the one who shone in the room. The low back made Quincy imagine softly stroking her fingers down Holly's spine, while kissing her shoulder.

The thought made every part of her ache and she forced herself to shake off the feeling. Thoughts like that distracted her and were ultimately pointless. Holly quite obviously couldn't stand her, as their conversation before coming here was testament to, and some part of her was saddened by that reality. But that pain was a warning as to why she couldn't afford to engage with anyone, not even on a friendly basis. When she cared and showed her feelings, it caused problems.

It was hard to simply be polite to Holly. Most were put off by her brusque attitude, but Holly kept coming back and trying, and trying again. In a way she envied Holly. Everywhere Holly went, she was upbeat—she sang, danced, talked to everyone, and kept everything fun.

That was totally alien and tantalizing to her.

After a drinks reception, everyone sat down to a dinner. She was sitting beside Lali, who told her the meal was ten thousand dollars a plate, and that George had paid for them. They were incredibly lucky to be living the life they were now. It was just the two of them at a table of actors and a couple of directors, since George and Bea were at the head table, and Cammy patrolled the perimeter of the room with Inspector Lang and his team.

As the dinner things were being cleared away, Holly looked over to a table she'd had her eye on the whole evening, where Story St. John was sitting. She didn't disappoint in the flesh—she was utterly gorgeous, especially so in her dinner suit. She wore it so differently to George, Cammy, and ever-so-boring Captain Quincy. Story wore it almost ironically. It was a little too big for her in a sweet, awkward way, and she wore trainers with it instead of dress shoes.

Story wasn't tall and had a lanky boyish figure, but she had muscles in all the right places, a fact she loved to show off on her social media accounts that Holly followed religiously. Her hair was delicious as always, short back and sides, but long on top, choppy and flopping all over the place. Story was so gorgeous.

She sighed out loud.

"I can guess who that sigh is for," Lali said.

Holly smiled. "No one else could make me sigh. You have to admit she's delicious, Lali."

Lali looked over to Story's table. "She is, but you don't look at someone all day in a relationship—you need so many more ingredients to really lose your heart to someone."

"This from the woman who fell for the dashing Captain Cameron."

Lali lifted her wine glass and sipped. "But Cammy did more than simply look good—she romanced me and showed me that she had all the wonderful loyal characteristics that I needed. She chased me for a long time. I needed to be sure it was real. I think your Story is probably loyal for the space of a night, then moves on to pastures new."

"Maybe," Holly said smiling, "but what a night."

Lali laughed and shook her head. "Get ready, they're starting the auction."

The organizers had some fantastic prizes donated, and the auction would make a fortune for the film foundation.

"Look at lot six," Lali said.

Holly looked down at the booklet and scanned the prizes. Then she saw it. A dinner date with Story St. John.

"Wow! If only I was rich," Holly said.

Lali laughed. "Remember, you're supposed to be the straight girl in our group, Holls."

"Yes, I remember, but...It doesn't matter anyway. Some rich bitch is going to bid for this."

Lali squeezed her hand. "Let's bid as high as we can, just to make sure the rich bitch pays top dollar."

Holly laughed. "Yes, great idea, Lali."

George gave a speech to begin the evening. And as George talked, Holly had the strange sensation someone was watching her. She turned around and saw Captain Quincy looking. As soon as Holly caught her glance, Quincy looked away quickly.

Strange, thought Holly.

After the speeches, Holly eagerly awaited the auction. They got to lot six, and Story St. John swaggered up on stage. The master of ceremonies gave her the microphone and she said, "Hello, ladies. Let's make lots of money for the foundation, and I'll give you the time of your life." Story ended her introduction with a wink.

Some women in the audience squealed, while Holly laid her head on Lali's shoulder. "Oh God! I think I'm melting."

Lali laughed and pushed her upright. "Pull yourself together, Holls, or Ms. Rich Bitch is going to win Story."

"Lali, there's no way we can even compete."

"Don't be so defeatist. Come on," Lali said firmly.

The flamboyant master of ceremonies started the auction. "Shall we start bids for the gorgeous Story St. John at one thousand?"

Holly had a rush of excitement. She wasn't rich but she had some savings, and one thousand she could bid. Her initial excitement was dashed when nearly every woman in the room's hand shot up.

"My, my, Story is popular, ladies," the master of ceremonies said. "Shall we get serious? Five thousand?"

This time half the bidding hands went down, including Holly's. "That's me out."

Lali's hand remained up.

"What are you doing, Lali? I don't think Cammy will be pleased at you spending your life savings on another woman."

Lali just smiled. "You'll see."

She watched the auction with interest and couldn't understand why Lali kept bidding, or where she was getting the money from. It finally came down to Lali and one other woman.

Holly couldn't believe her eyes. "Lali, this is serious. You're going to be left owing a fortune."

The master of ceremonies said, "The bid is with you at the back, ma'am. Can you top ten thousand?"

Lali giggled and shouted, "Fifteen thousand."

Holly clasped her hand over Lali's mouth. "Lali—"

Lali shook her head and held up her bidding card.

"Congratulations, ma'am. You are the highest bidder. Come up and meet your date."

"Off you go then," Lali said, pointing first to Holly and then to the stage.

Holly had no idea what was going on. This was crazy. "What do you mean?"

"You won. A present from your friend and your Queen," Lali said.

Holly could hardly speak. "Bea?" She looked up to the head table, where Bea was smiling broadly at her, and then blew her a kiss and pointed up to the stage.

"I'm going to kill her, but not before I kiss her."

"Up you come, miss," the master of ceremonies said.

Lali gave her a push and Holly finally stood. She felt every eye in the room on her as she walked up to the stage. She couldn't meet Story's gaze when she stepped up.

The host asked her name, then said, "Holly Weaver, you have won a dinner date with Story St. John."

Story walked over to her with a huge smile and kissed her on her cheek. As she did she whispered, "I'm so glad you won, babe."

Holly placed her palm on the cheek that Story kissed and was led off the stage by her. She still hadn't said a word.

"Let's get a drink at the bar and swap details," Story said.

Holly could only reply, "Okay."

The film star Story St. John was leading her by the hand to the bar to have a drink. This must be a dream.

Quincy walked around the room, keeping an eye on any new people coming in and out. She had watched the auction with interest and surprise. What these women saw in that young butch actor who didn't know how to wear a suit, she had no idea.

She got even more of a shock when Holly walked onto the stage as the winner. The gossip from the personal staff was that the Queen had paid the winning bid for her friend. The excitement on Holly's face when she met Story confirmed she must at least be interested in women and was not as straight as she presented. Why Holly would waste her energy on Story, Quincy couldn't understand.

Quincy found herself walking around the perimeter of the room, towards the bar. As she did she heard Holly's unrestrained laughter, and that was exactly how she would describe Holly. Unrestrained in all she did. Quincy hadn't known her long, but she had never met someone who appeared to enjoy life and express emotion like Ms. Weaver.

Every day Holly sang joyously as she walked to Queen Beatrice's room, lifting the mood of everyone who came in contact with her. It was intriguing to be around someone so polar opposite to her. Quincy didn't want to feel, tried to stop herself from recognizing the tortured emotions, because she wished to keep her sanity and her job. But Holly *felt* every moment of every day, it seemed.

She stood a few yards away from the end of the bar and heard Story give Holly every line in the book. Quincy contemplated for a moment what it would feel like to be Story St. John and enjoy an active sex life with lots of different women, in and out of her life and her bed. The very thought made Quincy panic.

Yet it was funny to think that Holly Weaver had a more active lesbian sex life than she did, when Quincy was the one who was openly gay.

Sex and relationships were something that tantalized but terrified her. Quincy wasn't someone who could just have sex with someone for its own sake. In one way it was the old-fashioned side of her. She thought sex was something that came with commitment, like the bond her friends Jacob and Helen shared. This was just the way she saw the world. But at the core of her decision not to explore the sexual side of herself was self-protection. Deep down, Quincy knew that she was a person who felt deeply and was frightened that she wouldn't keep those feelings out of any romantic encounter she might have. It was safer to keep things uncomplicated, ordered, controlled—the way the admiral had brought her up.

Then she noticed Holly looking at her with furrowed eyebrows, and Story gone. Quincy quickly looked the other way and walked off.

George hung up her bow tie and unbuttoned her shirt. Bea walked into the bedroom area of the hotel suite from the adjoining nursery.

"How is my little Teddy bear?" George asked.

Bea smiled and said, "She and Nanny Baker are sound asleep."

George watched as Bea went to her dressing table and took off her jewellery. It always made George's heart ache to watch Bea take off her finery after an evening engagement. She had done countless events like these on her own, and it had been exceptionally lonely to come back and get ready for bed on her own. Now she was never alone.

She thought about how excited Holly had been after they returned to the hotel. She and Bea had talked for ages.

"You know what I don't understand?" George said.

"What don't you understand?" Bea said as she walked over to George. Bea turned her back to her and said, "Unzip me, Bully?"

George stroked her fingers over her wife's bare shoulders. "Why did you buy that auction lot for Holly? I know you said you suspected Holly was bi"—George unzipped Bea's gown—"but surely a Lothario like Story St. John isn't who you want for your friend."

Bea chuckled as her dress pooled at her feet. "Lothario? You really are old-fashioned, Bully." Bea stepped out of her dress and lifted a clothes hanger from the bed to hang it on. "Story does tend to go through women like there's no tomorrow, but it's just stage one in my matchmaking. Hang this up for me, will you, sweetheart?"

George barely heard her. Her gaze was glued to Bea's breasts encased in her silk lingerie. She never noticed much when her wife's breasts were in front of her. She adored them so.

Bea gave her a gentle poke in the stomach. "Eyes up, Your Majesty. Will you hang up my dress?"

"Sorry, of course I will, my darling." George carried the dress over to the large walk-in wardrobe and hung it up, ready for Holly to attend to in the morning.

When she turned around, Bea crooked her finger and bade her come back to her quickly. George's heart began to thud...amongst other things. She simply loved her wife's body, and to think Bea had worried that she wouldn't be as turned on by her after the baby... well, it was the complete opposite. George loved her body more, and as she had said before, Bea had carried their baby, and that was even more exciting.

She put her hands around her wife's waist, and Bea said, "To answer your question—"

"What question?" George pulled Bea close and nuzzled her neck.

Bea pushed her back gently. "Why I paid for Holly's auction prize?"

"Oh...that." George sounded as if she'd wished she'd never asked. "Tell me in the morning."

"Nuh-uh." Bea put both hands on George's chest to hold her back. It was funny but oh-so satisfying that George still wanted her as badly as their first night together. "It's important. Lali, Greta, and I have suspected that Holly was bi over the years, but in the last year it has seemed like something she really wants to explore. She went gaga over Captain Quincy at the polo, and she's always been gaga over Story St. John."

George looked confused. "What? She likes Quincy?"

"No...well she did at the polo match, but she certainly doesn't now."

"Why? What's wrong with Quincy? She's a fine officer. Decorated for bravery. She's a *real* action hero, not a pretend one like bloody Story St. John. I don't think you'd find a better—"

Bea put a finger over George's lips. "Yes, she's very nice, but there was a mix-up, and well, it's too much to explain to you, Bully, but Quincy doesn't exactly engage anyone in conversation. She's a little quiet."

"Quincy has been through an awful lot for this country, Bea," George said seriously.

That stopped Bea in her tracks. "Is that the reason why she won her Victoria Cross?"

George nodded. "It was a classified operation. I know what happened, and I could tell you but—"

"That's all right," Bea said quickly. "You can keep Quincy's confidence. She has more going on beneath the surface than I thought. Anyway, you've distracted me. The first stage of Holly's matchmaking?"

"Oh yes, of course. Do tell," George said, smiling.

"I want Holly to find love like the rest of us have, and she has tried and tried to find the right man over the years, but I have the feeling she should have been looking for the right woman. Just a hunch."

Bea traced her fingernail down George's chest and over the surface of her sports bra, making George's nipples rock hard.

George pulled off her shirt and bra, obviously hoping that would hurry Bea along. "And? Where does Story fit in?" George said breathily.

"Story is fun, full of life, extremely confident in her sexuality— the perfect person to help Holly explore that side of herself."

Bea unclipped her bra and dropped it on the floor. George's hands immediately went to cup her breasts.

"Then stage two swings into action." Bea didn't think George heard her any more, as George had dropped to her knees and started to kiss her stomach.

She stroked her fingers through George's hair. The feeling she had when she looked at George was what she wanted for Holly. Stage two was for Holly to find the one who would love her completely and with unwavering loyalty.

Bea felt George inch down her underwear, kissing her flesh as she went. She stepped out of her panties and said to George, "Bed, Bully."

George stood with the biggest smile on her face. She picked Bea up and carried her over to the bed. Bea pulled George to her and kissed her deeply.

She ran her hands over George's shoulders, back, and upper arms. Bea loved the strong muscles she always found there. She didn't need to fantasize about action heroes like Story St. John because she had her own real soldier ready to make love to her whenever she wanted.

George kissed down to her breasts and spent time licking and sucking all around her nipples. That was always her partner's favourite place to be, and that suited Bea since she loved any attention there.

Bea was throbbing, wet, and desperate for George's touch. She took George's hand and pushed it down to her hot centre.

"Georgie? Make me come while you suck me here." Bea squeezed her own breast.

George grinned and slipped her fingers into her hot, wet folds. "My pleasure. Watch me?"

She groaned at George's touch. This was going to be quick. George licked all around her nipple while she repeated the motion with her fingers around her clit.

Bea's hips started to move as she watched George's wet tongue tease and tantalize her. "Oh God, yes."

From slow stokes George changed her pace to fast by flicking her tongue on the tip of Bea's nipple, her finger matching the speed and barely touching her clit. It was so good, but frustrating at the same time.

"Please go inside. I need you," Bea pleaded.

"Anything for you," George replied.

George sucked her nipple right in her wet mouth and slid two fingers deep inside her at the same time. Bea threaded her fingers through George's hair and thrust her hips in time with the fingers inside of her. She could feel her orgasm building deep inside of her as an electric current of pleasure ran from her nipple down to her clit with every suck and roll of George's tongue.

"Just like that, Bully. Going to come," she gasped.

Bea reached down and placed her hand on top of George's. She wanted to feel every sensation as George fucked her. The ball of heat building inside her reached a peak and tumbled over into an intense orgasm.

"God," Bea shouted as her hips thrust, trying to get George as deeply inside her as possible.

Then she slammed her thighs shut, trapping and stilling George's hand. "Enough."

George let go of her nipple, gave a few final kisses to her breast, then came up to kiss Bea.

"That was so good, Georgie."

George smiled and placed little kisses all over her face. "I love to make you come."

Bea stroked the dark hair from George's eyes. "You're welcome to do it whenever you want, Bully."

George eased her fingers out and pulled her on top of her. Bea looked into George's blue eyes and sighed with happiness. "You have no idea how gorgeous you are, George. Every part of you makes me want you, but especially this." Bea put her hand on George's chest. "Your heart, the love that you have for Teddy and me, makes me the luckiest woman on the planet."

George smiled. "Most of the people at the event tonight wished they were taking you home, so I think I'm the luckiest."

Bea reached down and felt how wet George was. "I'm going to make you feel lucky, Your Majesty. You need to come."

"Oh yes, I do," George said.

As Bea started to kiss her way down to George's sex, the computer monitor on the bedside table lit up, and they heard Teddy crying.

"Mum, Mum! Want Mum!"

George sighed with frustration. Bea rested her head on George's stomach and giggled. "The joys of parenthood."

"I wouldn't have it any other way," George said, "I'll go." She sat up and pulled on some boxers and a T-shirt.

Bea pulled the covers over herself. "I won't forget where we were."

George smiled. "I'm counting on it."

Inspector Lang gathered the protection squad in the lounge room. They all sat around on the couches while Lang went over the night's events, all except Quincy who remained standing with her hands clasped behind her back.

"Tonight went like clockwork, everyone. Well done. Next up is Washington, DC, where the royal party will be met by the president and her husband on the White House lawn. Again, we are only there for two days before moving off to the main tour. We'll be working in concert with the American secret service, so be cooperative.

"Quincy, you will lead a team with Clayton when Queen Beatrice and Princess Edwina have a private day at the natural history museum, while the rest of us will accompany Queen Georgina to the marine base. On the security front, everything is quiet, apart from the usual throwaway threats. There's been nothing substantive."

Garrett didn't like what she was hearing. She should be on point, and Queen Beatrice should be her principal, with that child Clayton under her, looking after the royal brat. It had been her job, she was told, until the bloody Queen stepped in.

No matter how much things moved on, there was still a culture of the upper-class old boys' network in Britain, and Garrett hated it. From what she'd heard, Quincy should have been discharged out of the marines, but her mother's influence swept her assault on her comrade under the carpet. Now she was given the prize of being Queen Beatrice's protection officer, just because she was the Queen's old friend.

Her cold gaze moved onto Quincy, standing there as if she was on parade. Everything about Quincy was aggravating. The way she stood as if she had a stick up her ass, the way those around fawned on her just because she had the Victoria Cross, no doubt given for nothing, but because of her friends in high places.

Garrett's phone beeped with a text message: *I heard someone took the job you were promised.*

Unknown number. Who could be texting her out of nowhere, and how did they know about her job?

She typed out a reply: *Who is this?*

About thirty seconds later a response came: *Someone who shares your hatred. Call me when you get to Washington if you want to help me and get rid of the war hero, and don't bother trying to trace this phone. I'm fifty steps ahead of you.*

Garrett looked up nervously, and the meeting was over. Everyone was filing out to go to bed. Her heart was hammering in her chest. She should report this, she really should.

Garrett watched Inspector Lang walk up to Quincy and pat her on the shoulder. Why did everyone think she was so bloody wonderful?

She looked at her phone. She should report it, Garrett told herself, but then simply put her phone in her top pocket and walked out of the room.

Chapter Five

Queen Georgina and Queen Beatrice were making their way to the White House for the official welcoming ceremony. The line of armoured cars containing the royal party and their staff drove slowly, flanked by police outriders.

Bea took a handkerchief out of her bag and wiped Princess Edwina's mouth. "We shouldn't be taking Teddy, George. She'll be so bored."

George was sitting on the other side of the car reading over her speech. "I know it's not ideal, but both the British and American officials were quite eager to have Teddy with us. The American officials are keen to emphasize the easy-going family element that President Watson has brought to the White House, and our beloved prime minister wants the good publicity that we, as a family unit, bring Britain PLC. Basically, they all want the photo op of us all together. The president's son and daughter will be there too."

"I don't like the idea of our daughter being a photo opportunity, Georgie," Bea said with an annoyed tone to her voice.

George put her papers to the side and leaned over to take Bea's hand. "I know that, and I want to protect you both on this trip as much as possible. Bo Dixon was insistent, so I negotiated. Teddy attends with us for this ceremony, and I get to do some of the visits on my own when we get to Chicago, and you and Teddy get to stay at the hotel and rest."

"If we must, we must then," Bea said. "I'm looking forward to meeting President Watson. She's quite a reformer."

George smiled. "Like someone else I know and love."

The window to the front of the car opened and Quincy said, "We're just pulling in to the White House now, ma'am."

"Thank you, Quincy," George said, then turned back to Bea. "So I'll get out and lift Teddy from her seat. You get out the other side and walk around to meet us."

Bea nodded. "And you'll pass Teddy to me once we go up onto the podium?"

"Yes. Don't worry—everything will go swimmingly," George said.

Bea smoothed down her dress. "I'm actually quite nervous, even after all the events and speeches I've made before. Maybe it's because we're taking Teddy. How many will be there?"

"There'll be seven thousand there on the south lawn, plus photographers," George said.

Bea glanced nervously at Teddy who was chewing on the ear of her bear. "That's an awful lot of people for Teddy."

The car rolled up to the reception area on the south lawn of the White House. They could hear the loud noise of the military band playing, and the chatter of people eagerly awaiting their arrival.

George straightened her tie and gave Bea a reassuring smile. "It's only for a couple of speeches, a few handshakes, then we'll go inside for lunch. Nanny Baker will help look after her."

Bea quickly checked her make-up in the mirror, and the car stopped.

"I love you, Bea."

George's reassuring strength always calmed her down. But then she knew that her presence did the same for George. Bea could only thank God they'd met.

She leaned over and gave Teddy a kiss. "You be a good girl, okay, sweetheart?"

Quincy opened her door and she got out. Bea was immediately hit by the noise that seemed to travel everywhere they did. She walked around the car and joined George who was already shaking hands with the president, along with Teddy.

Bea smiled as she watched President Laura Watson shake hands with Teddy and make a big fuss over her. She did come across as a very easy-going woman.

Her husband was a handsome, warm man who, along with their two teenage children, welcomed George and Teddy just as happily.

Bea approached the president who shook her hand and said, "I'm so pleased to meet you, Your Majesty. Your daughter is adorable."

"Thank you very much. We're delighted to be here."

The president leaned over and said in a conspiratorial low voice, "How about we get all this show over with so we can go back in, kick off our heels, and have lunch?"

Bea laughed softly. "Sounds perfect."

The president was greeted by her husband and children, then they led Bea, George, and Teddy across the south lawn. The sounds of the cameras and the spectators filled the air.

Before they ascended the platform, they all stood as a group, facing the press pack, to give the world the perfect photo op. The two most well-known families in the world, standing side by side in friendship. The royal tour had truly begun.

The next day Queen Beatrice and Princess Edwina were having a private day, while Queen Georgina went to tour the local United States Marine Corps base. Quincy wished she was going there instead of accompanying Queen Beatrice to the natural history museum. The museum had been recommended to them as an excellent choice for a day out. It was indoors and, after the reconnaissance Quincy had done the evening before, easy to make secure.

She and Clayton were standing guard as usual, while they waited on the royal party getting ready, which usually took some time.

Just like clockwork, she heard Holly before she saw her, as she sang her way towards them. Her voice was full of energy and happiness. Everyone said that Holly set the tone of the day. This kind of unrestrained, easy-going attitude was so alien to Quincy and worried her. Yes, that feeling when she was in Holly's company, deep in the pit of her stomach was *worry*…she was sure.

Holly approached holding her make-up kit. "Good morning, Clay."

"Morning, ma'am," Clay said with a huge smile.

"It's Holly, Clay. What a lovely morning it is."

Throughout the whole exchange Quincy kept her steady gaze forward. She then heard Holly say to her, "Good morning, Grumpy, do you ever smile?"

Grumpy? Quincy was immediately aggravated. She kept looking forward and didn't show her aggravation one bit.

"Good morning, Ms. Weaver."

Holly gave an exasperated sigh and said to Clayton, "Does she ever smile? My God, Quincy, you are hard work."

Luckily for Quincy she then went in to the Queen. Grumpy? *I'm not grumpy. I'm professional.*

Quincy felt her anger rising and her heart started to beat fast. The anger made her panic. She couldn't afford to let that out. She closed her eyes, took a breath, and she was back in control.

About ten minutes later Queen Beatrice asked her to join them. When she went into the lounge area of the suite she found Queen Beatrice and Holly on the floor, playing with Princess Edwina and her toys. Nanny Baker was sitting on the couch.

Anyone who saw Beatrice in her jeans playing with the princess on the floor would never believe she was a Queen Consort—they would think she was a normal mum. In the short time she had worked for Beatrice, she had seen what a great mum she was.

She turned her gaze to Holly and stopped breathing for a second. The sunlight coming through the window was hitting Holly's beautiful reddish-blond hair, giving it a golden warmth that made Quincy want to run her hands through it. Holly was beautiful.

"Quincy, we want to make a slight change to the visit to the museum," Beatrice said.

Now Quincy was starting to worry. Changes to the schedule were never good. "What change, ma'am?"

Bea looked to Holly and smiled. "It was actually Holly's idea. We thought it would be a much better idea to go to the zoo than a museum. I think Teddy is a little bit small to appreciate dinosaur bones."

Quincy tried her utmost to keep her tone light and not show her annoyance and worry. "Ma'am, the museum has been finalized and fully checked for security. Every one of the staff has been background checked. The police dogs have been through it, and I myself have personally checked the entire building."

Beatrice turned to Holly and said, "Maybe she's right."

Holly furrowed her eyebrows. "No, Bea. Don't let Grumpy here dictate how you spend your free time—you get little enough as it is. Teddy's only one year old. She's not going to be interested in a pile of dusty dinosaur bones."

Holly picked up Teddy and said, "You want to see the lions, don't you, Teddy?"

"Lions!" Teddy replied excitedly.

Quincy could hardly contain her annoyance and frustration. "Ma'am, the zoo is an open-air site, packed with members of the public. I can't—"

She was cut off by Holly who stood up and walked over to her quickly. "Listen, I want to keep Bea's and Teddy's lives as normal as possible. The zoo is the perfect place for a one-year-old."

Quincy used everything she had to say as calmly as possible, "It is *my* job, Ms. Weaver, to keep Queen Beatrice and Princess Edwina safe. Need I remind you that the King and the Crown Prince of Denbourg were assassinated last year. The world is a dangerous place."

"No one is a threat to Bea and a little child," Holly said furiously.

Strangely, the angrier Holly got, the harder Quincy's heart beat. She decided to say nothing. She wasn't going to win this fight with either of these two women, and she wanted to calm the tension she was feeling inside.

"As you wish, ma'am. I'll get the team organized." Quincy bowed her head and walked out as calmly as she could muster.

As she shut the door she heard Holly say, "What is wrong with her? She just gives in and stomps out, after I've been arguing in her face…"

Quincy turned to Clayton, who stood guard in the corridor. "Clayton, stay here. There's been a change of plan. I'm going to brief the team Inspector Lang left us, then I'll be back."

"Yes, ma'am."

❖

Quincy walked down the corridor towards her bedroom. Hopefully most of their days wouldn't be as chaotic as today had been. The stress of not having done reconnaissance before the zoo visit was really intense. Quincy's need for order and control was ripped to shreds.

Holly Weaver was obviously going to be a bad influence and a problem on this tour. She lived life without rules and expected everyone else to do that, but Quincy couldn't let Holly's influence affect Queen Beatrice's safety.

She turned the corner and bumped right into Holly coming the other way. "Evening, Stompy," Holly said.

She had now gone from grumpy to stompy. Quincy didn't know which one was more annoying. Quincy took a breath and said, "Good evening, Ms. Weaver."

Holly didn't seem happy with that. Unlike Quincy, Holly couldn't hide her displeasure. She sighed with annoyance and walked off.

About ten seconds later, Holly came hurrying back, looking really peeved. "What is wrong with you?"

"Excuse me? I don't understand, Ms. Weaver," Quincy said.

Holly growled. "Oh, stop calling me *Ms. Weaver* like we're in some sort of Jane Austen novel. I argued with you today, and you just stood there like a statue. I say good morning to you every day, and you stand staring forward like a statue. Have I done something to you? Why don't you show any sort of emotion? Anything, even anger, shout at me, *anything*. It's so annoying. Show what you're feeling, even for a good morning. Look at me at least."

Quincy saw fire and a passionate anger in Holly's face, and felt her own body react to it. Her heart sped up and heat radiated through her body. No matter the cause of Holly's passionate reaction, Quincy enjoyed basking in its warmth and heat.

Holly awoke a longing Quincy didn't know she had. She wished she could let herself truly feel and show emotions the way Holly did, and Quincy admired that quality in her.

She took a moment and a breath to calm her hammering heart, then looked Holly right in the eyes and said quite coldly, "I don't let myself feel, Holly."

Holly looked at her searchingly. She obviously hadn't been expecting that response.

Quincy had to get away, so she simply said, "Goodnight, Holly," then walked away leaving Holly standing there. When she lay in bed that night, Holly's fiery, passionate eyes were stuck in her mind. Holly's fiery eyes morphed into real fire in her mind as she drifted off to sleep.

Quincy coughed and spluttered as she desperately tried to find her men and women in the smoke-filled warehouse. She could hear their screams, their desperate shouts, and she felt powerless as she tried to navigate the smoke-filled rooms.

"Jacob?" she shouted, hoping her friend would reply.

The smoke and the heat of the flames licking around the structure were becoming overwhelming, and she had to fight the choking feeling and her instincts to run the other way.

She shouted again and followed the cries of pain closest to her. She found the room and saw someone she didn't recognize because of the effects of the blast and fire lying on the floor. The entrance to the room was on fire and she needed to run through to get him.

Quincy didn't think, she just acted. She took off her jacket, held it over her head, and ran into the inferno. She screamed as she caught fire, the pain and the panic so intense.

Until she woke up gasping.

"Jesus."

Quincy grabbed for her water, to try to calm herself. Her hands and her whole body were shaking.

"Keep control, keep control," Quincy said like a mantra.

She couldn't lose control again.

CHAPTER SIX

Another day, another aeroplane journey, that's what it felt like to Holly, and this was only the start of the tour. They had been to Toronto, stopped briefly in Washington to be greeted by the president, and now were on to their main engagements.

Holly was in the bedroom area of the plane helping to dress Queen Beatrice before landing in New York.

"This is really beautiful, Holly," Bea said as Holly zipped her into her dress.

"Thanks. I hoped you'd like it. I know Jaq Dillard is a really new designer on the block, but her designs are stunning, I thought."

Bea smoothed her hands down the sky-blue dress and sat at the dressing table. "It's perfect and fits the brief I gave you. British designers, and especially up and coming designers. If every picture of me on this tour is going to be captioned with, *Queen Beatrice was wearing*...we might as well give some publicity to our home-grown talent."

Holly leaned on Bea's shoulder. "I bet you never guessed when you were studying so hard at university, that you'd end up being a fashion icon."

Bea laughed. "Never in my wildest dreams. I wasn't the least interested in fashion back then, but it's all worth it if we keep raising as much money as we have been."

Holly opened her make-up kit and started to prepare what she would need. "I don't envy you, Bea. You have to keep up this pace for the rest of your life."

Bea sighed. "I know. At least we're going to be in New York for a whole week. Besides, we're doing good, and I'm doing it with the love of my life."

"You're lucky," Holly said with a hint of sadness in her voice.

"What's annoying you?" Bea said.

"How do you know anything is annoying me?" Holly said defensively.

Bea raised an eyebrow to her friend. "Holls, we usually can't shut you up, and you've been really quiet on the plane journey."

Holly let out a breath and started to retouch Bea's make-up. "It's something that happened the other night. I met Quincy in the hotel hallway, the day we went to the zoo, and I confronted her about the day."

"What did you say?" Bea asked.

"I was just frustrated. No matter what I said or did that day—cracked a joke, be angry at her—she just gave me nothing back. She's like one of those Greek statues."

"And what did she say?" Bea said.

"Nothing at first, which made me even more frustrated. Then I shouted—*Just show me you feel something, anger even, just something.* She looked at me directly in the eye for the first time and said she doesn't let herself feel."

"Nothing?" Bea said.

"Yeah, that's what I thought. It's a really strange thing to say. How can you not let yourself feel emotions? They just are—they just happen."

"I shouldn't really say this Holls…" Bea said.

Holly stopped dead in her tracks and sat on the edge of the dressing table. "What? You know something about her?"

Bea looked as if she was struggling with what she could say. "I don't know all the details, but you know she won the gallantry medal?"

Holly nodded. "Yes, I know all the security people really look up to her."

"Well, all I know is that she went through a lot to get it. Quincy was in hospital for a time after her mission. George says she was a real hero. She saved lives in the face of danger. I think that's why

George asked her onto our team so suddenly. Something happened, and she had to get away from her regiment."

"Wow," Holly said, as her mind was imagining all sorts of situations.

"Promise you won't say anything to anyone, Holls?" Bea said.

"I promise, Bea. You know you can trust me," Holly said.

Holly remembered the incident in Toronto, when the boy lunged at Bea. Afterwards at the hotel, when Quincy didn't think anyone was watching, her hand was shaking uncontrollably. There was something under that stony façade, Holly thought, and she was going to find it.

What she didn't tell Bea was when she confronted Quincy, and she gazed back at her, Holly had observed that Quincy's eyes looked as if they had seen more than anyone ever should.

She feels. I know it and I'm going to coax it out of her.

Holly was nothing if not determined and persistent, and it felt like a challenge to unearth the emotional side of Quincy. No one who tried to take care of others and was prepared to die for her comrades felt nothing. There was a torrent behind those steady controlled eyes, and Holly had to unleash it.

George was sitting with Teddy on her knee in the seating area of the plane, going over her schedule with Cammy. Sebastian approached the table and showed her some papers.

"Ma'am, these are the amendments the foreign secretary would like to make," Bastian said.

Nanny Baker got up from the seats across from them and said, "Would you like me to take Teddy for you, ma'am?"

To anyone else, her situation would have seemed absolute chaos. She was reading important documents and making notes while Teddy was singing along with the characters she was watching on her computer pad, but this was what George had always dreamed of. She remembered taking part in these tours with her mother and father, and she had never ever been pushed aside for official business.

"It's okay, Nanny Baker. Teddy's being as good as gold—aren't you, Teddy?"

Teddy just continued singing, and Cammy laughed. "Teddy and Queen Beatrice are the only ones who can get away with ignoring you, ma'am."

George chuckled. "Very true." She turned back to Sebastian. "These changes are fine. Thank you, Bastian."

As he walked away, she glanced over at Captain Quincy. She was looking at her phone and appeared agitated. Then Quincy got up and quickly walked to the front of the plane.

"Cammy, is Quincy settling in all right?" George said.

"I think so. The team respect her as far as I know. I'm sure she probably finds this a big change from military life."

George smiled. "I can imagine. This is organized chaos compared to what she's used to. Guarding a family isn't easy, I know. You manage well, Cammy, but Quincy is so much more reserved."

"She's had a hard time, but being with her friends can only help," Cammy said.

❖

The quickly arranged meeting was frustrating Quincy. Neither Garrett nor Inspector Lang seemed to be taking her worries seriously.

During the flight she had received what she perceived to be a threating text message to her phone: *Can you keep Queen Beatrice safe? We'll find out...*

Inspector Lang said, "There are no serious threats against Queen Beatrice. Military intelligence keeps us abreast of any internet chatter, and there's nothing. We'll keep an alert eye on this, but the threat seems more personal to you, Quincy. We'll have this looked into when we land and get set up."

"Sir—" Quincy started, but Lang walked out of the meeting room, ready to land.

Garrett walked up behind her and laughed. "A bit jumpy, Quincy, aren't you? We haven't even started the tour, and you're already causing trouble."

"Listen, Garrett. I don't care what you think of me. I care about keeping Queen Beatrice and Princess Edwina safe. Keep your feelings of job disappointment away from duty, okay?"

Garrett gave her a dirty look and walked off.

❖

The plane door opened, and Holly watched as the security team waited to lead the way. She couldn't help but zero in on Quincy. Despite her neutral facial expression, she could see Quincy's breathing was heavier than normal, and on instinct she looked down to Quincy's hands. The one she could see was balled into a tight fist, but she was sure she could see a slight tremor.

You feel too much, I think.

They travelled to the hotel, and once the royal party were taken up to their rooms by the manager, the staff were taken upstairs by a very officious assistant manager with a computer pad.

"Follow me, please."

He set off at a rapid pace. Holly nudged Lali. "Remind you of anyone, Lali?" Holly joked.

Lali nudged her back. "Oh, shush."

He led them through the grand marble entrance of the hotel. The hotel felt out of place in a modern New York, a hotel from a bygone era when the rich and famous were treated like royalty themselves.

The assistant manager led them to a set of gold elevators. Inspector Lang was already placing men and women at the bottom of them, and she presumed there were guards on the floor where they were staying.

When the elevator opened onto their floor, it was already busy with staff milling about. It reminded her that she had still so much work today, after a long day of travelling. There was Bea's and Teddy's luggage to deal with, and Bea's clothes to be steamed for tomorrow.

She saw Captain Quincy and Cammy organizing their security teams. Quincy looked up from her computer pad as she passed.

What was going on behind those eyes? Holly wondered, but her mission on this tour was to work Quincy out. A national hero, someone who would think of others before herself, could not be this stony person she presented. To care and to risk yourself for others— you had to care a lot.

❖

Holly ate her dinner in her room, checked her email, and called Greta back in Britain with all the news. She had already set out Bea's clothes for tomorrow morning. It was a dressed-down visit at a kids' program in the city, before two more formal events in the afternoon and evening, so there was a lot to get ready.

She decided to go and check out the lounge area the other staff had told her about. The rec room, as it had been christened, was a meeting room situated on this floor, and re-allocated for their use.

The corridor was quiet, with only the guards on night shift at the floor entrance. The rest of the staff had gone out for a night in the Big Apple.

It was nights like tonight when she felt the loneliest, and her thoughts turned over and over in her head. Mainly she thought about her sexuality and questioned if she was ready to start dating women again. Could her heart take more heartbreak? She would get a chance to test her theory on her dream date with Story St. John at the end of the week.

She wandered into the rec room, spotted a coffee machine, and made her way over. She heard a noise and looked around to see Captain Quincy sitting on the couch in the far corner of the room, doing something or other with a paintbrush.

Quincy looked up and said, "Good evening, Ms. Weaver."

Holly had to admit that her low upper-class accent was quite sexy. It was just a shame it belonged to such a frustrating person.

"Hi, Stompy," Holly said, just to be annoying. Aggravatingly, Quincy gave her a small smile in return.

Holly looked around the room. People sat here and there, talking and sharing stories, and she felt sorry for Quincy sitting all by herself. These were her colleagues, yet she sat alone.

Don't do it, Holls, she told herself, but in spite of that, she poured another coffee and started walking towards Quincy's table.

Quincy stood politely when she saw her coming. "Can I help you, Ms. Weaver? Is there something wrong?"

Holly sighed and plonked herself down at the table. "There will be if you don't stop calling me Ms. Weaver. It's Holly."

"Sorry—Ms. Holly," Quincy said with the ghost of a smile.

"Wait, was that a joke?" Holly said. "Not from you, Stompy."

Quincy gave her another smile. Two smiles in one night? She was privileged.

Holly put both cups of coffee on the table and noticed a few other cups there, along with a case of paints, various brushes, water, and a box of unpainted figures. What was Quincy doing?

"I brought you a coffee, but I see you've had a few already," Holly said.

"Thank you. I could do with another," Quincy replied.

"You'll never sleep, you know."

Quincy cleared her throat nervously and said, "I don't sleep much."

There was a silence, and Quincy went back to her painting of her little figures and Holly took a sip of coffee.

"Ugh, it's not the best coffee, is it."

Quincy never looked from her painting. Holly couldn't help but gaze at Quincy's slow, methodical brushstrokes. She was so precise.

"Compared to the coffee brew kits in marine rations, it's top notch," Quincy said.

Top notch? She sounded just like George. So posh. Holly chuckled to herself. "I couldn't live without my coffee. When I'm in London, I love to get mine on my way to work, but since we've been on tour, I've been too lazy to get up early enough to go out and get it."

Another silence sat between them. Quincy wasn't much at making conversation. Why had she come over here in the first place? Holly thought.

As if reading her mind, Quincy said, "Thank you for bringing me coffee, but don't feel obligated to sit with me."

Holly sat up quickly and said defensively, "I don't feel obligated."

Even though she did, but she wasn't going to let Quincy think she was right and make herself look bad.

"So, what are you doing here with your paints and brushes?" Holly was going to have a conversation whether Quincy liked it or not.

Quincy put down the figure she was holding and set her fine paintbrush in a cup of water.

"I paint model soldiers and—"

Holly burst out laughing. "You paint toy soldiers? Like the kind kids play with?"

"I do not paint *toy* soldiers," Quincy said defensively. "I paint metal figures. It's very precise and difficult work. I do it to relax."

Relax? She painted toy soldiers to relax? My God, she would have never imagined that drop-dead gorgeous polo player she had seen a year ago would paint soldiers for fun. Maybe all military officers were dull—after all, Queen Georgina made model ships and planes. She had a whole room dedicated to it at Windsor. Beatrice found it endearing in George, but the silent Captain Quincy was a different matter.

She had seen George with Bea in private, and they had such a passionate energy. Quincy didn't appear to have passion or anger in her. Captain Cameron was never dull either, so it couldn't be an officer thing.

"…in the Big Apple?" Holly caught the tail-end of Quincy's question but had been so lost in her thoughts she missed the rest.

"Sorry, what did you say?"

"I said, I thought you'd be spending time with your friends tonight, or out with the other staff? Clay couldn't wait to go out and experience an evening in the Big Apple." Quincy took a drink of her coffee.

"You mean Bea and Lali?" Holly said.

Quincy nodded.

"Well, they all were having a dinner and movie night. To relax before the workweek really starts. But Lali has Cammy now, so it's a couples thing. I didn't want to be a third wheel. Bea and Lali tried to insist, but no. My friends have all coupled up and I'm the last single one. It's awkward sometimes."

Holly realized how open she was being. She hadn't admitted that to anyone, not even her friends.

"I understand. Why didn't you go out on the town? I'm sure Clay would have been delighted to escort you," Quincy said quite seriously.

"Escort me?" Holly laughed softly. It was like having a conversation with someone from a Regency romance novel. "I don't need an escort, and anyway Clay is too young for me. She is gorgeous eye candy though."

Quincy looked down quickly and tensed up. She clearly found that sort of talk embarrassing. She wondered what it would take to ruffle those posh, awkward, dull feathers.

Holly had wanted to keep talking to Quincy to prove a point, and Quincy was intriguing, like a puzzle she had to work out. No one who looked as good as she did in a polo uniform could be that dull.

"Anyway, we've got a lot on this week, and I need all my beauty sleep for my date on Friday."

"Your date?" Quincy looked up.

"My auction date with Story St. John. Have you seen any of her films? She plays a soldier a lot and holds a machine gun like no one else." Holly smiled and winked.

Quincy looked at her impassively. The small amount of light-heartedness they had shared during the conversation had disappeared.

"No, I haven't. I don't see many films or TV unless they're documentaries."

"I thought you'd say that." Holly stretched and yawned. "I better go and get my beauty sleep."

When Holly stood, so did Quincy. Politeness was ingrained in her it seemed. "Good night, Ms. Holly."

"Night, Stompy," Holly said and walked off.

CHAPTER SEVEN

Quincy got her usual couple hours of nightmare-filled sleep and went out for a run before her duty shift started. The busy, noisy New York streets were the perfect antidote to the dark movies that played and replayed in her mind.

It was going to be a busy day for the royal couple with three events packed into the day. She prayed they would get through the day and this tour without incident. George, her friend, had entrusted her wife and her child to Quincy, and Quincy felt the pressure every day, especially after the threat she had received.

Inspector Lang took the text seriously enough, but she suspected the rest of the team had listened to Garrett's insinuations after the incident in Toronto. They thought she had a hair-trigger response at least, and who knew what they said about her when she wasn't there.

She had to be vigilant. She'd let down her comrades on their last mission, and she wasn't going to let it happen again, no matter what her colleagues thought.

Quincy stopped when she came upon a coffee shop. It was the chain that Holly had mentioned being her favourite, that she was never up early enough to get.

I wonder what she likes?

Her first instinct was to bring her something, but she had no idea what to order and, going by the menu she could see through the window, the list was extensive.

She decided to make it her mission to find out. The conversation they'd had last night revealed a lot to her about Holly. She wasn't just the larger than life party girl. She was kind, that was certain. There was no way Holly came over to talk to her last night through interest in her. It was undoubtedly through kindness, when Holly saw her sitting on her own.

Quincy wasn't one to share a joke or sparkling conversation, she knew that about herself, and while she busied herself with her model painting, she wasn't the most likely to attract a friendly companion. That suited Quincy. Friends or lovers wanted something she couldn't give—feelings, affection. Feelings made you ineffective to your task, as her mother had taught her, and as she had learned, feelings could take your life, everything you held dear, away from you.

She knew she inspired loyalty from those who served under her, simply by her conduct, her bravery, and fairness, and she had cared about all those who served in her unit like brothers and sisters. That was why it hurt so much, and why she had to keep iron control on herself.

She arrived back at the hotel by six a.m. Plenty of time to get showered and changed. Then her phone pinged with a text.

Nobody believes you, do they?

Holly thought she had broken the ice with Quincy last night, but this morning she was back to her unapproachable, stompy self, and when she tried to talk to Quincy, it seemed like her head was in a completely different place. It was almost like she had let a tiny sliver of personality show, then reined it back in quickly. Why was she frightened of showing what was clearly underneath the surface?

At the first visit that morning the Queen, Bea, and Teddy went to a children's charity project. Bea thought it was particularly important to include this charity when they had made the plans for the tour, since it was for children who'd suffered bereavement, a subject very close to Beatrice's heart.

Bea had never appointed ladies-in-waiting, as such, so Lali and Holly pitched in whenever they were needed—like today, when Bea thought she might need some backup help with Teddy.

They met a group of about twenty-five children and the charity's staff. George and Bea went around to every one of them, listening to their stories and telling them how brave they were.

Holly was so proud of Bea. All the children were nervous about meeting her until she hugged them and put them at their ease. Once the first few kids had a hug from Bea, a line for her hugs developed, so much so that George joked that no one wanted her hugs. Of course, the kids then ran to her.

After watching a play about bereavement, put on by the children, they were invited to take part in a game of indoor kickball.

Holly hovered around the edge just in case George or Bea would need her to take Teddy. She saw Garrett standing a few feet away and took the opportunity to walk over.

"Hi, Garrett, it's going well isn't it?"

Garrett grinned. "Yep, no problems, just like I said."

Holly turned to her quickly. "Why? Was there supposed to be?"

Garrett whispered, "According to our Captain Quincy, there's threats to Queen Beatrice around every corner on this trip. She keeps trying to convince Inspector Lang, anyway."

That was the argument she must have overheard on the plane. Holly played dumb. "Why would anyone threaten Queen Beatrice?"

"That's what nobody in the team knows apart from the brave Captain Quincy, so it would seem."

Holly detected a large dose of jealousy from Garrett. She did know the job of Bea's security person had been earmarked for Garrett, until the Queen unexpectedly chose Captain Quincy.

Maybe she could use Garrett to find out some more info on Quincy. "What do you know about Quincy, Garrett?"

Garrett gave her a slightly suspicious look. "Why are you interested?"

"Because Queen Beatrice is one of my best friends, and I want to know she is in safe hands, and Captain Quincy has barely acknowledged me since she started working with us. I'd like to know if she has a problem."

"Yeah, you're Queen Bea's close friend, aren't you?" Garrett appeared to grasp that she might have someone with the Queen's ear. Garrett leaned over and said, "When she was appointed, I heard lots of rumours, so I made enquiries. She's been in the marines since she left boarding school and worked without incident until after she won her Victoria Cross."

Holly turned her head to catch sight of Quincy and found the captain's eyes already on her. That was a few times she had caught her doing that. Did she aggravate Quincy that much?

Garrett continued, "Her mother is the highest ranking woman in the armed services."

"Wow," Holly said. "Is she in the marines too?"

"No, a vice admiral in the Royal Navy. Not hard to understand Quincy's quick rise through the ranks, or her medal."

That comment was a step too far. Any good friend of George's and Cammy's would be loyal, hardworking, and never take a leg up. As quiet and unassuming as Quincy was, and maybe conservative in her tastes, she wouldn't believe that of her.

She thought she'd heard enough. "Well, thanks, Garrett."

And as she went to walk away, Garrett grasped her arm and said, "But you haven't heard the best bit. After she won her medal, Captain Quincy beat a fellow officer to a pulp. Put him in hospital. She should have been court-martialled out of the service, and but for her mother and the Queen riding to her rescue, she would have. Now she has the cushy and extremely well-paid job of protecting Queen Beatrice and the heir to the throne. Nice, eh?"

Just as Holly went to reply, Garrett's mobile rang. She looked at it and said, "I have to take this."

Then walked off. Holly considered their exchange as she watched Garrett whisper into her phone.

I don't think I like you. She didn't buy Garrett's assessment of Quincy one bit, although it was interesting to find out some of Quincy's background. Having a vice admiral for a mother must have been interesting.

Holly looked over to Quincy again. She didn't know why she was so interested in what made Quincy tick. She supposed it was because she hadn't met anyone so controlled—and apparently without much of a personality—before. There must be some fire in there. Somewhere, surely.

"Walk to Holls." Bea was walking to her, with Teddy leading the way, and Bea supporting Teddy with her hands.

Holly crouched down and opened her arms to her. "Come on, then. Walk to me."

Teddy shuffled towards her with a big smile on her face.

Holly grasped her up into her arms and twirled Teddy in the air. The little girl giggled, and Holly brushed her dark hair from her deep blue eyes.

As Bea joined her, Holly said, "This one is going to break some hearts, Bea."

Bea smiled and said, "If she's anything like her mum, she will. We came for your help, didn't we, poppet?"

Teddy nodded and said, "Help, Holls."

"We can't let Mum win, can we Teddy?"

They both looked over to George, who had two kids by the hands. "Hurry up, you three."

George smiled, and Holly heard Bea sigh lovingly. "You're still as loved up as when you met, aren't you?"

Bea nodded. "I never thought I could be this lucky."

"I wish someone would make me sigh like that," Holly said.

Bea gave her a cheeky smile. "Story St. John did."

Holly kissed Teddy's brow. "That doesn't count. She's unattainable, and I am supposed to be the great man-eater, remember?"

"Supposed to be. Let's go, Teddy."

After two engagements in one day, it was back to the hotel to get a quick meal and prepare for the royal couple's evening event. Once Queen Beatrice was safely in her suite, Quincy went in search of Inspector Lang in the rec room, where the team were getting some food during their break. She'd reported the text message as soon as she got back from her run this morning and Lang had said it would be traced while they were out.

Quincy strode into the rec room and saw a group of agents around Garrett, who stopped talking when she entered. Clay was eating with one of the other staff members, and Lang sat at one of the tables looking over his computer pad.

"Sir?" Quincy said.

He looked up. "Ah, Captain. Make sure you eat before we head back out. It's going to be a late one by the looks of it."

"Sir, did you trace the text message?" Quincy said.

Inspector Lang cleared his throat. "Yes, we did. It was a cheap prepaid phone, discarded in a bin—"

Garrett, whom she hadn't heard approach, said, "A bin that happened to be on your jogging route this morning. Imagine that."

She turned to her quickly. "Just what are you insinuating?"

Garret smirked at her. "What do you think, Captain Fantastic?"

Quincy felt a hot surge of anger course through her system, and it took everything in her not to respond in kind.

"That's enough, Garrett. Go," Inspector Lang said.

When she walked off, Lang put a supportive arm on her shoulder. "Listen, Quincy. I checked and rechecked with intelligence, there is absolutely no chatter or any threats to Queen Beatrice. If this is a threat, it's someone working on their own."

"That's all it takes. One person, sir," Quincy said.

"I know, and we will monitor the situation and be prepared until we know more," Lang said.

"I think we should tell the Queen, sir."

"No," Lang said firmly. "I know Queen Georgina is your personal friend, but I don't want her worrying over something that will most likely be no threat."

"Of course, sir." Even though she disagreed, Quincy would never go above Inspector Lang's head and disregard the chain of command.

"Now get something to eat," Lang told her before getting back to his work.

Quincy felt so frustrated. How could no one see what she did? There was so much at stake.

Clayton walked up to her and said, "Captain, come and eat with us?"

"Not tonight, Clay. I think I'll just go back to my room for a while."

Holly watched Bea finish feeding Teddy in her high chair, then lift her out and give her a big kiss.

Nanny Baker came and took Teddy from Bea, then said, "Let's get you ready for your bath, Your Royal Highness."

Bea said, "The Queen is doing her boxes, but let her know when Teddy's ready, Nanny Baker. She always likes to bathe Teddy."

"Of course, ma'am."

Bea flopped down on the couch beside Holly and hugged her cushion. "Can you believe I have to go out again? I'm exhausted after today's visits."

"A Queen Consort's work is never done," Holly quipped.

"You're not joking. The kids ran rings around me today. It's amazing that children who've been through so much can still find it in themselves to laugh and play. It's inspiring, makes me feel bad for even daring to complain. Forget I said I'm tired. Tonight I will have the biggest smile on."

"That's the spirit." Holly looked at her watch. "I'm starving. I hope Lali hurries up."

When they'd returned, they'd agreed to have dinner together while George caught up on work. Lali said she would organize dinner.

"She's probably caught up with Cammy," Bea said.

Holly rolled her eyes. "No doubt. Honestly, she spent months insisting that she wasn't interested in Cammy, and now she can't keep away."

Bea laughed. "She was always interested—Lali just didn't want to admit it. Now on to important matters. What are you going to wear for dinner with Story St. John?"

Holly's head hit against the back of the sofa. "Don't ask. I'll need to go shopping. Maybe on Thursday when we've got the day off, Lali could come with me."

"And what about me?" Bea said.

"I thought you'd want to spend it with George and Teddy," Holly said.

"I do, but this is your big date with Story St. John, Holls."

Holly took Bea's hand. "I'd love it if you came. I'm so nervous. I know I'm going to say or do something stupid."

"Holls?" Bea said seriously. "Why have you never explored this side of yourself before?"

"What do you mean?" Holly said.

"Oh, the fact that you're attracted to women. You are, aren't you?"

Holly nodded. She couldn't lie to her friend. "Yes, I have always been."

"Why did you never tell us? I mean you've always made comments about women, and I've seen the way you look at some, but it's always been men you've chased."

Holly sighed. How to explain this? "I found men didn't often expect a lot from me emotionally, and that suited me. A few wanted to take things further, but I just broke it off then."

Bea looked confused. "Why did you?"

"I didn't want to fall in love. I was in love once, and she broke my heart. Remember, I met you guys at the LGBT group on campus. You advertised for helpers for an event?"

Bea looked as if she was thinking hard for a minute. "Oh yes, you came with that gorgeous looking girl, what was her name—"

"Sade, that's her. She dumped me right after that meeting. She had been seeing someone else. I was so in love with her. I vowed that was the last time I'd fall like that."

There was a knock at the door, and Lali led in a couple of hotel staff with food for them. Once the staff left, Lali said, "Sorry I'm late. What did I miss?"

Bea said, "Holly's bi."

Quick as a flash Lali replied, "I already knew that."

It was so good to laugh with her friends.

Quincy slammed the door to her room. It was only in the safety of her room that she could let her feelings rise to the surface. She sat on the bed and held her head in her hands. Her anger was simmering inside of her, while a feeling of impotence and frustration paralyzed her.

Her mobile beeped and her heart sank. When she picked it up she read: *I'm watching and waiting.*

She threw the phone on the floor in frustration. Why were these threats so personal to her? What the hell was going on?

Why could no one see what she could? There was a threat, a clear threat to Queen Beatrice's safety, and no one was doing anything. As she sat with her eyes closed, movies of fire burning flesh and the screams that haunted her played across her mind. When the fire started, burning heat spread across her body, and she jumped and opened her eyes.

Quincy tried to take deep breaths to calm herself. Would these episodes ever get any better? Would she always be this defective? That was how she thought of herself. A marine who couldn't control themselves was defective. She managed to fake her wellness to the psychiatrist, but she knew herself that she didn't only have scars on the outside of her body. Months of trying to keep these episodes under wraps during her close protection training had been hard but doable.

Now that she was on the job, a job with stress and lots of other staff members making things harder, keeping a lid on the episodes was difficult. Stress amplified her problems.

Her gaze fell to the computer pad on her desk. Maybe speaking to Helen would help clear her mind. She walked over to her desk and made the call.

Helen's face appeared on screen. "Hi, Quin. It's great to see your face."

Quincy let out a breath. "It's good to see you too."

She had always envied that strong bond of love that Helen and Jacob had. Since he had been injured, Quincy was sure that Helen's love was the only thing keeping Jacob alive.

"How's the tour?" Helen said. "We've been watching it on the news at the hospital. Princess Edwina looks the sweetest." Quincy was silent in response, but Helen must have seen the tension on her face because she added, "Is everything okay? Are you coping, Quin?"

"Of course…well, I can't really talk about it," Quincy said.

Helen smiled. "I'm well used to military secrets, living with Jacob. Tell me the gist of it."

"There's a certain threat to the royal party, I think, and no one is taking it seriously. The security team appear to know all about my disciplinary incident and think I may have a screw loose, it seems."

"I see. Well my advice to you would be to use your initiative. You have lots of resources. Use them," Helen said.

Quincy had never thought of that. "You mean Blade?"

Helen smiled. "I'm sure she could help you with some non-official enquiries."

Blade, a hacker, had been an officer in military intelligence when Jacob and Quincy first met her. Now out of the military and working freelance, she could be called on for help.

"Thanks, Helen. That's a great idea." Quincy's stomach churned with guilt as she contemplated asking the next question. She looked down and said, "How's Jacob?"

Helen gulped hard and put on a smile. "He's doing as well as could be expected."

The shame slithered around inside her body. *It should have been me.*

"How are you doing, Quin?" Helen asked. "Are you sleeping all right?"

She couldn't lie to Helen. "As well as could be expected."

"It doesn't help Jacob when you don't sleep, you know."

Quincy didn't want to reply, so she just said, "I better go, Helen. We have an evening engagement tonight. Thank you for talking to me."

"Anytime, Quin. Take care."

"You too. Goodbye," Quincy said.

As soon as the call ended, there was a knock at her door. It wasn't usual for anyone to come to her bedroom.

She went to the door and opened it to find a smiling Holly Weaver. Bright and smiling Holly Weaver, that's how she thought of her.

"Good evening, Ms. Holly. How can I help you?"

"Queen Beatrice asked me to come and talk to you about a day out we're planning. We promised we wouldn't spring anything on you without notice again, so here I am." Holly had been expecting to be asked in, but Quincy hadn't as yet. She tried to look over Quincy's shoulder and saw a room sitting absolutely perfectly. Almost like there was no one living in it. Holly's room was a mess every day until the maid service came, her bed sheets all over the place, computer pad and mobiles strewn around the room. But at least it had personality. She'd added pictures of her mum and dad, her brother, her life, basically. From what she could see, there was none of that in Quincy's room.

Yet another mystery about Captain Quincy.

"Where would the Queen Consort like to go?" Quincy said.

"Well, you know I'm going out with Story St. John on Friday night? I have nothing to wear, so I thought we could go shopping to one of the amazing department stores here. Maybe Saks or Bloomingdale's, although I don't know if I can afford the prices there—"

"No," Quincy said firmly.

Holly stopped midsentence, not quite believing what she was hearing. "Excuse me?"

"I said *no*. Going to a department store is absolutely out of the question. I did say I would work with you to try and enable Queen Beatrice to have some normal days out on this tour, but a shopping trip cannot be made safe."

Holly was furious. How dare Quincy say no to her as if she was in charge. She took a step into Quincy's space and said, "I don't know what you think is going on here, Captain *I'm in charge of everything*, but this is not the marines. You can't just command me and I'll do what you say, and you most certainly can't command Queen Beatrice, so I would start making plans if I were you."

Holly stopped speaking and expected Quincy to shout back at her, but instead she just stared into Holly's eyes like a statue, her jaw clenched tightly.

She waited and waited, but Quincy said nothing. "What is wrong with you? Say something."

Holly was getting angrier by the second. What would it take to make Quincy loosen up and act like a human being?

On impulse she grabbed Quincy's tie, pulled Quincy the few inches towards her, and kissed her. She gave Quincy the deepest, most passionate kiss she could muster, but after a few seconds Quincy's mouth softened and Holly got the same feeling she'd had the first time she had ever seen Quincy at the polo match. Her stomach flip-flopped and twisted and turned in the most amazingly delicious way. Then she remembered she was angry and who she was kissing and pulled back right away.

Quincy appeared shocked, but everything about her was softer looking. Her body had relaxed, her jaw and face were not hard like a marble statue, and her eyes didn't look dead any more. There was a glint of fire and passion there, she was sure of it.

They both stood there saying nothing. Finally, Holly couldn't stand it any more, so she said, "We're going shopping on Thursday. Make plans for it."

Then she walked away, without looking back.

Quincy strode purposefully to the Queen's dressing room. She had called Cammy and asked if she could have a word with the Queen.

Her whole body was thrumming with anger, and something else she hadn't encountered before. She was sure Holly had kissed her simply to annoy and torment her, but as soon as Holly's lips touched hers, a fire was lit low in the pit of her stomach.

Did all kisses make you feel like that? Whether freely given or simply to annoy? Quincy had no idea, and no experience—well, apart from some kisses shared with her friend at school, on a camping trip. That had been nice, but terrifying too.

Quincy got to the Queen's dressing room and nodded to the guards on the door. She knocked and was told to enter. Cammy was holding the Queen's suit jacket while she slipped into it. Tonight's program was a formal event for the arts, and another black-tie affair.

"Come in, Quincy," George said.

Cammy started to use a clothes brush on the Queen's jacket.

"Thank you, Your Majesty. I wondered if I might have a quick word?" Quincy said.

"Of course. Fire away." George walked in front of the mirror and fiddled with her bow tie.

"I've been informed that Queen Beatrice and her friends, Ms. Weaver and Ms. Ramesh, wish to go shopping on Thursday."

Queen Georgina smiled. "We had heard something about that, hadn't we, Cammy?"

"Aye. Holly's big date with Story St. John." Cammy rolled her eyes. "The lassies are all aquiver about it. What they see in that boyish floppy-haired actor who plays at soldier, I'll never know."

"Quite right," George agreed. "She needs a good haircut and a dose of a ten-mile march, up to your knees in mud, with a hundred-pound kit bag on her back. Then she'd know what being in the military was like. Anyway"—George smiled—"there's no accounting for taste."

The Queen didn't seem to see the seriousness of the matter, and Quincy couldn't impart the information about the text threats. "Ma'am, a New York department store is swarming with people. It would be impossible to make secure and keep secure."

George seemed to see the problem. "Yes, true. But I would like Bea to enjoy our days off and have as normal a time as she can." She turned to Cammy. "Is there a way to make it safe?"

Cammy blew out a breath. "We could do it. Quincy, if you and I work together, we could organize it with the store's cooperation."

"We don't have much time." Quincy wished she could tell her comrades the truth about the threats, but she was bound by the chain of command. The knowledge would be her burden to carry, and she would keep the Queen Consort and Princess Edwina safe, no matter the cost, or what people thought of her. "Yes, ma'am, I'll start on preparations with Cammy tomorrow. Excuse me. I have to meet with the protection squad before we leave."

When she walked out of the Queen's dressing room, she spied Holly exiting the consort's room, holding her large make-up kit.

They looked at each other silently for around ten seconds before Holly turned away and walked off. Quincy got that same excited feeling she'd experienced before, when she kissed her, and she had no idea what to make of it.

CHAPTER EIGHT

By Thursday, all the arrangements had been made, and Bea, Holly, and Lali were in the car, on their way to Saks. Holly drummed her fingers on her bag nervously while Lali read out Cammy and Quincy's instructions.

"From the car we will be met by the store manager and senior store staff. We will then be conducted to the designer floor, which will be closed off to the public for the duration."

"I hate causing all this disruption, Lali," Bea said.

"At least it's not the whole store," Holly said pointedly, looking at Quincy sitting in the front seat of the bomb- and bulletproof vehicle.

Originally Quincy had wanted the whole store closed off, but Bea insisted that she didn't want to inconvenience the shop that much, so a compromise was reached. The designer floor would be closed off, with members of the protection squad at each of the elevators and staircases, stopping any unauthorized visitors.

Lali continued, "I wouldn't worry, Bea. The store bosses will be overjoyed at the publicity. News clips of you shopping here will be broadcast all over the world in seconds. I also understand that some of the staff and other well-wishers are waiting behind barriers at the front door."

Holly raised an eyebrow. "And this is meant to be your day off?"

Bea smiled. "I'm getting used to it. As George puts it, the royal team are always on parade, and as the Dowager Queen says"—Bea imitated George's grandmother—"We must always have a bright smile and a wave for anyone we meet."

Lali laughed, while Holly went back to drumming her fingers. "I don't know why I came up with this idea. I don't fit in a place like Saks, plus I'll probably only be able to buy a scarf at their prices."

Bea covered her hand and squeezed. "You fit in as much as me. I'm only Queen Consort because of George, and you will get the most beautiful dress in here. It's a gift from Lali and me."

Holly was shocked. "What? No, you can't buy my dress. Bea, you already bought me the auction date."

Lali took her other hand and said, "It's our gift to you. We want you to explore this side of yourself and find happiness if you can."

Holly looked nervously to the front of the car and saw Quincy looking right back at her in the rear-view mirror. If only her friends knew she had already started exploring, with the most unlikely of candidates. What she had done was impulsive. She was used to doing impulsive things, but kissing Quincy, which she had done out of pure frustration, had started impulsively, but then she found herself melting into Quincy's lips.

She had imagined it would be like kissing a statue, since that was how Quincy presented herself, and she'd insisted she didn't feel anything, but the kiss was anything but.

Holly quickly dispelled the thoughts from her head. She was going out with the most gorgeous charismatic film star, and she couldn't wait.

They arrived at Saks, and as much as the Queen Consort had promised to keep to the plan Quincy had devised with Cammy, it immediately broke down. As soon as Beatrice got out of the car, she didn't simply wave to the crowds—she walked over to them, making her way down the crowd, shaking hands and receiving flowers. Quincy was on high alert and kept extremely close to the Queen Consort.

Her gaze darted around the crowd, her heart thudded, and her breathing became heavy. Every person could be the one who sent the messages. The one who could hurt the consort and show what a failure Quincy was.

They made it into the store, and Quincy breathed a sigh of relief. She was in command today, since the Queen and Inspector Lang weren't with them. Everyone knew where they had to be positioned, but she visually checked all the entrances and exits as they made their way to the elevators.

She looked to her side and saw Clayton's eyes roving around the luxurious store, rather than on the principal.

"Eyes front, Clayton."

"Sorry, ma'am. I've never seen anything like this," Clay said.

Quincy could quite understand Clay's excitement and awe at all these new experiences she was having. It was a world away from East London where she was from.

Once they got up to the designer floor, the party was taken to a comfortable seating area, with two changing cubicles and a raised podium between them.

Quincy and Clay took position at the back of the room close to the door and watched as the staff fawned over Queen Beatrice and her friends, bringing them drinks and nibbles.

Never in a million years would she have thought that a highly trained marine would end up here, in a dress shop, protecting the Queen Consort, while her friend chose an outfit. How her life had changed.

Quincy's gaze was meant to be trained on the exits and the consort, but she couldn't help as her scrutiny drifted to Holly. Surprisingly, Holly appeared nervous. She had expected the excitable life and soul of the party to revel in this, yet she wasn't.

She remembered what Holly had said in the car, that she wouldn't fit in here. Quincy didn't know why she could ever think that. She was beautiful, bright, and would shine anywhere she went. Had no one told her that before? Had no one told her how beautiful she was?

Quincy hoped that Holly would meet someone who told her that. Then Quincy thought about why they were here. Holly was going out with Story St. John. She doubted an egocentric film star like her would make Holly feel as special as she should be.

When she had met Holly's eyes in the car, that hungry, excited feeling returned, if only for an instant. She tried to shake the memory away. It was distracting her, and as her mother always warned, *Never let feelings impinge on your duty.*

So she looked away quickly.

❖

Holly shuffled her way into the next dress and called Lali in to zip her up. This was the second dress she'd tried on, and as glamorous and gorgeous as it was, it just didn't suit her. It would have been perfect for Bea, but she was different.

Lali zipped her in and said, "Okay, Holls, go out and see what you think."

Holly stepped out in the white evening gown, and up onto the podium. Bea gasped. "You look beautiful, Holls. What do you think, Lali?"

Lali smiled. "She's gorgeous."

Holly sighed. "I don't think it's me, girls."

"Why, what's wrong?" Bea asked.

Holly turned around on the podium, looking at every angle, then threw her hands in the air. "I don't know. I can't explain. It's just not me."

Lali said to the personal shopper, "Do you have anything a bit more…bohemian. A more unconventional designer, maybe?"

"Of course. I'll bring you back some new choices," the personal shopper said.

She returned smiling, with a few dresses and some shoe boxes. "I think I've got just the thing, Ms. Weaver."

"I have a good feeling about these, Holls," Bea said as Holly stepped off the podium.

When Holly went back into the changing room Bea got ready with her phone to take Holly's picture. She looked around and saw Clay and Quincy talking by the elevators. It was strange—each time Holly had come out with a new dress on, she had noticed Quincy looking at her intently. She couldn't read that stony gaze of hers, but there was *something*.

Was it annoyance? After all, Quincy hadn't wanted this trip and fought against it. She and Holly did appear to be like chalk and cheese. Quincy was a lot like George, conventional, unwavering from rules and regulations, but George was not shut off from her emotions, although she had tried to hide her panic attacks after her father died. Bea had helped her through that time.

Perhaps it was the boarding school and military upbringing that made it difficult for them to deal with negative emotions.

Just then the elevator dinged, and a young woman emerged with mineral water and glasses with ice, as Bea had requested. The young woman got quite a fright when Quincy jumped in front of her and demanded to see her clearance ID.

"It's all right, Quincy. I asked for some water to be brought up," Bea shouted over.

Quincy stepped aside and took up her original position.

The young woman nervously curtsied. "I brought some water, Your Majesty."

Bea gave her a warm smile and looked at her name badge. "Thank you so much, Chloe. Just leave it there, and we'll help ourselves."

Chloe's face beamed with happiness. "Thank you, ma'am."

Bea had never had such an attentive security officer. Garrett and some other of Lang's men who had accompanied her had kept their distance, but Quincy seemed so uptight and nervous of the crowds they talked to all the time. She hoped Quincy would relax over time.

The dressing room doors opened, and this time a smiling Holly walked out and stood on the podium. She was wearing a ruffled black silk dress, with an asymmetrical hem, and to complete the more unconventional look, a pair of tall lace-up patent-leather designer boots.

Bea clasped her hands to her mouth. "Yes, that's the one. It's gorgeous, and so you, Holls."

"It is, isn't it?" Holly said happily. "I love it."

She twirled around the podium and Bea got to see that the back of the dress was completely bare, with only a lace tie around her neck, and the zip starting at the waist.

Lali came and sat beside Bea. "It's perfect for Holls."

"Perfect," Bea said, then quickly turned her head and saw it: Quincy gazing at Holly with what she could only describe as attraction.

My, my, Captain. You aren't made of stone after all.

Holly came down from the podium and skipped over to them. "Do you think Story will like this?"

Bea laughed. "I think you're going to knock Story St. John's socks off!"

❖

When Quincy returned from the Queen Consort's excursion, she went back to her room and took the opportunity to call her former comrade, Blade. Blade had been recruited by the intelligence services for her exceptional skills, after she hacked into the Ministry of Defence computer files.

Three years' service, and many, many missions behind her, she decided to go out on her own, in civvy street.

Quincy took off her jacket and sat down at her desk. She dialled the number Blade instructed her in a text.

The phone connected but no one said hello. "Blade? It's me—Quincy."

She heard a laugh on the other end of the line. "I'd know that gravelly voice anywhere. Hi, Quincy. Is this line secure?"

"Probably not," Quincy replied.

There was a short silence and Blade said, "It is now. How's life? I see you have a very different posting now."

Quincy switched her phone to speaker and laid it on her desk. She walked over to the hotel window and looked over the New York skyline.

"Yes, it's very different, but an honour that the Queen has asked me," Quincy said.

"And Jacob?"

At the mention of her friend's name, her mind played the movie of her pulling him out of the building, his flesh burning, and Jacob screaming.

She gulped. "He's as well as can be expected."

"I'm sorry. I can't imagine your pain, Quincy," Blade said.

Quincy didn't want to think about it any more, so she asked, "I need some help with something, Blade. It's top secret."

"Of course. Name it," Blade replied.

"I've been having some threats to the Queen Consort texted to my mobile. Only me, which is strange. Our commanding officer says there's been no internet chatter about any threat, and to be honest I don't think they're taking it seriously."

"I see. You want to know who, and why you?" Blade said.

"Yes. There must be a reason why I'm the only one getting the messages," Quincy said.

She heard Blade typing in the background. "Any enemies you can think of?"

One face came to mind. The face that sneered and sniggered as she punched and punched until the skin on her knuckles became bloody and sore.

"Lieutenant Rodwell. He was court-martialled out of the marines on my evidence. He is vindictive enough, but I seriously doubt he'd have the courage to do this."

"I'll check it out. I've got your mobile details. I'll monitor it and try to track this person down," Blade said.

"Thanks, Blade. I appreciate it," Quincy said.

When Quincy hung up she let out a long breath. At least now she had someone on her side, and someone who believed her totally.

When Bea returned to the hotel, she discovered Princess Edwina was coming down with a cold, so she and George decided to retire to bed early and try to get her to sleep.

Bea finished up in the bathroom and walked back into the bedroom. She stopped dead at the sight of Teddy lying in bed clutching her Rupert Bear, with George in her sleep shorts and T-shirt lying alongside her, stroking Teddy's brow, and talking softly to her.

Bea's heart melted at the sight. George was such a good mum, and together they both made a loving pair to take care of Teddy. They hadn't talked about it, but Bea realized she wanted another baby. How could she not want George's babies?

"How is she?" Bea asked as she lay down on the bed.

"A little hot and stuffy." George wiped Teddy's nose with a tissue.

As soon as Teddy saw Bea, she reached out for her. "Mummy."

Bea pulled her into her arms and kissed her head. "You not feeling well, my little Teddy bear?" Teddy shook her head and buried her face in Bea's chest. "Did the doctor say she could travel?"

"Yes. He said she should be fine by the time we're scheduled to go. I hate to see her unwell." George moved closer so she could take them both in her arms and pulled them to her chest.

"I know," Bea said. "I don't think we can take her out on engagements the rest of the week. It wouldn't be fair."

George started to stroke Teddy's back as she lay on Bea's chest. "No. It's best to leave her. So how was the big shopping trip today? Did you all have fun?"

Bea smiled. "We certainly did. Holly got the most amazing dress. She is going to look stunning for Story."

"Hmm," George said with annoyance in her voice.

"Oh, don't be all huffy about Story," Bea said.

"Anyone with the audacity to have the name *Story* has an ego a mile wide."

"Well, ego or not," Bea said, "Holly fancies the pants off her, so she's perfect for stage one matchmaking. Which reminds me, has Quincy had many big relationships, or is she more of a one-night stand kind of person?"

George looked at her quizzically. "Well, we don't tend to talk about relationships, past or present, but I don't know of anyone. When we were stationed together, she always stayed on board with me when the ship docked. It was Cammy who enjoyed the nightlife. Why do you ask?"

"Just something I saw in her eyes when Holly came out in her dress. I wondered if maybe—"

"Holly?" George said. "I doubt it. When she came to see me about the shopping trip, she was really angry about Holly's plans. Plus, they're not exactly a good match anyway. Quincy is a rule driven officer, Holly is…"

"A fun-loving free spirit?" Bea offered.

"Exactly," George said.

Bea wasn't convinced. George wouldn't see emotions if they were right in front of her nose. But Bea saw something. She knew it.

Teddy started to grizzle and cry, so George asked the computer to play her favourite lullabies, and they put off the light to try to soothe her.

As they lay in the dark, Bea said, "George, when we get back from this tour…"

"Yes?"

"Let's have another baby."

George squeezed her in a hug. "Nothing would make me happier, Mrs. Buckingham."

❖

Holly sat on her bed gazing at her new dress. It was more than she could have ever hoped for. She felt nervous and slightly uneasy at the thought of her date. She was never usually nervous before dates. She was always the one on the front foot. She had confidence and picked up men very easily wherever she was. She'd even famously once managed to find the only straight man in a gay bar, on one of her nights out with Bea and Lali.

This was different. With men she exuded confidence. She knew how their minds worked and used that to have them eating out of her hand, and if anyone got too close or wanted something more, she moved on.

Women were different. Holly had only ever loved one person, a woman, and she had been so head-over-heels in love, that she had let her girlfriend lead in all things, and in the end she got her heart broken in two. Did she have the courage to start dating women again?

She knew it wouldn't be Story St. John. This date was bought and paid for—Story probably couldn't wait to get it over with—but it was what the date represented that was more worrying.

Holly was dipping her toe back in the water with probably the biggest lady's woman she could think of. That made her laugh.

Holly threw herself back on the bed. She couldn't stare at these four walls all night. George and Bea had settled in for the evening because Teddy wasn't well, and Lali and Cammy had gone out to a movie.

She got up and made her way along to the rec room. When she entered she saw Captain Quincy over in her usual corner, but this time she was sitting with Clay. She felt her throat tighten as she looked over at her. Why had she done that stupid kissing thing? Now everything was going to be more awkward than it already was.

Maybe she could just walk back out without being noticed. She got to the door and Clay shouted, "Holly? Come and sit with us."

Oh God. She couldn't get out of this now.

She put on a forced smile and pointed to the coffee machine. "I'll just get some coffee first."

Her heart started to beat fast as she poured out three mugs of coffee. What was Quincy going to say? Would she embarrass her and talk about the kiss in front of Clay?

Holly put the mugs on a tray and added sugar and milk. She took a breath and said to herself, *Just brazen it out, Holls.* She sauntered over, and Clay jumped up and took the tray from her.

"I thought you two could use some coffee."

Quincy glanced up to her, then quickly looked away. "Thank you, Ms. Holly."

Yes, things were definitely awkward, and it appeared as if they were both going to ignore that the kiss ever happened, which suited her very well.

"Are you happy with your nice new dress, Holly?" Clay said.

"Yes—well, I hope it's nice," Holly said. "I don't know if I can pull it off."

Clay gave her the biggest smile. "You were gorgeous in it." Clay turned to Quincy. "You saw her too, Quincy. How did she look?"

Holly's heart sank. Why was she asking her? Quincy wasn't even looking when they were there. Now she was either going to have to be ever so polite or be as blunt and stony as she usually was.

To her surprise, Quincy looked up at her and said, "She was beautiful, Clay. Beautiful."

Holly stopped breathing for those few seconds because she could see the sincerity in Quincy's eyes.

But as quickly as it was said, Quincy's attention went back down to her soldiers.

Clay said, "Are you nervous about going out with Story?"

Holly kicked off her shoes and brought her legs up on the couch. "God, yes. I'm going to make a fool of myself—I just know it."

"Story's films are amazing. Her last one, *Dogs Of War*, I saw about ten times, I think," Clay said.

Holly let her gaze fall on Quincy, who appeared not to be interested in their conversation. "I know. I loved that one. There's something about her, in her army gear, holding a gun, that makes me swoon."

Clay laughed. "I don't know about that. She's not my type, but her film was great." Just then someone called Clay's name across the room. "Sorry, I said I'd play cards with the guys. See you later, Holly, ma'am."

Holly panicked. *Don't leave us alone!* "Bye, Clay." Great. Now it really was going to be awkward. Holly drummed her nails on her coffee mug, searching for something to say. "Drink your coffee before it gets cold."

"I will in a minute. I just have to finish painting this part of the face," Quincy said.

Holly watched her intently. The bristles on this brush were longer than a conventional paintbrush, and she made each stroke with such consideration and purpose, that it was almost meditational.

"You having fun?" Holly joked.

Quincy put down the soldier to dry and dipped her paintbrush in a glass of water, mixing it around. "Yes, I know you wouldn't understand it, but it is fun for me. It's how I unwind."

"So do you have a room at home full of model ships and planes like Queen Georgina?" Holly asked.

Quincy lifted her coffee mug and took a drink. She knew she was going to send Holly running off in boredom. "I don't build ships and aeroplanes. I like to paint the soldiers and scenery for famous battles."

Holly scrunched her nose up in such a cute way. Story the pretend soldier had better show Holly a good time. She deserved it.

"What, you set them out on a table or something?" Holly asked.

Quincy shook her head. "You either make or buy the template for the battlefield, then paint it, and add in bushes, shrubs, and grass. A bit like model railway enthusiasts do." Oh God. She'd just mentioned model railways. Holly was going to think she was even more boring than she'd originally thought.

"Yeah, I know what you mean. My dad has a model railway set up in their attic. He goes there to escape me, Mum, and my brother when we're getting too loud."

Quincy smiled. "You know what I'm talking about then. It's like that, only you set up famous battles."

"Have you got one set up at home now?"

As soon as Holly said it, Quincy felt sadness engulf her, and the atmosphere changed, to a more sombre one. "No. I don't have a home at the moment. I came straight here from barracks."

"What about your parents' home?" Holly said.

Quincy thought about her mother's house in London, its decor a testament to all the Quincys who'd gone before her, and all that she had to live up to. Her mother's house was only a place to visit, not to stay, or she might suffocate.

"I just have a mother, and I haven't lived at home since I was seven years old." Why had she said that? She never talked about her life to anyone.

"What?" Holly said with surprise.

"I was at boarding school." Quincy thought that would explain everything.

"I forgot you were posh," Holly joked. "But seriously, you need your mum when you're seven. How could you be away at school?"

Quincy felt embarrassed trying to explain her mother, and her family. She said defensively, "That's just the way my family works."

"All right. Keep your hair on, Stompy." Holly sat back in her chair, and the conversation stopped.

This was why Quincy didn't have friends. She couldn't traverse the conversations and observe the niceties. She tried to think of something to make it better, and she picked up one of her unpainted soldiers and offered it to Holly.

"Would you like to try?"

Holly looked confused. "You want me to paint? I can't even draw the easiest pictures."

Quincy offered her hand more closely. "Try, it's very relaxing."

Holly took the soldier and their hands touched. Quincy looked at their hands and then at Holly. What did she see in Holly's verdant green eyes that intrigued her so much? Maybe it was the openness in them. They hid nothing, unlike hers or her mother's. When Holly was angry, she could tell, and when she was unsure of herself, like while in the dress shop, she could tell. She envied that in Holly.

Holly pulled the soldier and her fingers away, and Quincy could still feel the radiance of Holly's touch in her fingers, her arm, and her chest. Just like her kiss that her mind replayed in her head often. It made a change from the awful memories.

"Can I have a brush?" Holly said.

Quincy shook herself. "Oh, sorry. Hang on a sec."

Quincy got her a brush, put the paints between them, and propped up her computer pad on the table. "This is the picture of how the soldiers are meant to look, so if you can, follow that as a guide."

Holly held the brush as if she was unsure of what to do.

"Start with the uniform, it's easier."

Holly sighed and dipped her brush in the red paint. "I'll mess it up."

"It doesn't matter, Holly. It's the process of painting it that's important. It helps you calm and settles your mind. Besides, mistakes help us to learn."

Holly laughed. "Well, I'll be doing a lot of learning then. What soldiers are these anyway?"

Quincy picked up her own figure again. "Grenadier Guards. I'm working on a battle from the Napoleonic Wars," Quincy said.

Holly started painting and they worked away in quiet contemplation for a while. There was no awkwardness during their silence. It felt nice, and easy. Quincy loved the look of concentration on Holly's face.

She didn't hold back from the task, and in fact attacked it with as much enthusiasm and gusto as she did everything else, making the occasional joke, or laughing at herself when she made a mistake.

It was endearing, and as time went on, Quincy found herself watching Holly rather than working on her own figure. Holly was everything Quincy was not. She sat cross-legged on the couch completely at ease, singing or humming as she painted. It was so attractive.

Quincy wished she could be that open and feel that much at ease. She felt like she had been on parade her whole life, and since the mission, since she'd lost her men and her friend was injured, things had gotten so much worse.

Holly yawned and stretched. "I'm tired, but this was great, Quin. Can I help you again?"

"Of course. I have a whole infantry division to paint."

Holly looked at her quizzically. "I've never met anyone like you, Quin."

"No?"

"No," Holly said simply.

She stood and Quincy said politely, "Goodnight then, Holly."

Holly chuckled. "Night night, Stompy."

Quincy's heart thudded as she walked away, and she reran the kiss in her head. "Stop this."

As soon as Holly left, she gathered up all her things.

"Well, well, Captain." She hadn't heard Garrett approach her table. "Who'd have thought you would find the nerve to chat up a girl."

Quincy gave her a pointed look. "I wasn't chatting up anyone. She expressed an interest—"

Ignoring her and butting in, Garrett said, "Oh well, she's going out with someone who can entertain her a lot better tomorrow night. Story St. John won't bore her to death with toy soldiers. She'll probably talk her into bed in an hour."

Quincy slammed down her things on the table. "What is your problem, Sergeant? May I remind you that you are talking to a superior officer?"

"Losing a bit of your famous control there, Captain. I better watch out. I don't want to end up beaten to a pulp."

Quincy reined in her anger quickly. *Don't lose control. Don't let them see.*

She said nothing, so Garrett leaned in and said with contempt, "Yes, ma'am."

CHAPTER NINE

The next day was a busy one for George and Bea, but not for Holly. Bea wouldn't be back for any changes of clothes, so Holly helped Nanny Baker with Teddy. Suffering with a cold, Teddy wasn't the easiest to take care of.

For most of the day Holly sat on the couch with Teddy lying across her lap watching her favourite children's shows while Nanny Baker fussed around getting Teddy, food, medicine, and anything else she might need.

Holly looked at her watch, then stroked Teddy's head. "It's nearly time, Teddy. Do you want to see Mummy and Mum?"

Teddy sat up. "Mummy?"

Holly pulled her onto her knee and told the TV to turn to the financial news channel.

George and Bea had been in the financial district, promoting British business. They attended a reception in the morning and early afternoon, and now they would be ringing the closing bell.

Teddy sat up and looked at the TV. "Mum? Mummy?"

"They are just coming. I promise," Holly said.

Sure enough, after about a minute George led Bea up onto the platform where the bell was rung.

Teddy spotted them and began to bounce up and down. "Mum, Mummy."

She saw Quincy standing in the background. No one else would have noticed the security people, all the focus was on George and Bea, but Holly couldn't take her eyes off her.

Quincy looked tense. Her head went from side to side, as if she was expecting trouble at every turn. Holly thought about how different Quincy was when they'd painted the toy soldiers together. She was calm and relaxed, and at ease.

That was something Holly believed Quincy rarely felt—to be at ease, and relaxed. Holly felt this pull, from somewhere deep inside herself, to help Quincy feel that way, and that was confusing.

Quincy was such a complex person, despite the bland, grey appearance she tried to portray. If anything of what Garrett told her was true, Quincy had a lot of troubled waters underneath.

What was she thinking? It was not her job to ease those troubled waters.

"Mum, Holls?" Teddy said.

Holly gave her a tight hug and kissed her head. "Don't worry, Mum and Mummy will be back soon. They're just doing their queeny thing."

Yet Holly couldn't deny that she found Quincy attractive. She looked down to Teddy and said, "Why did Stompy have to be so gorgeously good-looking, and troubled? It's a deadly combination, Teddy."

The day of Holly's big date finally arrived. Bea and Lali had gathered in her hotel room to help her get ready. She poured herself into her dress, and Lali zipped her up. She turned around so Bea could see her. "What do you think?"

"Beautiful. Story is going to be stunned," Bea said.

"Hardly, did you see her last girlfriend? Kiki Lavante? She had legs up to here"—Holly raised her hand above her head—"and had breasts out to here." She held her hands in front of her chest as if she was holding a pair of melons.

"Well she's an ex for a reason. Maybe she doesn't like breasts out to there," Lali said.

Bea added, "Besides, your breasts are fabulous."

Holly gave her friend a lopsided grin. "Thanks for the support, girls. Do you think these earrings work with this dress?"

Bea tapped her finger on her chin. "Hmm. I think we could do better. I've got a pair that would go perfectly with your outfit. Bring your handbag, and we can stop at my suite on your way out."

They made their way there, and when they rounded the corner they saw Quincy talking to one of the younger protection officers on the door of the Queens' rooms.

Bea turned her head and winked at both Holly and Lali. "Captain Quincy? You're just the person."

Oh God. No, Bea, Holly thought.

Quincy bowed her head. "How can I be of service, ma'am?"

"Holly here won't believe how good she looks for her date tonight. What do you think?" Bea said.

Holly cringed. She could see by Quincy's tightening jaw how uncomfortable she felt. Quincy stood with her hands behind her back, ramrod straight, as if on parade.

"Ms. Holly looks very smart, ma'am," Quincy said.

That was not the kind of response Holly was expecting. She glared at Quincy silently.

Quincy bowed her head again and excused herself.

"Smart? I'm smart? Does she think she's inspecting the troops or something?" Holly said.

"Don't worry about her, Holls," Lali said. "It's just her way."

"She wouldn't know an emotion if it came up and kissed her on the face," Holly said.

Bea and Lali laughed, but they didn't know that it was true. Holly's impromptu kiss had no effect on the stuffy, stompy Quincy.

Who cared, Holly told herself. She had a date with a film star.

Quincy was frustrated on so many levels this evening. As she ate dinner, another text message threat arrived: *You never protect those you care about, do you? Remember Denbourg? It only takes one shot.*

Quincy went back to her room. She couldn't keep her fear of what might happen from showing. She paced around her room waiting on Blade's call.

Her phone rang. "Blade? Have you found anything?"

"Yes and no. The messages are easy to trace, but they are all prepaid phones with no account attached. I'm sure if you followed the coordinates I have, you'd find the phone dumped in a bin again. It's only a few miles away. I saw you got another text?"

"Yes, I take it you're tracking my phone?" Quincy said.

"Of course. I'll monitor your incoming messages and see what I can find out. I'm trying to trace where the prepaid mobiles were purchased. If I can do that, then I can hack the store's security cameras, and we get our man," Blade said confidently.

"Okay. What about Rodwell?" Quincy didn't know if it was her prejudice that was driving her to think it was him. That was why she needed Blade's clear-headed opinion.

"Yeah, I've tracked his phone, hacked his computer, and found nothing out of the ordinary. He's living with his mum after leaving jail. But if he moves, I'm on him. I promise I'll help you get whoever this is, Quincy."

Quincy ground her teeth together through pure stress and frustration. "Thank you, Blade. I appreciate it."

Quincy threw the phone on her bed and held her face in her hands. She needed to cool down, or this was going to drive her crazy. "The rec room."

She'd go to the rec room and check and recheck the protection squad's security files to see if there was something she had missed. Then she could also check that Holly got back safely from her date.

The past few nights she had spent painting her models with Holly had been the most relaxing and enjoyable nights she could remember. Holly's positivity and cheerful personality were infectious, but tonight she was going out with someone else. Someone she could never compete with.

I'm not trying to compete. I can't afford to feel that way, Quincy told herself firmly.

❖

A limo picked up Holly outside the hotel and conducted her to the restaurant where she was having dinner with Story. Lali had told her it was quite an exclusive restaurant, where the rich and famous mingled.

That made Holly even more nervous. She was just a working-class hair and make-up artist. How was she meant to walk into a roomful of these people and not look out of place? She let out a long, nervous breath. Someone would probably try to give her their drinks order.

The car stopped, and the driver said, "We've arrived, ma'am." Holly felt sick. She couldn't do this.

But before she knew it, the driver had opened the door. Some paparazzi took her picture before they realized she was no one famous, and they returned their attention to the windows of the establishment.

Holly reached into her small clutch bag to get a tip for the driver, but he said, "Don't worry, ma'am. Ms. St. John has taken care of everything."

"Oh, thank you," Holly said, surprised. Story was a good date.

She walked to the restaurant door and a doorman conducted her inside. A snooty looking maître d', who stood by the lectern in the reception, said, "Name please, ma'am?"

Holly had to squeeze her clutch bag to stop her hands from shaking. "I'm here to meet Story St. John?"

He looked her up and down, as if astonished that she could possibly be Story's guest. "Name?" he repeated.

"Holly Weaver."

"Ah, yes, Ms. Weaver. Follow me."

Holly was led into the dining room and felt every eye upon her. She felt worse when she recognized some very famous film and TV actors. *God, I shouldn't be here.*

Then she saw her—Story St. John, the woman of her dreams, at one of the tables waiting for her. When Story saw her, she stood and gave her the sexiest smile, then surprised Holly by saying very loudly, "Holly, great to see you." Holly was again surprised when Story pulled her into an embrace and said enthusiastically, "You look absolutely gorgeous, babe."

Holly's very, very warm welcome was rather overwhelming, and before she knew it she was sitting down. She looked around and got some envious looks from women around her.

Story must have seen how uptight she was because she stretched her hand across the table and squeezed hers. "Hey, relax, babe. You're too beautiful to look worried." She ended that sentence with a cheeky wink.

Holly smiled. At least someone thought she looked nicer than smart. "Thanks, I've never been to a place like this for dinner."

"Hey, it's nothing. You work in a *palace*. All these people who like to think they're important are nothing to your boss."

"I suppose. You look nice too, by the way," Holly said.

Story grinned and swept back her gorgeous floppy front fringe of dark black hair with her fingers, in that sexy way she had. "Thanks." Story was wearing a black suit and a white open-necked shirt, but with a pair of distressed-looking but clearly expensive sneakers.

"Oh, before I forget." Story got up and walked behind Holly. "We need to get a selfie. Smile." Story lifted the mobile on her wrist.

Holly smiled. She smelled Story's cologne, and oddly at a time like this, the date of her dreams, she said to herself, *Not as nice as Quincy's.*

That was weird.

She was soon distracted by flashes coming from the restaurant window. Holly turned and saw a whole bank of cameras trained on them.

"Don't worry about them, babe," Story said. "They follow me around. Let's order, huh? I'm starved."

Holly opened up her menu to choose her food, then a thought occurred to her. If the cameras followed Story around, why get a table here? Why not a booth at the back of the restaurant where they could have privacy?

They began to eat, and Holly hadn't laughed so much in her life. Story was very entertaining. Her tales of her childhood and getting into the film business were really funny. Story's informality was like a breath of fresh air. Everyone in the royal court was so formal in their speech, and in their dress. Captain Quincy came to her mind. A masculine presenting butch lesbian, Quincy was even more conservative in manner and dress than Queen Georgina, and George was very old-fashioned as it was.

Quincy's bland dark suits and matching ties would hardly win any fashion awards, and that military short haircut which was simply combed to the side was so boring compared to Story's. Every time she saw Quincy's hair, she had the greatest urge to run her fingers through it and mess it up.

Plus, Story was so open, and anything Holly asked she would tell her without hesitation. She had learned more about Story in half an hour than she had heard from Quincy the entire time they had known each other.

Holly was surprised at Story's enthusiasm for the date. She had assumed that she would want to get the bought-and-paid-for date over and done with. But no, it did feel like a real night out. Story flirted with her constantly, and it was weird and exciting to be flirted with by someone who had always been an untouchable famous actress.

The only thing that gave her pause was Story's constant smiling looks to the cameras outside. Oh, and Story checked her phone, posting pictures on social media as they ate. It was almost as if they were sharing their date with the world. Story was never quite present with her.

"Enough about me. I heard you and Queen Beatrice were best friends from college," Story said as the waiter cleared away the main course.

"Yes, the four of us—Queen Beatrice, Lali the Queen's secretary, and Greta, our friend back in the UK. We all love your films, by the way," Holly said. "We have a girls' night at the palace every month, and we always watch your movies."

Story's eyes lit up at that comment, and Holly wondered if she'd said too much.

"Story St. John by royal appointment, huh? I like it," Story said.

Holly was a little uneasy. "Do you mind if I nip to the ladies'?"

"Sure." Story chuckled and took her hand as she rose to leave the table. "By the way, your English accent is so sexy. I could listen to you all night." Story winked at her. "Why don't I order us dessert, and then I'll take you on to a club I know. The women are hot, but not as hot as you in those boots."

Holly was lost for words. "You want to take me to a club?"

"Yeah, let's drink, dance, and have some fun, huh? You like to have fun don't you, Holly?"

Holly beamed, and her heart started to pound. "Fun is my middle name."

❖

Quincy looked up from her computer pad, gazed around the rec room, and realized she was the only one still there.

She looked at her watch. It was half past two in the morning. The only people who would still be up would be the duty officers on guard at the elevators and stairwells. She stretched and rubbed her face. She'd discarded her suit jacket on the arm of the couch, her top shirt button was undone, and her tie loosened.

She had been trawling through all the secret MI5 files on any previous threats made to the royal family. There had to be something in there, someone who was connected to the messages she was getting.

Quincy wouldn't discount Lieutenant Rodwell, but he wasn't in the country to cause any physical threat, and he wasn't the type of man who could afford to have someone do his dirty work for him.

The Queen's cousin, Viscount Anglesey, was another obvious suspect. He had committed treason to get his hands on the crown. She had met him at various polo and horse events over the years, and he was an obnoxious man with an inferiority complex as big as his ego, but he was still in a secure unit at hospital.

She supposed he might have the means or the influence to somehow get a hired gun, but that scenario was unlikely. Then there was Thea Brandt's network of criminal gangs. Thea Brandt had organized and succeeded in implementing one of the world's most shocking assassinations. Her people took down the King of Denbourg and his heir in one afternoon. Thankfully Thea Brandt had been apprehended and would never see anything but the four walls of a Denbourg jail for the rest of her life.

Queen Rozala had taken the crown, and was performing her duty beautifully, along with her Crown Consort, Lennox.

But again, Thea had networks of people who had never been caught, and she probably had resources squirrelled away. She had threatened to take her revenge on Queen Rozala's family, of which the Buckinghams were part. British intelligence and agents were involved in hunting her networks down and destroying her weapons stores.

Thea Brandt definitely required more investigation. She would ask Blade to try and find out what she could.

Quincy began to yawn. She looked over at the coffee machine and contemplated having another coffee, anything to put off going to sleep and slipping into the nightmares that lived inside her head, and her heart. But if she didn't sleep, she wouldn't be rested and alert for her job.

The prospect of her alarm going off at four thirty made her decision for her. She would be forced to face her nightly hell again.

She stood, and as she went to lift her suit jacket, Quincy heard the beep of the elevator. Instinct made her pull her gun from her shoulder holster. As she approached the rec room door, she heard the officers on the elevator talking to someone.

She heard laughter that she would recognize anywhere. It was Holly.

Quincy holstered her weapon. She had assumed Holly would have returned earlier in the night. She walked into the hall and saw a giggling, tipsy Holly, making the stiff protection officers rather embarrassed, with one boot on and carrying the other one in her hand.

Quincy strode up to them and offered Holly her arm. "Ms. Weaver? Let me escort you to your room."

Holly giggled. "You are so posh. Let's go, Stompy."

The officers looked at her strangely. Quincy's embarrassment forced her to move quickly. "Let's leave these officers to their work."

Holly saluted her. "Yes, ma'am."

Great. This she had not expected to do last thing at night. Of course, Holly was not falling down drunk, just sweetly tipsy.

"I take it you had a good night then," Quincy said.

"Yes! It was an amazing night. You should have fun sometime. We had dinner, then Story took me clubbing. Imagine? Story St. John taking Holly Weaver dancing." Holly twirled around and nearly fell, but Quincy kept her on her feet. "And she thought I was beautiful, not *smart*." Holly stabbed a finger in Quincy's face.

Through Holly's date and the haze of alcohol, she remembered that? Quincy felt put on the spot. She didn't know what to say, but her earlier remark must've annoyed Holly.

"Let's try and keep on our feet, Holly," Quincy said.

They made it to Holly's room door. Holly was giggling and telling herself to shush at the same time.

"Be quiet, Captain Stompy," Holly told her sternly. "You don't want to wake anyone up."

Quincy held Holly by the shoulders. She had helped more than one drunk marine back to their room and saved them from getting a bollocking for it.

"You need to sleep. We're travelling tomorrow, remember?"

"Oh yeah. Where are we going? Texas, LA? I'm confused."

"Chicago," Quincy told her.

"That's it. Oh, guess what? Story wants to take me out when we get to LA."

A small part of Quincy felt sad at that prospect. The memory of Holly's kiss still burnt brightly in her mind, and Story St. John, a woman she had learned ran through ladies like water, was not worthy of those kisses.

But she was glad the prospect of some more dates with this famous film star made Holly so happy. Holly was strong-willed, irresponsible with Queen Beatrice's safety, and she embarrassed her regularly, but she was kind, going out of her way to talk to Quincy when she didn't need to. Holly deserved to be happy.

"What are you thinking so hard about, Stompy?" Holly said.

"Just that I'm glad for you, and I hope you'll be happy," Quincy replied.

Holly looked intently into her eyes, as if searching them for something.

"What?"

Holly furrowed her eyebrows. "I don't know. There's something in your eyes. Something…" Then out of nowhere she said, "When I first saw you, I thought you were an Adonis, but you need to let me sort out your hair." She began ruffling up Quincy's hair with her fingers.

"What are you doing?" Quincy tried to pull Holly's hand from her head.

"I've wanted to do that since I met you. You need all your straight edges ruffled," Holly said, laughing.

Quincy pulled Holly's hands down, and Holly made a grab for her tie. As she did, she pulled Quincy's shirt open below the neck. Holly stopped dead and stared.

Quincy took a step back and hastily buttoned up her shirt. Panic spread throughout her body. No one had seen her scarred body. Not her mother, not that she would have wanted to. No one. Flaws and scars were meant to be hidden, especially these, because they marked her failure to her marines.

Holly slumped against the side of her door, apparently forgetting about what she had seen. "I'm so tired." She yawned and then her face went pale. "I don't feel so good."

Quincy looked left and right at the protection officers on the exits. She didn't want them to see Holly like this or worse. She took the few steps to Holly and lifted her into her own arms.

"Wait, what are you doing?" Holly asked with surprise.

"Taking you to bed." Quincy squeezed her eyes shut tight, realizing what that sounded like. "I'm helping you into your room."

Holly handed Quincy her key card, put her arms around Quincy's neck, and rested her head on her chest.

Quincy managed to walk through the doorway and carried Holly to her bed. "Sit there a second and I'll get you some water."

Holly felt good in her arms, too good, so Quincy hurried over to the minibar and got out a bottle of water. She was becoming more annoyed as time passed. That idiot actor obviously plied her with drinks. Completely irresponsible.

She brought back the water and knelt down in front of Holly. "Here, drink this."

Holly took a big sip.

Holly's beautiful auburn hair fell across her face, and without thinking, Quincy gently brushed it back with her fingers. Then she caught herself and pulled her hand back quickly.

What was she doing?

"You must think I'm an idiot," Holly said.

"Of course I don't. Everyone has a little too much sometimes."

That term *everyone* didn't apply to her. Alcohol, control, and anger didn't mix.

"Thanks for being kind to me," Holly said.

Quincy took her hand and said, "I'll always be kind to you."

Holly looked up with her drowsy, tipsy eyes and said, "I saw you before you came to work here, you know? It was at the polo. You didn't notice me though."

Quincy looked down at their clasped hands. "I'd better leave you to it. We have an early wake-up call." She stood, and when she reached the door she felt compelled to turn and right a wrong.

"Ms. Holly?"

Holly looked up.

"You didn't look smart. You were stunningly beautiful, and I did notice you at the polo match. I saw you."

Without giving Holly a chance to say anything, she walked out.

CHAPTER TEN

Q uincy woke from her sleep, gasping and sweating as always. Thank God for her alarm or else she would have been stuck in that terrifying nightmare. She could still hear the screams in her ears. Still feel the frustration that the fire and the heat kept her back from getting near to her men. Then the fire engulfed her clothes and skin as she pulled Jacob out of the building. It was so real that she could almost feel the heat radiating off her scars when she wakened.

Once she calmed and her breathing settled, she remembered one thing that was different about her dreams this time. As she'd pulled Jacob from the building, confusion and pain engulfing her, she saw Holly standing there. She was smiling, and Quincy felt deeply inside that if she went with Holly she could escape this nightmare.

Quincy didn't know what to make of it. Then she remembered last night and how she'd felt helping Holly to her room. The truth was, she didn't know or understand the feeling because it was new. She had trained herself to control every kind of emotion, but this exciting tingly feeling in the pit of her stomach was not something she had come across before.

She had felt attracted to people before, but this was completely different. This was not just attraction. This feeling was making her think and react in different ways, uncontrollable ways, and not knowing how to control something worried her.

She scrubbed her face and remembered what her first PT sergeant had told her. There was no problem or feeling that couldn't be managed with vigorous exercise.

Quincy got up, pulled on her running shorts and T-shirt, and left the hotel by four thirty to have a long run. The streets of New York were quieter than usual, but still busier with people than most cities. She looked down at her watch and saw her heart rate. She had to work harder. On her run Quincy passed so many coffee stands and shops, and they reminded her of Holly's love of a morning brew. After her late night, Quincy guessed that she would really appreciate coffee.

Clayton had sussed Holly's favourite coffee for her, but going into the world famous coffee shop and navigating the order was another thing. She didn't even understand the order when Clayton gave it to her. She only ever had black coffee, and she knew others added milk or sugar or both. That was all she'd needed to know about coffee orders until now.

She stopped outside the door of the shop and said to her watch, "Holly's coffee order."

The note was displayed, and she walked inside the shop. The first thing Quincy noticed was the noise and chatter, despite the early hour. Some of the patrons looked as if they had been out since last night. The busy, noisy environment was not one she could ever relax in.

Quincy stood in line and looked at the menu above the counter. It appeared to be written in some ancient script for all she could decipher.

As she moved up the line she kept reading and rereading her note so she didn't make any mistakes. Quincy arrived at the counter, and an overly bright-faced young woman was waiting for her.

"Hi, can I take your order?"

Quincy gazed down at her note and stuttered as she said, "A large wet extra shot almond-milk cappuccino."

She looked up at the server, hoping she had understood her stumbling order, and luckily, she seemed to, because she passed the order to the young man at the coffee machine.

"Would you like that in a stay warm cup?" she asked.

"Yes, please." Quincy replied. She had meant to ask for that with her order. A stay warm cup would keep the coffee piping hot for hours, which was essential since Holly would probably still be sleeping.

The young woman smiled and said, "You have the sexiest accent. Are you staying in New York long?"

Quincy froze. Was this flirting or just great American customer service? If it was flirting, it was totally outside her comfort zone.

"No, I'm leaving today actually," Quincy said quickly, hoping that would be the end of the conversation.

"Pity," she said with a wink. "Can I get you something else? Some pastries?"

"Erm…" Quincy looked at the array of cakes and pastries. She pointed at the almond croissants. She figured since Holly liked almond milk, she'd like almond pastries. She paid for her order by swiping her watch, then ran back to the hotel. She placed the coffee and pastry bag on the table just by Holly's door and went to get a shower.

Holly first became aware of a dull thud in her head as she wakened. As she opened her eyes, she realized she had gone to sleep in her clothes and one boot. Then she remembered her amazing date the night before. It had been more than she ever hoped for. She might have started off nervous and shy with Story, but that had soon changed.

Story was charming, open, telling her stories and anecdotes, and as she'd found out at the club, the life and soul of the party just like she was. They had danced and sung and had a few drinks, and had an all-round fantastic time.

"And she wants to meet up with me again."

Holly kicked her legs excitedly and all the covers fell from the bed. She turned onto her side quickly to make a grab for her phone on the side table, but her head and her stomach reminded her she'd had a few drinks.

She took a sip of water from the bottle on the table and then picked up her phone. She discovered she had lots of likes and comments waiting for her on social media. How weird. She had a wide circle of friends, but not enough for this.

Holly opened her social media app and saw picture after picture that Story had taken of them at the restaurant and the club. More of the night came back to her now. She recalled how Story was constantly on her social media, posting pictures of them. Sometimes it looked as if she wasn't quite with Story as her guest. Funnily enough, her job title, *Royal Dresser*, was captioned on the pictures more often than her name.

One headline caught her eye. *Story St. John by royal appointment. Sources tell us film star Story St. John's movies are a monthly ritual enjoyed by Queen Beatrice and her friends, much to Queen Georgina's annoyance.*

Holly smacked her forehead. "Oh God, Bea is going to kill me."

She sat up on the edge of the bed and kept her eyes closed until the spinning in her brain stopped. When she opened her eyes slowly and looked at the door, she had a flash of a memory. She was holding on to Captain Quincy around the neck and messing up her hair. "Please tell me I didn't do that."

Holly slumped forward and leaned her forehead on her hands. Then she saw in her mind's eye Quincy carrying her in her arms over to the bed and getting her the bottle of water that now was set on the side table.

She looked after me, Holly thought. Why would Quincy care if she was made of stone and felt nothing, as she said she did? And why was she still awake at that time?

As she asked herself all these questions, one memory stopped her in her tracks. When she had been ruffling Quincy's hair and tousling her tie, she had pulled down the collar of her shirt, and seen her skin was covered in burn scars. Did they cover more of her body? She did remember Quincy pulling her shirt up quickly, and the look of panic on her face.

What had happened to Quincy? Maybe this was why she'd left the Royal Marines. Queen Georgina did say she was a hero, and that was why she'd won the Victoria Cross.

Holly's heart ached for her. How did someone like Quincy, who was quiet and shut off from those around her, deal with the kind of hurt and pain she must have gone through?

Then she realized the answer. "By not feeling. That's what she meant by she doesn't feel."

But when Holly had kissed her, she had felt not only surprise, but passion coming back from her, and when she'd gotten the opportunity to gaze into Quincy's eyes, she saw a torrent of feeling.

There was a knock at the door. She went to answer it and found one of the hotel staff.

"Good morning, ma'am. I was sent to do the alarm calls, but I noticed these outside your door and thought you'd want to know someone left them for you."

The man handed over a stay warm cup of coffee and a bag.

"Where were these?" Holly asked.

"Just on the table here."

"Thanks. I appreciate it." Once she went back in, she took a look, and then a sip of the coffee. It was her favourite coffee, down to a tee. Then she looked in the bag and saw a sugar dusted almond croissant.

"God, yes. This is just what I need. Whoever you are, thank you."

George was up early, as was her habit, but she needed to be especially early today as they were travelling to Chicago. She wanted to get all her boxes done before they travelled, so she could learn her speech on the plane.

"Come," George said.

Bea walked in and over to her chair. She was still dressed in her silk nightdress and dressing gown.

George turned her chair, and as was their habit, Bea sat in her lap and wrapped her arms around her shoulders.

"What's happening in the world today?" Bea indicated to George's boxes.

George sighed. "The usual dispiriting fighting. Vospya is in turmoil again. Bo Dixon is looking rather silly for inviting the president for a state visit."

Bea laid her head on George's shoulder. "We could have told her that."

George kissed Bea's head. "Everything all right?"

"Yes," Bea said, "I'm just enjoying the calm before the storm, with you."

George wrapped her arms around Bea. "You're right. Is Teddy still sleeping?"

"Nanny Baker is just getting her out of bed. Do you still want to have breakfast together, or are you too busy?"

"I always want to have breakfast with you two. I'll make time," George said.

Bea sat back up. "Do you remember these trips with your parents?"

George smiled. "Yes, as far back as I can remember. One of my first memories was a visit to Australia. I remember being inside a car that was parading through the streets. Mama kept telling me to wave at the crowds. It was the noise I remember the most. It was so loud, that I put my hands over my ears. But then we met a kangaroo, and I thought it was the best thing that had ever happened to me."

Bea kissed her cheek. "That's sweet. I think these trips will be better for Teddy when she has a little brother or sister to play with."

"Yes, when Theo came along it was much more fun, although I spent most of my time trying to keep him behaving, I remember. He was more free-spirited than I."

"Teddy is extremely free-spirited," Bea said with a smile.

George squeezed her wife more tightly. Although Teddy was the spitting image of George, she had a lot of Bea's spirit in her.

"That's true. I think she might be a challenge as she grows older," George said.

Bea laughed softly. "I think that's putting it very politely, Georgie."

She took George's computer and called up an entertainment website. "Now that you've dealt with all your stuffy news, look at this."

George raised a questioning eyebrow. "What? You don't normally look at tabloid news stories—if you can call them that."

"This isn't about us this time. Look." Bea grinned.

George looked at the pad and saw pictures of Holly, taken through a restaurant window. Some showed her sitting normally at the table with Story St. John, and some showed them holding hands. The headline said: *Queen Beatrice's Royal Dresser caught having an intimate dinner with Story St. John in New York.*

"Why do they have to say *caught*? It was a charity auction date," George said.

Bea shrugged and shook her head. "You know what the media is like. Everything has to be sensational or lurid. The point is, she obviously had a great time, and I heard through the grapevine that she didn't get back here till two thirty. She must have gone on somewhere with Story afterwards. A good first start at exploring this side of herself."

"But Story St. John? I wouldn't trust my friend with someone who has a haircut like that," George said.

Bea gave George a kiss on the lips. "Don't be so old-fashioned, George." Then she added cryptically, "Besides, I think it will be someone else who will win Holly's heart. Sometimes the most quiet, unassuming people are the ones who will love you the fiercest."

The plane trip to Chicago was a short hop, but the plane had been forced to circle the airport because of a security alert on the ground. Luckily for Captain Quincy and the rest of the royal party, it didn't appear to be connected to their arrival.

Everyone was quietly reading or talking amongst themselves as they waited for the all-clear to land. Quincy spent her time going over the itinerary and the hotel plans, making sure she was familiar with everything before they landed.

She saw someone sit across from her out of the corner of her eye. She looked up and sighed inwardly. "Can I help you, Garrett?"

Garrett leaned forward on the table and said, "A little birdy told me you disappeared into Holly Weaver's room last night."

"Not that it's any of your business, but I was helping her to her room, not disappearing into it. You shouldn't listen to gossip from our little royal court."

Garrett leaned back in her seat and crossed her legs. "You need to be careful fucking around with the consort's best friend, Quincy. That's a friendly warning."

Quincy gave her a pointed look. "I would thank you to keep a civil tongue in your mouth. Especially with a young child toddling around."

Garrett laughed. "God, you sound like an actor in those old black-and-white films. I know you were born with a silver spoon in your mouth, but you're a big girl now. You can take it out, you know."

Quincy balled her fists, swallowed the anger she was feeling. "What exactly is it you want, Garrett?" Quincy said.

Garrett leaned forward and said quietly, "Your job. It was mine until you had your temper tantrum and beat your fellow officer senseless. Then of course the old boys' network cracked into action, and you were saved and given *my* job."

"You think you know it all, but you know nothing of my life," Quincy said firmly.

Garrett raised her eyebrows. "That mask is going to slip one day, Captain, and Mummy or the Queen won't be able to save you"— Garrett got up and adjusted her suit jacket—"and I'll be there waiting to step in. I wonder what Holly would think of your…transgressions?"

Quincy's anger was simmering. She knew she was being played with and she was never going to let someone like Garrett goad her into a display of anger.

She watched Garrett stop by Holly as she passed her seat, lean over and say something, then leave. That made her feel more anger than anything. She didn't want Holly to have a bad impression of her. It was bad enough Holly seemed to be avoiding her all morning. Perhaps she felt a bit embarrassed or awkward after last night.

Quincy returned to her work, and five minutes later someone sat down again. Her heart sank, as she thought it might be Garrett returning, but this time when she looked up she saw Holly sitting across from her, smiling. Her stomach did some kind of unusual flip.

"Hi, Quin," Holly said.

"Good afternoon, Holly," Quincy replied.

"I wanted to say thanks for last night, for helping me back to my room. I'm not usually a big drinker when I go out, but I was nervous. You don't normally go out with a film star every day," Holly said.

Quincy couldn't help but see the pictures of Story and Holly this morning. Clay had shown her them all. She envied how much Story and Holly could let go and have fun.

"I understand, and don't mention it. I'll always make sure you get home safely. If you ever need me, just call. You have my number."

Holly sat forward. That statement was said with such sincerity that it touched her deeply. Story had sent her home in a cab. She could look after herself, but still, she was in a strange town, with strangers around her. Holly didn't think Quincy would ever do that.

Holly's gaze dropped to Quincy's collar, and she thought of the scars she had seen the previous night. As with Quincy's personality, what might seem very ordinary and boring hid so much beneath the surface.

"How are you feeling now?" Quincy asked.

"Tired but okay. A night out like that used to be no problem for me to handle, but maybe I'm just getting old."

"I doubt that," Quincy said.

"So this is where the tour really heats up? Lots of visits, lots of travelling," Holly said.

"Yes," Quincy said flatly.

If she didn't know better, there was something worrying Quincy, despite how neutral she was trying to sound. "What's wrong?" Holly said.

"Excuse me?" Quincy replied, looking confused.

"I can tell you're worried about something. Your jaw flexes when you're worried." Holly didn't mention about the shaking hands. That would be exposing too much, and she didn't want to embarrass her.

"My jaw does not flex," Quincy said with a hint of anger.

Great, Stompy was back again. She decided to change the subject. "I've come up with a few places for Bea and Teddy to visit in Chicago, especially when Queen Georgina goes on her solo day visits." They had a busy schedule in Chicago and surrounding cities, and they were going to use the hotel as a base for the family, while Queen Georgina made some solo trips out of town. Holly continued, "I did promise you I'd keep you in the loop, so you could prepare."

"Email me the list and I'll let you know which ones are suitable." Quincy looked down at her computer pad and effectively dismissed Holly.

Stompy was definitely back. Holly couldn't understand how she could show such care and kindness like last night, and then go back to this stoic crap.

"What do you mean *which ones are suitable*? What could be unsuitable about a zoo or an aquarium?" Holly said.

Quincy didn't look up. "I need to contact the places you wish to visit and see if it's feasible to close to the public for the duration of the visit."

"Are you insane? If you do that every time they go somewhere, Teddy will think that it's normal for places to be devoid of people. Part of the fun is being around other people. I know you don't understand that, and you only like the company of your toy soldiers, but that's not what normal people do."

Quincy raised her gaze and said, "At least Princess Edwina will grow up safely. That is my job and only concern."

Holly gave a frustrated groan. "Listen, Stompy—"

That second Clayton interrupted them. "We have the all-clear, ma'am. We're to prepare to land."

Holly wasn't going to waste her breath any more. She got up and totally ignored Quincy by saying, "Thanks, Clay."

While the staff set up at their new base of operations, Quincy and the protection squad accompanied the two Queens to a Chicago rehabilitation hospital. Queen Georgina and Queen Beatrice talked to former military personnel and members of the public who had suffered in terrible accidents but were trying to get their health and their lives back, by the use of pioneering medical procedures.

For Quincy looking on, it was all a little too close to home. Especially when Beatrice sat with the wife of one of the patients who explained the effects of her partner's rehabilitation on the family. She began to cry, and Queen Beatrice pulled the woman into a hug, as she wiped away her own tears.

That picture would make the front pages of the news media worldwide. Quincy could only think of Helen, and her own guilt that she couldn't suffer in Jacob's place.

She used every ounce of her control to keep her mind on the job. Once they returned from the hospital, Inspector Lang asked to speak with her. Quincy walked into the room deemed the security operations room. Team members were setting up the equipment just recently delivered from the plane.

Lang saw her and said to the others, "Could you give us five minutes?"

They filed past her, and Garrett winked at her as she walked out. Quincy walked over to him and stood at attention.

"I just wanted a quiet word with you, Quincy. I understand Ms. Weaver has set out a few places she'd like to visit with the Queen Consort and Princess Edwina, while Queen Georgina is away."

Holly must have gone above her head. She couldn't believe it.

"Yes, I'm going to make enquiries to see if they can accommodate us."

"Loosen up a little, eh?" Lang said.

"Excuse me, sir? I don't understand," Quincy said.

"There's no need to clear out the general public for the duration of the visit. This is, after all, a goodwill tour, a chance for Queen Georgina to cement the good relations between the United States and Britain. The Queen's PR officer agrees it makes for great publicity in the media, for the public to see pictures of the Queen Consort and Princess Edwina amongst the crowds."

"If you'll forgive me, Inspector, I'm thinking of their safety, not of publicity. You know I've had more threats—"

"Yes, to you, Captain. It sounds to me more like a threat to you than the royal party. Our best people back home are constantly monitoring the internet and found nothing. I know you know that, because you've been checking the files."

It was beginning to sound as if Lang thought she was being a bit hysterical. Quincy had never been thought of as anything other than level-headed and the thought of being labelled in such an emotional way was horrifying to her.

"Sir, I'm just trying to do my job," Quincy insisted.

Lang patted her on the arm. "I know you are, Captain." His tone was softer now. "You may be a hugely experienced and decorated military officer, but you're new to protection. You have to let them breathe or they become suffocated. They might be the royal family, but at the end of the day they are a family."

"What do you want me to do, sir?" Quincy said through clenched teeth.

"Just remember they are a family and let loose your tethers slightly."

Quincy had no choice. She had to obey orders. "Yes, sir."

The corridors of the hotel were full of royal staff and hotel staff, trying to set up the rooms and organize the equipment and luggage the royal court would need during their stay. It was organized chaos, to put it kindly.

Quincy spotted Lali orchestrating everything. She was still furious at Holly for going over her head, and she determined to show her that was just not the way things were done.

"No, the monogrammed luggage to the dressing rooms, not the bedrooms," Lali said to the hotel staff.

As they moved away Quincy said to Lali, "Ms. Ramesh, do you know where Ms. Weaver is situated?"

Lali gave a small smile and said, "Of course, she's in the Queen Consort's dressing room. Let me get you the number."

She looked down at the computer pad. "Yes, it's room 1967. Two doors along from the presidential suite."

"Thank you," Quincy said.

As she marched along the corridor, she saw Nanny Baker walking with Princess Edwina. Just a few yards behind was Clayton. At least Clay knew the importance of her task. As she passed Clay, she said, "Keep alert. We haven't swept the rooms and corridors since this morning."

Clayton nodded. "Yes, ma'am."

This hotel was a lot bigger than the previous one in New York. She finally arrived at the room number and knocked.

"Come in," Holly replied.

Quincy walked in and found Holly surrounded by open suitcases and trunks. She was in the middle of hanging some dresses on big sturdy clothes rails that ran the perimeter of the room.

Holly hung up the dress she was holding and turned to face her. She sighed immediately. "Oh, this can't be good. Your jaw is clenching again."

Quincy's anger intensified. Holly had this uncanny knack of reading her emotions, even when Quincy was sure she was showing none. "I thought we had an understanding, Ms. Weaver," Quincy said. Holly rolled her eyes. "My God, it must be bad. We're back to Ms. bloody Weaver again. What understanding?"

"Our understanding that you would come to me with your ideas for the Queen and the consort's free time."

"And I did on the plane, then you didn't listen to me. You want to cut Bea and Teddy off from normal life. Meeting people on official royal events can't be the only time they meet the public. The public don't behave normally then. I remember the first time I met Queen Georgina. I was nearly—well you know what I mean, kacking my pants." Holly smirked.

"I did listen to you, and I compromised the best way I could, but you had to go over my head and speak to Lang, didn't you?"

"What?" Holly was confused for a second, then remembered asking Inspector Lang if he saw any problems with her ideas. "Oh, that? I just asked him—"

Quincy took a step to her and cut her off. "You broke the chain of command. I'm your liaison for the Queen Consort's movements."

Holly couldn't believe this change in Quincy. She was actually showing anger. Holly flicked her gaze down to Quincy's hands, and there it was, the tremor she had seen before.

Holly took a step closer. "Chain of command? I'm not a marine. I'm a civilian and I don't follow your rules or your orders. Got that, Stompy?"

Quincy didn't say anything, but she saw a torrent in her eyes. There was so much under that hard surface.

Quincy turned and walked out without saying another word.

As she shut the door behind Quincy, a memory stirred in her mind. The previous night, Quincy left her bedroom but stopped and said, *You didn't look smart. You were stunningly beautiful, and I did notice you at the polo match. I saw you.*

She saw her.

❖

Bea carried a bag full of Teddy's toys from one of the luggage trunks and set out a small play area beside one of the couches. All the furniture looked like it could have come from Buckingham Palace it was so grand.

Lali walked in with her ever-present computer pad and gave a quick curtsey.

Bea smiled and shook her head. "Will you ever stop doing that in private, Lali? You're my bloody friend."

Lali smiled. "I should hope not. You know how I love to follow rules, and at least I don't call you Your Maj like Holls."

"True. Did you organize the staff rooms as I asked?" Bea said.

"Yes. Why did you want Holls across the corridor from Captain Quincy?" Lali asked.

"Just a feeling. I saw her eyes glued to Holly when she was choosing her clothes for the big date."

Lali sat down on the end of the couch next to Bea. "Really? Now that is interesting. I've never seen an interest from Quincy in anyone, or about anything, since she joined us. Cammy can't talk highly enough about her, though."

Bea set out Teddy's toys on her play mat and joined Lali on the couch.

"Yes, George too. She seems to have qualities that those who serve with her really appreciate. Loyal, hardworking, and brave," Bea said. "Besides it's not just the shopping trip."

"Oh, do tell." Lali smiled.

Bea edged closer in a conspiratorial fashion. "Well, a little birdy told me Quincy escorted Holly back to her room last night, after she got back a little drunk and a little late."

"Really?"

Bea nodded. "Now anyone else, apart from Quincy, you would have expected something a bit naughty went on, but this is Captain Quincy. And Holly didn't tell me about it this morning. That tells me that at least she felt it was too personal to share."

"Or she can't remember." Lali laughed.

"Maybe, but I think it's the former. Have you noticed how annoyed Holls gets at Quincy? She tries to goad her to talking or arguing all the time."

"I suppose you've got to retain your crown as our group's matchmaker. First Greta and Riley, and don't think I didn't realize how much you encouraged me to give Cammy a chance."

Greta's partner Riley had been in one of their lecture groups at university, but Riley would have stared at Greta with puppy eyes and done nothing about it if Bea hadn't pushed her.

"Well, after their three kids and a long and happy marriage, I think I was right to, and don't tell me you're not happy."

Lali gave her a hug. "I couldn't be happier. So who was your little bird who gave you this information?"

"Clay," Bea said. "It was the talk of the protection squad this morning."

Lali sighed. "Clay…she's so sweet. If I was ten years younger and not engaged—"

"Lali!" Bea play hit her friend then said, "I know what you mean. So good looking, and so sweet."

"A bit like Captain Quincy," Lali added.

"Exactly."

The door to the suite opened and George walked in with Teddy on her shoulders. Lali immediately stood up and curtsied.

George looked at them both through half-shut eyes and said to her daughter, "I think we've missed something, Teddy bear."

Bea and Lali smiled at each other, and Lali excused herself.

George lifted Teddy down and she toddled to her mummy. "What did I miss, my darling?"

Bea captured her daughter in her arms and gave her a big kiss. "Nothing for you to worry about, Bully."

Holly finished with Bea's clothes and went to her new room. She didn't even have the energy to open her own suitcases, instead opting to lie on the top of her bed and try to take a nap. Try was the operative word—every time she shut her eyes, she thought about her argument with Quincy. She thought about all the things she should have said and didn't, but Quincy's open show of anger had flummoxed her.

Holly had been angry. She hadn't done anything wrong. All she did was get a second opinion from Inspector Lang on her ideas. It was a very casual, quick word, and Holly had no idea it would cause so much aggravation.

Then Clay had told her that the gossip amongst the protection squad was that Quincy got a bit of a dressing down, and Holly began to feel guilty. She realized what an embarrassment that would be for an officer like Quincy. Someone who followed the rules to the letter.

Holly threw her arm across her face and tried to clear her mind, but Quincy's face kept running through it. Especially Quincy and her scars, which she suspected were both physical and mental.

She sat up quickly. "I can't take this."

Holly rung Clay and asked what room Quincy was in. She was astonished to find out she was in the room across from her.

She got up and walked across the hall, really nervous all of a sudden. "I never thought I'd be apologizing to Stompy."

Holly knocked. She heard shuffling and low voices, but no one replied. Quincy wasn't in there with a woman, was she? The thought didn't make her feel any better. In fact she felt a little anger and she didn't know why.

She was determined not to be ignored, so she thumped the door harder. "Quincy, I want to talk to you—"

The door suddenly opened, and there stood a puzzled looking Quincy. Holly spotted a face on the computer pad behind her. A beautiful blonde.

"Can I help you, Holly?" Quincy said.

Holly wished she'd never come. Why she'd worried or cared if she'd hurt Quin's feelings, she'd never know.

"It doesn't matter. You're busy." Holly turned and hurried back to her room.

❖

That evening was the calm before the storm of engagements ahead, and all the staff were taking advantage of the fact.

The designated rec room here was as old-fashioned as the hotel—no gaming terminals or banks of computer interfaces—but there was an ancient table tennis table, and so competition ensued.

Holly had played table tennis a lot as she grew up and was so far beating all comers. Some of the security and other staff were gathered around, cheering on the participants, while others sat at tables reading and relaxing.

She was now playing Clay and beating her soundly. Clay hit the ball over the net and Holly smashed it back, winning the point. She jumped for joy and twirled around as the rest clapped.

Clay groaned. "You're beating me to a pulp, Holly."

"Yes, and I thought you were supposed to be an expert marksman, Clay?" Holly winked at her friend.

"Supposed to be," Garrett chimed in from the side.

Holly narrowed her eyes at Garrett. She never said anything if it wasn't negative, it seemed. She had a huge chip on her shoulder.

"Okay, match point. Let's go, Clay," Holly said.

Clay served, and a rally began between them. It was one of their longer ones, but just as Clay was starting to smile, perhaps thinking she had a chance, Holly smashed the ball clear of the table.

Everyone clapped, and Clay came around the table to shake Holly's hand. "Well played, Holly. You were too strong for me."

Holly gave her a quick hug. "We all have our strengths. Luckily for Bea and Teddy, yours isn't table tennis. It's the business of protecting that you are the expert at."

A voice from the other end of the table said, "My turn."

She looked and saw Garrett with the bat. Holly didn't want to play her—she could imagine that Garrett wouldn't take losing well.

"No, thanks. I think I'll finish while I still have my table tennis crown intact."

Holly walked away from the table and noticed Quincy sitting at one of the tables. She'd never even noticed her coming in.

She should take the opportunity to apologize like she'd wanted to earlier, but she felt awkward after interrupting Quincy's phone call. It had been such a strange sensation seeing Quincy engaged in an intimate conversation with an absolutely gorgeous woman. Funny—before, she couldn't picture Quincy in an intimate relationship, because she was so emotionally closed off.

But then, Holly reminded herself, she had seen hints of passion in Quincy, so perhaps some other woman had persuaded her to open up. It would be worth the effort, Quincy was—

"Oh no." Holly remembered another thing she had said last night. She had told Quincy she was an Adonis. She was, but you didn't just go and tell someone that. So embarrassing.

She decided just to apologize quickly and go to her room. She approached the table, and Quincy stood up politely. Quincy was every inch the well-mannered and handsome officer. She couldn't forget that.

"Hello," Quincy said.

"Hi." Holly leaned on the back of one of the upright chairs that circled the table and said, "When I came to your door earlier, I wanted to talk to you about something."

"Of course. Sit down." Quincy indicated to the chair.

So much for her quick getaway. Quincy had all her soldiers out on the table and her paints and brushes. One half-painted soldier was set off to the side.

"What's wrong with him?" Holly asked.

"He's the one you were working on. I kept him apart in case you wanted to complete him," Quincy said.

Holly was slightly taken aback. Despite their cross words, Quincy had still thought of her. Quincy being considerate was beginning to become a pattern.

"Um…thank you," Holly said.

Quin picked up a brush and handed it to her. She took it, and just like the first time, their fingertips lingered together. Why did such an apparently boring, stony-faced security officer have such magnetism?

Holly felt it strongly. She pulled her fingers away and picked up her soldier. When she began the paint strokes she got the same calm feeling as she did the last time.

This must be why she does it. It calms her mind.

"You wanted to talk to me about something?" Quincy reminded her.

"Oh yes, I wanted to apologize for earlier. I really didn't mean for what I said to Inspector Lang to cause such a big thing. After I spoke to you on the plane, I thought, maybe I'm wrong, maybe the places they visit should be closed off from the public. I only asked for his opinion, and he said no. I really didn't mean to go over your head, and I'm sorry if it caused you any embarrassment within the squad."

Holly looked up from her soldier and Quincy was gazing at her. "That's all right. I'm sorry I was...so forceful about it," Quincy said.

There was a silence as they gazed at each other, and then Holly looked back down to her task.

After a while she couldn't help but ask, "Did I interrupt you and your girlfriend?"

"Girlfriend?" Quincy said. "Oh no, that was Helen. The wife of my friend from the marines."

Holly was waiting on more information, but as usual Quincy's conversation was stunted. "Helen is beautiful." She pretended to concentrate on her task but watched Quincy out of the corner of her eye. Quincy had gulped and flexed her fists when she'd mentioned her friend. "Do Queen Georgina and Cammy know your friend?" Holly asked.

"No, I commanded Jacob's unit after I'd left the Queen's ship," Quincy said.

Again she didn't elaborate. It was such hard work having a conversation with her. "It's nice that you keep in touch with his wife—" Then Holly realized what might have happened. She reached out and covered Quincy's hand. "Oh God, he didn't pass away on duty with you, did he? I'm so sorry I've brought it up."

Holly could feel Quincy's hand trembling under hers. Quincy snatched her hand away.

"No, he didn't." Quincy started to quickly pack her paints, brushes, and soldiers away. "I think I'll head off to bed, Holly. I'm very tired."

God, she really had struck a nerve. "Listen, I'm sorry, Quin, if I—"

"No, no, it's fine. I'm just tired." Quincy took Holly's brush and washed it out. "You can finish your model another night. You're always welcome."

Holly was certain Quincy was not going to her room because she was tired. Every night they had been on tour, Quin had been the last one up, as if she didn't want to go to bed.

Quin gathered her things together and said, "Goodnight Holly. Sleep well."

As Quin walked away, Holly thought, *Well, that was a conversation stopper.*

That night Holly was awakened from her sleep by a loud noise. She gasped when she woke, as the noise gave her quite a scare.

"Bloody hell. What was that?" She sat up quickly and realized she'd fallen asleep with her computer pad on her chest.

She looked at the time. "Three thirty? I have to be up in a few hours."

Then she heard the noise again. It was like a muffled shout, but she couldn't quite make it out. It was coming from outside her room, so she got up and put on her dressing gown.

Holly opened the door a crack and peeped along the corridor. Luckily her room was at the end of the corridor and not near any entrances or exits, so there were no security personnel to see her in a state of undress. Just then she heard a whole series of shouts—shouts of pain, she was sure—and they were coming from the room across the hall. Captain Quincy's room.

"Quin." Holly hurried across the hall and put her ear to the door.

She heard heavy breathing from Quincy, then shouts of, "Jacob! I'll find you, I'll find you. Jacob, no, no!"

Holly's heart was thudding. She wanted to get in there and hold Quincy. She shouldn't go through nightmares like this herself. These dreams must be connected to the mission Quin got the medal for, that her friend Jacob had obviously been really hurt in.

She wished she could get Quincy to talk about this. Someone like her, who kept everything so locked up tight, must find it so hard to deal with these emotions. Holly took a step back and thought of the torrent of emotion she had seen in Quincy's eyes.

Quincy's words floated across her mind. *I don't let myself feel anything.*

But quite clearly, she did. It was all there, all this pain, tragedy, and emotion were just simmering under the surface. If Garrett was right, and Quincy had gotten involved in a fight, these were the emotions that were driving her anger.

Then she heard more screams of pain. "It's burning, burning!"

Holly closed her eyes and felt such an urge to soothe her pain. Should she knock and try to wake her up? It might make Quin feel worse knowing that Holly heard her. She was such a private person.

She was about to knock when she heard shuffling in the room. Quin was awake. Holly hurried back to her room. When she shut her door, she decided in that moment that she was going to help Quincy, whether she liked it or not.

CHAPTER ELEVEN

The next morning Holly desperately wanted to say something to Quincy, but she knew Quin would shut down if her team would be able to overhear them.

When she walked up to Bea's suite, she noticed that Quincy wasn't standing guard with Clay. Someone else was in her place.

"Clay, where's Quin?" Holly said.

"Morning, Holly. Queen Georgina wanted to speak to her."

"Oh, okay then." Holly had been so worried when Quincy wasn't there. Her mind had started racing, especially after last night. Quin had sounded so distressed.

Holly knocked and was told to come in. She curtsied when she saw Queen Georgina on the floor playing with Teddy.

"Morning, ma'am," Holly said.

"Good morning, Holly. What do you think of Teddy?"

Holly put her hand to her mouth and gasped. Teddy was wearing little white trousers, a polo jersey, and the tiniest pair of riding boots.

"Teddy!" Holly put her make-up case down on the table and dropped to her knees. "Teddy, you look so cute."

Teddy clapped her hands and said excitedly, "New boots."

"Come show me your boots then," Holly said.

Teddy toddled over to her slowly. Holly was sometimes struck by the enormity of what this little toddler had in front of her in her life. She would be Queen and travel the world just like they were doing now, with her own family, just as George's mother and father had done. A long, ever-stretching line of continuity.

George was dressed in her polo riding gear, and Teddy matched her, making the cuteness level ten.

They were visiting a city riding stable, set up for children with difficult home lives and children with certain challenges. The stables were founded by a US sister charity to the Queen Consort's own UK city farm charity. Queen Georgina was clearly looking forward to this engagement. Anything with horses, and she generally was happy.

Leaving Teddy and George to play, Holly walked into Bea's bedroom and found Bea ready and waiting, sitting at the dressing table. Bea was simply dressed in jeans and a jumper today.

"Morning, Your Maj," Holly said.

Bea chuckled. "Morning. I'm all ready for my war paint."

Holly put her make-up case down and said, "How cute is Teddy in her riding outfit? Just adorable."

"Oh, I know," Bea said. "She's so cute I could eat her all up, and she matches her mum too. I love George in her polo gear."

Holly knew that. She'd seen Bea mentally tear George's riding clothes off with her teeth.

"She is dishy," Holly said.

She'd started to apply Bea's make-up, when Bea said, "I hear you were ripping up the table tennis table last night, then painting some toy soldiers."

Holly stopped her dabbing into the powder. "You have very good sources don't you, Your Maj."

"Maybe." Bea grinned.

"Well, maybe you can use your sources to find out who's leaving my favourite coffee outside my door every morning."

"Really? I'll try to find out. So why were you helping Quin?"

"Uh, we had clashed a little bit over the plans I had for your days off, and I wanted to apologize. I was a bit…" Holly searched her brain for the right word. "I was a bit forceful in my argument."

"You? Never," Bea joked.

She was well known amongst her group of friends for being very fiery. "Okay, okay, do you want your make-up like Koko the Clown?" Holly gave her friend a mock glare.

"You win," Bea said. "Have you heard from Story again?"

"Yeah, she texted to apologize for the story in the media about girls' night. She said she just mentioned it to one of her friends. I need to be even more careful about what I say to people. I never want to expose your private life to the world."

"Don't worry about it. I know how hard it is. So are you looking forward to meeting Story again in LA?"

"Of course," Holly said quickly.

Their date had been so much fun, well, apart from feeling like Story wasn't present with her. It felt like every touch, every dance was set up by her to look good on her social media, but she was so much fun, and she talked and told her all about her life. Being with her wasn't hard work.

Holly said, "If she remembers. I'm sure she'll have some gorgeous actress to go out with by then."

"I'm sure she'll remember," Bea said.

As Holly rummaged in her make-up case, Bea said, "Regardless of Story St. John, do you think you'll explore a relationship with a woman?"

Holly stopped and turned to smile at her friend. "Yes, I think I will. I think it's a woman I'm meant to love. I don't mind saying I'm a bit scared."

Bea took her hand. "You can't go through life worried about getting your heart broken. You have to take some chances. Look at the chance I took. I stepped into the gilded cage for George, but she is so worth it."

"I'll try to be brave," Holly said. "Now which shade of lippy for a riding stable?" Holly held out a palette of colours for her.

Bea pointed. "This one, please." Then she said, "Oh, by the way, George, Cammy, and Quin are going to give the children a polo lesson."

"You mean Cammy and Quin will have polo gear on too?"

Bea nodded and grinned like the Cheshire cat. "Yes, they will, and you're coming with us. It'll be an informal day."

Holly gulped, and her heart thudded wildly. "Wait—didn't Cammy once say polo was for posh girls and boys?"

Bea giggled. "She's been persuaded to make an exception for the children."

Holly clapped her hands together. "I can't wait to see this."

❖

Quincy wasn't wildly comfortable doing this. During their visit to Appledown Riding Stables, she was to hand over the protection of the Queen Consort and Princess Edwina to Clay, while Queen Georgina, Cammy, and herself took part in a polo lesson.

In the run up to the tour, Queen Georgina's private secretary had been informed that the children who came to the stables were studying all the equestrian pursuits the Queen enjoyed, and polo was the main one.

The Queen suggested that they donate some children's polo sets to the stables and get involved with a lesson. Quincy had been reluctant, but the Queen had asked her as a favour, and so she couldn't say no.

It wasn't that she didn't want to get involved with the children, but she didn't like being the centre of attention, and now she was to be front and centre on every news broadcast around the world.

After her nightmares and bad sleep last night, she was surprised she could even function properly, far less play polo. Her nightmares had been particularly bad—it must have been talking about Jacob with Holly that had triggered them. Holly had pressed and pressed her for information, and all she could think to do was run. God only knew what Holly thought about her.

She was beginning to regret encouraging Holly to help her paint her model soldiers. It would probably be safer if she just gave the rec room a miss and stayed in her room.

The cars pulled into the stable courtyard, and all the children, the staff, and their families were waiting and waving a mixture of American and Union flags.

The Buckinghams were creating plenty of goodwill, just as their tour was meant to do.

Quincy was in the car behind the royal party. Clay was sitting in her stead with the Queens, where she would normally be. She was impressed with the new young recruit. Clay took her assignment very seriously, but had that happy knack of fitting in with the family aspect of the duty. Quincy didn't know if she would ever do that well.

The royal car stopped, and Quincy said into her body mic, "Clay? Look sharp. Don't relax just because this is an informal visit."

"Yes, ma'am," Clay replied.

Letting your guard down during such a small visit, with children as the main well-wishers, was an easy mistake to make. Any assailant would take this as an ideal opportunity to strike, and even though Quincy would be otherwise engaged, she would never switch off.

Quincy watched Cammy emerge first and open the Queen's car door, and the children and adults squealed as she stepped out. Then Clay opened the consort's door. She noticed Clay's gaze taking in the full perimeter as the consort got out.

Well done, Clay, Quincy said to herself.

Both the royals waved to the crowds before George leaned into the armoured car and took Princess Edwina from her car seat. There was an even bigger cheer. Princess Edwina had been a star from the moment the Queen and consort announced the pregnancy to the news outlets. Countless words had been written about the princess in her first year, and no doubt interest would increase as she grew up.

Then Quincy's attention was caught by Holly coming out of the car. The Queen Consort had asked Holly to come along to help with Teddy, to give Nanny Baker a break for this outdoor event.

When she saw Holly and gazed at that bright happy smile, she forgot to breathe.

She felt a touch on her arm and was knocked from her thoughts. It was Lali, summoning her from the car. Everyone had gotten out but her. Brilliant. After reminding Clay to stay alert and promising not to switch off despite her different role today, she had done just that. Holly stole her attention.

Holly, George, and Bea made their way down the line of children and staff, taking their time and making that human-to-human contact they were both so determined to bring to their roles.

Bea and George were shown the stables, and they talked to the staff about the challenges they encountered. Bea found it fascinating and explained to the staff why the city riding project was so close to her heart, and how much her sister Abigail got from it.

Then came the part Bea was most anxious about—Teddy was going to ride one of the smallest ponies in the stable. Riding was not for Bea, she and horses did not mix, and the thought of her baby on one didn't fill her with joy. But horse riding was ingrained in George and her family, and something Bea couldn't fight against.

George had put Teddy on the back of a horse before she could walk and took her out to play with the horses every weekend at Windsor.

In the stable yard a very small pony was led out, and Bea held Teddy just that little bit tighter. She didn't want to pass her anxiety to her daughter, but she couldn't hide her natural reaction. Her sister Abigail would be so proud that her niece was enjoying her own love of horses.

George must have noticed her worry, because she came over to her and smiled. "Let me take her. She's going to be fine, my darling. The stables have chosen a very mild-mannered pony, and I know what I am doing. Do you trust me?"

"Of course I do. I know you do this with her every weekend, but"—Bea shot a look to the bank of photographers waiting for their piece of today's visit—"if it wasn't in front of all of them, I'd feel better."

"I completely understand how you feel, Your Maj, but the paparazzi won't dare try anything sneaky with Teddy's mum in charge." Holly felt Bea's anxiety as she stood beside her. Since coming to work for her friend, Holly had come to understand that the royal family's life was a constant balance of negotiations with the media, so they could have some semblance of a private life.

Each public appearance, holiday, and family event was only possible if the press were given their photo op of the day, and this was it. Since Teddy had been born, photos with her were the most requested.

In order to have privacy later, the press were allowed this one shot outside, of George leading Teddy around on the pony. The pony ride went ahead without incident, and then George, Cammy, and Quincy set up the children's polo equipment and joined the children on horseback.

Holly joined Bea and Lali against the fence to watch. George and Cammy were really good looking in their polo gear, but she could not take her eyes off Quincy.

That day she had first seen Quincy at the polo, she had assumed Quincy was a confident woman who knew how good-looking she was, but now Holly knew that wasn't the case. Quincy's long, muscular legs in those polo trousers and boots almost made her drool, but the fact that Quincy didn't know how good she looked made her all the more enticing.

I'm lusting after Quin the dull, but then she corrected herself. She wasn't dull, she was intense. Intense emotions were held at bay behind those so troubled but gorgeous blue eyes. Holly couldn't imagine hiding her emotions. If she wasn't happy, everyone knew it.

If someone could break Quincy's self control, what would they unleash?

She saw one of the children struggle to manage her horse, and Quincy trotted over quickly and gained control of the reins.

Holly gave a long sigh.

Bea said, "Was that a longing sigh, Lali?"

"I think so," Lali replied.

Bea had Teddy in her arms. "That only begs the question, which one of our gorgeous polo players made our best friend sigh, Lali?"

Lali smiled and played right along. "I would hope it wasn't either of ours, Bea, so that only leaves Captain Quincy."

She'd been rumbled. "Oh, shut up, it's just the polo uniform."

Just then Quincy jumped off her horse, took off her helmet, and looked right at her. Holly felt her knees turn to jelly. She grasped the fence tightly.

George called to Quincy and she looked away from Holly and walked the child's horse over to the other side.

That had never happened to Holly with anyone, male or female. She was sure it was the thought of that torrent of passion that was under Quincy's hard surface.

She was sure because she had felt it when they'd shared that awkward forced kiss.

Bea bumped her shoulder. "I think she caught you looking, Holls," Bea said while bouncing Teddy on her hip. "Auntie Holly likes the captain, doesn't she, Teddy?"

Holly said, "Haven't you got some queening to do or something?"

"You better watch it," Lali said. "Story will get jealous."

"As if? Listen, Quincy is good looking, okay? I admit it," Holly said.

"I've seen her looking at you, Holls. I think she likes you," Bea said.

"Come on, she does not look at me. I aggravate her, cause her trouble, and generally annoy her. Besides, every time I try to talk to her, it either ends in me arguing, or long silences. It's like trying to get blood out of a stone."

"Holly," Lali said, "you can talk more than enough for both of you."

Bea leaned over and whispered, "Sometimes the most quiet, unassuming people are the ones who will love you the fiercest. I found that out."

That comment took her by surprise. She looked at Bea, then back to Quincy. She had promised herself she would break through that tough outer surface. Her attraction to Quincy was just going to make her more determined.

You just need to be unravelled, Stompy.

Then Lali said, "Oh, by the way, your coffee fairy? You're looking at her."

"What? Quin gets my coffee?" Holly said with surprise.

"Yes, I asked around. She got Clayton to find out what you like and picks it up on her morning run."

"But that first time we'd just had a big argument," Holly said.

Quincy happened to look across and Holly said to herself. "What is going on inside you, Captain?"

CHAPTER TWELVE

The week they were spending in Chicago was frenetic. Some days they had four engagements in a day, and starting tomorrow Queen Georgina was leaving Bea and Teddy and making some solo visits to neighbouring cities. Luckily at the end of this week they would be headed to Kentucky, where after a public appearance at the Kentucky Derby, the royal party would be staying for a week-long break at the Castleford Ranch, owned by a horse breeder friend of the Queen.

Holly didn't get the chance to spend time with Quincy in the rec room for another few days, since Bea and George had evening engagements, but this evening was free.

She waited in the rec room for an hour and Quincy never came in. Clay went out for the evening so she couldn't ask her where her commanding officer was. Holly thought back to their last conversation here. She had asked, prodded, and probed about her military life and her friend in the marines, and then Quincy had run away.

Was Quin frightened to talk to her? Maybe she thought Holly'd keep asking things she was too uncomfortable to talk about. She would, she conceded, but she would approach things differently this time. First she had to find Quincy.

She went to Quincy's room, but first she went to her bedroom for a quick change. Instead of her comfortable wool jumper, she put on a little tight low-cut top. Holly hadn't tried her hand at gaining a woman's attention in a long time, and her first and only girlfriend had pursued her, but she knew from her relationships with men, a little distraction could oil the wheels of a conversation.

Happy with her appearance, she walked across the hall and knocked on the door. A surprised looking Quincy opened the door, and her eyes momentarily flicked down to her cleavage and then quickly back up.

You are human then, Stompy.

"Can I help you, Holly?" Quin said.

That posh voice was sexy, Holly did have to admit. "I was waiting for you in the rec room."

Quincy looked even more surprised. "You were?"

"Yes, I thought we were painting your toy soldiers together." Holly pushed past Quincy and found a table set out with all her paints and soldiers. "Are you trying to hide from me, Captain?" Holly said with a hand on her hip.

"No, I—I didn't think it was a regular appointment."

Holly laughed and flopped down onto one of the chairs around the table. "Appointment? We don't have an appointment. I just thought it was something we were doing together. Are you sure you're not hiding from me?"

"No, of course not. You're welcome to join me," Quincy said.

Holly could feel Quincy's awkwardness pouring off her. "Relax would you? I'm sure I'm not the first woman who's been in your bedroom."

Quincy never replied to that, but said, "Can I get you a drink?"

"White wine, please," Holly said.

Holly watched Quincy nervously get her a drink from the minibar. She'd never seen her so off kilter, or her iron control slipping so.

It was because she was in Quin's private space. Outside that door she was Captain Quincy, the unflappable Captain Quincy, but in here…That was the question. Who was the real Quincy?

Holly wouldn't make the mistake of asking direct questions about her friend Jacob and the problems she was sure powered Quincy's nightmares. She had to be clever and gain her trust first.

"Your wine, Ms. Holly." Quincy handed the glass to Holly. Quincy was so nervous that she had to hope Holly didn't notice the slight shake to her hand. She had imagined that by staying in her room, she would avoid Holly and her questions. Now here she was in Quincy's most private of spaces.

She sat down and Holly pointed at the mug on the table. "You drink too much coffee, Quin."

"No, it's camomile tea. I thought I'd try it. A friend recommended it to me—I don't sleep too well, you see." Why had she said that? *Don't tell her anything.*

"Okay, I'll let you off then. Is this my guy?" Holly picked up a soldier from the box.

"Yes, that's the chap," Quincy said.

Holly chuckled and leaned forward to pick up her brush, giving Quincy a closer look at her cleavage. "You say things in such a funny way, Quin."

Quincy's heart thudded wildly. She remembered the feel of Holly's lips, and then imagined what kissing and licking her way over Holly's plump breasts would feel like. Her mouth watered, and her sex ached.

Quincy had never felt so attracted to someone before. She had worked with a lot of women, and many had tried to seduce her, but she had always, politely and quite easily, brushed them off. None of them had made her feel like this.

"Quin? Are you listening to me?"

"Sorry?" Quincy said.

"I was talking to you, but you were miles away," Holly said.

Holly had distracted her again, this time with her body. This was becoming a pattern. Quincy chastised herself.

"Sorry, what did you say?"

"I said, are we all set for the aquarium tomorrow?" Holly said.

Quin nodded. "Yes, I sent a team there today to recon the place, and the local police will sweep the place tomorrow." She'd had no choice but to relax her preferred choice of closing the building, after Inspector Lang talked to her.

"Great, now paint." Holly pointed to her models.

"Oh yes." Quincy lifted her brush but was so tense that she couldn't relax and paint as she normally did.

Holly was sitting in her room.

She never had anyone in her private space. She felt obliged to speak, but her mind was blank. Holly was used to sparkling conversation, no doubt, and all Quincy could do was gulp hard, and could find no words.

"What army people did you say these were?" Luckily Holly filled the silence.

"The Grenadier Guards. One of the oldest infantry regiments. They were raised in 1656," Quincy explained.

"Wow, that's a bloody long time ago," Holly said.

Quincy couldn't help but smile at that response. "I suppose it is. They served King Charles II, then—" Quincy stopped short. "I won't bore you with the history."

Holly looked up from her soldier. "You're not boring me. Are your marines as old as that?"

"Not quite. The Royal Marines were officially founded in 1755. But we have a long, proud history."

"Do you miss it? I suppose it's a once a marine, always a marine kind of thing?" Holly said.

Despite all the pain and the terrors of her dreams, Quincy did miss it. "Yes, I'll always be a Royal Marine commando. I miss the day-to-day work of looking after my unit. Training and working hard."

Holly smiled. "At least you get to run in some nicer places now."

"It's not the same…" Quincy's mind wandered to training with her men in the wet moors of Scotland. "I remember running for miles, with full kit, in the driving rain and cold of the Scottish Highlands, but then the sheer exhilaration of finishing, setting up camp, and sitting around the fire together."

Holly screwed up her eyes. "How can that be fun?"

"It's hard to explain. You push your body to its limits, to the point when you think you might collapse. You think the harsh reality of nature is going to break you, but then you realize that every one of your men and women is feeling the same pain, the same hopelessness."

Quincy could see herself running beside Jacob, could see his struggle, and everyone else's.

"You know you can't let them down, and you keep going. We pull each other through. There is no *one*, there's only together. We go on together or not at all."

She had to stop speaking and clear her throat. "That's what being a Royal Marine is all about."

When she looked up, Holly was gazing at her with a certain look that she couldn't decipher.

"It must bring you all so close together," Holly said.

Quincy could only nod and think about Jacob. *Put me out of my misery, please, Quincy. I can't be the man I was.*

She closed her eyes and tried to dismiss the memory.

"You said the best bit was setting up camp." Holly filled the silence again—she always seemed to. "Did you have to eat bugs and stuff?"

Quincy chuckled. Again Holly had pushed away her sad thoughts, with just her words. What else could she do? Her heart started to thud, and she had the urge to touch Holly and run her fingers through that reddish-blond hair of hers.

"Yes, we had to eat the odd bug, the odd fish eye—"

"Yuck," Holly interrupted her, "you didn't have to tell me in detail."

"Sorry, but I loved camping out overnight. Whether in the wet Highlands or the stifling dry heat of the Middle East. The night always ends the same, making a fire and having a cup of tea."

"That sounds nice. I've never been camping, but my gran had a real open fireplace, and I always lay in front of it and watched the flames. I was fascinated."

"There's something about a campfire that connects with somewhere deep inside the human soul, I believe. It heats us, gives us hope. It's primal somehow."

"That was beautiful," Holly said breathily.

The atmosphere in the room had changed and she never even realized it. Holly's lips were slightly parted, and her chest was moving more rapidly.

She'd never intended her words to have such an effect, but they had. If she was a braver woman, she would go over to Holly and kiss her, but she wasn't, so she just put her attention back to her model figure.

After about thirty seconds Holly said, "When we get to the ranch in Kentucky, will you show me how to make a fire?"

Quincy wanted to say no. She was already too close, and Holly had the ability to get her to talk about things that she didn't want to. But Quincy couldn't say no.

"Of course I will."

"Excellent. Quin? Did you always want to be in the marines?"

"Yes, I was in the marine cadets at boarding school. My mother wasn't too happy," Quincy said. She'd done it again. Said more than she should.

"Was she worried about you getting injured? Fighting on the front line?"

"God, no. It was a bit beneath the family name, that was all. My family has a long tradition in the Royal Navy, but we captain fleets of ships, not fight like common soldiers, as mother put it."

Holly furrowed her brow. "I think you're brave choosing the Royal Marines. Can I see a picture of you in your uniform?"

Quincy was not expecting that question. "Erm, I don't think I have—"

Holly put her brush down, came over to her chair, and crouched down beside it. "Come on. I know you've got to have some, and I'm not leaving you alone until you show me."

The smell of Holly's perfume was intoxicating, and she couldn't tear her eyes from her breasts that she could now see, up close and personal.

Just show her. Then she'll leave you alone.

She reached over to her bed and picked up her computer pad and opened up her photos. "This is me, during officer training." She was dressed in full fatigues, with green beret, gun, and black war paint on her face.

Holly scooted closer and leaned her arm on Quincy's leg—for balance, she assumed, but it sent heat throughout her body.

"God, you look so butch I could eat you all up." Holly giggled.

"Excuse me?" Quincy said with surprise.

Holly smiled that cute way she had that wrinkled her nose. "Just a figure of speech. Next pic, come on."

Quincy's hands were starting to tremble slightly, but it was nothing compared to how hard her heart was thumping. How could something feel so exhilarating, turned her on so, and at the same time make her want to run.

"Do I scare you, Stompy?" Holly asked with the sexiest smile.

Yes. "No."

She flicked onto the next pic and it was of Quincy in her dress uniform, meeting and leading the Queen around the parade ground.

"Soon after the Queen took the throne, she visited all her regiments, and I was given the honour of accompanying her to inspect the men."

Holly gave her a strange look. "You really believe that Honour for Queen and Country stuff, don't you?"

"Of course. The Queen was and is my boss. Everyone in the military feels the same. We aren't the prime minister's forces—we are the Queen's." Quincy continued, "It's been ingrained in me my whole life. It's my greatest honour to serve my country, as a Royal Marine, or as a protection officer."

There was a silence before Quincy turned to the next picture. She was in desert fatigues in the Middle East, standing with her friend Jacob.

Don't ask, Quincy said to herself.

"Is that Jacob?" Holly asked.

Quincy nodded, and Holly didn't say another word, or push her further. She got up and walked back to her chair.

"I want to finish my little soldier man before bedtime."

Quincy didn't say anything, and they worked on in quiet companionship for another hour before she started to yawn.

"You better get some sleep, Quincy," Holly said to her.

"I need coffee, more like. This camomile tea makes me too sleepy."

"Isn't that the point?" Holly said.

Quincy was sure it wasn't the tea. It was Holly's company. She felt more at ease just sitting in silence with Holly than she could remember with any other person. She had no need to hide from her. Holly seemed to have backed off from the really personal questions, and that made Quincy able to just enjoy her company, which she did immensely.

She was able to hold a conversation herself it seemed, and Quincy found Holly's chatter soothing. Yes, this she could cope with.

Quincy could admire from a distance and not feel the fear of getting closer. Because any closer was the unknown, and the unknown frightened her.

❖

The next day Queen Georgina took an early flight to an event in Cleveland, Ohio, and Quincy led a team of protection officers to the aquarium Queen Beatrice and Princess Edwina were visiting. She and Clayton hovered a few feet behind Beatrice, Lali, and Holly, who were looking at the fish in the tanks, with five other members of her team, including Garrett, spread out behind them.

There was a carnival atmosphere at the aquarium. They happened to arrive on the one day a month that the aquarium put on a special event for school excursions. Busloads of kids made the place much busier than expected and made Quincy nervous.

Quincy looked over to Clay and saw she was very focused and surveying the scene. She then looked behind and said through her body mic, "Stay alert, everyone. It's getting busier."

They all nodded. Quincy disliked this busy environment. Children and their parents would edge closer to try to get a look or a word with the consort.

Queen Beatrice was so open and approachable that she would drop down to one knee with the princess and talk to anyone and everyone. Quincy had lost count of how many hugs she had given to the little children she met. Hugging seemed to be Queen Beatrice's thing, but it made Quincy nervous.

Everyone seemed like a threat. Staff members wandered about in shark and whale costumes, entertaining the kids by juggling, making balloon animals, and goofing around with them.

Compared to a normal royal event, this was chaotic, but Quincy had to try and remember this wasn't an official visit, rather a private day out, although not so private. The people around them had their phones out filming them.

They made slow progress along the tanks. At one point Holly looked back at her and smiled. The tension that she was holding was eased for that moment, and she smiled back. Holly's smile could melt any heart.

She was so caught up in Holly's smile that she bumped into someone as they walked along. She'd been distracted again. This was becoming a dangerous habit.

❖

"Do you see the big blue fishy, Teddy?" Bea said to her daughter. Teddy pressed her hand against the glass of the fish tank. "Fishy."

Holly couldn't resist looking back over her shoulder. The last time she did, she was rewarded by a smile from Quincy. Quincy so rarely gave out smiles that it seemed all the sweeter. But this time she wasn't smiling. She was looking around the room nervously. It was getting very busy, and people were getting quite close. Holly knew how much that stressed Quincy out. Maybe she had given Quincy too much of a hard time when she'd resisted these days out for Bea and Teddy.

"Caught you looking," Lali said to her.

Holly nudged her. "Stop it. I'm just looking around."

Lali smiled. "Of course you were."

They looked down when Teddy said, "Fish, fish," and started to pull Bea.

"I think she likes it here," Bea said. "Great idea, Holls."

Teddy kept pulling, and they looked up to see someone in a cartoon shark costume coming towards them.

"You want to see the shark?" Bea said.

"Uh-huh," Teddy said.

They all started to move. As they got closer to the costumed staff member, the shark lifted its fin to reveal something small and black. Before Holly could even see what it was, Quincy shouted, "Gun!" then ran over just as it was fired, and a cascade of silver glitter fell.

Bea already had Teddy up in her arms, and Clay was in front of them, shielding them both from what Quincy had shouted. A gun.

Quincy held the staff member to the floor while he shouted, "It's just a glitter gun. It's just glitter."

The rest of the protection squad surrounded them, and she heard Garrett say, "Hair trigger again, Quincy?"

Everyone around them had their cameras trained on Quincy and were laughing, as she stood up covered in glitter.

Oh no, thought Holly.

CHAPTER THIRTEEN

As soon as they got back to Bea's suite, Holly said, "I need to speak to Quincy, Bea." The clip of the glitter explosion had gone viral on social media. Holly's stomach sank as she imagined everyone laughing at Quincy, especially Garrett. Bloody idiot.

She asked around but all anyone knew was that Quincy had left the hotel. Without any clues, Holly got the elevator downstairs and walked outside. Where would she go? Most people in emotional distress would head for a bar, but Quincy didn't drink—well, except coffee.

Then she spotted a diner on the corner. On a hunch Holly went in, and there in a booth up at the back wall of the dinner sat Quincy, staring into her cup of coffee.

Quincy looked more emotional than she had ever seen her, and that was probably because she didn't know anyone she knew was watching her. Holly's heart ached for her. She was isolated enough as it was—apart from Cammy and Queen Georgina, she didn't seem to have any real friends, and she didn't think tough military people like them talked about feelings. Plus, she didn't have any friends in the protection squad. Clay hero-worshiped her, but that wasn't the same as having one of your peers to confide in.

Quincy needed someone, and like it or not, Holly was going to be the one she would confide in. She slipped into the booth and faced Quincy. "Buy me a coffee?"

Quincy appeared astonished to see her.

"Holly, what—?"

"Why did you run off? The Queen Consort and I wanted to speak to you," Holly said.

"Funnily enough I wanted to be alone," Quincy snapped.

Holly held up her hand and said, "Snappy, tight jaw—uh-oh, Captain Stompy is here."

"Look," Quincy said, gesticulating. She appeared about to lose her temper, show anger and emotion at last, but then she took a breath and laid her hand flat on the table. "Could you just leave me alone?"

Holly saw the tremor in Quincy's hand. She covered it with hers and squeezed. "I'm not going anywhere. I want to be your friend, and you're not going to scare me off. I know you're embarrassed—"

"Embarrassed? The whole aquarium was laughing, the whole world was laughing at the protection officer who bravely jumped in front of a gun, a gun that fired silver glitter. I'm a laughing stock. Everyone already thought I had a hair trigger."

"Maybe Garrett, and people like that, but the people who know you, who care about you, Bea, me, Lali, we're all grateful and proud of what you've done."

"Proud? How could you be?" Quincy said.

"That glitter gun could have been a real gun—"

"But it wasn't," Quincy interrupted.

"But it could have been, and you heroically stepped in front of it. It was a stupid thing for their staff member to use when royalty were visiting."

"I'm no hero." Quincy tried to pull her hand back, but Holly wouldn't let go. "Let me go, Holly." Quincy's jaw was tightening more than ever.

Holly just smiled at her and put her second hand on top of Quincy's. "Remember, Stompy, I don't do what I'm told. I'm not a soldier-marine-type person. I'm Holly Weaver, and I don't do well with authority."

Holly's statement appeared to confuse Quincy. "What do you want from me?"

"This is our last night off in Chicago. The next few days are packed with visits, so come out with me tonight and forget that today ever happened."

"No, I can't. I—" Quincy flustered.

Holly raised her eyebrow in suspicion. "Why not?"

"Because I have my models to finish, and security plans to finalize," Quincy said.

Holly rolled her eyes. "No, you don't. You can play with your toys another night—I'm helping you, remember? Anyway, I know you and Lang already have your security plans sorted out. You're coming."

Quincy had no answers for her. Holly presumed she wasn't used to being told what to do.

"Good, that's settled then."

"What will we do? Won't I need to book us a table somewhere, or try to get us tickets for something?"

Holly chuckled. She knew what a planner Quincy was, and a stickler for keeping to times and plans.

"What I'm going to say is going to shock you to your very core. We are going to go out and just see where the night takes us. No plans, no preparations, just get dressed and go out into the Chicago night."

Quincy gulped. "We won't get in anywhere in a big city like this."

"So then we get a hot dog in the street and walk through the park. We'll find somewhere. Come on."

Holly finally let Quincy's hands go, and they got up from the booth. Quincy still appeared to be startled by this new turn of events.

I'm unravelling you, Stompy.

Holly brushed some glitter from Quincy's suit jacket. "Tonight, we tell the world and that bloody arsehole Garrett that we don't care what they think."

"I don't know if—" Quincy's words died away as Holly started to brush Quincy's cheek.

"You have some glitter here." Holly looked into Quincy's eyes and saw more than she ever had before. Quincy's barriers were dropping. She could see intense sadness, confusion, hurt, and want in those beautiful blue eyes. She was mesmerized by Quincy's eyes. They weren't like any shade of blue she had ever seen, almost like the colour of the deep, dark blue of the open ocean. The whites surrounding them were so milky she felt she could dive into them. Holly realized she was still touching Quincy's cheek, only now she wasn't brushing away the glitter, she was caressing. She pulled her hand away and said, "Let's go and get ready."

❖

Quincy stood in front of her mirror on the wardrobe, trying to come up with excuses why she couldn't go out with Holly tonight. The last thing she wanted to do was go out into the public after being made a fool of today, but strangely, as awful as that sounded, the thought of being with Holly gave her tingles of excitement in her stomach.

She straightened her grey tie and said to her reflection, "Ms. Holly, there's a security matter that—No, she won't buy that."

She then picked up her comb and, even though her hair was sitting perfectly combed to the side, did it again.

Quincy racked her brains, but nothing was coming to her. She jumped when she heard a knock at the door.

"Just tell her no. Look her straight in the eye and say no," Quincy told herself.

She opened the door ready to say no, and Queen Georgina was standing there. Quincy quickly bowed her head.

"Your Majesty. Please come in."

George walked in and said, "I can't stay for long. I've just gotten back from Cleveland, and I want to put Teddy to bed."

"Of course, ma'am."

"I wanted to talk to you about today," George said.

Quincy's heart sank. "George, I'm so—"

George stopped her and put her hand on Quincy's shoulder. "No, Quincy. I know you've had to put up with a few jokes and laughter today, but I can't thank you enough. You put yourself between a threat and my wife and child without thought for yourself. It might have been a misunderstanding, but it could have been so much worse."

Quincy let out a breath. "I think some of my team think I'm overly cautious." Overly cautious were the only words she could use without telling her friend about the threats she'd had and betraying the chain of command. "Both Your Majesties are extremely popular, but there are a lot of bad people out there. Pockets of Thea Brandt's organization still exist all over the world. We still need to be ready for anything."

George nodded. "I agree with you. I can't imagine the pain that Queen Rozala went through. If I lost Bea or Teddy I—" George's voice cracked. "I don't know how I could go on."

"I promise you, George. I will protect them with my life."

"I know. I'm going to have a word with Lang. That episode today gave me quite a fright. If a normal member of the public could get that close with a real weapon, then God only knows what they could do. I think things have been a little lax since we got to North America."

Thank God someone was finally listening. "I think that's a good idea, George," Quincy said.

George nodded. "Well, you must excuse me. Teddy is waiting for me to read the next story in her *Winnie-the-Pooh* book."

Quincy smiled. "Duty calls, then."

"Indeed. Have a good night, Quincy."

"Goodnight, ma'am."

Quincy walked back to her bed, sat down, and looked at her watch. Maybe Holly had a change of heart.

Just as she thought that, there was another knock at the door, and a voice shouted, "It's time to come out to play."

It was Holly. Despite her horror at the thought of going out, she felt a huge ball of excitement in her stomach.

She opened the door, and Holly stood there with the most gorgeous smile. She was beautiful. The feeling Holly gave her hit Quincy forcefully, straight in the chest.

Holly was wearing skintight ripped skinny jeans with black heels, a very low cut black strappy top, and her biker jacket tied around her waist, with lots of tribal style wristbands and three beaded necklaces in different sizes. Nothing about Holly was regular, or predictable.

Holly looked her up and down, then screwed up her eyes. "I like the suit. Bespoke, I'd guess?"

"Yes, I have them made in a little tailor's in Savile Row," Quincy said.

"Nice, but you need to liven it up a bit. Can I come in?" Holly asked.

"Of course," Quincy said.

As Holly walked past her, she realized there was no back on her top—it simply tied at the neck. She had an overwhelming urge to run her fingers down Holly's back as her excitement grew.

"Let me look at you," Holly said.

Holly had this way of biting her lip that Quincy found adorable. She jumped when Holly quickly undid her tie, but she caught Holly's wrist in her hand before she unbuttoned her collar button.

"No, I don't wear my shirt open," Quincy said in panic. She never thought for one minute Holly would remember the quick look she'd gotten of her burn scars, the night she'd helped her back to her room.

Holly looked at her silently, then said, "That's okay. We can liven you up in other ways. Let me see your wardrobe."

"Excuse me?" Quincy said.

"I need to look at your selection of ties," Holly replied.

Without waiting to be invited, Holly bounced over to her wardrobe and opened the doors.

Quincy was there in a second and pushed one door shut. She was more than a little angry at anyone invading her privacy.

"Do you trample your way through the lives of everyone you meet?"

Quincy expected an angry response, then maybe they could bring an end to this charade, but Holly just chuckled and pushed her in the chest. Amazingly Quincy found herself moving as meekly as a mouse.

"Not everyone, but you, Captain Stompy, need your life ruffled up," Holly said.

Once Holly got a proper look at Quincy's wardrobe she said, "Bloody hell."

There were about ten suits hanging in suit bags, and ten white shirts hanging perfectly beside them, and about the same number of ties, sitting perfectly in a row, in various shades of grey.

Holly turned her head and said to Quincy, "You are so straight Quincy, in an un-gay way."

"Un-gay? What does that mean?" Quincy queried.

"I made the word up just for you. If you weren't so deliciously butch I'd worry you weren't gay."

"Who says I am?" Quincy said sharply.

Holly rolled her eyes. "Oh, please. You outstud most men." Holly then walked out of the room saying, "I'll be back in a couple of minutes."

❖

Holly left Cammy and Lali's room clutching a selection of coloured ties. She'd had to put up with a few jibes about going on a date with Quincy, but this wasn't a date. Was it?

No, she was just trying to make Quincy feel better. The look of shame and embarrassment she had seen on Quincy's face today hurt her heart. She had wanted to run to her and gather her in her arms, but she couldn't.

No one who watched today's events could know the pain and the mental scars Quincy carried. No one knew she didn't want to sleep because of the pain that awaited her. If they did, no one would have laughed.

Whatever Quincy had gone through to win her medal haunted every breath she took, and the strange thing was, Quincy didn't know how Holly understood her. She didn't know that Holly had heard the dreams that tortured her.

Holly had to get Quincy to talk, but she had to do it a little at a time. If she didn't, Quincy would run.

She arrived back at Quincy's room and walked back in with a big smile. "I have donations from Captain Cammy's wardrobe." Holly held up the ties, which were a few different shades of red. It seemed military people didn't go wild when it came to expressing themselves through colour.

"What's wrong with my tie?" Quincy asked.

Only half listening, Holly held up each tie to Quincy's collar until she found one she liked. "You need something less grey and more cheerful."

"What do I have to be cheerful about?" Quincy asked stubbornly.

Holly ignored that question for the moment. "This will do."

She picked a red tie with navy blue flecks through it. Holly slipped the tie around Quincy's neck and went to lift up her collar, but Quincy grasped her hands and said, "I think I can do my own tie."

Holly's breath caught as she felt the strength and warmth coming from Quincy's hands. As she looked into her intense eyes, Holly felt in danger of falling in, so she took a step back and took a deep calming breath. When her heart rate returned to normal, she said to Quincy, "You are going out with me."

Quincy looked up. "What?"

"You asked, what did you have to be cheerful about? You're going out with me, that's what. My friends will tell you—where the fun is, you'll find Holly Weaver."

The corner of Quincy's mouth lifted into a smile that reminded her of the moment they'd locked eyes at the polo.

"Is that right?" Quincy said.

"Yeah, it is. Now that we have that sorted, how about your hair?" Holly said.

"Oh no. I draw the line there," Quincy said. "This is a regulation haircut."

"Regulation this, regulation that. I don't know about you, Captain. You need a little un-regulation in your life."

"Un-regulation? Is that like un-gay?"

Holly burst into laughter. "You've got it, Stompy. Let's go."

Quincy got a few strange glances and a few envious looks from members of the protection squad. It made her feel good—in a strange way—to be pulled along by this energetic, enthusiastic woman. Jacob had a similar outlook on life as Holly and was always telling her to enjoy herself.

Once they got outside the hotel, Holly put on her leather biker jacket, and Quincy said, "So where to now?"

"Let's get in a taxi and go to the river. It's first on my list," Holly said.

"List?" Quincy queried. "I thought Holly didn't make or follow plans?"

"I don't. I just made a list of things I'd like to do while I'm in Chicago. That's all. Apart from that, we'll play it by ear."

Holly waved down a taxi and pulled Quincy in. They had a minor scuffle at the other end when Quincy insisted on paying for the taxi. When they got out, Holly scowled at her, as she put her wallet away. "I asked you to come out with me. Why did you have to do that?"

Quincy straightened her tie and said, "There are some rules I will not bend about, and one is that a lady never pays."

Holly strolled up to her and grinned before stroking a finger down her tie. "So what does that make you, then?"

That one simple act turned her on so much. She was feeling so many new and intense feelings around Holly.

Quincy responded quickly. "An officer."

Holly giggled. "And a gentlewoman? How can I argue with that? Let's go."

They made their way down to the walkway and started to stroll slowly along.

"This is beautiful isn't it?" Holly said.

"Beautiful," Quincy said, looking right at Holly.

Holly stopped and looked at her. "You never say a sentence when one word will do, do you?"

She smiled and said purposely, "No."

"Very good, Stompy."

Quincy said, "I leave all the words for you—you seem to need so many." She offered Holly her arm, and she took it.

"True." Holly smiled.

They strolled along, admiring the boats on the river as they went.

It felt so easy being with Holly. She didn't feel the need to think of making conversation. Holly carried the conversation for them both. Listening to her incessant chatter and commentary was strangely comforting. It was a relief, and at the same time frightening, how easy this was. Feeling comfortable in someone else's presence was a foreign experience.

"Are you listening?" Holly said.

"Sorry, what did you say?"

Holly should have been annoyed that Quincy wasn't listening, but the small smile on Quincy's face made her annoyance disappear. Whatever thoughts were making Quincy smile, they had to be good.

"I said, why don't we hop on one of these little cruise boats? You'd like that, being a marine navy-type person."

"If you'd like to."

Holly shook her head as she laughed softly. She had never seen Quincy smile so much and be so compliant.

"You're actually smiling tonight, and not arguing with me."

"I don't go out of my way to disagree with you, Holly. I'm just trying to do my job," Quincy said.

"I know. You're not as grumpy and gruff as you make out," Holly said. "I think I always knew that."

Holly thought back to when she'd kissed her out of anger. It had been intense, and she'd never forgotten it. In that brief moment, she'd found that Quincy had passion buried deep down inside her.

Quincy seemed uncomfortable after Holly's revelation, and they remained silent until they got to the little jetty area, where the boats were all moored.

They picked one that went out for a half-hour ride and climbed aboard, Quincy insisting on paying again. They walked up to the front of the ship and leaned against the railing.

Holly lifted the phone on her wrist and said, "Quincy, smile." She moved in close to Quincy and took a selfie. "I'm going to put this on my social media, if you don't mind?"

"That's fine." Quincy closed her eyes and took a big breath of air.

"Do you miss the sea?" Holly asked.

"Yes, sometimes," Quincy replied.

Another short reply, but if Holly wanted Quincy to talk about more painful things, she had to play the long game. One thing was certain—Quincy had to talk about her pain, or it would eventually destroy her.

"Okay, how about this, you ask me a question about my life, then I ask you one," Holly said.

"Why would you want to know about me?"

Holly sighed. Despite being one of the most polite people she had ever met, Quincy had zero social skills.

"It's what friends do. We're going to be working together for a long time," Holly said.

"If you like." Quincy looked terrified at the prospect.

Holly thought she'd start easy. "You ask first, then."

"Um…" Quincy looked as if she was thinking hard. "Why did you change from a psychology degree to hair and make-up?"

Holly was completely surprised by that question. "How did you know that?"

"It was in your security file," Quincy said flatly.

"You read a security file on me?" Holly said, annoyed at the idea.

"Don't worry. There's nothing bad in it," Quincy said.

"I should think there isn't. I've got nothing to hide." Holly didn't like the idea of Quincy having an advantage over her, but then she remembered that she knew about Quincy's nightmares.

"Okay, well, I was always really into hair and make-up, but I did well at school, and my parents, well my dad, was really keen that I go to university. I think it was something my dad regretted missing. He was really clever, always finished the *Times* crossword and difficult puzzles in no time, but his parents weren't so supportive."

"And so you felt obliged," Quincy said as if she understood.

"Yeah, but my heart wasn't in it. Although I met the best friends I could ever have at uni, I was unhappy in my work. Dad saw that and told me to follow my heart," Holly said.

Quincy looked in her eyes. "And you did?"

Holly nodded. "And look where it led me."

"Quite." Quincy smiled.

Holly rubbed her hands together. "My question next. You went to Queen Georgina's boarding school in Scotland?"

"Yes, the Queen was two years above me, but we were in a lot of the same afterschool groups. My mother went there and grandfather. That's the Quincy family career path—boarding school, then officer training school," Quincy said.

Holly sensed a sadness in that answer but didn't want to pursue it and scare Quincy off. The wind rushed through her hair and she shivered.

Quincy must have seen her because she unbuttoned her suit jacket. "Here, put this around you." Quincy draped the jacket around her shoulders.

"Quin, no, you'll be cold," Holly said.

"I'm used to being up to my eyeballs in freezing mud. I think I'll survive." Quincy gave her the sexiest smile that made Holly shiver down to her toes.

The thing was, Quincy didn't know what a sexy smile was—it was just natural and of the moment. She thought back to her date with Story, and she felt Story probably practised her sexy smiles in the mirror.

Holly pulled the jacket tightly around her and inhaled Quincy's cologne.

She moaned, and Quincy said, "Sorry did you say something?"

Holly was caught out. "Um…just commenting about how polite and well brought up you are."

"I don't know about well brought up, but we had politeness drummed into us at boarding school."

Holly slid closer to Quincy on the rail of the boat, so their elbows were touching. "And you just love following rules?"

"Indeed," Quincy said. "Rules make a military unit work, keep the wheels turning, and keep everyone safe."

Holly sensed they were delving into dangerous territory, so she tried to lighten the mood. "You want to know where we're going next?" Holly said.

"Tell me?" Quincy smiled.

"The one thing every visitor to Chicago has to experience." Holly leaned in close to Quincy and whispered in her ear, "Deep dish pizza!"

After their boat ride, Quincy got them a taxi, and Holly asked the driver where the best pizza place was. He drove them to a place called Daisy's Deep Dish, and they found themselves in a long line waiting for a table.

"I told you we should have booked a table, Holly," Quincy said.

"Oh, live a little, and have some faith," Holly said giving her a wink.

Quincy groaned internally. A wink from Holly had a similar effect to when she'd whispered in her ear on the boat. Then Quincy had to hold the boat's rail tightly to stop herself from visibly shaking. The thought of Holly's breath and kisses on her body made her wet.

No one had ever done that before, and they were such new emotions to deal with—attraction and frustration. She started to shuffle from one foot to the other and tap her hands against the sides of her legs.

Quincy looked at the length of the line ahead of them and said, "Look, let's find somewhere else."

"Have some patience, Captain. We're in no hurry—unless you're desperate to get away from me and back to your toy soldiers?"

Quincy's evening would be a lot calmer if she was back at the hotel with her model soldiers. Being here was scarier, but Holly's enthusiasm for life silenced her demons for a time.

"No, I have all the time in the world for you."

"Great." Holly smiled brightly and looped her arm through hers. Holly was someone who didn't respect boundaries and was openly affectionate, and that was so foreign to Quincy, but she was beginning to like it.

Holly took out her phone and showed her how their selfie on the boat had gotten so much positive feedback.

"You have a lot of friends and followers," Quincy said. She didn't participate in social media. The thought of sharing her life and private thoughts with the world made Quincy shiver.

"They're not really true friends. I picked up so many new followers when I became Bea's dresser, and then when I went out with Story, it went a bit mad."

Just then a message popped up on her screen: *Hey, babe, give me a call. I've got some great plans for when you come to LA.* Holly stuffed the phone in her pocket quickly.

She was obviously better acquainted with Story St. John than she'd said. Quincy stiffened and felt a tightening in her stomach. She had felt the same emotion when Clay had shown her the pictures of Holly and Story together after their night out.

How could she compete with a film star? Quincy realized what she had just thought and chastised herself. She was not in any competition for Holly or any woman.

A silence hung between them until one of the restaurant staff came up to them and said, "Ma'am, if you'll follow me, I'll take you to a table."

Before they could question him, he walked off. Holly yanked Quincy's hand. "Come on."

"We can't jump the queue," Quincy said.

Holly laughed. "Stop being so British, Captain. Come on."

She was dragged along and they were seated in a booth near the back, and given free drinks. Apparently, they recognized Holly as being the Queen Consort's dresser who went out with Story St. John.

Holly looked around the restaurant and smiled. It was full of sports memorabilia and Americana. The walls of their booth had a chalkboard surface, and many people who had sat there had left messages.

"Great table, isn't it? I've never been a celebrity by association before."

"People must be fascinated by your relationship with Story St. Clair," Quincy said.

"St. John," Holly corrected her but thought she'd detected a note of annoyance in Quincy's voice. "I have no relationship with Story. I've only heard from her twice since I went out with her. Once to apologize for the newspaper headlines about the Queen Consort, and tonight, as you saw. Story has more glamorous and more beautiful women than me to keep her company."

"I doubt that," Quincy said then looked down at her menu equally as quickly.

Holly was taken aback at that comment. Her stomach was going all sorts of crazy. There was something magnetic about Quincy, some force pulling her to this quiet, troubled soul. She was desperate to know more about her, and after they ordered Holly said, "We hadn't finished our questions game."

Quincy clasped her hands in front of her tensely. "If we must, but it was my turn next."

"You can have a double go next time. What are your parents like?" Holly asked without waiting, so as not to give Quincy much time to think.

Quincy now stared down at her tightly clasped hands. "I didn't know my father. My mother never talked about him."

"Didn't you ask her?" Holly asked.

"It's complicated, and we don't have that kind of relationship," Quincy said flatly.

Holly couldn't believe a kind of mother-daughter relationship where you couldn't talk about these things.

"Someone must be named on your birth certificate," Holly said.

Quincy looked up sharply. "That's a very personal question. Most polite people would not ask that."

"Ugh, stop with the stuffiness, Quin. It's a harmless question, and you know you can trust me, don't you?"

Quincy remained silent. She looked as if she was fighting with herself.

"There's that tight jaw again," Holly said. "Listen, anything you say to me will stay between us, I promise. I mean, I've not told anyone about your nightmares, have I?" Holly said that without thinking. She'd forgotten for a moment that Quincy didn't know that she knew. Quincy's eyes were wide, her jaw as tight as Holly had seen, and Quincy looked as if she was about to flee.

She grabbed Quincy's hands and squeezed them. "Look, I'm sorry I mentioned the nightmares. I won't ask anything about them, I promise. Please, don't run."

"How did you know?" Quincy asked.

"I heard you one night. I woke up and wondered what the noise was. I went out into the hall and heard the noise coming from your room."

"You've told no one?" Quincy said with a sense of panic.

"No one. I'd never do that to you. Believe me, I would never break your trust, and I won't ask you about them, but if you ever want to talk about them, I'm here."

Quincy let out a long breath. "Thank you for not saying anything. I don't want anyone to know. My superiors might question my effectiveness."

Holly smiled. "I promise."

Their pizza order arrived and brought their conversation to an end, and there was an awkwardness hanging between them. Holly had to get Quincy back to enjoying her night and not thinking about her pain.

"This pizza looks amazing. I bet a posh officer like you isn't used to eating pizza."

She was rewarded by the smallest of smiles.

"You're right," Quincy agreed, "but this is delicious."

Holly looked into Quincy's eyes and said, "Let's just enjoy tonight and forget about everything else. Okay?"

Quincy nodded. "Okay."

CHAPTER FOURTEEN

George closed the *Winnie-the-Pooh* book when she saw Teddy had drifted off to sleep. She pulled up her covers, then stroked her brow with the back of her hand.

"Sleep well, Teddy bear."

She heard the door open slowly and Bea crept in. "Is she asleep?"

"Yes. Snug as a bug in a rug."

"The prime minister's on the phone for you," Bea said.

George frowned. "It's late for her to call. Did it sound serious?"

"I don't think so, but you know Bo Dixon. She's slippery, and so hard to read."

"I'm just coming." George followed Bea out of Teddy's room and gently closed the door. She went over to the secure computer terminal on the side table and pressed her fingerprint to the screen. "Prime Minister?"

"Forgive the late hour of my call, Your Majesty. I hope I didn't disturb you and the Queen Consort?"

George sighed inwardly. Bo Dixon couldn't sound more insincere if she tried. "No, not at all. How can I help, Prime Minister?"

"First of all I have to congratulate you and the Queen Consort on a highly successful tour so far. The press and public are delighted on both sides of the pond. I hear President Watson was over the moon with her popularity polls after your visit. You are leading Team Britain remarkably well, ma'am."

George felt her anger starting to simmer. Bea must have noticed, because she came over and sat on the couch beside her and took her hand. As if she needed Bo Dixon's condescending approval.

Bea mouthed, "What?"

George just shook her head. "I feel a *but* coming, Prime Minister."

"Not a but. As I say, Team Britain is being well represented, and we have some very important business engagements coming up on your tour, and we can't afford to have any weak links in the team."

"Weak links?" George played dumb, but she could feel what was coming next.

"I understand Captain Quincy was made to look quite a fool today, and the video went viral. I hear whispers that she may not be quite sound. We can't afford to have our officials or security personnel look like fools. I did counsel you that she might not be the best choice for the Queen Consort—"

George couldn't hold her tongue any more. "Excuse me, Prime Minister, but you are talking about a recipient of the Victoria Cross. A marine who without a thought for herself went through hell to try to save her team."

Bea could now get the gist of what was being said. She stood up, crossed her arms angrily, and mouthed, "Tell her to bugger off."

George almost burst out laughing. She could always rely on Bea.

"Ma'am," Bo Dixon continued, "I don't mean to be disrespectful. I'm only trying to look out for your best interests, and not have your triumphant tour marred by someone who is not capable of the job."

"Prime Minster, you know why she left the marines. She was a hero yet again, saving a young woman from harm. Captain Quincy does nothing but give of herself to her country, and to its people. She put a dangerous predator behind bars."

There was a long silence, then Bo said, "You also know what happened after she saved that woman. It's up to you, ma'am. I've given you my best advice, and the rest is up to you."

"Captain Quincy stays," George said firmly. "Goodbye, Prime Minister. End call," she instructed the computer. "Bloody fool."

Bea came and put her arms around George's waist. "Did bloody Bo Dixon want you to get rid of Quincy?"

"Yes. She didn't want Team Britain to be embarrassed like it was today."

"Quincy was just doing her job. When it happened, I thought it was a gun. I got the fright of my life, but Quincy didn't hesitate to jump in front of us."

Bea rested her head on her chest, and George wrapped her arms around her. "She never would hesitate. That's just who she is. A selfless, brave, and honourable officer."

"I heard more than I was meant to, I think. Who was the woman she saved?" Bea asked.

"After she received her medal, she rescued a young marine from a sexual assault. The man was given a jail sentence for it."

"What a hero," Bea said.

George said, "The real heroism is living with the aftermath of tragedy, and that's what Quincy has done."

Holly and Quincy left the restaurant and Quincy hailed a cab. "Back to the hotel, Holly?"

"Not likely. There's still one thing on my list."

They got into the cab and Holly gave the driver the name of a place and smiled at her. "Have you ever been to a gay club, Quin?"

Quincy wasn't expecting that. "No, no, I haven't."

"Don't look so terrified. I'll keep the hordes of women at bay." Holly chuckled.

"Hardly, I'm not the type to attract attention," Quincy said.

Holly furrowed her eyebrows. "Have you seen yourself in a mirror?"

"I don't know what you mean."

Holly shook her head. "It means you are really good looking, tall, brooding—the women will lap you up."

"Then I'll open my mouth and bore them to death," Quincy said.

Holly play hit her on the arm. "Bloody hell, Quin. Have a little faith in yourself."

The cab couldn't stop outside the club, so it dropped them on the corner and they began to walk.

Again Quincy offered Holly her arm, and Holly took it. Quincy loved the feeling she got when Holly hung on to her or touched her. It was exhilarating, exciting, and gave her a warm feeling inside. Despite their very different personalities, she'd learned that she and Holly had the same fundamental principles, of loyalty, discretion, and responsibility.

They walked into the club, and Quincy's eyes and ears were assaulted with noise and lights.

Holly led her through the throng by the hand. The array of strange haircuts, similar to Story St. John's, were abundant.

They arrived at the bar, and she bought some drinks. Quincy had a lot of trouble being heard by the bartender over the music.

Holly took a sip of her drink and said, "What do you think?"

Quincy looked around at the room of women and men, shouting, singing, and gyrating to the music, and generally acting like a bunch of drunk young people.

"It's very loud," Quincy said.

Holly laughed and was moving to the music while sipping her drink. "I bet you never did this at officer school."

"Not quite. Did you go to clubs like this when you were at university?" Quincy asked.

"Oh yes, especially after I broke up with my first girlfriend. I got my heart broken, and I decided I would live life without worrying about love."

"I always thought you were straight," Quincy said.

"Most people do. I'm bisexual, but after that heartbreak…well, I somehow knew inside I wouldn't lose my heart to a man, but I could have a lot of fun with them."

Holly was dancing more and more on the spot, and Quincy just stood rigidly against the bar. She wasn't exactly showing Holly a good time. She didn't know how to do these things, be charming and entertaining. "I bet you had much more fun when you were out with Story St. John." Why had she said that? *Don't compare yourself to her—you'll never win.*

"It was a lot of fun. Meeting a film star is always going to be a night to remember, but I never quite felt I was there with her, if you know what I mean. She was constantly checking her social media, taking pictures of us and posting them online. She wasn't present with me, not like you and I have been tonight. All your attention has been on me, and you've never once looked at your phone," Holly said.

"I'm not on any social networking sites," Quincy said.

Holly took a step closer and said, "Still, even if you were, I doubt you would be so involved in yourself that you would forget you were with me."

"I'd never forget I was with you." Quincy's heart thudded.

Holly took her hand gently. "Come and dance with me."

Panic spread through her. "No, I can't dance, not like that."

Holly laughed. "Yes, you can. Queen Georgina said the same thing when we took her to a gay club."

Quincy couldn't believe it. "George danced to this sort of music?"

"She had a good reason to—Bea."

Quincy hesitated, and a boyish looking woman approached.

"Are you two together?" the woman asked.

"No," Quincy said quickly.

Then the woman asked Holly to dance.

Holly replied, "No—"

"No, on you go, Holly." She didn't want her to go, but she didn't want Holly to feel obliged to stay with her when she had wanted to dance since they got here. "Enjoy yourself."

Holly gave her a slight scowl but followed when the other woman led her to the dance floor.

Quincy felt tense and annoyed, and she couldn't take her eyes off Holly as she began to dance. Holly danced just like she did everything else in life, with vigour and enthusiasm. She felt the smile creep up on her face as she watched Holly. It was nice to see her dance. She appeared to absorb the music and really feel every word. Quincy envied Holly's ability to feel so freely. It was tantalizing.

The picture changed when her dance partner got closer and closer to Holly, then put her hands on her hips.

Quincy zeroed in on the hands on Holly's hips, and she hated the sight. Jealousy was another new emotion to add to her list, and she didn't quite know how to handle it.

She closed her eyes and tried to bury it, like she did every other emotion, but this clearly didn't work. When she opened her eyes, she saw Holly pushing the hands off her, just for her dance partner to put them back, on her buttocks this time.

Quincy didn't know what happened, but her legs just started to stride over. When she arrived at the couple, she tapped Holly's dance partner on the shoulder.

"May I cut in?" Quincy said.

"What do you want, buddy?" the woman said.

"I'm dancing with Ms. Holly now. Find someone else to play with." Quincy towered over the woman.

Holly said, "I'd listen to her, if I were you. She's in the marines."

The woman's eyes went wide, and she hurried off. Quincy took Holly in her arms, the way she had been taught to dance at school. It was the best she could do.

"Thank you for saving me from Miss Wandering Hands."

"You're welcome," Quincy said.

"You're so funny." Holly felt right at home in Quincy's arms, despite her awkward dancing.

"Why? My dancing?" Quincy asked.

"Well, that too, but the *May I cut in*? It's like being in that eighteenth-century romance novel I mentioned before," Holly said.

"I've been brought up in a very privileged, rule-driven circle. It's just who I am."

"I wouldn't want you to change," Holly said.

And Holly *didn't* want her to change, just loosen up a bit, for her own good more than anything.

"Listen," Holly said, "why don't you get us some more drinks while I visit the ladies'?"

"Okay."

Holly slowly made her way back from the ladies through the throng of people. It was then that she thought maybe her clubbing days were behind her. She'd had more fun talking to Quincy on the boat, in the pizza place, or painting her models than she was having here, but she'd wanted to show Quincy all the things she'd missed out on. Her evening with Quincy had been much more understated than her time with Story, but much more fun. She just wished Quincy would open up more.

She finally made her way back to the bar and stopped dead when she saw a woman standing very close to Quincy. Her first reaction was anger, then annoyance. She couldn't leave Quin for five minutes. Wait, why did she care?

Of course I care.

The woman took another step closer and put a hand on Quin's chest, but instead of being more annoyed, Holly chuckled. Quincy stepped back to the bar as far as she could go, and then leaned back, desperately trying to put distance between her and the overeager woman.

"Looks like you need rescuing, Stompy," Holly whispered to herself. She walked over and put her arm around Quincy's waist. "There you are, sweetie. Making new friends?"

Quincy looked at her with pure panic in her eyes. "Ah—"

Holly pulled Quincy closer and placed her other hand on Quincy's stomach, claiming her with both hands.

"She's taken, honey," Holly said to the woman.

The woman took a few steps back and gave her a forced smile. "Lucky you. I wouldn't leave her alone for long. She's gorgeous."

Holly clung to Quincy more tightly and inhaled the sexy scent of Quincy's cologne. It turned on all her senses.

"Oh, I know she is. That's why I have two arms around her, and I'm not letting go," Holly replied.

Once she was gone, Holly said, "You can breathe now, Quin."

Quincy let out a long breath. "Thank you for rescuing me. I just froze."

Holly reluctantly let Quincy go. "You've never been chatted up before?"

"Once or twice, but it's easier to blame protocol in the military, and then run." Quincy straightened her tie.

It occurred to Holly then that maybe Quincy had never had a girlfriend. She had to have slept with someone, but maybe Quincy had never been in a relationship.

"Well, don't worry, if you're with me, I'll save you." Holly was more than happy to keep women away from Quincy. Delightfully happy.

Quincy handed her a drink. "Here, I got you another fresh orange and lemonade. Are you sure you don't want something stronger?"

Holly took a sip of her drink and shook her head. "No, contrary to what you saw after I went out with Story, I'm not a big drinker, and besides, I'd rather have a clear head with you."

"Why?" Quincy asked.

"I suppose because I was so nervous when I was out with Story and her entourage, the drinks went down quickly, and she always had a fresh bottle of champagne at the table."

"And you're not nervous with me?" Quincy asked.

Holly laughed. "Don't be daft. You're Captain Stompy. You make me aggravated, angry, sometimes, when we argue, frustrated…" Holly took a step closer. *You also make me feel like I want to kiss you, again.* She noticed Quincy didn't step back, when she stepped into her space. As an experiment, she took another step, then another, and Quincy didn't move. Their bodies were touching, and Quincy was simply gazing at her. She wished she knew what was going on behind those gorgeous eyes of hers.

"Question game again," Holly said.

"I think you'll find I'm owed double."

"Psh, I'll owe you triple next time. Have you ever had a girlfriend?"

Quincy shook her head, and Holly's heart sped up. She heard the music in the club change to a slow love song.

She grasped Quincy's tie gently. "Have you ever danced to a slow love song?"

Quincy's lips parted, and her eyes dropped to Holly's. "No, never."

"Well, I better teach you, so the next time somebody chats you up, you'll know what to do."

Holly walked ahead and pulled Quincy behind her. When they got to the dance floor, Quincy held her hands up as if she was going to waltz. Holly chuckled and placed Quincy's arms around her waist. "Like this, and just move slowly."

"Just this?" Quincy shuffled awkwardly.

"Nearly. Just relax more." Holly slipped her arms around Quincy's neck. She felt Quincy stiffen slightly. "It's okay. It's just me. Annoying Holly who doesn't follow rules. I'm not scary."

"You think?" Quincy said.

"Come on. Relax a bit and just go with it," Holly told her.

"Relax and go with it?" Quincy said. "I don't know how to do that."

"Yeah, you do. Look in my eyes. When you're dancing slow, you've got to make eye contact." Holly was a little selfish telling Quincy that. She wanted to gaze into her eyes without fear of Quincy thinking she was an idiot.

Quincy locked eyes with her, and Holly sighed with longing. Why did Quincy make her feel this way? She'd never met anyone so beautifully handsome, and yet so obviously damaged. There was a deep longing in Holly to soothe Quincy's pain.

Holly scratched her nails down the fine shaved hairs on the nape of Quincy's neck and felt her shiver. Holly saw passion blossom in Quincy's eyes.

"I'm owed some questions," Quincy said, her voice breathy.

"Go ahead," Holly said.

"Why did you kiss me that time when we were arguing?"

Holly ran her nails slowly down Quincy's neck again. "Because I wanted you to show me some emotion—anger, passion, anything."

"I—" Quincy was struggling to speak, and Holly was frightened she was pushing her too far for one night.

"Just dance with me, Quin. Don't worry about anything else tonight."

Holly leaned in to Quincy and laid her head on her chest. Quincy was stiff at first, but gradually they began to sway together quite naturally.

Quincy felt like she was walking on air as they walked from the taxi into the hotel. They'd danced together for a few songs at the club, and then they decided to head back to the hotel, as it was getting late.

Being so close to Holly on the dance floor was exciting, scary, and overwhelming. In the past Quincy had always found ways to brush off any attention she got from women, but she just couldn't say no to Holly Weaver.

They didn't say much as they travelled home in the taxi. There was a tension between them now, as if they were on the verge of something new, only Quincy didn't know if she was brave enough to take the leap.

When they got into the hotel, Quincy felt obliged to say something. "Thank you for tonight, Holly. You really took my mind off what happened today."

"You're welcome," Holly said, as she took a step closer. "I had a great time too."

Out of nowhere Quincy felt compelled to say, "I trust you."

Holly scrunched up her eyes. "What—"

Unfortunately, the lift doors opened and Holly was interrupted. Quincy saw Stephens and Daniels flanking the lift, and the easy-going feeling was replaced by her stiff on duty persona. She had probably been the laughing stock of the squad tonight, but she was their commanding officer.

Quincy straightened her tie and said, "Any problems, Stephens?"

"No, ma'am. All the principals are in for the night."

"Very good," Quincy said then turned to Holly and said, "I'll escort you to your room, Ms. Weaver."

Holly gave her an angry look but followed her to her room.

When they got to Holly's room, Quincy said, "Goodnight."

"Why have you changed?" Holly said with annoyance in her voice.

Quincy didn't understand. "What do you mean, changed?"

"We had a great night, you were so relaxed, and we were close, then you talked to the guards just now, and you're back to Captain Stompy."

Holly's voice was rising by the second, and she didn't want Stephens and Daniels to hear. "Let's talk about this another time," Quincy said.

"We bloody won't." Holly opened her room door and pulled Quincy in by the tie and slammed the door.

"Why did you do that?" Quincy said.

Holly prodded her in the chest. "Because we are not finishing a lovely night that way. Why did you change?"

"Because we can't all be like you, dancing and singing their way through life. I'm an officer of the Queen's protection squad. I need to appear professional. They already have had a good laugh at me today."

"Oh, stop being so stiff-necked. You're out of their earshot now, so tell me, what were you going to say?"

Quincy's moment of bravery deserted her. "I can't remember what I was going to say."

"For God's sake, Quin. You do remember. You said that you trust me, and then you were going to say something else." Holly scooted around her and pressed her body against the door. "I won't let you go until you do."

"Don't be so childish. It's been a long day. I want to go to my room," Quincy said. She was starting to realize how vulnerable she had made herself to Holly tonight. She seemed to lose control of her emotions when Holly was around.

"Nope," Holly said with a sinister smile, "you don't pass until you tell me."

Quincy was getting really angry now. She should have stayed in tonight and painted her model soldiers.

"No. Let me go. That's an order," Quincy demanded.

Holly laughed. "That's an order, is it?" Holly took a step towards her and ran her nail down from her chin to her collar. Quincy shivered. "I don't follow orders, Captain."

If Quincy wanted to get out of this, she had to tell her. Holly both tantalized and terrified her. "Earlier when you asked about my parents, and I wouldn't talk about it? You asked if I trusted you, and I do trust you. It's just hard to talk about."

Holly's demeanour softened, and she placed her palm on her chest. "You can always talk to me."

"My adopted mother is Vice Admiral Quincy, the highest ranking woman in the Royal Navy," Quincy said.

"You're adopted?" Holly asked.

"Yes, Admiral Quincy is actually my aunt, but she adopted me at birth. My father isn't listed on my birth certificate. That's what I was going to tell you."

"Thank you for trusting me," Holly said. Holly had never wanted to kiss someone more in her life than in that moment. Quincy was being so open and vulnerable with her, and she knew how hard that was for her.

She wanted to kiss all of Quincy's hurts away. She leaned in close and parted her lips and saw red hot passion in Quincy's eyes. Seeing that want in someone careful and stoic made Holly even hotter.

Just before their lips met, she slipped her fingers through the buttons of Quincy's shirt. She didn't think about it—it was just instinct.

Quincy stepped back like she'd been burned, and the passion in her eyes was gone. In its place were the solid, emotionless walls that Quincy usually kept erected.

"I think it's time for me to go," Quincy said coldly.

Shit, shit, shit, I've blown it. Why had she touched her there? She reached out for Quincy but she had already reached the door. Holly tried to grasp her hand.

"Quincy, talk to me."

"There nothing to talk about. It's time to go. I have duty early tomorrow morning." That cold emotionless tone had crept back into her voice.

"Quin, I didn't mean—"

Once those walls of Quincy's went up, they were impenetrable. Quincy turned the doorknob.

"Look, I'm sorry, Quin. I know you're sensitive about that area of your body. I saw you had some burn scars that night you brought me back to my room. I just forgot, okay?"

"It's fine," Quincy said stiffly.

Holly squealed in exasperation and stood in front of her. "Oh, bloody hell! Be angry at me or something. Don't go back to this emotionless rubbish."

"I told you before—I don't let myself feel."

"You obviously do, or you wouldn't have nightmares about what happened to you, and you wouldn't jump like a cat on a hot tin roof when I touch you on the chest. If you talk to me about what happened to you, it can help you. I'll never betray your trust."

Quincy said, "Stop trying to change me. I'm not going to be your pet project. I don't want or need any more friends, certainly not ones who trample though my life thinking they know best. Just leave me alone."

Pet project? "You can bet I'll leave you alone. I've wasted enough time trying to be a friend. Go and wallow in your pit of despair, punish yourself for whatever you think you've done. I don't care any more."

Holly slammed the door shut.

❖

Quincy fell down onto her bed and put her hands over her face. The pain and guilt inside her were overwhelming. After this afternoon's debacle, she had thought that Holly had quietened down the demons that gnawed at her soul. She had actually loved being out with Holly and had begun to feel like a normal person.

Holly made her feel more than she had her whole life, and for a short time tonight she'd given her a glimpse at a normal life. The frightening thing was, when Holly touched her, she brought some light to the dark places inside. That made her feel guilty, and she'd taken her guilt out on Holly. All Holly had done was give her an evening out, to take her mind off today, and she had taken her guilt out on her. Yet more guilt to pile up on her.

She pulled her hands away from her face and the tremoring was back. She laced her fingers together so that she could keep control. Holly, it seemed, was determined to fix her, and she couldn't be fixed. How would she ever hope to live with this guilt bearing down on her? But then, had she ever lived? Apart from the good times she'd had with Jacob, George, and Cammy, had she ever lived?

She'd lived for her career, just as her mother taught her, always striving for the next rung of the ladder, the next rank, the next medal, but where had that left her?

Now she had no career, and only George and Cammy as friends, but they had their own lives to lead, while she had nothing. Before she'd left the UK, Jacob told her to live every moment for him, and what had she done? Hidden away, painting her soldiers and trying to scare away the one person who wanted to be her friend.

Maybe it was time to try to change. Quincy remembered Helen once telling her that if she couldn't articulate how she felt, then she should write it down.

She went over to the writing desk and pulled over the hotel notepad. Once she lifted a pen, Quincy tapped it repeatedly on the paper. Could she do this?

Yes, it was a safe way to let out her feelings before they boiled over. Quincy began to write all the things she wished she could say to Holly. A letter that she would never give her.

Dear Ms. Holly,

I wanted to apologize for this evening. I'm sorry I can't be the friend you deserve or expect. I just want you to know that I see you. I've seen you ever since that fateful day at the polo match.

You think I'm emotionless and that I don't notice you, but my eyes adore you when you don't know I'm watching. I love the way you live each breath of your life with fun and enthusiasm, feeling every moment. Sometimes when I look at you, I stop breathing and wish I could be the one who makes you smile and laugh, but how can I be that for you when I can't feel? If I let myself feel, I would—well, I don't know what I would become, but it is terrifying to me.

CHAPTER FIFTEEN

Holly was in Bea's dressing room steaming Bea's outfit for today. Her anger and annoyance were bubbling under the surface. She could hardly sleep last night, going over and over her conversation with Quincy. They'd had a great evening, and Quincy was more open than she had ever been. Holly had managed not to spook her the whole night, but then she'd made one mistake. And she'd apologized. What Quincy had said about her hurt. She was trying to help Quincy because she cared, not because she was a project. Maybe at first Quincy was a challenge, but never a pet project. How could Quincy think that?

Holly's phone rang. It was Story St. John, and unlike before she didn't have that nervous excitement that made her nearly faint.

"Hi, Story," she said with a sigh. How crazy was she? A film star was calling her, and she was almost annoyed.

"Hey, babe. It's nice to hear your voice again. I'm not interrupting you, am I?" Story said.

Story must have noticed the tone of her voice. "No, sorry, I'm just in the middle of some work, but it can wait. How are you?" Holly walked over to the window of the hotel and looked over the Chicago skyline.

"I'm great. I just wanted to make sure you still wanted to meet up in LA. I had a few ideas of where I wanted to take you but—"

"But what?" Holly asked. Story was actually planning and thinking about what they could do together. It should be a fairy tale, but why didn't it feel that way?

"I wanted to check that I wasn't stepping on anyone's toes. That's not my style, despite my rep," Story said.

"Why would you think that? I told you I was single," Holly told her.

There was a pause, then Story said, "I saw the picture you posted last night. You were with someone, and I thought maybe things had changed for you."

Things had changed. Her burgeoning feelings for Quincy were subduing her excited attraction for Story, but what did that matter? Quincy didn't want or need anyone to help or care for her.

"What? No. That's Captain Quincy, Queen Beatrice's security officer. We went sightseeing on our night off. Why did you think things had changed?"

"The way you were looking at each other in the picture. And when I met you at the charity dinner, the same woman in the picture couldn't keep her eyes off you. I notice these things."

That took Holly by surprise. Even back then there had been something. "If you want to take me out on a date, then I'm free and single. There is no one else who wants me in that way," Holly said.

"Great, I really enjoyed spending time with you. I'll get back in touch and we'll arrange when to meet," Story said.

At least someone wanted to spend time with her, someone who didn't hide from every feeling they'd ever had.

"Thanks, I'm really looking forward to it."

A few minutes after Holly hung up, Lali popped her head around the door and said, "Morning, Holls. How did the big date go?"

Holly scowled. "There was no big date, and it was a disaster."

Lali's smile faltered. "Oh."

Bea walked up and down Teddy's bedroom, holding Teddy in her arms. She had been difficult to put down tonight, as George wasn't going to be back from her engagement till late. Teddy was so attached to George it made her heart melt, but it also made things difficult when George wasn't there to read Teddy's bedtime story. It was their routine, and Teddy did not like her routine to change.

Bea stroked Teddy's back and sang to her. She began to hear Teddy's breathing slow and deepen.

"That's my poppet. Mum will be home soon."

She wanted to see George as much as Teddy. These solo engagements were hard on them both. She knew George got her confidence from Bea standing with her, but it would have been unfair to drag their baby girl around all the engagements the prime minister's office had arranged for them. Bo Dixon used them like her personal staff, the royal department she used to ingratiate herself to foreign powers, even if they were foreign powers she and George fundamentally disagreed with. Luckily, that was not the case on the North American tour.

She put Teddy into her cot and went to bed. The big suite felt even larger with George not here. She wasn't due to be back until the small hours of the morning.

Bea made sure the baby monitor was on, then slipped under her sheets and pulled George's pillow to her. If she closed her eyes she could imagine George was here with her.

Tomorrow they would leave for Kentucky, and Bea couldn't wait. She and George would have the main ranch house to themselves, and Bea had insisted there would be no staff looking after them. She wanted it to be just George, Teddy, and her, like a normal family.

Heaven.

Her thoughts turned to Holly. Lali had told her that Holly was livid with Quincy after their date, and she didn't want to talk about what went wrong. That spoke volumes to Bea. She could see on a daily basis how Quincy looked at Holly, and how Holly looked at Quincy.

Quincy was a tough nut to crack, even worse than George had been. Maybe it was time to take the matchmaking up a notch.

Bea heard the door to their suite open, and her heart started to flutter. No one got by their guards, so it had to be George. She sat up, and a few seconds later George quietly tiptoed through the door. George had been to visit a naval base and so was dressed in her Royal Navy uniform.

"I'm awake."

"Did I wake you?" George said as she put her cap down on the dresser.

"No, I've just gotten Teddy to sleep. She's a nightmare when you're not here," Bea said.

"I'm sorry I missed story time. I hate being away from you both." George started to undo her uniform buttons.

"So did you have fun playing with the American boat?" Bea asked.

George narrowed her eyes. "Ship, Bea. You know this by now. You just try to annoy me, I know."

Bea chuckled. "Ship, then. Did you have fun?"

George took off her watch and her wrist phone. "I had a fantastic time. The size of the American aircraft carriers is astonishing. The sheer engineering is—" She looked at her and smiled. "I'm boring you, aren't I."

Bea smiled. "No, I think it's sweet when you geek out over things like that. Anyway, I could never get bored watching you in that uniform."

Bea got up and walked over to her. George opened her arms. Bea stepped into them and tenderly stroked George's cheek. She loved the way George still shivered at her touch.

"You know, I missed you so much that I was hugging your pillow."

"I'm here now."

George leaned in to kiss her, but Bea dodged her kiss and whispered in her ear, "Let's play sailor."

George groaned. She loved how passionate and exciting Bea made their love life. George had no experience with women before Bea, although she had gained a lot of confidence since their first time. Bea seemed to genuinely love her body, and the knowledge that a beautiful woman like Bea lusted after her gave her confidence in herself. Bea gently led them to where they both wanted to be. "Yes, I'd love that."

"How long have you been at sea, Sailor?" Bea smirked.

George's heart was already beating out of her chest. She loved Bea for this. A long day away from her family, missing them both, but knowing when she got home, she would need this with her wife.

"Six months," George said.

Bea slid her hands inside her jacket, and George couldn't help but gaze lustfully at her wife's breasts, peeping over the top of the lace-topped silk nightie.

"All that time without a woman?" Bea slipped her hands under her belt buckle.

"Yes," George breathed. She wanted Bea to keep teasing her, but at the same time, George was so turned on, she needed to come soon.

"And how did you find me, Sailor?" Bea said while she slipped off George's jacket.

"An officer told me about you. He said you were the best."

Bea laughed and took hold of her tie. "Oh, I am, but can you afford me?"

It was time for George to show a bit of arrogance. "I'm from a very wealthy family, madam. I can pay you anything you like."

"Good." Bea took off her tie, threw it to the side, then took her hand. "Then I'm going to make you feel so good."

When they got to the side of the bed, Bea kissed her, a deep, passionate kiss that made her need to come even worse.

Bea took off her nightdress and underwear. George reached out to touch her breasts, but her hand was swatted away. Bea moved close and whispered in her ear, "Now, now, Sailor. You came to me to take care of you, and I will, okay?"

George gulped and nodded. Despite being the more dominant sexually, it was only by her wife's will, and at her lead. Bea had the capacity to make her feel like a fumbling virgin about to get their first sexual experience, or a strong, powerful warrior taking her wife as she pleased.

That was what made it exciting and why Bea was the love of her life. She simply didn't work without her.

Bea unbuttoned her shirt slowly and said, "When was the last time you slept with a woman, Sailor?"

George felt a hot surge of passion spread throughout her body. This was so good, and she wanted to make it even hotter. "Never. This is my first time."

A big smile erupted over Bea's face. "Oh, poor sailor."

Bea threw George's shirt to the side and unbuttoned her trousers. George stepped out of them, and Bea put them onto the chair behind them.

George slipped out of her sports bra and threw it to the side.

Bea smiled and sidled up close. "You have such a gorgeous body, Sailor. How would you like me to teach you how to make love to a woman?"

She could hardly breathe because Bea was stroking her fingers down her abdomen. "But I've only paid for an hour," George said, playing along.

"Make love with me, and you can have the whole night for free. Yes?"

"God, yes," George said quickly.

Bea chuckled and said, "Lie down on your front, Sailor."

George lay down, and Bea straddled the small of her back. George groaned and gripped the sheets when she felt Bea's wetness painted on her skin, as Bea moved.

Bea put her hands on George's shoulders. "First I'm going to make you relax, then I'm going to take care of you, Sailor."

As if Bea's fingers and hands massaging her back didn't feel good enough, Bea leaned over as she moved, and her breasts and nipples brushed over George's skin.

"Jesus," George said. Her sex was throbbing.

"Do you like that?" Bea asked.

"God, yes. I want to touch and kiss your breasts so much," George said, hearing the desperation in her own tone.

Bea massaged down to her buttocks and told her to turn over. Bea sat astride her hips and leaned over, saying, "I've been aching to do this."

She kissed George and brought George's hands to her breasts. Bea was loving this game, but she was so wet and turned on, that it was so hard not to say, *Make love to me*, and let George take control. She couldn't help but thrust her wet sex onto George's hard stomach.

Through wet, passionate kisses, Bea said, "I want you inside me, but I've got to take care of you first."

She kissed her way down to George's hard clit. George was so wet and turned on, and it was all because of her. Sometimes she just couldn't believe her luck. To have someone as handsome and good looking as George want her so desperately was more than she could have ever hoped for.

Bea licked all around George's clit but didn't touch it yet.

George's hips bucked, and she groaned. "Please, Bea, I can't take it."

Bea looked up at her partner and said, "Now I'm going to make you feel so good, Sailor."

She gave George's clit a few teasing licks, then sucked her all in.

George cried out, "Oh, fuck," and grasped the back of her head, encouraging her.

Bea kept up her speed until George's whole body went taut, and she shouted, "Christ."

She kissed her way back up George's shaking body. Bea looked in her eyes and stroked her sweaty brow. "I love you, Georgie."

George finally got her breath back. "I love you, my darling. You always know how to make things interesting."

Bea chuckled and traced George's lips with her finger. "I try, but you know what?"

George shook her head.

"I'm so wet, and I don't need a fumbling first-timer. I need you to fuck me like you know what you're doing."

George grinned and immediately flipped Bea onto her back, and held her wrists above her head. "I think I can help you with that. Don't move a muscle."

George got up and went over to the wardrobe. She grasped a backpack and pulled out an intelliflesh strap-on. This dildo allowed her to feel everything. George loved to use it and was glad Bea loved it too. Once it was attached, she walked back over to the bed and found Bea lying on her side, with a big smile on her face.

"How do you want me, Your Majesty?" Bea said sexily.

George pumped the strap-on a few times in her hand. It was now working and had become an extension of her clit. She wanted Bea to have a deep, powerful orgasm, so she asked for Bea's favourite position. "On all fours," George said.

Bea grinned and jumped into position. George climbed onto the bed behind her and immediately saw how wet her wife was. She stroked her hands down Bea's spine and over her buttocks. Bea groaned when she dipped her fingers into her wetness and circled her clit.

Bea looked back at her and said, "Fuck me, Georgie, don't tease."

George's sex pounded wildly at that request and she took hold of her strap-on. She now had full sensation.

Bea groaned as she pushed her way inside.

"Christ," George breathed when she was fully inside. It felt incredible, but she had to concentrate on making it feel good for Bea, first and foremost.

She started with some small thrusts until Bea got used to the fullness.

"It feels so deep." Bea moaned.

"Are you okay?"

George got her answer when Bea's hips started to undulate and encourage her. "Yes, just fuck me. I need you."

George held on to her hips and started long deep thrusts, then every so often she would hasten the thrusts. She could hear and feel Bea's orgasm building up. It felt so good. George had to close her eyes and concentrate on not coming, when all her body wanted to do was come.

When they both got near the edge of orgasm, she stilled and slowed her thrusts.

Bea called out with an almost painful cry, "Please, George, don't. I was so close."

"Soon, my darling." George built up her long slow thrusts again, and as she got faster, she knew her body wasn't going to let her stop this time.

Bea thrust her hips back into George and moaned almost continually. "Need to come, please?"

George thrust fast, her breathing hard and the orgasm building up in her sex. She could feel the walls of Bea's sex start to flutter. When Bea let her head fall onto the bed and pushed her hips up higher into her, George knew they were both going to come in seconds.

Their hips slapped together as she thrust hard, and then Bea's moans started to become higher pitched until she cried out, and George's orgasm exploded in her sex and through her strap-on.

"Christ," George shouted as her hips jerked in orgasm.

They collapsed onto the bed, breathing heavily. Bea pulled her into a kiss.

"Hmm, that was so good, Sailor," Bea said.

"Thank you, ma'am," George replied.

Bea laughed. "Can you tell I really miss you when you're gone on your own?"

"Just a bit." George winked.

George reached down to take off her strap-on and Bea's hand stopped her. "Oh no. I'm not finished with you yet, Your Majesty."

❖

Bea traced her fingernails around George's nipple, making it hard.

"Don't tease me, my darling. You've exhausted me."

"All right." She laid her head on her chest, and George stroked her hair. This was Bea's favourite place in the world. She sighed.

"What was that sigh for?" George said.

"It was a happy sigh. I couldn't be happier. I have you, and Teddy."

"And hopefully a little one on the way when we get home," George chipped in.

Bea kissed George's chest. "Don't worry. I haven't forgotten. I can't wait to have a little brother or sister for Teddy. I know she'll love being a big sister. Just like you."

George wrapped her strong arms around her and hugged her tightly. "I don't know what I did to have you fall into my lap. I'll never forget the first time I saw you at Timmy's and you scowled across the table at me. I think I started to fall in love then and there."

Bea leaned up on her elbow and looked down at her. "I thought you were gorgeous but that you'd be some stuck-up, overprivileged fool."

George stroked a strand of hair behind Bea's ear. "And what did you think when you got to know me?"

"I thought you were the kindest person I'd ever met, and I lost my heart to you very quickly. Do you know who reminds me of us?"

"Who?" George asked.

"Holly and Quincy," Bea said.

George furrowed her eyebrows. "Quincy? I don't think—Holly would terrify her. Then again, you terrify me sometimes."

Bea gave her a play hit. "Stop it, you. They've been getting close. I think Holly is getting her to open up, and I think we should help."

"Is this the stage two you were talking about?" George said.

"Exactly. I want Holly to be as happy as Lali and I are."

George pursed her lips and Bea said, "What? You don't think it's a good idea?"

"It might not be the best time for Quincy. She's been through hell the past couple of years. I can see the torment in her eyes. I've seen it in other military personnel. They hide it very well."

"But Holly makes her smile, and you know how hard it is to get Quincy to smile. Give it a try," Bea said.

"What can I do?"

"When we have our girls' night at the ranch in Kentucky, you were going to have a card game with Cammy and Quincy. Talk to her, about how she feels. Encourage her."

"Talk…about how she feels? That's a private matter. We're comrades—we don't talk about feelings."

Bea rolled her eyes. "Well, just do it this once." She leaned down and gave George the softest kiss, the kind of kiss that made George moan. "Do it for me?"

"Oh, all right, just kiss me. I've regained some of my strength." George rolled over so that Bea was underneath her.

Just as they were about to kiss, Bea said, "One more thing… about where Quincy stays at the ranch…"

CHAPTER SIXTEEN

Holly didn't know what to expect from a ranch house, but her mind had conjured up some quaint wooden place, like she had seen in the old Western films. This was not that.

The ranch house was more like a mansion that happened to be in the country. She had no idea how big a plot of land it was, but the fields went on for miles. The pool house where she was staying was bigger and nicer than her flat in London.

Bea did say the owner was really big in horse breeding and extremely successful. While George and Bea were here, the owner was moving out to another one of her houses, simply to give George and Bea their privacy, somewhere the press couldn't get them.

She walked from the pool house up the long driveway to the front of the white stone ranch house. Nanny Baker had called her for some assistance with Teddy. Holly rang the bell, and a housekeeper opened the door.

"Hi, I'm Holly. Nanny Baker asked me to come over."

"Oh yes, she's in the den." The aged housekeeper led her through the marble floored home. She was shown into a room dominated by a big comfortable leather couch and all the latest gaming tables and computer terminals.

Nanny Baker was on the couch trying to comfort a crying Teddy.

"Thank goodness you're here, Holly. I can't seem to settle her," Nanny Baker said.

"Hey, hey, what's all these tears, Teddy?" Holly sat down and opened her arms to the little girl.

Teddy climbed into her arms. "Want Mummy." Teddy snuffled.

Nanny Baker sighed. "I think her parents going to all these engagements is catching up with her. When she got off the plane, I think she thought they were all coming here to visit the horses."

Holly hugged her and wiped away her tears. "Mummy and Mum won't be long, Teddy. When they get back from the races, they won't leave you all week, I promise." Holly looked up and spotted the TV terminal. "Surely the races are on TV, Nanny?" Holly said.

Nanny Baker clapped her hands together. "Of course. Let's see."

"We'll try to find Mum and Mummy on TV, okay?" Holly said to Teddy.

Teddy nodded and nuzzled further into Holly's chest.

"There," Nanny Baker said when she found the right channel.

They were just in time to see Queen Georgina and Queen Beatrice, standing in their viewing box. Both were cheering.

"Mum! Mummy!" Teddy shouted. "Home soon?"

Holly stroked her soft dark hair. "They will be."

Her gaze fixed on the moody looking security officer standing behind them, and her heart ached. *Quincy.*

Once George and Bea entered the main house, Lang said, "Follow me, team. We'll get you settled into your quarters, and then we'll have a meeting."

Quincy followed Lang and the team to a large converted barn.

"This place is amazing, isn't it?" Clay said.

It looked as if it would have everything they needed. "Yes, looks great."

She was just about to put her bags down when Lang said, "No, Quincy, you're in the pool house at the back of the main house."

Garrett and a few of the others stopped in their tracks.

"What? Why, sir?" Quincy asked.

"The Queen's orders. Get going." Lang entered the barn, and Garrett said, "Privilege strikes again, eh, Captain Fantastic?"

Quincy turned away and walked in the direction of the pool house. Why had the Queen done this? She didn't want to be made different from the others. She would need to talk to George later at their card game and get switched back.

She found the pool house, which from the outside looked very much like a beautiful self-contained cottage.

Quincy walked through the front door and found an expensively decorated open-plan first floor, with a lounge area with the biggest, comfiest looking sofa she had ever seen, and to her right, a big kitchen. She noticed a kettle was nearly boiling and a cup sitting, waiting to be filled.

Someone was already here. Then she heard footsteps on the stairs, which led into the lounge area.

Quincy's heart thudded when Holly came bouncing down the stairs.

Holly stopped dead when she saw her. "Quincy? What are you doing here?" Holly said with surprise.

"I was told to report here for the duration of my stay. I didn't know you would be here," Quincy said.

"I was told to expect someone else to stay here, but I didn't think it would be you. Your bedroom's up the stairs on the left," Holly said.

"I'll ask to be moved." Quincy couldn't help but admire Holly, dressed in little denim shorts and a tiny strappy top. To Quincy, Holly's body was just perfect.

Holly put her hands on her hips. "Why do you want to be moved? Can't stand to be around me?"

"No, no, it's not that. I just thought you would prefer that," Quincy said.

Holly gave her a slight smile and joked, "No, it's fine. I'm sure we can keep ourselves from fighting and killing each other for a week."

Fighting and killing weren't really what Quincy was frightened of—well, maybe fighting. An angry Holly strangely turned her on. Seeing the fire burning in Holly's eyes made Quincy want to kiss her so badly.

"You're right of course." Quincy's eyes lingered on Holly's chest a little too long, and she was sure Holly caught her, by the smile on her face. "Well, I better put my clothes away. See you later."

Quincy ran up to her room as quickly as she could.

❖

That evening, Holly was having girls' night with Lali and Bea in the family room of the ranch house. They called Greta and made sure she knew they were missing her. This was the first girls' night she wouldn't be with them.

Instead of a film they decided to play Scrabble, so they could talk.

Holly put down her last letter on the board, and said, "Yes! Triple letter score."

"That's not a word," Lali said.

Bea looked at the board. "Hurple? That's definitely not a word, Holls."

Holly smirked. "I thought I might just get away with it."

"Not on my watch," Lali said as she totted up the scores.

Holly rolled her eyes at Bea. "Of course not."

"So who won, as if we didn't know?" Bea said to Lali.

Lali smiled. "Me."

Holly drank the rest of her glass of wine. "Do you have to be efficiently brilliant at everything?"

"Yes." Lali and Bea laughed and sat back on the couch.

There was something Holly had been desperate to ask Bea all night, but it never was the right time, so she topped up their glasses and went for it. "Why am I sharing a house with Quincy?"

Bea looked to Lali and said, "Talk about changing the subject."

"Well?" Holly took her glass and sat cross-legged on the couch.

"There wasn't enough room for all the security people in the barn," Bea said.

"I know that's not true. What are you two playing at?" Holly said.

"Well…" Lali was obviously trying to think of something. "So you can paint your little toy soldiers together."

Holly picked up a cushion and threw it at her friend. "You're a terrible liar. The pair of you are trying to play at matchmaker, aren't you?"

Bea giggled. "Maybe. Quincy is so sweet and gorgeous, and she needs a good woman to make her smile. The only woman we've seen make her smile is you."

Holly took a sip of her drink. "I'm sorry to disappoint you, but Captain Quincy is not interested in a love affair. And apparently, she doesn't want to smile. She doesn't want to feel anything. That's her trouble."

"Oh well, you're both there now," Bea said. "By the way, have you heard from Story?"

"Yes." Holly sighed.

"That didn't sound like a happy sigh," Lali said.

"It's just a feeling. I mean, I should be ecstatic. A film star who I had a crush on is calling and texting me a lot."

"*Had* a crush on?" Bea said.

Holly didn't know if she could say she was crushing on Story any more. She should have, but she wasn't sure. After meeting Story, and talking with her, there were more than a few things that bothered her, plus her crush had been eclipsed by her attraction to a moody marine, who hardly said two words. But she wasn't going to admit that yet.

"*Have* a crush on. It's just that I've heard from her a lot since I posted the picture of me and Quincy, and she's asked about Quincy too."

"Do you think she's jealous?" Lali asked.

Holly laughed. "I don't think Story St. John does jealousy. No, I think more of a turf thing. She's on social media a great deal talking about you, Bea, and that I work for you. I think she's more interested in the publicity it would get her to go out with the Queen Consort's friend. I might be wrong. I don't know."

"I suppose you'll find out when we get to LA," Bea said.

"I suppose." Holly sighed.

Bea leaned over and patted her thigh. "In the meantime you might as well paint toy soldiers with Quincy."

"Oh, stop it."

"Full house," Cammy said with a huge smile.

Both George and Quincy threw their cards into the centre of the card table. The house had a bar and den downstairs with a fully equipped gaming room.

"She's too good," George said while Cammy pulled her winnings towards her. They were only playing for matchsticks and pride.

"She is indeed," Quincy agreed.

Cammy began to shuffle the cards. They'd enjoyed a pleasant evening talking about old times, officers they had known, and some of Cammy's exploits with the ladies she'd met, but all the time Quincy wanted to ask about the pool house.

"George, why did you have me billeted with Ms. Weaver?"

George and Cammy looked at each other quickly. "Uh, Bea didn't want Holly staying there all alone. She supposed she and Lali would be spending most of their downtime with us"—George pointed to Cammy—"and you had been spending time together, so...I could have Garrett take your place."

"No, no, don't do that," Quincy said a little too quickly, she realized. "I mean, she doesn't like Garrett, I don't think. I'll keep her company."

"As you wish," George said.

"You know, Quincy," Cammy said, "you should take her out riding or something."

"What? Why?" Quincy asked.

"Three cards, please. Well, model soldiers are excellent in their own way, but they don't keep a woman's interest in the long term."

"I don't have any interest—"

Cammy put her cards down. "Come on. Anyone can see how you look at her."

Quincy felt her cheeks burning, so she put her head down. "I can't. It's not possible for me."

George patted her on the shoulder. "I know how hard things have been, Quincy, but a lifetime is a long time on your own. I nearly lost Bea because I never spoke up and told her how I felt."

There was silence for a few seconds before Cammy said, "I didn't have that problem with Lali. I told her how I felt from when I first met her—she just didn't believe me."

They laughed and George recounted some of the stories about how Captain Cameron won the heart of Lali Ramesh that Quincy had missed.

Could she do that? There was a burning desire inside her to do so. Quincy just didn't know if she was brave enough.

❖

Holly was walking back to the pool house when she heard a voice behind her. It was Quincy.

"Holly? I'll walk you back," Quincy said.

She looked back and saw Quincy running towards her. Holly had to admit she loved her dressed-down look of jeans and checked shirt.

When Quincy caught up she said, "Did you have a good time with the consort and Lali?"

"Yes, you?" Holly asked.

"Yes. Yes, I did. George, Cammy, and I played cards, and… chatted." Quincy stumbled over her words.

Things were a little strained between them, hardly surprising since the last time they talked they'd been arguing.

Surprisingly Quincy was the first one to break the silence, with, "I wanted to talk to you about the last time we spoke—"

"And argued," Holly finished for her.

"Yes. I apologize for what I said. I know you were trying to be kind, but I'm just not used to someone being so close. And when you touched me there, I became…Well, I'm sorry."

"That's okay. I made the mistake. I know you're sensitive about your body there, and I didn't think. I was trying to be your friend, and I don't think of you as a project."

They arrived back at the front door to the pool house, and Quincy said, "I know—it was a stupid thing to say. I'm not good at personal relationships."

Holly led the way inside and flicked the kettle on. "Coffee, tea?"

"Coffee, please."

Holly got the cups out. This was her chance to mend some of the damage she had done to their friendship. "Why don't you go and get your soldiers, and we can paint while we drink our coffee?"

A huge smile broke out on Quincy's face. Bea and Lali were right. She did make Quincy smile.

"I'd love that. Give me a second." Quincy hurried to the stairs, then stopped on the first step. "Holly?"

Holly turned around and said, "Yes?"

"The night we went out in Chicago? It was the best night of my life," Quincy said, then hurried upstairs.

Holly was gobsmacked. Did Captain Stompy actually just say that? Or was she dreaming? Maybe Quincy was unravelling at last.

❖

"Finished!" Holly exclaimed.

Quincy and Holly were sitting together on the couch, painting their model soldiers.

Holly had finally finished her first one and was enormously pleased. Since they had started painting together, Quincy had completed about six, but Holly was only a beginner.

"Well done," Quincy said.

Holly compared her soldier to one of hers. "It's not nearly as good as yours, Quin."

"Don't be silly. It just takes practice. In any case, when I set up my battle scene with these men, I'll always remember the happy time I had with you painting them," Quincy said.

Holly, who was sitting right next to her on the couch, turned to her and smiled. "Have you really had a happy time?"

"Yes. Are you ready for another one?" Quincy held up an unpainted soldier.

"Thanks. What happens when we finish these?" Holly asked.

Quincy smiled. "We move on to a different regiment. There were quite a few at the battle." Maybe Holly would lose interest eventually, but she was determined to enjoy this time she had with Holly before someone who didn't have a whole lot of demons to hide swept her off her feet.

"Excellent." Holly asked the computer to play a playlist from her phone through the speakers, and she sang happily while she painted.

Quincy just adored how free and fun-loving Holly was. She was exactly how she imagined her real mother to be.

"What were you thinking?" Holly said.

"Sorry?"

"You were gazing at me and looked as if you were thinking hard," Holly said.

What would she say? Quincy didn't want to run the risk of upsetting Holly again and pushing her away. She had missed Holly when they weren't speaking.

"I was wondering if you were like my mother, actually."

Holly scrunched up her face. "The vice admiral?"

Quincy smiled. "No, my birth mother. I was adopted, remember."

"Oh, that's right—your adopted mother is your aunt, isn't she," Holly asked gently.

She's probably frightened I'm going to run. But Quincy didn't want to. She wanted to talk about her mother, for the first time in her life. "It's okay. You can ask about her. I'd like to tell you."

"Did you always know you were adopted?" Holly asked.

"Yes, my aunt told me about my birth mother since I can first remember. She wanted me to know so she could teach me not to follow her example."

"Why?" Holly asked.

"I told you about the normal career path for a Quincy? Boarding school, and then naval officer school? That was the way, as far back as anyone can remember. Well, my birth mother didn't take that path. According to my aunt, my birth mother partied, drank, took drugs, and generally disappointed the family. My aunt called my birth mother *the Quincy who got it wrong.*"

"What happened to her, Quin?" Holly pulled her legs up on the couch and sat cross-legged.

Quincy kept painting her model in an effort to keep calm. She'd never talked like this before, but she didn't want to run from Holly again.

"My birth mother died when I was born. She had been at a party and got into a car with a drunk driver. There was an accident. I was saved, my mother was not."

Holly immediately put her hand on Quincy's thigh. "I'm so sorry, Quin." She could see the pain on Quincy's face.

"Thank you." Quincy went quiet, then said, "I wished I could have known her, just to make my own mind up about her."

"Why, what did your aunt say?" Holly asked.

"She used her as an example of what my life would be like if I didn't follow rules and the path set out by the Quincys before me. When any part of my character showed any sign of being like her, like my anger, she warned me that I would turn out like my birth mother."

"You have a temper? Never!" Holly joked.

Quincy smiled and then rubbed her face with her hands. "I try so hard to keep it in check, but you seem to disrupt my control."

Holly chuckled. "Good—like I said, you need to be ruffled up, Stompy. So your aunt adopted you at birth?"

Quincy nodded. "Don't get me wrong, the admiral has always given me everything I needed. I wanted for nothing, but she tried to mould me into another version of her, like I was one of her junior officers on deck, but I was different from her. I handled things differently."

Holly guessed those differences were the way Quincy handled emotion. Despite her protestations to the contrary, Quincy did feel, and feel strongly, and that was why she was so scarred.

"The admiral?"

"My mother. I've always called her that," Quincy said.

"She must have been so proud that you got the Victoria Cross."

Quincy smiled. "Yes, I was only the second Quincy to win a VC. Mother was very proud, until…It doesn't matter."

Holly decided to let her off with that. Quincy had opened up enough for one evening. She could talk to her more through the week.

They continued to paint in comfortable silence, then Quincy said, "I didn't mean I thought you might be like my mother because of the drinking and partying, but because I thought she would have been fun-loving, just like you."

Holly bumped her with her shoulder. "I know that, silly. Look at my guy's horse." She held up her model. "Do you think that's the right colour for him?"

"It's perfect," Quincy said. "You just reminded me, Holly. I wondered if you would like to go horse riding tomorrow? I'm fishing with Clay in the morning, but after that I'm free."

"Me? Ride a horse?" Holly said with shock. "I don't ride horses. I'm a city girl."

"I'll teach you. I thought if you practised with me, towards the end of the week we could ride out with a picnic, and I could show you how to make a fire like you wanted me to."

Holly couldn't believe the change in Quincy. She was being so open and friendly. Holly wondered if the Queen had said anything to her.

She put down her model and rinsed her brush in the glass of water. "Quin, has the Queen asked you to keep me company or something?"

"No, not at all. I want to—you gave me such a nice night in Chicago—but if you don't want to, I'm not the best company, and—"

"Shut up, you. Of course I want to. I'm just scared of the horse part."

Quincy had the biggest grin on her face. "I'll look after you, I promise."

Holly was genuinely scared, but if Quincy was offering to actually do something sociable, she wasn't going to turn her down.

"I'll agree if you let me cut your hair." Holly winked at her.

Quincy appeared terrified. "My hair? But I…"

"Those are my terms," Holly insisted.

Quincy let out a breath. "Okay, but nothing like a Mohawk or anything."

"I promise. You just need to be ruffled up and unravelled. It's a date, then," Holly said.

She watched Quincy gulp and her eyes dart around the room. Holly knew she was thinking about it being a date. That thought probably scared her as much as the haircut.

They painted their models for a while longer, and Holly noticed Quincy yawning. "You tired? We can stop for tonight."

"No, I'm okay. You go if you want," Quincy said.

She never slept properly, because of those bloody nightmares, Holly thought. She wished she could slip into bed, take Quincy in her arms, and soothe her to sleep. Unfortunately, that wasn't on the cards. Maybe she could get Quincy to relax on this big, sumptuous couch.

"Why don't we put a movie on and put our feet up on this rather expensive-looking coffee table?" Holly suggested.

"If you like," Quincy replied.

They put away the model kits, and Quincy got them drinks while Holly chose a movie.

When Quincy returned she was surprised that the lights were off, but Holly explained it was nicer that way, like a movie theatre. But she was really trying to set everything to help make Quincy dozy. She wanted her to fall asleep and get some rest.

Quincy seemed to accept that, and they began watching. Holly kept glancing to the side and caught Quincy's eyes getting heavy.

Holly decided to be bold and took Quincy's hand. She initially stiffened and looked at Holly, but Holly just smiled back and squeezed Quincy's hand.

She relaxed and they continued watching, Holly rubbing her thumb rhythmically on the back of Quincy's.

Eventually Quincy dozed off. Holly carefully put her arm around her shoulder and eased her head onto her lap. Holly stroked her fingers through Quincy's hair, and it felt so good. So good that she dozed off herself.

CHAPTER SEVENTEEN

Quincy opened her eyes and felt more rested than she ever had. It took her a few seconds to realize she was lying on Holly's lap. She sat up quickly and rubbed her face. Holly was still sleeping and looked so beautiful at rest.

They must have fallen asleep watching the film, but how she got onto Holly's lap, she had no idea. As she thought about it, she remembered wakening slightly, feeling Holly's fingers running through her hair, loving the feeling, and falling back to sleep. Quincy then realized she hadn't had a nightmare. This was the first night since the mission happened, that she didn't have her nightmares.

Quincy felt unsettled and confused—she needed some space. She hurried upstairs to her room and jumped into the shower. As the water hammered down on her back, she thought about the feel of Holly's fingers running through her hair, then she imagined them touching her body, and a heat spread across her skin, and want and need burned in her sex.

Then she looked down at her scarred body. *I can't let her see this. I failed the ones I care about.* Quincy immediately turned the shower ice-cold. *I can't feel this way.*

She remembered her mother drumming into her that emotion would destroy her life, her career. She'd already had her second chance, and she wouldn't get another, especially with the admiral.

Quincy got out of the shower and dressed quickly. Maybe these horse-riding lessons weren't a good idea.

She looked at the time on her watch and walked over to her computer pad on her desk.

"Computer, call Helen." Helen was the only one who could understand what pain she carried.

Helen's bright face appeared on the screen. "Good afternoon, Quin. Or good morning where you are."

"Good morning, Helen."

"Where are you now, exactly?" Helen asked.

"We're in Kentucky. The Queen's friend owns a large ranch, so we're having a week off."

"Good, you should relax more," Helen said.

Quincy heard the sound of Helen's kids in the background. "How are you and the children, and Jacob?"

"Me and the kids are doing well. Jacob is a little brighter—he had some more skin graft surgery, and it seemed to go well. We're hoping it's going to work out. The kids and I will be going to the hospital later, and I'll tell him you called."

Quincy nodded. At the mention of Jacob's name, her guilt washed over her. Guilt for having a good time with Holly when some of her men were dead, and Jacob was in constant pain.

"Don't, Quincy. I know that look," Helen said.

"What look?" Quincy didn't think Helen could read her that well.

"That guilty look. You're a hero, Quincy. You saved my husband. Do you think that I'd rather he was dead? I would have given anything to have him come back to us, and you did bring him back."

Jacob had asked her to end his life. As he lay in the field hospital, he'd begged her, but she couldn't do it. She couldn't hurt her friend.

"But he has a family, he has you. It should have been me in Jacob's hospital bed," Quincy said.

"Why are you feeling this today? Has something happened?" Helen narrowed her eyes. "Have you met someone?"

How did she know that?

A smile crept onto Helen's face. "You have. You *have* met someone. Tell me about her."

"I haven't. You know I don't feel that way," Quincy said.

"Don't give me that rubbish the admiral drummed into you. You loved Jacob, and that means you can feel love."

Quincy sighed and looked down. "It's just a friend who's been kind to me. It's nothing romantic."

"Who is she?" Helen asked.

"How do you know it's a she?" Quincy said more sharply than she meant to. "I'm sorry. I'm a little off kilter."

"That's okay. Feelings can make you be like that. I know it's a woman because your eyes wouldn't flit about like that for a man friend. What's her name?"

"Holly Weaver. She's the Queen Consort's royal dresser and friend."

Helen's face lit up. "The woman who went out with Story St. John?"

"Yes. That's her." The mention of Story St. John made her uneasy.

"She's gorgeous, Quincy. What's she like?" Helen asked.

How could she describe Holly? There didn't seem to be enough words to describe her, or the feeling in Quincy's heart when she thought about her.

"She's spirited, and she doesn't like rules, regulations, or following instructions."

Helen laughed. "You must have crossed swords with her, then."

"Yes, at the start, but she's persistent, kind, giving to those she loves, and she likes spending time with me painting my models."

"She must like you if she's doing that," Helen joked.

"Holly just decided she was going to be my friend. I've done everything I can to push her away, but nothing appears to dissuade her. She's the most persistent woman I've ever met."

"Sounds like a woman after my own heart. Good for her. Hence the guilt. You're thinking, how can I live and enjoy myself when Jacob is in pain, and your other men died. You wear your own scars, Quincy, both inside and out. Jacob told you to live life to the fullest. You promised him."

"I know I did, and I've failed miserably so far," Quincy said.

"But now you have a chance?" Helen said.

"Maybe." Quincy sighed.

"Listen to me, Quincy," Helen said seriously. "If you have the slightest chance to live and love, you have to grasp it with both hands, because you never know when it will be taken from you. To do anything else would be betraying the memory of your marines who died, and Jacob. If he could, he would give you a swift kick up the backside."

Helen was right. She could just imagine what he would say to her. She could see herself falling for Holly, and she had to at least try. Although if she had to compete against Story St. John, she didn't think she could win. After everything Holly had done for her, she deserved a nice time this week, and the Queen had asked her to keep her company. So she would do that and more.

❖

Quincy fixed bait on her hook and watched Clay cast her line in the river.

"You've done this before, Clay?" Quincy said.

Clay grinned. "Yeah, my grandpa used to take us to Margate to sea fish on the holidays. I used to love it. Getting out of busy London and breathing in that sea air. It was brilliant."

The river the stable staff had directed them to was only a ten minute walk from the ranch. It was warm, beautiful, and quiet. Just perfect to start the day. They left very early, but Quincy felt bright and rested, something she hadn't felt in a long time, and all because of Holly.

Even though she was only half awake, the feel of Holly's fingers stroking through her hair was heaven. Although socializing was difficult for her, Holly deserved her effort, because Holly was trying so hard with her.

Quincy made sure she left the coffee pot ready to use this morning, and a cup and spoon ready for when Holly woke.

Clay set her fishing pole down and lifted up a flask. "Tea, ma'am?"

Quincy smiled. "I think you can call me Quincy now, Clay."

"Sorry, Quincy, thanks. Tea?"

"Yes, please."

Clay poured out the tea and handed it to her. The mug was warming and comforting. She looked over at her fishing pole. There hadn't been a movement since she had cast out first thing this morning, but Clay had a few bites.

"I don't think I'm ever going to get a bite," Quincy said.

"Part of the fun of fishing, isn't it? Sitting here, enjoying the quiet, no bites," Clay joked.

Quincy chuckled. "You're right."

They were silent for a few minutes, then Clay said, "Quincy, have you had any more of those messages?"

"No." Quincy sighed. "They've dried up. Maybe it was just some crank."

Clay looked at her seriously. "But you don't think so?"

"No. Something tells me it's serious, but there's no evidence. The one man who has something against me is living quietly with his mother in the UK, and there's no intel on any direct threats to the Queen Consort."

"I know the rest of the team aren't taking it really seriously, but I trust your instincts, Quincy. If you need anything from me, just say."

It meant a lot to Quincy that Clay would say that. At least she had one ally. "I appreciate that, Clay. Between you and me, I have someone looking into it. A former military intelligence officer, who was a good friend. She's making enquires and tracking the messages."

"Great. No one's getting past us, boss. If we're out on an engagement and something happens. I'm ready to follow your lead."

"Thank you, Clay."

"So what are you doing this afternoon?" Clay asked.

Quincy started to laugh softly. "Something that will be a great challenge. Teaching Holly to ride."

"Quin, I don't want to do this. Let me down," Holly said.

Holly had been terrified when Quincy took her over to the stables to meet the horse she had picked out for her. Holly was expecting a pony like Teddy had been on, not this gargantuan beast.

At the start she refused point-blank to mount, but eventually Quin persuaded her to at least walk down to the training ring with the horse and see how she felt. Now she was up on its back, and her life was flashing before her eyes.

"Quincy, let me down. This horse is a giant," Holly pleaded.

Quincy had hold of the reins and was patting the horse's neck. "I'll let you down if you really want, but I thought you could at least have a trot around the ring, see if you get used to it. The stable staff assure me Honey is a very tame girl, and she's not that big. Not as big as mine."

Holly could see how important this was to Quincy. She wanted to take her out riding, have a picnic, and light a fire. To do that, Holly had to ride.

"Honey? Is that her name?" Holly said.

"Yes. Give her a pat and talk to her. This isn't a car you're driving. It's a highly intelligent animal. Let it know you care."

Holly held on to the pommel of the saddle with one hand, and with the other scratched behind the horse's ear. "Hi, Honey. I'm really scared, but I hope you will take care of me."

Honey whinnied. "You see?" Quincy smiled. "Honey likes you."

"Hmm, we'll see."

Quincy started to lead them around the training ring, and Holly held on with all the strength she had.

Quincy slowed and bowed her head. "Afternoon, Your Majesty."

Holly was so focused on her fear, that she hadn't noticed Bea was standing at the side of the training circle.

"Afternoon. How is she doing, Quincy?" Bea said, grinning.

Holly scowled at her, and Quincy said, "She's doing well, ma'am."

"I hate this, Bea. Honey here is a giant," Holly said.

"Oh, be brave, Holls. You can do it," Bea said.

"I don't see you ever riding." Holly grasped the reins tighter as Quincy led off the horse again.

Bea winked at her. "I don't need to ride a horse. I ride in carriages."

"Bitch," Holly said jokingly, and Bea just laughed.

That evening Holly was getting her wish to cut Quincy's hair. Her bravery with the horse and persistence had persuaded Quincy. After they ate dinner together, she sent Quincy to the shower to wash her hair and told her to wear something other than a shirt, while she set up to cut.

Holly pulled a chair away from the kitchen table, and every muscle in her body ached. "Ouch!"

"You're going to be even sorer tomorrow, Holly."

Holly looked up, saw Quincy at the top of the stairs, and stopped breathing. Quincy was standing on the stairs, in shorts, a sleeveless T-shirt, and bare feet, with a towel around her neck. She had never seen Quincy so casual or seen her bare arms or legs. They were muscular, but lithe, just right in Holly's eyes, and her wet hair made her even sexier.

She was a bloody Adonis.

Quincy walked down the remaining stairs and lifted the chair for her. "Where do you want this?"

Holly took a breath and tried to regain her senses. "Um, just next to the table where my kit box is."

She followed Quincy over, still feeling her aches and pains, but also some new aches and needs. Her mind kept picturing Quincy's body lying on top of hers, and her hands touching her.

"Is everything okay, Holly? Is this okay?" Quincy pointed at her T-shirt.

Holly noticed it had a high neckline so as to hide Quincy's burn scars. Everything about Quincy came back to the scars and the pain she'd gone through. Holly wished she could kiss every scar and show Quincy that love could heal the pain.

Did she just say love? *You're crazy, Holls.*

"I'm fine. Sit." Holly took Quincy's towel and shook it out, then wrapped it around her shoulders. As she did she inhaled the scent of Quincy, fresh from the shower, and the gorgeous smell of Quincy's cologne. It made her want to bury her face in Quincy's neck, and kiss and bite it.

It was such a strong urge that she let go of Quincy and turned away, pretending to sort through her scissors in her kit box.

"Holly? You will keep it simple, won't you? Nothing like Story St. John, please?"

That comment made Holly laugh and regain her control. "I promise. You're not a Story."

"Is that a bad thing?" Quincy wasn't sure what Holly meant by that, but she had to know.

Holly walked to her with scissors and comb. "What?"

"Not being like Story St. John," Quincy said.

Holly stood in front of her and started to comb her wet hair. "No, it's not. I like you just as you are, Stompy."

Quincy's spirits soared, and as Holly cut her hair and ran her fingers through it, she closed her eyes and enjoyed the peaceful feeling. Normally when she closed her eyes, Quincy was bombarded by bad movies in her head, but not when Holly touched her. Holly soothed her demons, and she greedily soaked up her attention.

After Holly had snipped for a while, she said, "Head up, let me see you."

Quincy opened her eyes and watched as Holly checked all the lengths of her hair. Her eyeline just happened to be at Holly's cleavage, and as Holly bent over, Quincy got a teasing look. Holly's breasts were soft and round. Holly wasn't skinny—she had a gorgeously proportioned body, with lush hips and thighs that made Quincy crazy.

Then Holly looked her right in the eyes, while her fingers stroked though her hair.

"You have the most beautiful blue eyes, Quincy," Holly said breathily.

Quincy didn't quite know what to say to that. She'd never had such a compliment before, and she was caught in Holly's gaze.

Holly's lips were parted, and she wet them with the tip of her tongue. Quincy felt lust like she never had before. She wanted to pull Holly onto her lap and suck on Holly's teasing wet tongue.

"Do you remember when I kissed you, Quin?" Holly asked.

"Yes." Quincy remembered every second of that kiss.

"I'm sorry if it made you uncomfortable," Holly said.

Was Holly trying to gauge whether Quincy would welcome another? "I'm glad you did. It was my first kiss." Holly stood up sharply and the moment was gone. Had she said the wrong thing?

"I'll just put some wax through your hair, and you can look at it in the mirror."

"Did I say something wrong?" Quincy said.

"No, no, not at all," Holly said, as she vigorously waxed and styled her hair.

That obviously meant she had. Why would her first kiss be a bad thing?

"Go and look in the mirror."

Quincy got up and walked over to the mirror hanging above the fireplace. She looked in the mirror and found a thoroughly modern haircut looking back at her.

Holly came up behind her. "What do you think?"

It was nice and short, just how she liked it, but choppy on top, with messy spikes going in all different directions.

"I think Clay will approve. I'm finally modern," Quincy said.

Holly stepped closer and leaned her head against Quincy's shoulder, while looking in the mirror. "But do *you* like it? It's not Story St. John, like I promised."

Quincy laughed. "No, it's not Story St. John. I like it. Honestly. It ruffles me up a bit, just like you said."

"Great." Holly was full of smiles and seemed back to normal after their little blip. "I'm so glad you trusted me to do it."

Quincy turned to Holly and took her hand. "I trust you. I wouldn't let anyone else as close."

She hoped that would convey how much she cared about Holly. She was not good at these kinds of relationships, or any relationships. Quincy didn't know how else to say she wanted something, something more with Holly.

"I know. I understand you more than you realize," Holly said enigmatically.

"Do you?"

Holly smiled and nodded. "Why don't we eat dessert on the couch, and then paint some toy soldiers? It's fast becoming my perfect evening."

"Model soldiers," Quincy corrected her with a smile. "Nothing would make me happier."

She knew in that moment that Holly and no one else understood her and made her happy.

CHAPTER EIGHTEEN

Holly left the pool house as soon as Quincy left to have a meeting with the protection squad. She had to talk to Bea. Last night had left her reeling. She was feeling more and more for Quincy and had almost told her, but then Quincy had to go and reveal that the kiss they had shared was Quincy's first.

Was Quincy's apparent interest in her real, or would it be just her first experience of many? She'd given her heart once and had it broken, and she couldn't take it again.

Holly rang the bell and waited for the housekeeper. Last night she had lain awake and listened to Quincy's tortured dreams. Every moan or shout hurt her deep inside, and she had to physically stop herself from going to Quincy, but she knew Quincy would be embarrassed, and she didn't want to frighten her away just as she had gotten her to open up.

The housekeeper opened the door. "Morning, Miss Holly."

"Hi, could I speak to Queen Beatrice please?"

"Of course, they're in the kitchen. Follow me."

When she walked into the large ranch kitchen, she found the sweet domestic scene of a family breakfast. George had Teddy on her knee, and was feeding her bits of toast, and Bea was making some coffee. Bea smiled when she saw her.

"Holls, come in and have coffee."

Holly curtsied to George and said, "Morning, Your Majesty. I'm sorry to interrupt you both."

"Not a bit of it." George wiped Teddy's mouth with a napkin and said, "Teddy and I were just off to feed the horses. We'll leave you two to chat."

"Horsey, Mum," Teddy said.

George lifted Teddy up into her arms and said to Bea, "Do you have the bag ready, Mummy?"

Bea lifted a cloth bag from the kitchen counter and handed it over. "Apples, carrots, and a bag of sugar lumps. The horses will love that."

Bea kissed her daughter and then gave George a lingering kiss. "Be good—both of you."

"Will do. Let's go, Teddy bear." George strode out and Bea gave a big happy sigh.

"You look a happy woman," Holly said to her.

"I am." Bea brought over the coffee and told Holly to sit. "This was the best idea ever. A whole week, just me, George, and Teddy, no servants, no officials knocking at our door at any time of the day or night. I can just be a wife and a mummy."

Holly knew the strain not living a normal life put on her friend. She was such a free spirit, and being in the gilded cage alongside George was hard, even harder since Teddy came along.

"I'm happy for you, Bea." Holly sat down gingerly and groaned.

"Saddle sore?" Bea said while pouring her coffee.

"Just a bit. I don't know how I'm ever going to go on this picnic at the end of the week, but I promised Quin."

"And that's important to you?" Bea said.

"Yes. I don't want to let her down. She might look like this tall, strapping, tough soldier, but deep down she's really quite sensitive." Holly didn't want to mention Quincy's nightmares, that was too private, and she wouldn't break her confidence.

"You really care about her, don't you," Bea said.

Holly took a sip of her coffee, as if that would give her the courage to say the words out loud. "I think I might be falling for her, but—"

Bea clapped her hands together with glee. "Yes, I knew it. Aren't I always right? Wait, what's the *but*?"

"Well, it's going to sound stupid now, but after one of the first times I'd argued with Quin, I went to confront her."

"And?" Bea wasn't following her.

"I was frustrated because she wouldn't be angry, annoyed, show any emotion or anything, so I kissed her on a whim."

"You kissed her?" Bea laughed.

"Yeah, it was out of anger and stupid, and afterwards we just pretended it never happened," Holly said.

"But you've talked about it since?" Bea asked.

"Last night, that's the thing. I was cutting her hair—"

Bea slammed down her cup in surprise. "Wait, Quincy let you touch her regulation hair?"

Holly nodded, and Bea blew out a breath. "She must care about you."

"The thing is, she told me that stupid, done in anger, joke kiss was her first ever."

"Aw, how sweet!" Bea grinned.

"It stopped me in my tracks. I mean, I've had more experience with women than her, and maybe I'll be the first of many. I was in love once and got my heart broken. I'm older and ready to settle down, and I don't want to play around."

"Holls, Quincy is straight as a die, in a nonsexual sense. Does she seem like someone who would play with you for a bit, then move on?"

Holly took another sip of coffee and said, "If she was Story St. John, yes, but Quincy, no. Then again, who knows? She's kept her emotions locked up for so long, who knows what she will feel when she explores her sexuality? I'd be her first."

"First and last, I would say. Let me tell you a secret no one else knows."

"What?" Holly inched closer.

"I'm George's first, and only. She never so much as kissed a woman before I met her. She got it right the first time when she picked me," Bea said quietly.

"Wow, you're George's one and only?" Holly allowed herself to think that maybe this could work.

Bea took her hand and said, "Maybe you are just Captain Quincy's one?"

❖

For the rest of the week, Holly spent all her time with Quincy, trying to gauge if Quincy really wanted what was growing between them. On Friday, after nearly a week of basic training in riding, Holly had promised to ride a trail to a nearby lake for a picnic with Quincy. Her riding hadn't improved a great deal, but enough so she could go on a short ride. So Quincy said, but Holly was still scared of the prospect.

Holly checked her appearance in the mirror in her bedroom. The jodhpurs one of the female stable hands gave her were just tight enough to catch Quincy's attention. She smiled, remembering catching Quincy looking at her bum a few times during their riding lessons.

She was determined today they would talk about what was between them, and if Quincy was slow on the uptake, she would just need to kiss her and ruffle her feathers.

"Are you ready to go, Holly?" Quincy shouted upstairs. Holly knew she had been waiting for a while.

"Just coming," Holly shouted back.

"I'll go and get the horses saddled up. Could you bring my wallet? I left it in my bedside table," Quincy said.

"Okay, see you soon." Holly walked next door to Quincy's bedroom and chuckled when she saw how tidy it was. She quickly opened her bedside table and lifted Quincy's wallet. Underneath was a neatly folded piece of paper with her name written on it.

Holly knew she was invading Quincy's privacy, but she just couldn't not look at it. She sat on Quincy's bed, opened up the piece of paper, and started to read.

Sometimes when I look at you, I stop breathing and wish I could be the one who makes you smile and laugh, but how can I be that for you when I can't feel? If I let myself feel, I would—well, I don't know what I would become, but it is terrifying to me.

When Holly finished reading, she lowered the letter. "Bloody hell."

"Holly, relax. You're doing fine," Quincy said.

Holly was holding on to the reins with a death grip, and her thighs were gripping her horse like steel.

"We're not riding far, are we?" Holly said.

"Not too far. Don't worry." Quincy was leading them down a wooded forest trail that led to a lake. It was only a fifteen minute ride usually, but with the slow pace they were doing, it would take a lot longer.

"I'm really proud of you, Holly. You've faced your fear."

"It's worth it to spend time with you, Quin." Holly managed a smile through her tension.

That meant so much to Quincy. Holly was doing this just to spend time with her, boring Captain Quincy? Quincy's heart thudded with new feelings of love and hope, something she hadn't felt in...she couldn't think when. All because of Holly Weaver.

They rode on through the woods until they came to a small clearing. "We're here. I'll get you down."

Quincy jumped down from her horse with ease and tethered it to a tree next to some grass, then went to Holly. Her knuckles were white from holding the reins so tightly.

"I hate this bit, Quin," Holly said.

Quincy stroked Holly's horse to keep her calm. "You only have to slip your leg over, and then slide. I'll catch you, I promise."

Holly closed her eyes. "I can't. It was different at the stables. I don't like this."

Quincy reached her arms up to her. "Just slip one leg over, and I'll catch you. You trust me, don't you?"

Holly opened her eyes and looked at her. "Yes."

"Okay, then. Hold Honey's mane and slide your leg over. I promise I won't let you fall."

After a few false starts, Holly finally slid her leg around, then started to panic. "I'm going to fall, I'm going to fall."

"No, you're not." Quincy put her hands on Holly's hips. "Can you feel my hands?"

"Yes," Holly squeaked.

"I've got ahold of you, so just slide into my arms." Quincy stepped as close as she could, and Holly inched down her body slowly.

Quincy felt slightly guilty about the feelings Holly's body was inciting in her, since she was so scared. But when Holly's backside slid into her groin, it lit a heat inside of her. Holly was on the ground now, but neither moved. Their bodies were tightly pressed together, and Quincy kept her hands on Holly's hips. She had an insatiable urge to pull Holly even tighter into her groin.

"I feel safe now." Holly moved her head back so that her hair was brushing Quincy's cheek.

Quincy closed her eyes and pressed her nose into Holly's soft hair. When she felt Holly press her bottom back into her, she snapped out of her lustful daze. "Um…I'll see to the horses if you want to walk down to the shore."

Holly smiled teasingly. "All right, Stompy."

Quincy showed her how to build a fire, and she helped light it by getting down low on the ground and blowing on the tinder. It was exciting to see the fire burst into life.

They got the tea on the fire and started to eat their picnic. Holly was fascinated by the flames dancing in the fire. She didn't think she'd ever been so content, sitting here on a log by a lake, with a cup of tea, next to Quincy. That was the best part. It was funny. Even though Quincy was much more relaxed, she still didn't say much, but that didn't matter because her body was relaxed, and her whole demeanour was different. Being talkative just wasn't her way.

The only way she was able to express herself was in the letter she had found.

Wait. Had Quincy left that letter visible, so she would find it and read it? It was strange that she'd forgotten her wallet. Quincy always remembered and planned for everything.

"Do you want more tea?" Quincy asked.

"No, I'm fine," Holly said.

She saw Quincy tap her fingers against her tin teacup, as if she was nervous.

"Holly?" Quincy cleared her throat. "Have you ever been in love?"

Holly nearly spat out her mouthful of tea. "My God, Quincy, you stay silent all this time, and then open with that?"

Quincy looked down at the pebbled ground. "We are trained in the military to only give and receive the important information."

"That's an important piece of information to you?" Holly said.

Quincy threw the rest of her tea on the ground and stood. "It doesn't matter. Let's get packed up."

Holly grasped her shirt and pulled. "Hey, sit down. This date isn't finished yet. I learned to ride—well, not ride, but survive riding on a horse for you, so sit."

Quincy appeared surprised by her reprimand but sat back down. "I'm sorry if it's personal. I'm just interested."

"Why?" Holly pushed her. She wanted to see if she could get Quincy to tell her how she felt.

Finally Quincy looked her straight in the eyes and said, "I wanted to know how a beautiful, vibrant, fun-loving woman like you wasn't in a relationship like your friends Queen Beatrice and Lali."

"I haven't wanted to fall in love for a long time. My first love broke my heart, as I told you." Holly gave her a brave smile.

Quincy narrowed her eyes. "What did she do?"

"We were at high school together, went to the same university, and made all these plans for our future—but one day she told me she'd met someone else, and my world fell apart. You know what she told me? Let me go and make me miss you, and then we could maybe have another chance someday."

"Bloody fool. She really said that?" Quincy asked.

Holly nodded. "Yep. She really said that. You know, sometimes I wish I could grab my younger self and give myself a shake for even shedding a tear over her."

"What did you say to her?" Quincy asked.

"With tears rolling down my face, I told her to shove it up her arse and walked off."

Quincy burst out laughing, which was rare for her. "Good for you."

"Yeah, I might have been a fool in love, but I wasn't an idiot. After that I didn't want to feel that way again. So dependent on someone, so out of control. I mostly dated men and tried to live up to my man-eater reputation."

Quincy unexpectedly took her hand and said, "She wasn't worthy of you."

Holly looked down shyly. "I don't know about that."

The conversation stopped there as if both of them were scared of saying what was quite obviously hanging between them. Holly was trying to build up the courage to tell Quincy how she felt when Quincy stood up.

"We better get the horses back to the stables."

Shit. *You've lost your chance, Holls.* She got up and watched as Quincy very carefully doused the fire and made it safe.

Holly followed her up to the bank of the lake and Quincy offered her hand. When she took it, she knew this would be her last chance. When they got back they were having dinner with their friends.

"Quin?"

Quincy turned around. "Yes?"

"I wanted to thank you for today before we get back." Holly moved closer and pulled Quincy to her by grasping her shirt.

And then they were kissing.

"Are you kissing me because you want to ruffle me up again?" Quincy pulled back and asked. Quincy was surprised at first, but then she began to kiss Holly back. She'd wanted to feel Holly's lips again so badly, and now she had them.

Holly traced her finger across her lips. "No, I'm kissing you because I needed to. I needed to taste you and see if it felt as good as the last time."

"And did it?" Quincy asked.

Holly nodded. "Oh yes."

Quincy moved in to kiss her. She couldn't get enough of the taste of Holly. Their kiss became passionate, and Quincy walked them back against the tree behind them.

Quincy's barely restrained passion was pouring out and she couldn't stop. She ran her fingers through Holly's hair. She'd been dreaming of doing that practically since she met her.

Holly held on tight around her neck, and Quincy ran her tongue along Holly's lips and inside her mouth. She tasted with her tongue and lips, the way she wished she could have the first time.

After a life of trying not to get involved with her feelings, Quincy was now revelling in them.

Holly grasped Quincy's hands and put them around her waist. Quincy didn't hesitate to slip them under the hem of Holly's T-shirt and stroked her bare skin. Holly moaned into the kiss, and Quincy pulled their hips together, desperately seeking relief from the tension that was throbbing inside of her.

They finally had to break apart to breathe, and Holly said breathily, "You're good at that. You sure you have never done that before?"

"No. Never. I've never needed or wanted to, until you."

"Wow, you really are one of a kind. A girl's dream," Holly said.

Quincy suddenly felt an anxious fear deep inside of her. She knew if she ever made love with Holly, she would disarm her and demand that nothing be held back, and Quincy didn't know if she was brave enough for that. Yet.

The horses picked that moment to start fussing, and Quincy took the opportunity to press pause. "We'd better get the horses back."

Quincy could see a look of disappointment in Holly's eyes.

CHAPTER NINETEEN

When they got back to the pool house they had to get ready for dinner with their friends, so Holly couldn't get Quincy to talk about what had happened between them again. The longer they didn't mention it, the more awkward it got, plus Bea and Lali weren't exactly subtle over dinner in their encouragement for them to get together, which made things more awkward.

They got back to the pool house after a silent walk from the ranch house. It was as if after showing all the emotion and passion, Quincy was a little bit scared. Holly knew painting her model soldiers always brought calm to Quincy, so she suggested spending the rest of their evening painting.

Holly sat cross-legged on the couch next to Quincy, who had relaxed a good deal.

"I'm getting better at the faces," Holly said, holding up her soldier.

Quincy smiled. "So you are."

"I had a great day today, Quincy. Thanks for making it special. Teaching me to stay on a horse was a great feat."

Quincy said seriously, "I had the best day I've ever had."

Holly looked up and met Quincy's eyes. She didn't know quite how to respond to that. "Thank you."

Then out of the blue Quincy said, "Helen told me not to feel guilty for having a good time with you."

Holly took her hand. "Jacob's wife?"

Quincy nodded and turned her gaze back to her soldier. Holly wondered of Quincy needed to talk about this before they could explore what they felt, because whatever had happened weighed Quincy down like a stone.

"What happened to Jacob?"

Quincy looked up, and then the walls behind her eyes began to shut, so Holly quickly grasped her hand. "Don't run away from this. Tell me what happened, and then you'll be free of it."

Quincy pulled her hand back, got up, and said angrily, "I'll never be free of it."

Holly tried to keep calm. She had to show Quincy she wasn't going to be scared off the subject. "I care about you, Quin. Nothing you say is going to change that. Come and sit down."

Surprisingly Quincy responded and sat back down.

"I know you're fighting against a lifetime of training from the admiral, but you can trust me. You will feel better if you share it."

Holly took her hand and kissed it. Quincy looked at her, but Holly could see in her eyes that she was somewhere else.

"After the King and Crown Prince of Denbourg were assassinated, my unit was on a mission to destroy one of Thea Brandt's weapons stores. It was a warehouse near the water, so we made an amphibious landing. We entered the building and spread out. That's when we realized there were hostages there. Human shields for her weapons."

"Oh my God," Holly said.

"They were ordinary men and women from the local village. Jacob was my second in command, then there was Lieutenant Rodwell, and three other marines. Six went in, three went out."

Holly moved closer and put her hand on Quincy's back.

Quincy continued, "Rodwell had a grudge against me ever since officer training school. He never liked me, and I graduated top of the training group. He was transferred to our unit a year and a half ago, and he hated being under my command."

"So what happened?" Holly asked.

"We had fire support in the hills surrounding the warehouse, but Brandt's people had a lot of firepower guarding it. I remade the plan. We were to split up, get the hostages, and get out the way we came, via an unguarded dock at the back, where our motorboat was waiting."

Holly saw Quincy's hand begin to shake as she recounted her story.

"Rodwell was vocally against the new plan. He didn't care about anyone but himself. He was a coward forced into the marines by his father. Not fit to wear the green beret. I ordered him in no uncertain terms, and we split up."

"Bloody arsehole. Did you get any hostages out?" Holly asked.

"Come with me. You'll be safe." Quincy untied two female hostages on the second floor and led them downstairs. She met Jacob, who was leading a male hostage from behind some crates.

Then they heard gunfire, and the main warehouse doors burst open.

"They know we're here," Quincy said, then shouted into her body mic, "Cover fire!"

Quincy and Jacob made their way to the back of the warehouse while exchanging gunfire with Thea Brandt's men.

Jacob said into his mic, "Phillips, Rodwell, Logan, where are you?"

"Logan here, sir. Phillips and I have two hostages, on our way down."

Quincy looked at Jacob. "Where's Rodwell?" Then she shouted, "Rodwell report."

"Ma'am, look." Quincy turned around to the back of the warehouse, while Jacob fired at those attacking them.

Rodwell was running out their escape route alone. "Rodwell, get back here."

Rodwell looked back and said over the radio, "I'm not dying here in this godforsaken warehouse, just because you want to play hero and rescue villagers who no one cares about."

Then he was out of sight.

"You're a cowardly fucking bastard, Rodwell," Jacob shouted.

It was then that all hell broke loose. They heard explosions all over the large warehouse and screams through their earpieces.

Quincy shouted over the din of the explosions, "This place is wired. Let's get these two out, and then double back for Phillips and Logan."

Jacob nodded, and they made their way to the back exit. Luckily the heavy fire had died down since the explosions, but the wooden warehouse was starting to burn.

When they got the three hostages out the back door, they saw Rodwell, already sailing off in the motorboat, towards their pickup point around the cove.

"He's taken the launch. He's taken our escape!"

Jacob was fuming, but it was Quincy's job to keep them calm and alive.

"We'll deal with that coward later. Now we keep our minds on the job." She spotted a rowboat attached to the small wooden pier where they'd made their landing.

Quincy turned to the hostages and said, "Go down into the boat, and if we're not back in ten minutes, row for shore over there." She pointed to the beaches and habitations a few miles down the coast.

They got them safely into the boat and made their way back into the warehouse. The place was starting to fill with smoke. They could hear their marines shouting for help.

"Let's split up," Quincy said. "Let's get our people."

Jacob smiled and bumped fists with her. "In together, out together."

Quincy said, "Remember, if I don't get you back to Helen, she'll kill me."

Quincy heard a voice pulling her out of her memories. "Quin, Quin, take a breath. Stay with me."

Holly. Holly made her calm, her only light in the darkness. She reached for a bottle of water and took a drink.

"Tell me how your story ends, Quin, but stay with me," Holly said.

"I searched everywhere I could, and then heard Phillips and Logan trapped up the stairs. They were screaming in agony. The stairs had collapsed under the fire, and I couldn't get to them. Then I heard Jacob screaming for help. The smoke was overwhelming me and everyone else, it was hard to search, but then I saw him in one of the rooms. A wooden beam had fallen on his leg, after an explosion. I had to get to him, but the fire was covering the entrance to the door."

"You didn't—you didn't run *into* the flames did you?" Holly said.

"I took my gear off, down to my vest, then put my jacket over my head and ran to him. I got burned but I could cope. Jacob had detonated one of the blasts, and he was badly burned, really badly."

Holly couldn't stop tears—she felt for both Quincy and Jacob. She did all she could think of and put her arms around Quincy.

"I got the beam off his leg. He was screaming for me to put him out of his misery. He asked me to shoot him—he looked me in the eye and pleaded with me to shoot him. I couldn't, I just couldn't. I promised Helen I'd keep him safe."

Holly saw tears starting to pour from Quincy's eyes, and Holly hurt for her even more. "How did you get out?"

Although Quincy was crying, her face was quite like stone. She obviously had such trouble dealing with this.

Quincy turned and looked right at her, tears falling from her eyes. "I put him over my shoulder and moved as quickly as I could. I had to run through the fire to get out the front of the warehouse. Luckily our cover forces had wiped out the enemy and come down from the hills. The last thing I remember is rolling on the ground trying to put out the flames on my body. Then two medics came and knocked me out."

"Oh my God." Holly cupped Quincy's face with her hands and wiped her tears with her thumbs. "I'm so sorry. You've had so much pain, but I'm here for you."

A different look appeared in Quincy's eye, and it was hungry. Quincy kissed her unexpectedly and forcefully. The kiss caught Holly by surprise.

It didn't feel right. It didn't feel like Quincy.

"Quin I don't think—"

Quincy suddenly stopped and said, "I'm sorry. I'm not...I need some space."

She got up and walked out the front door, leaving Holly lost for words, but one thing she did know. Captain Quincy was the most honourable, noblest, bravest person she had ever met.

When she looked in Quincy's tear-stained eyes, she knew she was in love with her.

❖

Quincy walked and walked till she calmed. Sharing her story had been one of the hardest things she'd ever had to do. But as she calmed, unusually for her, instead of running from offered comfort, she wanted to run to it. She wanted, no, she ached for Holly.

Quincy walked back, but Holly had gone to bed. Probably disgusted with her. She went up to her bedroom and changed into her boxers and T-shirt, sat down on the end of her bed, and rubbed her hands together. Quincy wanted to go apologize to Holly, but she was scared.

Jacob's words floated across her mind. He told her to make a life, to grab any chance she got, and to be brave. She got up and walked out of her bedroom and knocked on Holly's door.

"Come in," Holly said.

Quincy took a breath and opened the door. She found Holly lying in bed, looking beautiful as she always did.

"I'm sorry for earlier."

Holly sat up. "For what?"

"Kissing you and then running, pushing you away," Quincy said.

"That's all right," Holly said.

Quincy was longing to go over to her, but she was afraid.

"I've never talked about this before, and it's hard to control what I feel," Quincy said.

Holly pulled back the covers and said, "Don't talk to me from there. Come here."

She patted the bed. Quincy hesitated for a few seconds, then walked over but didn't get in. She had never shared her bed with another woman before, and this wasn't any woman. This was Holly Weaver. She went into the bed but lay quite stiffly on her side looking at Holly, unsure of what to do next.

Holly reached out and stroked Quincy's cheek. "I don't want you to control what you feel with me. I'm Holls. You know I'll never betray you, or use your feelings against you. I know you trust me. Don't you?"

Quincy answered from her heart. "You are the only light in the darkness inside of me."

Holly had never heard anything so painfully beautiful. She scooted closer and said, "Then don't run from me." She inched closer and placed tiny, tender kisses over Quincy's face. Quincy moaned when Holly ran her tongue teasingly over her lips.

Something in Quincy was unleashed in that moment, because she kissed Holly feverishly, and put her hand on Holly's hip to pull their pelvises closer.

Holly wanted to feel Quincy as close to her as she could. She pulled off her nightie and lifted Quincy's hand onto her breast. Quincy touched her breast so softly and tenderly, as if she had been given a special privilege.

"Holly? I want you so much, I need you." Quincy turned them over so Holly was underneath her. Holly loved the feel of Quincy's solid body on hers. She opened her legs, so Quincy could slip between her thighs.

Holly was careful not to touch Quincy's upper body and make her run. She pushed down the sides of Quincy's boxers. "Take them off, Quin. I want to feel you touch me," Holly said, between kisses.

Quincy kicked off her boxers and their sexes came together for the first time. They both groaned, and Quincy said, "You're so beautiful. I want to make you come."

Holly encouraged her by holding onto her backside and pulling her closer. "You're going to. Don't you feel how wet I am?"

"Yes." Quincy grasped both of Holly's plump breasts, and then put her mouth on one, sucking the nipple into her mouth.

Holly tensed and grabbed Quincy's head. "Oh yes, just like that." She knew this was Quincy's first time and wanted to be as vocal as she could to give her lover confidence that she was doing the right thing.

Quincy rolled her wet tongue around her nipple slowly, teasing and sucking. It was driving Holly's desire to new levels, and all she wanted was to feel Quincy inside her.

Quincy started to kiss her way back up Holly's chest and neck, but Holly pulled her back to her lips, then took Quincy's hand and pushed it down to where she wanted it.

"Go inside me, baby," Holly breathed.

Quincy closed her eyes when her fingers slipped between Holly's slick folds. To think that Holly wanted her that much, despite being emotionally challenged and mentally scarred, was more than she deserved.

She stroked all around Holly's clit, her fingers always moving but never directly touching. Quincy was going by how she touched herself, although she hadn't done for such a long time.

"Quin—" Holly hips moved around desperately.

She finally pushed two fingers inside Holly. She loved the way Holly looked when she experienced pleasure. She lived every ounce of what she was feeling.

That was so attractive to her, considering she found living life to the fullest difficult. Holly pressed her leg between Quincy's and said, "Together, Quin."

Quincy hesitated. Letting go herself sexually and emotionally was a scary thing, until Holly placed her hand on Quincy's face and said, "Look at me, and don't be scared. Together—we'll be safe together."

In that moment she believed Holly. She would be safe with Holly, always. Quincy thrust against Holly's thigh while she thrust her fingers inside her. Holly pressed her nails against her backside, making Quin hiss and thrust harder.

She could feel her orgasm so close and was frightened it was going to overwhelm her. She felt the walls of Holly's sex begin to flutter.

"Faster, Quin. I'm going to come. Together, Quin."

Quincy thrust harder onto Holly's thigh and pressed her face into the sweet-smelling hair that had so tantalized her, and her hips began to buck as her orgasm took control and washed over her.

"Fuck, fuck, Holly," Quincy shouted.

A lifetime of tension and sadness that overwhelmed her poured out unrestrained. Holly gave her neck a death grip, and her fingers were gripped by Holly's walls as she came with a cry.

She felt cheated that she couldn't see Holly's face as she came, so she raised herself up and started to stroke Holly's clit with her thumb.

"Bloody hell, Quin," Holly said.

"I want to see you," Quin explained.

Quincy soon felt Holly's walls start to flutter again, so she started thrusting.

Holly said, "Jesus, Quin—" Then she went still as her orgasm washed over her.

Quincy was blown away by how beautiful she looked. As Holly calmed, Quincy eased out her fingers and simply cupped Holly's sex with her hand protectively.

"Do you know how much you mean to me, Holly?" Quincy asked.

Holly shook her head. "No, will you tell me?"

"You've made the light come to the dark places inside me and made me see beauty in the world again. Hope."

Holly pulled her down into a kiss and rolled them over so she was on top. "If you let me, I'll care for you forever." Then she crawled down Quincy's body and was only starting to kiss her, when she got to her hips and then her sex.

Holly opened her up, and she felt Holly's wet tongue lick all around her clit. It felt amazing, and she slammed her head back against the pillow.

"Oh my God."

Holly gave her one big lick and looked up at her sweetly. "I'm going to show you how beautiful the world is, baby."

Holly was awakened by a noise. As she came to, she noticed Quincy was tense, sweating, and quite obviously dreaming.

She looked at the clock. It read four in the morning. "Poor baby."

Quin had been through so many emotions last night, that it was no wonder she was having nightmares, even though she was with her.

She did the only thing she thought she could. She leaned over her and stroked her brow, then her arm. "Shh, it's okay. Quin, you're safe with me," Holly whispered.

Quincy started to thrash. "Get off me. I'm burning!"

Before she knew what was happening, Quincy had flipped her and held her arms by her biceps painfully.

Quincy was big and strong—she had to wake her quickly. "Quincy, it's me!" she shouted.

Quincy's eyes opened suddenly. Her breathing was heavy and laboured.

"It's me, Quin. You're just dreaming."

Quincy looked down at the way she was holding Holly and pulled back her hands immediately. "I'm sorry, I'm so sorry. What have I done?" *You've hurt her. You've hurt Holly.* "Please forgive me. I was dreaming about the medics holding me down. I—"

Holly made a move towards her. "It's okay, Quin. It was just a dream. You weren't trying to hurt me."

She could have killed the woman she loved. She did love Holly, and she had to get away from her. Quincy jumped up and pulled on her boxers.

Holly walked to her.

"No, stay away from me, Holly."

"It was just a nightmare, a reaction to telling me everything that you told me about. Please don't run away. I'm falling in love with you, Quin."

Holly reached out to touch her, but Quin grasped her wrist. "No, I can't be trusted. When I show my emotions, I can't be trusted. This has followed me my whole life. I can't feel."

Holly pulled away from her hand. "Don't give me that crap your bloody admiral mother has fed you all these years. That's why you have so many emotional problems."

Quincy felt that almost like a slap. "I can't love you—I can't love anyone. Don't follow me."

"Run away then. Do whatever you want, Captain," Holly shouted.

Quincy went out Holly's bedroom door and took refuge inside the safety of her own room. She let her head fall back against the door.

She closed her eyes and saw herself holding Holly down, hurting her. If Holly hadn't woken her up, God only knew what would have happened.

I'm not capable of loving someone.

With a lifetime of practice behind her, she tried to force down everything that she felt and shut herself off.

But she'd never tried to shut down love before.

Her mobile on the bedside cabinet beeped with a message. Her heart sank with dread, and she walked over to read it.

I'm back. Are you ready?

CHAPTER TWENTY

Holly woke up and reached for Quincy, but then remembered she was gone. She sat up and looked around the room and remembered what happened last night.

"Argh! One step forward, three steps back."

She pulled on a top and walked downstairs. She saw all of Quincy's bags set at the front door of the pool house. They weren't leaving till late this afternoon, but Quincy was eager to leave.

Holly made a cup of coffee and walked outside onto the porch area and sat down. She watched the ranch staff coming and going. Everyone was busy. She smiled when she saw George walking out the front door of the house with Teddy on her shoulders. George was such a good parent, and Bea had said they would be trying for another baby soon. George and Bea were the perfect couple, and the perfect family, something for them all to aspire to.

Could she have that with Quincy? That was up to Quincy, but if she ran every time they had a problem, especially with all the battle scars Quincy carried, what chance did they have?

One thing was for sure, she was falling for Quincy big time. She heard footsteps and looked up, expecting to find Quincy, but instead she saw Garrett walking towards her.

"Morning, Holly."

"Garrett." Holly hoped Garrett would keep on walking, but she didn't.

"I hear you've spent a cosy week with Quincy? Word on the grapevine is that you're together."

"How is that any of your business?" Holly said sharply.

"I did warn you. She was drummed out of the marines for violence, and she's starting the same shit here. Quincy is unhinged."

Holly put down her coffee and jumped to round on Garrett. "Don't you ever say that in my presence, Garrett. Quincy is a hero, who has gone through hell for our country."

"Oh, touchy. She's over there trying to convince Inspector Lang there is some grand conspiracy to harm the Queen Consort, but surprisingly the only one who has any threats is Quincy. Funny that, eh?"

"What are you talking about?" Holly couldn't believe what she was hearing.

"What?" Garrett held her hand to her chest in mock surprise. "Captain Fantastic didn't tell you there's been lots of apparent new threats texted to her?"

Holly said nothing but inside she was angry, both at Garrett and at Quincy. She thought last night Quincy had completely opened up to her. Why would Quincy keep these threats to her best friend a secret? She had thought there was just the first one Garrett had told her about and no more.

"I'll take your silence as a no, then," Garrett said. Then she looked her up and down, and said, "She been violent to you too?"

"What? No," Holly said angrily.

Garrett pointed down to her arm. "Are you sure?" Then she walked off.

Holly looked at her arm and saw fingermarks. Shit, if Quin saw those, she would be even more upset than she was last night.

Quincy returned from the direction of the barn, presumably where she'd been meeting with Lang. "What did Garrett want?"

"Why didn't you tell me about the threats against Bea?" She hadn't told Quincy she knew about the first. Holly noticed she was back to wearing her grey suit and darker grey tie, and she didn't have her hair done as Holly had styled it. It was back to combed over to the side.

Clearly the holiday was over, and she was back to Captain Stompy.

Quincy didn't answer. She walked into the pool house and took a bottle of water out of the fridge.

"Well?" Holly followed her.

Quincy took a sip of water. "You didn't need to know, and you shouldn't have known. I told my commanding officer."

"And? What happened?" Holly said. "Bea is my best friend."

"Lang didn't take it seriously, and so I made my own enquiries. Whoever it is has been sending me messages. They stopped when we came here, but last night they started again. I told Cammy, and now Lang is furious that I broke the chain of command. There, you know everything, happy now?"

"No. Why did you run last night. We—" Holly remembered the marks on her arm and covered them up quickly. "We shared something so special. You told me all the pain you had been carrying, and we made love."

"Then I hurt you," Quincy said. "I told you, it's not safe for you. I can't be with anyone—I'm too scarred."

Holly felt the tears start to roll down her face. "What? Of course you're safe." She took a step towards Quincy and put one hand on Quincy's chest while the other cupped her cheek. "I understand the pain you carry, but you can share it with me. I'm falling in love with you."

Quincy closed her eyes and rested her forehead against Holly's. "I want to protect you from everything, even me."

Holly kissed Quincy softly. "You could never hurt me."

Quincy opened her eyes and began to say, "I want—" Then her eyes wandered to Holly's arm. "What is this? These are from last night, aren't they?" Quincy said with real panic in her voice.

Holly was frightened that Quincy was going to run, but what could she do but tell the truth? "Yes, but it was a one-off. It was just because you talked about your mission for the first time."

Quincy recoiled with a horrified look on her face. "I'm so sorry, so sorry. You are the last person I would hurt."

"I know. It's okay." Holly tried to reach out to Quincy but she backed away. Holly saw all the walls she had knocked to the ground rise before her very eyes.

A cold stillness came upon Quincy. She adjusted her tie and said, "The admiral was right. Only bad things happen when I let my emotions rule me. I can't be with you in that way, Ms. Holly. Last night was a mistake."

"A mistake?"

Quincy nodded and walked out the door.

Holly gazed at Quincy across the plane, and she wouldn't meet her eyes. *She's scared.*

"Don't push her, Holly. She'll come to you. She has a lot on her mind," Bea said.

Holly, Bea, and Lali were sitting together on their plane trip to LA. Queen Georgina was in conference with Inspector Lang and Cammy.

Holly hadn't told Bea or Lali about Quincy's nightmare, and the real reason she had run. It was far too personal, and they might not understand. She only told them that they'd slept together, and then Quincy had backed off from what she felt.

"She's a bloody idiot," Holly said. "You know her mother made her this way? Punished her for showing emotions?"

"The admiral?" Bea said. "Yes, George told me about her. Sounds like a frightening woman."

Holly lay back in the seat and let out a breath. "It's so hard to break though the indoctrination the admiral gave her."

"But you want to keep trying, don't you?" Lali said.

"I'm not giving up on her, no matter what she thinks."

Quincy could feel Holly's eyes boring into her from across the plane. She gazed at her hands and felt such shame that these hands could hurt the woman she loved. Maybe the admiral was right—only bad things happened when you let emotion rule you, just like her birth mother had.

Both her personal and private lives were under stress this morning. After receiving the new message last night, she'd contacted Blade first, who'd said she might have something and asked for more time, and then she had to go and talk to Cammy.

Breaking the chain of command was taboo to Quincy, but she felt like she had no other choice. She spoke to Cammy, who was concerned and immediately took it to the Queen.

George had then summoned Inspector Lang for a meeting back at the ranch house. Lang was annoyed with her, and the protection squad were not happy with her either.

At the moment Lang, Cammy, and the Queen were having a conference call with their liaison at the CIA, asking for their help with these anonymous threats.

"You did the right thing, ma'am."

She looked up at Clay who was sitting at the other side of the table. "I hope so. No matter what happens, we have to keep on our toes."

"Yes, ma'am."

CHAPTER TWENTY-ONE

"Garrett?" Quincy's rage surged through her. "I can't believe it."

When they landed in LA, Quincy had a message to call Blade as soon as possible. She didn't get that chance till the afternoon, as the Queen and the consort went to the Los Angeles County Museum of Art, where they were opening a British art exhibition.

As soon as she was assigned her room at the new hotel, she called.

"I've been monitoring everyone in your team, just as a matter of course. Garrett received a call yesterday evening, then left the barn and walked out into the woods. I hijacked the ranch's security cameras."

"You are good, Blade. Why would she turn against her Queen?" Quincy asked as she paced up and down.

"She's working with someone. Following instructions. I'm trying to hack into her messages, but they are heavily protected. Hold fire until I know more. Don't let her know you are on to her."

Quincy hung up and threw the phone on her bed. There was a knock at the door. She opened it, and Holly walked in.

"Hi, I hoped we could talk," Holly said.

"I really don't want to talk," Quincy said.

"You never do. Don't be so cold and closed off to me again. We spent a lovely week together and we slept together, if you remember. We need to talk about us."

"I remember. There is no us. I can't be with you," Quincy said firmly.

"You love me—I know you do. You're just scared."

"What I'm doing is protecting you. I don't want to hurt you. Besides, I don't have time for this. I've got lots of other things on my mind."

"Oh, you do, do you?" Holly looked furious. "I never thought you'd be the sleep with them and run type."

"Like your precious Story St. John? Despite the fact she sleeps with everything that moves, you and your friends giggle about her like schoolgirls. I sleep with you once and don't want to see you any more, and I'm bad?"

"Story St. John hasn't slept with me and dumped me, only you," Holly said.

"Well, give her time. She's taking you out to the gala dinner in a few days. I'm sure she'll get her chance then."

Holly felt tears starting to roll down her face. "How could you say that? You don't expect that I'm going out with Story after what we've shared?"

"You should go out with her. I don't want a relationship. Could I make that any clearer?"

Holly hurried to the door, and Quincy stopped her. "I don't mean to be so harsh. I just can't be the person who made love to you. I can't afford to let myself feel."

Holly wiped her tears away and said, "Jacob told you to grab any chance you had at a life and love, but I suppose you just want to ignore your best friend and wallow in your pit of despair for the rest of your life. The admiral, mark two."

Holly walked away and slammed the door. Quincy rested her head against the wall. It was destroying her to be so cold to Holly—she was everything to her. But Holly's safety was more important.

❖

Quincy stood outside the Queen's room with Clay, waiting on the royal party. Tonight was the UNICEF gala. The gala that Holly had been invited to by Story. Cammy had told her she was a bloody idiot for trying to get away from Holly. But encouraging her to go out with another woman seemed like a good idea at the time. Now the churning inside of her was killing her. The worst of it was she was going to have a front row seat.

Holly came from the consort's dressing room. She looked utterly breathtaking in her dress for this evening. Holly stopped and gazed at her. She didn't look happy.

Holly walked up to them and said, "Clay, can I steal Quin for a few seconds?"

"Sure. You look beautiful by the way, Holly," Clay said.

"Thank you, Clay."

Clay tactfully took a few steps away, and Quincy said, "You do look beautiful, Holly."

"Tell me not to go, and I won't, Stompy," Holly said.

Quincy was taken aback. She really was still willing to fight for her after she had pushed her away? Holly deserved so much more than Quincy could give her. She thought of how Holly's body felt in her hands, and when she imagined someone else touching her like that, she felt sick, but she couldn't be what Holly needed emotionally.

Quincy kissed her forehead and said, "Have a good time."

A look of sadness and anger came over Holly. "Don't worry. I'll make sure I have a bloody good time."

Holly gazed at the beautiful art on Story St. John's walls. It was exquisite, as was Story's penthouse flat. It was like an apartment from an interior decorator's magazine.

There was a large comfortable couch beside her and an open fireplace in front of her, with a mantel at shoulder height, then above that a gorgeous art print.

After the gala Story had asked her back for a drink, and she accepted just so she didn't have to go back to the hotel. It was funny—a few months ago the thought of being in Story St. John's penthouse would have made her faint, but not now. Now her heart ached for someone else.

"Here we go." Story walked towards her with a bottle of champagne and two glasses. She looked adorably sexy with her bow tie hanging undone around her collar.

"You have a beautiful apartment, Story, and your art is amazing," Holly said.

"Thanks." Story gave her a glass and poured out some champagne. "I don't know anything about art. It's all my interior decorator's work."

Holly took her glass and sipped the champagne. "I suppose all the women say that to you."

Story grinned. "No, normally any woman who comes up to my apartment goes straight to the bedroom. Art isn't the main thing on their mind."

Holly laughed. "But not me."

"Not you, you're different, Holly." Story indicated for them to sit down.

Story had been so attentive tonight and hadn't checked her social media once.

"Why am I different?" Holly asked.

"You don't treat me like a film star, just like a normal person."

Holly was intrigued. Story had definitely lost some of her bravado. "You seem different tonight, Story."

Story looked down sheepishly. "I was looking forward to seeing you again. I really enjoyed meeting someone who wasn't in my circle. It can be so tiring being Story St. John."

Holly smiled. "It must be. So there's another Story?"

"You could say that. I feel more at ease with you. You're real, and the people I socialize with are never real."

"It all looks so glamorous, your world, but I suppose there are downsides," Holly said.

Story looked at her glass and swirled the champagne around. "I had hoped we might be able to see each other again, but then I saw the way you were looking at Queen Bea's bodyguard."

Holly gulped. She hadn't meant to be impolite and look at another woman all night, but she was just drawn to Quincy.

"I'm sorry. When you called me to ask about us, there really was nothing going on, but then we got closer."

Story smiled. "That's okay, babe. You win some, you lose some. She was looking at you just as much. I wish someone would look at me that way."

Holly raised an eyebrow. "Story, women more than look at you all the time. They lust after you."

Story shook her head. "They don't look at me the way she was looking at you, Holly. She is so into you."

"We're not even together. I thought we were, but she's frightened of feeling," Holly said.

She saw a flash of hurt in Story's eyes. "Sometimes people can be so scared of love, babe, they lose everything. Give her a chance to come around."

"Are you speaking from experience?" Holly asked. She couldn't believe Story looked so emotional. She was nothing like the film-star Story.

"Yeah, even Story St. John was in love. I fucked it up. People do stupid things when they're scared of what they feel. Give her a chance?"

Holly smiled and took Story's hand. "I'll try. You should show this side of you more often."

"That's not what everyone I meet wants. They want the woman you met on our first date."

"I hope you get another chance, Story." Holly kissed her on the cheek. "Thank you for tonight."

As much as it killed Quincy, she sat up in the rec room waiting for Holly to get back, just to know she was safe. She'd gone somewhere with Story after the gala and hadn't come back with the royal party.

Clay had gone to bed a long time ago, and she was left alone. Would it always be this painful watching Holly be with someone else?

In the long term it probably wouldn't be Story, but someone would come along and give Holly what she couldn't.

Jacob and Helen would be so disappointed in her. A chance at happiness, and she was walking away from it. Sharing herself, all of her body and soul, was just too hard, and she wasn't that brave.

She tried to console herself that when they were back in London, she wouldn't see as much of Holly, only during the workday. It wouldn't be like here, where they were thrown together constantly.

Quincy sat staring at her computer pad, trying to work and reply to some emails, but her head was just filled with images of Holly and Story together.

She heard the lift doors open, and she knew it was Holly. Quincy looked at her watch. It was two thirty in the morning. Had Holly slept with Story? The thought killed her.

The last time they were in this position, Holly was giggly drunk, and she'd helped her back to her room. This was so different.

Holly walked into the rec room. She wasn't giggly this time. She looked sad.

"Why are you still up?" Holly asked.

"I wanted to know that you got home safely," Quincy said.

Holly sighed inwardly. Quincy quite obviously cared for her, she was in as much pain as she was, but she wouldn't give in to love.

"Well, I'm home safely," Holly said.

She could see in Quincy's face how much she wanted to know about what had happened with Story.

"Did you have a good time when you left?"

Holly strode to her. "You want to know if I slept with Story, so that you can heap more pain on yourself, wallow in it, and feel safe that nothing will ever come of your feelings, of the fact that you love me. Because I know you do. Well, bad luck, Captain. I spent the evening telling Story about the woman I love, the woman I want more than anything in the world, and the fact that she doesn't want me. So, no, I didn't sleep with her."

Quincy appeared shocked at her outburst and said nothing.

Holly wasn't stopping. "Remember these words? *You think I'm emotionless and that I don't notice you, but my eyes adore you when you don't know I'm watching. I love the way you live each breath of your life with fun and enthusiasm, feeling every moment. Sometimes when I look at you, I stop breathing and wish I could be the one who makes you smile and laugh, but how can I be that for you when I can't feel? If I let myself feel, I would—well, I don't know what I would become, but it is terrifying to me.* You can't keep those feelings locked up."

She turned around and hurried to her bedroom.

CHAPTER TWENTY-TWO

When Holly got behind her bedroom door she threw her handbag on her bed. Tears were spilling over, and she was sick of being emotional. This wasn't Holly—Holly was the life and soul of the party, always having a smile on her face.

This Holly was a lovesick fool, just like the last time she had loved a woman. She should never have gotten close to another woman in the first place. Her heart being ripped in two was not what she'd had in mind. She couldn't even enjoy a date with Story because of bloody Captain Quincy.

She fell down on the bed and growled in frustration.

There was a knock at her door. She got up and opened it, and Quincy walked straight in. She stroked Holly's cheek. "I'm sorry for the way I am, and I'm sorry I told you to go out with Story—it killed me. I want to be different. I love you, Holly, and I want you to help me."

Holly was not expecting this. It was her dream come true, but dreams so often turned into nightmares. Holly pushed Quincy gently. "I can't do this again and have you run away. I can't go through a broken heart again, Quin."

"I won't run. I was scared that I would hurt you," Quincy said.

"I told you that nightmare was a one-off. You'd just spent the evening telling me things you probably didn't even tell your doctor when you got home. Am I right?"

Quincy nodded. "No one knows all of what I told you, and you're right, since I told you, I feel lighter. Maybe I felt guilty because of that and looked for excuses. I got a medal for bravery, and I wasn't brave enough to give you all of myself."

Holly was surprised when Quincy started to undo her tie.

"I have to be brave enough to show you everything, my scars on the inside and out." Quincy took a step towards Holly and placed her hands on her buttons. "I'm ready. I want to be yours, if you still want me, after you've seen everything."

She was actually going to lay bare everything, and that trust meant so much to Holly. "Thank you for your trust. I love you."

Quincy still tensed and looked scared as Holly opened the first button on her shirt. "It's okay. You're safe."

Holly undid the buttons one by one. Underneath the shirt was a high necked vest. She threw the shirt to the side and inched the vest up slowly.

As Quincy's scars were revealed, Holly couldn't stop the tears from falling. Quincy's shoulders and arms were muscular and well developed. She was a soldier through and through. Her pink burn scars ran from her belly button and stopped just at her collarbone, but they weren't unsightly in any way. They were the mark of the brave heart that beat inside Quincy's chest.

Quincy tensed, and Holly stopped her. "No. You went through so much for your men and women, for your best friend."

She dropped the vest and now Quincy was naked from the waist up. Holly ran her fingers over her scars reverently. "How could you ever think you weren't capable of emotion? Love gave you these battle scars."

"But my men are dead, and Jacob is—" Quincy's voice cracked.

"You see these scars as if they represent your failure, but as I see them, they represent your bravery, your love for your unit. You gave everything in you to save them, and I love you for it."

The more Holly touched Quincy's chest the more Quincy relaxed. She ran her fingertips over Quincy's breasts, which didn't have as many scars, and then brushed her nipples, and they hardened.

"You're beautiful and handsome, Captain. Everything I've ever wanted." Holly turned around and said, "Take me out of my dress."

"Anything you ask." Quincy unzipped the dress and it pooled at Holly's feet. Quincy was captivated and released from all restraints. She had shown Holly everything and she still wanted her.

She felt so light, like a huge tonne weight was suddenly gone, and as long as Holly loved her, it would not return.

Quincy watched Holly step out of her underwear and unclasp her bra. The sight of Holly's body was too much for Quincy. She held Holly's hips and kissed her. Now that Quincy had let go, her love, want, and need were like a torrent that would never be sated.

Quincy lifted her, and Holly wrapped her legs around Quincy's hips. She walked Holly over to the bed and laid her down.

When Quincy began kissing down her belly, Holly pulled her up and said, "No, just kiss me, just kiss me. I want you to kiss me until we come."

Quincy gazed at the love shining from Holly's eyes and was transfixed. "I can't believe you love me and gave me another chance. I'm sorry for how I treated you the last time."

Holly cupped her face and locked her legs around Quincy's backside, drawing their bodies as close as she could get. Their lips were barely touching, and parted, each breathing in the other, and Holly said, "I couldn't do anything else but love you. There is no one else in the world I could have fallen in love with, Quin."

Their lips met softly and tenderly, not with the feverish want that had marked the first time they slept together. Quincy followed Holly's lead and sank into her. Nothing had ever felt so intense or all encompassing. This was not how she'd ever imagined sex. This was love, and Quincy was never going to let go.

Quite naturally their hips started to move together slowly, to match their soft wet kisses. Quincy felt like she was melting into Holly, who kept her legs tight around her, squeezing them together. Their tongues danced, loving and giving, and Quincy was becoming lost.

Her orgasm built, and she thrust her hips faster. She could feel Holly's wetness on her sex, mixing with her own. They were melded together now, and nothing was hidden.

She pulled her lips back from Holly's and said in a shaky, breathy voice, "I'm going to come. I can't—"

Holly wrapped her hands around the back of her head, holding Quincy close. "I want you to come. Just let me look at your gorgeous blue eyes."

Quincy nodded, rested her forehead against Holly's, and hastened her thrusts. Holly kept her hands on Quincy's cheeks, and she felt more connected to Holly than she could have thought possible.

Her orgasm soared and crashed across her body. When she cried out, Holly kissed her, taking all she had to give.

Holly began to surface from sleep. Images of Quin touching her, loving her, floated across her mind. It had been perfect, and Quincy had allowed her to touch her most scarred places, emotionally and physically. But even before she opened her eyes, there was a big part of Holly that expected Quincy to have left her bed.

She cracked open her eyes, and there, with her arm and leg draped across her body and gazing at her with big open eyes, was Quincy.

"Good morning, darling Holly."

"Morning, Stompy." Holly was tense and frightened that anything she might say would cause her to run.

Quincy smiled and stroked Holly's hair softly. "Your hair is even more beautiful tousled than styled."

"Hardly. It'll be a mess. I never even brushed it last night," Holly said.

Quincy shook her head. "You know, the first time I saw you, I wanted to run my fingers through your hair."

"You did?" Holly was surprised Quincy wasn't tense, she wasn't running, and she was still naked, and not hiding her scars.

Quincy nodded, and Holly caressed her cheek. "It was your eyes. The first time I saw you, as grumpy as you were, I was lost in these blue eyes that were beautiful but had seen terrible things. I wanted to soothe your pain. Plus you're an Adonis, so that helps."

"But I tried to stop you at every turn," Quincy said.

Holly giggled softly. "I just had to unravel you first."

"Given our positions, I think you have," Quincy joked.

Holly pushed Quincy onto her back and leaned over her, smiling. "Was that a joke, Stompy?"

Quincy pulled Holly on top of her and stroked her fingers up and down Holly's bare back.

"I think so, but then I'm so unaccustomed to humour, I couldn't be quite sure. But you always know what I'm feeling, so I defer to you," Quincy said.

When she had woken up and felt Holly's arms, Quincy felt safe for the first time in her life. Which was astonishing, given that she had shown not only her deepest feelings, but the scarred body that she was so ashamed of and which caused her such guilt.

Holly had loved her, loved all of her battle scars, as Holly put it, and when Quincy fell asleep, she hadn't dreamt her nightly terrors. She wasn't naive. Quincy knew her past was something she would always live with, but now her pain, her fear, were subdued by the love in her heart.

And yet there was still one secret she hadn't shared. Garrett.

"What are you thinking?" Holly said.

Quincy didn't know if she could verbalize what was in her heart. She tried, but she stuttered and stammered.

Holly, sensing her difficulty, filled the gap. "You know, nothing happened with Story last night."

"I know. You told me," Quincy said.

"Yeah, but I mean *nothing*. When we were dancing at the gala, she saw me looking at you and guessed that I was involved with you."

Quincy was surprised. She had met Holly's eyes a few times, but she didn't think she had distracted Holly from her date.

"Involved?" Quincy questioned what that meant.

Holly traced her fingernail down around Quincy's eye to her lips. "I told her I was in love with you."

Quincy could only say, "You did?"

Holly nodded. "She understood. Story's quite nice to talk to, actually, when she's not with her entourage or worrying about her publicity. She asked me back to hers to talk, and we did. That's all."

"Because you were in love?" Quincy repeated.

Holly nodded. Quincy knew she had to share what she knew about Garrett. Holly had given so freely to her, and she had to do the same. Queen Beatrice was her best friend, after all.

Quincy rolled them over so she was on top. "I have to tell you something, but you must promise not to tell anyone, not Queen Beatrice, not Lali."

Holly looked worried. "What? Why, what's wrong?"

"Do you promise? This is really serious, Holly," Quincy said.

"I promise, just tell me."

Quincy sighed. "You know the messages I've been getting?"

"The threats to Bea? Yeah, what about them?"

Quincy rolled off Holly and sat up against the headboard, and Holly did the same.

"I've had an old friend from military intelligence looking into it, and she's found out the messages are coming from Garrett."

"Garrett?" Holly said loudly. "That bloody creepy Garrett is plotting to hurt Bea? I'm going to kill her."

Holly went to get up, but Quincy caught her. "Hang on, Supergirl. Listen to me—she's taking her orders from someone else. We need to find out who, so we can't let her know we are on to her."

Holly sat astride Quincy's lap. "You mean I have to look at her, be around her, and not let her know I want to kill her for threatening my friend?"

Quincy took Holly's hand and kissed it. "Yes. I know keeping your feelings to yourself is a hard thing for you, but this is so important."

"Was that another joke?" Holly smiled.

"Yes, I'm getting better at it. Please, Holly, I shouldn't even have told you," Quincy said.

Holly leaned forward and pressed her hand to the middle of Quincy's chest. "Oh no, Captain Stompy. You tell me everything. Do you promise you'll keep Bea safe?"

"I promise you. No one will hurt Queen Beatrice."

"I love you," Holly said.

"I love you, darling Holly. Thank you for last night. You chase away the darkness inside me. You make the sun come out."

Holly stroked her cheek. "You are heartbreakingly beautiful. What a lucky woman I am."

CHAPTER TWENTY-THREE

Bea watched Holly in the mirror, as she straightened her hair for her. She looked miles away, but not in a happy place, which was strange since she and Quincy were together now. "Holls? Are you all right? I thought you would be happy as a pig in mud now that you and Quincy were together."

"Sorry, I am. I—it's just some of the things Quin told me about her mission are playing on my mind."

"The mission she won the VC for?" Bea asked.

"Yeah, that's it," Holly said a little too quickly.

Holly finished with her hair and began to touch up her make-up. "So is your Adonis everything you hoped she would be?"

Holly giggled and snapped from her concerned looking mood. "Oh yes, and then some."

Bea wiggled her eyebrows. "I bet."

Queen Georgina walked into the dressing room holding Princess Edwina.

Holly curtsied. "Morning, Your Majesty."

"Good morning, Holly."

Bea said to George, "We've just been talking about Captain Quincy and what an Adonis she is."

George raised an eyebrow. "Indeed?"

Bea looked George up and down and said, "Cammy let you wear jeans today? My, my."

"Special dispensation since we are going to Story Park. I'm told not to get used to it," George joked.

They all laughed. Today the royal party was touring a large theme park and opening a new part of the attraction. Princess Edwina was very excited to meet all her favourite characters from Story Park.

"Are we nearly ready? Teddy here is getting a bit fed up," George said.

"Mummy," Teddy whined and reached her arms to Bea.

George carried her over to Bea. "Tell Mummy who you want to meet, Teddy."

Bea took hold of Teddy and kissed her head. "Tell Mummy who, Teddy."

Teddy looked at her with the same blue eyes as George and said, "Big Bear."

Big Bear was one of Story Park's most famous characters. "I'm sure we'll meet him, and Mum will buy you a cuddly Big Bear to be friends with your Rupert Bear."

"Yes, yes!" Teddy said excitedly.

There was a knock at the door, and Lali walked in, holding her ever-present computer pad, and curtsied.

"Morning, Your Majesties. I just wanted to go over the itinerary for today again."

Holly rolled her eyes. "Again, Lali? I think we know what we're doing."

"Fire away, Lali. It never hurts to go over one's battle plans again," George said.

"Are we expecting a battle, Georgie?" Bea joked.

"A figure of speech."

Holly was looking forward to today. Bea had asked her to go and help with Teddy since the theme park and the crowds would be a bit much for Nanny Baker. She wouldn't have to count the hours till they got back to see Quincy again, although she was worried about Garrett and whatever she was up to. And tonight, when they got back to the hotel, Quincy promised to take her out to a swish LA restaurant—but the more Holly thought about it, all she wanted to do was have dinner here, paint some soldiers, and make love.

Lali began to read out the plans. "We will be met at the entrance by the Story Park executives and park manager. After introductions, a young member of staff will come forward with flowers for you Bea, and a toy for Teddy."

"You hear that, Teddy?" Bea said.

"Hey, I hope I get a toy too," Holly said.

Lali continued, "Next, you'll be taken to the new section of the park. There will be a stage where you, Queen Bea, Princess Edwina, and the execs will sit. Queen Georgina, you will be introduced, and then you'll make a speech—"

It was then that they heard shouts and commotion outside.

"What the devil is that?" George hurried to the door, and Holly followed. They found Quincy being dragged off Garrett by Lang and the team.

"Get her off me," Garrett shouted. "She attacked me. She's a psycho."

Lang held Quincy back. "I'm sorry to disturb you, ma'am."

George said, "What on earth is going on here?"

"A petty squabble taken too far," Lang said. "Quincy, go back to your room and stay there."

Holly was furious. To get Quincy to react like that, Garrett must have said something very bad.

"Yes, sir." Quincy looked at Holly before starting to walk off.

"No, Inspector Lang, Garrett—" Holly started to say.

"No, Holly." Quincy cut her off. "Just leave it."

Holly had to wait for what seemed like hours, but was only half an hour, to see Quincy. Inspector Lang and the Queen had to speak to her first.

Quincy opened her door and Holly jumped into her arms. "Oh my God. I thought I'd never get to see you." She gave Quincy a kiss on the lips. "What happened, baby?"

"Come and sit," Quincy said.

They sat on the bed and Holly held Quincy's hand. "Tell me."

"I'm sorry for letting my temper get the better of me, especially after me telling you not to react to Garrett," Quincy said.

"I know it takes a lot for you to lose control. What happened?" Holly asked.

"Ever since our security briefing this morning, Garrett had been chipping and chipping away at me. It was as if she was determined this was going to happen. In fact when I grabbed her and pushed her against the wall, she smiled at me."

"Why would she want to do that?" Holly said.

Quincy shrugged. "I should have been the bigger person. I should have kept control."

"What did she say?"

"There was a lot of gossip about us. Other staff members saw me leaving your room this morning. She made comments, and I don't want to repeat them."

"I'm a big girl, Quin. Tell me?"

"She made comments about your reputation with men, and being with Story, then me, in the one night, and that she'd be happy to take my place with Queen Beatrice, and with you, once I've been kicked out of the squad. In not as nice language, of course."

"So basically, I'm a bit of a slut who was fucked by Story and you in one night, and she'd be happy to as well?" Holly said.

Quincy put an arm around her shoulder. "I was trying to put it in nicer language."

"Bitch," Holly said angrily. "I wouldn't touch her with a ten-foot bargepole. I know you were defending my honour, Quin, but you gave her what she wants—the team to think you're a loose cannon."

"I know. The Queen and Lang want me to take a few days off, until they see what's going to happen."

"What? You're not going with us today? But that will mean Bea is protected by Garrett, the one who sent the threats."

"Apparently the Queen got some pressure from the prime minister after what happened in Chicago but fended her off. This makes it harder."

Suddenly the penny dropped. "You don't mean you might be replaced permanently?"

Quincy nodded. "Maybe, we don't know yet."

"They can't send you away." Holly cupped Quincy's cheeks. "I've just found you, Stompy. I want you here with us in the royal court, or else how often would we see each other? I'm going to George and Bea."

Quincy stopped her. "Stop. I want to let this play out, find out who Garrett is working with. I want you to go today and be alert. Watch her, and Clay will be doing the same. She knows about this."

Holly flopped down onto Quincy's knee and put her arms around her neck. "Okay, but just for a few days. I'm not going to let Garrett do this to you."

"I love you, Holly," Quincy said.

Holly laid her forehead against Quincy's and said, "I love you too, baby."

❖

Quincy paced around her room. The royal party had left, as well as Holly. How had she let her anger control her again?

Her phone rang—it was Blade. "Quincy."

"Quincy, I've found it. Garrett received a message to get you out of the way today. Where are you?"

"I'm at the hotel. Garrett and I had a confrontation. The Queen Consort is being protected by Garrett. They're visiting a theme park today."

"God, that's a busy, big open space. You need to get there. Lieutenant Rodwell left the UK for the US yesterday."

"Shit."

Quincy hung up and phoned Holly as she ran down the hall of the hotel.

"Holly? Where is the Queen Consort?"

"She's meeting with some of the staff before they go onstage for the speeches. Clay and I have Teddy—she was being bad tempered and wanted to stay with Big Bear. What's wrong?"

Quincy looked at her watch. Could she even get there in time?

"Tell Clay to stay with you and Princess Edwina no matter what," Quincy said. If she passed the intel to Clay and asked her to alert Lang, too many people would be involved, too much potential for leaks. Rodwell might pick something up and act earlier.

"Quin—" Holly said.

"I need to go." Quincy hung up and ran.

CHAPTER TWENTY-FOUR

Quincy pushed her way through the crowd. Her heart was pounding with fear, the fear of failing, just as she had failed Jacob and her men and women.

She finally saw the stage. The Queen Consort was making a speech, while George sat and watched. The audience around the stage was thick with people. She needed some height.

Quincy looked around and saw some fencing close to the stage. She climbed up and scanned the crowd. She heard her name called and looked down. It was Holly with Teddy, and Clay.

"I told you to stay where you were," Quincy said sharply.

"Sorry, Captain. Holly wanted to find you," Clay said.

"What is this all about, Quin?" Holly said.

Then Quincy saw him. The face she would never forget, the face that left them to their deaths, and he was pushing towards the front to the stage.

Quincy jumped down and took Teddy from Holly and gave her to Clay. "Clay, go back to the car, and lock yourself in with the princess. Don't stop, don't look back, no matter what you hear. Do you understand?"

Clay held Teddy protectively. "Yes, ma'am."

"What in God's name is going on, Quin?" Holly said.

"Lieutenant Rodwell is here. Stay back. I love you."

"Quincy, don't!" Holly called after Quincy as she ran to the stage.

Holly knew that Quincy would give her life for her friends, and this might be the last time she saw her.

She watched with horror as people in the crowd screamed. Quincy ran onstage, grabbed Bea, and turned her back to the crowd. Shots rang out, and Quincy and Bea fell. Holly screamed, "No!"

Pandemonium broke out.

Quincy heard distant voices and beeps as she began to awaken. Then the pain started to awaken her more. She opened her eyes and she saw Holly's smiling face, and her chest was filled with love.

"Hey, you're back with us, Stompy." Holly looked happy but had tears running down her cheeks.

Quincy could do nothing more than croak the words, "Love you."

Holly leaned over and kissed her so gently. "That's quite a few times you've said that, so it must be true."

She tried to remember what had happened, and images of running onto a stage and shots fired at the Queen Consort filled her mind.

"Bea…Queen—" Quincy tried to sit up, but pain seared through her chest and ribs.

"Don't, Quin. Calm down." Holly helped her ease back and she sat and held her hand. "Bea is absolutely fine. You saved her."

Quincy finally rested her head back on the pillow. "What happened?"

"Lieutenant Rodwell shot at Bea, but you grabbed Bea and took the bullets instead of her," Holly said.

Everything started to flood back to her. Grabbing Bea to the ground, the hot pain as the bullets entered her body. Lang and the others pulling Bea and George away from the scene. Cammy cradling her, while shots were fired again.

"Did they get him?"

"Yes. He's gone, and Garrett is in custody," Holly said.

Quincy nodded. "I heard you shouting for me," Quincy said.

Holly used a tissue to wipe away her tears. "They wouldn't let me through. I struggled and shouted, and eventually Cammy saw me and waved me over. I was more scared than I ever have been in my life. I held you till help arrived, and I warned you that if you died, I would kill you."

Quincy laughed and groaned in pain. "Don't make me laugh."

"Don't ever try and die. I've just found you." Holly kissed her hand.

"Hey, I'm here. I'm not going anywhere, if I can help it. I love you, Holly."

"I love you, Stompy." Holly stood and kissed her. "The Queen is outside waiting to see you. I better go and get her."

Holly left and George came in by herself. Quincy bowed her head. George smiled. "Any excuse for a lie down, eh?"

"Your Majesty, I would get up if I could."

George sat down beside her bed. "You had us all very worried, Captain."

"How long have I been out?" Quincy had never thought to ask Holly. She had assumed it was only hours.

"A week," George replied.

"Bloody hell."

"How do you feel?" George asked.

Every part of Quincy hurt. "Oh, you know. No more than a forced march through the Highlands in the driving rain."

George smiled. Quincy knew the Queen knew she was putting a brave face on the situation. Then the Queen looked serious. "Lang would like to see you too. He's very sorry he didn't listen to you."

"That's okay. Garrett did make it look as if I'd lost my marbles."

"Quincy, I cannot begin to tell you how much I am in your debt. I—"

"You don't have to thank me, ma'am," Quincy said.

"No, I do. When Queen Rozala lost her father and brother, I thought if tragedy like that touched my family, it would be me who was the target. I knew Bea would be distraught, but she would have Teddy, and Theo, to get her through. But I never, ever thought Bea would be the target. If she had died—" Tears came to the stoic Queen's eyes.

Quincy had never seen such emotion from George before. "Ma'am—"

"No," George said. "I have to finish. If I lost Bea, my world would fall into tatters. I really don't know how I would go on. She's my strength, you see."

George looked down at her own clasped hands for a second and said, "Nobody knows this, Quincy. Not even my brother Theo. When my father died, and I was thrust into this life of service, I fell apart inside. I would turn up to events, put on my best smile, and gulp down my pain over my father's death, and the enormity of inheriting the crown far too early. I thought I'd have years and years before duty called."

In all the years she had known George, she had never heard her talk about her emotions before. Maybe she wasn't the only officer who struggled.

George continued, "I would gulp it down so much that I started to have panic attacks. When Bea met me, she recognized them and helped me through them. For some reason I trusted her to see my vulnerability. She's my rock and keeps me balanced, so that when I go out into the world, I can appear to be strong and together. Bea is my strength, and without her I—Well, you can imagine."

"That's why you asked for me, didn't you?" Quincy said. "You knew what demons I was fighting and you understood them."

George clasped her hand. "We military people don't talk as much as we probably should, but I think we all understand each other's demons. I only wish I hadn't bowed to pressure and made you stay away from the park. If you hadn't gotten there, I would have been lost."

"Don't think about that. I got there. I wasn't going to let anyone take Queen Beatrice away from you. You gave me a second chance, George. I was facing losing my commission. You knew that, but you gave me this chance, and I met someone who has made me want to share my feelings and my life for the first time."

George smiled and sat forward. "My wife the matchmaker was right."

"What?" Quincy was confused.

George sat back and crossed her legs. "Bea thought she saw a spark of something between you and engineered the rooms, and generally tried to play cupid."

Quincy shook her head and smiled. She could see it all now. The rooms suddenly next to each other, the encouragement at every turn.

"Please thank the Queen Consort for me," Quincy said.

"You can tell her yourself. She'll be along to see you this evening. But one thing, Captain," George said seriously.

Quincy furrowed her brows. "What?"

"Wounded or not, I'll kick your backside from here to Buck House, if you let what's in here"—George pointed to her head—"interfere with what's in here." She then pointed at Quincy's chest. "That young woman has only left this hospital to go back to the hotel to shower and change. She's slept here and hardly eaten, and she took some very interesting calls from the admiral, all because she loves you."

Quincy couldn't quite believe she was worthy of such love and dedication. God only knew what the admiral thought of Holly. They would be like matter and antimatter.

The Queen stood and fastened her suit jacket. "I don't know what goes on between you and Holly when you're alone, Quincy, but I suspect she is the only one you let see the pain, the uncertainty, the fear, just as I do Bea. She deserves all of you."

Quincy smiled. "Don't worry. I'm sick of running from my feelings and my demons. Besides, my demons have no chance against Holly. She'd scare them to death."

George laughed. "Very true." She patted her shoulder and said, "Thank you again for risking your life and going through all this pain for my wife."

"It's my honour to, Your Majesty," Quincy said with absolute sincerity.

"You can be sure I'm going to thank you in a very special way."

Quincy's heart sank. "You know I don't like fuss, ma'am."

George just winked at her and said, "Bea will be in later."

CHAPTER TWENTY-FIVE

Holly waved off Lali and Cammy at the front door to her building and shut the door. Two months of rehabilitation in America were behind Quincy and Holly, and they could finally return home to Britain. Cammy and Lali volunteered to pick them up from the airport and help Quin get back to Holly's flat with the bags and suitcases. Quin was better, but she was still in recovery and banned from lifting anything heavy, much to her annoyance.

They had agreed that while she was recovering, Quincy would stay at Holly's flat so she could look after her, and then they would talk about what came next in their relationship. That was what Holly was worried about, as she shut the door and walked back up the stairs to her flat.

"What now?" Holly sighed.

She and Quin weren't a normal couple. They hadn't dated or done any of the normal things new couples would do. They were thrown together in the royal court, fell in love, and then Quincy was nearly taken from her by the bullets of a jealous, vicious ex-marine.

Holly had been through hell waiting to see if Quincy would survive, then had lived every day at the hospital while she was rehabilitated. Would things be different here at home? Would what they shared in the bubble of the royal court work in their real everyday lives? Holly wanted it to more than anything, but Quincy had never been in a relationship, and she had been really quiet on the plane trip home. Maybe this would all be too much for her?

Holly trudged upstairs to the front door of her flat. She'd left Quincy in her small kitchen and when she walked in, she found Quincy leaning against the countertop, rubbing her side.

"Are you in pain? You're meant to be sitting down," Holly said.

"I'm fine and I'm sick of sitting down," Quincy said.

There was an atmosphere between them, and Holly couldn't work it out. She had put up with a few bad tempers while she helped Quincy with her rehab at the hospital, but this felt different.

She doesn't want to be here.

"Sit down and I'll put the kettle on," Holly said.

"Holly—"

"Just please sit," Holly said a little sharply.

Holly went to make the tea. She heard Quincy sigh and do as she was told.

"It'll be time for your pain medication in ten minutes. I'll get you tea, then your meds, then—"

"Holly, you're fussing," Quincy said calmly.

"I'm not." Holly slammed the teacup down.

Quincy rubbed her forehead. She didn't want to be constantly reminded of her injuries. She wanted to be the strong woman Holly had fallen in love with. That was if Holly still loved her. In the few days before they'd left the hospital and on the journey home, Holly had been different. She had been taking care of her perfectly, but her kisses had been chaste and not like a lover's.

Maybe Holly had changed her mind? If the tension in the kitchen was anything to go by, then there was something wrong, and Quincy wanted to know what but was terrified of the answer.

"Holly? Please come and sit down. I want to talk to you."

Holly came and flopped down in the chair. "What?"

"Normally it's you who wants to talk. There's something wrong, and I want to know what," Quincy said.

Holly nervously tapped her fingers on the table.

"Do you not want me here?" Quincy said.

Holly looked up at her quickly. "Are you insane? I love you and I've just found you. Of course I do."

Quincy reached across the table and took her hand. "What is it, then?"

Holly sighed. "I'm worried this isn't what *you* want. I mean, we've never been domestic before. How do you know you won't feel suffocated? This is just a small one-bedroom rented flat, and you've lived in barracks all your life."

Quincy let out a sigh of relief. All the dreams and plans she had made before leaving the States could still come true.

She took a breath and remembered what Queen Georgina had said. Holly had stood by her and deserved all of her.

"Holly, I've never had a home. I went from boarding school to the marines, then to my regiment. Now I've found you, a love I never thought I'd have, and I don't want to miss a thing."

"What are you saying?" Holly asked.

"I'd like to have a home with you. I'd like us to buy a house together. A place we can make a home."

"Really?" Holly jumped up in shock and excitement and rushed over and sat on her lap. "You would?"

Quincy felt her side ache but wasn't going to let Holly know. She wrapped her arms around her. "Yes, I want that more than anything," Quincy said.

Holly kissed her with passion for the first time in months and lit a fire that had been smouldering in her since she'd recovered.

Holly pulled back and looked at her quizzically. "Why were you so tense on our way home then?"

"That wasn't tense, just nervous maybe about something else," Quincy said.

Holly screwed up her face. "What?"

"Well, I want to live with you, but as you always say I follow rules and regulations and I'm old-fashioned. Reach into my pocket."

"What? Why?" Holly asked.

"Just follow one order in your whole life, Ms. Weaver."

Holly reached into her pocket and pulled out a ring box. Her eyes went wide.

Quincy opened the box and said, "If I'm living with you, I want you to be my wife. No half measures."

Holly just stared at the ring with a stunned look on her face. "When? When did you get this?"

"Remember the day before we left America? I had a security briefing to go to? I decided I wanted to ask you to marry me the day I woke up in the hospital. My friend Jacob told me to make a life, and I finally want to do it with you."

Quincy took the ring out of the box and held it to Holly's finger. "Will you marry me and make a home with me, Ms. Weaver?"

"Yes!" Holly shouted.

Quincy pushed on the ring and Holly gave her kisses all over her face. Quincy kissed her lips and deepened it, slipping her tongue into Holly's mouth and tasting her. She pushed underneath Holly's top and caressed her sides.

Holly pulled away and rested her forehead against Quincy's. "Don't touch me like that when we can't do anything about it."

"Do you realize how long it's been since I've touched you like this?" Quincy said.

"Two months, six days, and eight hours, give or take," Holly joked.

"I'm sick of waiting. I want you." Quincy stood up with Holly in her arms. She felt a sharp pain in her side but said nothing.

"Put me down." Holly struggled in her arms. "The doctor said you're not to carry anything heavy—you're on medical leave."

"I don't care. I'm carrying you to bed, and I'm going to make love to you," Quincy said.

Holly gave in, wrapped her arms around Quincy's neck, and kissed her. Quincy carried her into the hall and said, "Which door?"

"The one at the end," Holly replied through her kisses.

Quincy carried her to the door and pushed it open with her foot. Once they were through, Quincy put Holly down and shrugged off her suit jacket. Holly busily pulled at her tie.

"I've missed this so much with you," Holly said.

Quincy looked around the bedroom. It was beautifully decorated, as she would have expected from Holly. Then something on the wall caught her eye. It was a moving poster image of Story St. John.

Holly followed her gaze and said, "Uh…that's just a silly thing. I'll take it down. I've got a real action hero now. You're my hero and all I need."

Quincy just smiled. "I know. Don't worry, we'll move her later. You love me and that's all that matters."

Holly pulled off Quincy's shirt and eased the compression vest up her body. Holly must have seen the grimace on her face because after Quincy was naked from the waist up, Holly said, "Are you sure this is a good idea, Quin?"

Quincy caressed Holly's face. "I lay in that hospital bed praying for the day I was well enough to touch you again. You stayed by my bed and my side when others would have run."

Holly ran her hand over the new scars that joined her burns, caused by the bullets meant for Queen Beatrice. "Of course I did, I love you. You're the bravest, most noble person I've ever met."

"I love you, Holly, and I need to show you how much," Quincy said.

Holly slowly took off her top and her bra, and kicked off her jeans, all while keeping her gaze on Quincy.

"Show me then, Captain," Holly said.

Quincy's mouth watered at the sight of Holly's plump breasts, and the fire that had been lit in the kitchen roared into life. She stepped forward and traced the back of her hand between Holly's breasts.

Holly gasped and her nipples hardened. Quincy's confidence was buoyed by the fact that she could have this effect on her lover. She cupped one of Holly's breasts and kissed her. They both walked back as they kissed until Holly's legs hit the bed.

Holly sat down and immediately started undoing Quincy's belt buckle. "Take these off."

Quincy helped her and shrugged off her trousers and jockey shorts. Holly put her hands on Quincy's hips and leaned her head against her stomach.

"I thought I had lost you, Stompy. I've never been so scared," Holly said.

Quincy lifted her head. "I'm not leaving you now I've got you. I've got a life to live."

Holly lay back on the bed and extended her hand to Quincy. "Show me."

Quincy lay on top of Holly and started kissing her. Her thigh slipped between Holly's legs and found her sex hot and wet.

Holly moaned and Quincy felt better than she had in months. Giving Holly all of her gave Quincy strength, mentally and physically. She pulled her lips away and ran the tip of her tongue around Holly's, making her moan.

Quincy's sex was pulsing and she wanted to come so badly, but more than that, she wanted to watch Holly come. She had dreamt about that all the time she was laid up in the hospital. The thought of Holly's love and what they had together kept her going.

Quincy moved her hand down and cupped her lover's hot sex. She looked deeply into Holly's eyes and spoke from her heart, showing the emotions that she never thought she'd be brave enough to show. "I never knew touching someone could feel like this."

Holly traced her fingers across Quincy's face as if taking in every part of her. "No one has ever touched me like you."

Quincy slipped her fingers onto Holly's clit and circled around it, teasing and making her lover's hips buck.

"Inside, Quin. I want to come with you inside me," Holly moaned.

Quincy didn't hesitate. She eased two fingers inside Holly, loving the feeling of the warmth she found there.

"You're so wet." Quincy groaned. Her own sex was pounding, demanding she thrust into Holly and seek the release she'd been craving, but she concentrated on the pleasure on Holly's face.

Quincy's slow thrust was punctuated by her thumb grazing Holly's clit, making Holly grasp at her hair.

"Faster, baby," Holly pleaded.

Quincy thrust deeper and harder and couldn't help but kiss and suck Holly's breasts as she did. She heard Holly's moans become louder and felt the walls of her sex start to flutter, so she raised herself up so she could watch every moment of Holly's pleasure.

"Come for me, Holls. I want to watch you."

Holly put her hands around Quincy's neck and, as she came, dug her nails into her neck. Quincy didn't care. She kept her eyes on Holly as her orgasm waved over her, locking Quincy's fingers tightly inside her.

"Jesus!" Holly said as she tried to get her breath back.

Quincy's heart was so full that she felt it might burst. "You are so beautiful."

Holly pulled her head down and kissed her repeatedly. "I love you, baby. That was so worth waiting two months, six days, and eight hours."

"It was worth waiting a lifetime. I love you."

Holly rolled Quincy over so she was on top, then placed her hand on Quincy's scarred heart. "Thank you for trusting me with your heart. You never need to worry about showing me what's in here. You'll always be safe with me."

Quincy reached up and gently touched Holly's chest. "You are the first woman in my heart, and the first to touch me, and there'll be no other."

"I'm glad you waited on me to show you the ways of love." Holly smiled at her and winked. "We've got so much to explore."

"I can't wait." Quincy chuckled.

Holly gave her a saucy smile. "I bet you'd love to use intelliflesh."

Quincy's eyes went wide, and her heart and sex started to thud. "You mean the—"

"Oh yes, I do, baby. Let me show you what I'd do if you had one on." Holly crawled down her body.

The feel of Holly's hair brushing between her legs was almost enough to make her come. Holly opened her up then met her eyes with a grin.

"Imagine you've got it on."

The moment Holly sucked Quincy's clit into her mouth, Quincy thought she would come immediately. She raised herself up on her elbows and imagined what Holly had said, while enjoying every moment of the sensation and watching her head bob up and down.

She knew she wouldn't last long, and she didn't. Quincy put her hand on Holly's head and threaded her fingers through her hair. She felt her orgasm surge over her body and her heart, washing away any last darkness, scars, and doubts from her soul.

"Fuck. Holly, Holly."

Holly climbed up her body and held her as she shook, cooing and reassuring her. "It's okay, baby. I love you."

Quincy opened her eyes and took Holly's hand. She kissed the engagement ring on her finger that looked like it was always meant to be there. "You are the dazzling light that led me out of the darkness, Holls. I will never stop loving and worshiping you."

Holly smiled and lowered her lips to inches from hers. "And I'm never going to let the darkness take hold of you again. It's got no chance against me. I love you, Stompy."

EPILOGUE

Windsor Castle was packed with crowds which lined the route from Windsor to St. George's Chapel and the streets beyond. The royal bands played, and the Household Cavalry lined the streets, waiting for the spectacle of the Order of the Garter ceremony. Two TV presenters stood in front of the camera and spoke to the people watching at home.

What a fabulous atmosphere we have on this warm August day at Windsor for this year's Order of the Garter. The normally large crowd has swelled this year, because we are to watch the investiture of a special new member. A hero who bravely saved our beloved Queen Consort from certain death. Captain Quincy, a winner of the Victoria Cross for gallantry, will be only the second person in history to be honoured with a VC and be made a Knight of the Garter, and the first woman, of course. Steven, can you tell us about the Order and what will happen today?

A cheer went up from the crowds as some cars processed into Windsor Castle, carrying some of the royal family.

Yes, of course, Crispin. The Order of the Garter is the oldest and most senior order of chivalry in the United Kingdom, given to those who have given extraordinary service to the nation, and is the gift of the monarch. It was founded by King Edward III who was inspired by the tales of King Arthur and the round table to create his own in 1348. It had always been a way for the monarch to honour politicians and aristocrats at the top of society, until Queen Georgina's grandfather took the throne.

He modernized the Order and made it an honour for every part of society, for people who have bravely helped their nation in time of need. It is normally celebrated in June, but the Queen postponed it, so the hero of the hour, Captain Adelaide Quincy, VC, would be recovered enough from her injuries. Buckingham Palace has said that the Queen wishes the nation to give thanks to the bravest woman she has ever met, and Captain Quincy will be taking part in the carriage procession afterwards, normally reserved for the royal members of the Order. It will give the crowds attending this historic ceremony a chance to thank the woman whose name has not been off the front pages and everyone's lips since the shooting. I understand Captain Quincy is not someone who seeks the limelight, but she is a hero. Back to you, Crispin.

❖

Holly watched with amusement as Quincy fidgeted with her green and yellow Royal Marine Commando tie. No more grey for Captain Quincy.

Quin was well used to ceremony, but being at the centre of it didn't sit well with her.

They were standing outside the door of the Windsor throne room, waiting for the Garter investiture to begin. Holly batted Quincy's hands away and straightened the tie herself.

"It's sitting perfectly. Calm down, okay? Everything will be fine."

Quincy sighed. "This isn't me, Holly. I hate being the centre of attention. It would be bad enough going through this ceremony normally, but George has made it all about me, this hero's parade. The world is watching."

Holly knew full well how anxious Quincy had been, so tense that she'd spent much of last night trying to keep her mind off it.

"George wants to thank you on behalf of the nation. She was so scared after the shooting. While you were unconscious in the hospital, she went through a difficult time, and Bea had to help her through it. The thought of Bea being taken away from her really terrified her, and she has you to thank for saving her. Let her honour you in the spirit it's intended."

Quincy let out a breath. "You're right. I just can't wait to get this over and done with, and then we can go home and paint some soldiers and set up our battlefield."

Since buying a new home and moving in together, Holly had surprised Quincy by having a whole room decorated and set up for her model building. She was forever disappearing into her battle room, as she called it. Quincy was so happy with them living together. Holly was pleased to have given Quincy her first real home.

Holly leaned in and whispered in Quincy's ear, "Or I could paint a marine with body paint and lick it off?"

Quincy shivered. "I like that idea."

"Well then, no more Captain Stompy," Holly said then looked over Quincy's shoulder. "Heads-up, Admiral on deck."

Quincy turned around and saw her mother walking towards her in full dress uniform. She saluted immediately. "Thank you for coming, Admiral," Quincy said.

Ophelia gave Quincy a peck on each cheek. "Well done, Addie. I have never been prouder of you. A Quincy has never been made Knight of the Garter, and a VC too. You've exceeded all expectations. Keep up the good work."

That was as emotional as her mother could be. It was her way, and she was happy that she had made her mother proud, despite all their problems.

Admiral Quincy turned to Holly and offered her hand. "Miss Weaver, I hear you are to become a Quincy soon." She held Holly's hand and looked at the diamond engagement ring there.

"Yes, that's right," Holly said.

The admiral and Holly had met quite a few times now, as Quincy recovered in the hospital. They would never be best of friends, but Ophelia had gained a grudging respect for how much Holly loved her daughter.

Captain Cameron, Lali, and Clay appeared at their side. Cammy said, "We're on parade, Quincy. Their Majesties are here."

Clay shook Quincy's hand. "It's an honour to be your friend, ma'am. Good luck."

"Thank you. I'll need it," Quincy replied.

All the guests filed in to take their seats at the back of the room. Holly hung back for one last kiss. She framed Quincy's face in her hands and said, "I love you."

She kissed her and Quincy replied in panic, "I love you, but there are cameras in there. I'm going to be on every news channel."

"Just think of me painting a marine commando in body paint," Holly said teasingly.

"You promise?"

The throne room in Windsor Castle was a long ornate chamber, with portraits of great kings and queens of the past looking down upon it. At the front was a raised platform with a throne on top. The knights and ladies sat along each side of the room, in their rich navy cloaks embossed in gold, the garter badge embroidered on the right side.

At the back of the room, next to the doors, were seats for guests, and that was where Holly and her friends were. Next to Holly sat the admiral. She leaned over and said, "Addie is as content and calm as I have ever known her. I think I have you to thank for that."

"I try my best. I love her." That was as good a compliment as she would ever get from the admiral.

"I hope she finds happiness like I never could," Admiral Quincy said.

Holly imagined the admiral never looked for happiness.

The doors of the throne room opened, and everyone stood as Queen Georgina and Queen Beatrice walked in procession behind the Black Rod and the Garter King of Arms.

George and Bea wore the same navy cloak and navy velvet caps with white feathers as the others. Two young pages, one boy and one girl, wearing gold medieval livery, held their trains as they walked. As George passed she glanced at Holly and winked.

This honour was a gift from George personally, and not the government. Bo Dixon was not part of the day, although she would have loved the publicity.

George was proud that she could give this to her friend. There was no greater thing than to sacrifice yourself for your Queen, and George understood the bravery that took. Twice in Quincy's life she had run into danger, rather than run away, and she deserved more honour than George could ever give her.

George had planned out the day herself, with the help of her private secretary, Bastian, and made changes to make it a more personal affair. She'd postponed the traditional luncheon to the end of the day, so they could get right out there amongst the people and have a longer procession. George wanted the country to praise Captain Quincy the hero.

When George reached the throne platform, she helped Bea into a chair at the side and ascended to the throne. Then she stood and said, "Garter and Black Rod, pray summon the Companion Elect."

The doors opened and the Black Rod and the Garter King of Arms led Captain Quincy in, flanked by one other knight, Prince Theo, and Lady Musgrove, a lady of the Order. It was tradition that the new knight be helped by two members of their choice.

As they approached, the Queen said, "Pray be seated."

Everyone sat except Quincy and her helpers. George smiled at Quincy, whom she could see was tense.

The girl page brought over the black garter with gold lettering and attached it around Quincy's leg. This was the beginning of dressing the new knight, while the bishop read the historical passage that went with the ceremony.

Then the Queen took the blue sash of the garter and placed it over Quincy's left shoulder, and it was fastened by Theo. Next the page brought her a silver badge on a red velvet cushion, the Garter Star. She took it and pinned it onto Quincy's jacket.

The navy blue garter mantle was then brought over, and with the help of Theo and Lady Musgrave, George draped it over Quincy's shoulders.

Finally the long, gold collar was brought over on a cushion. George lifted the thick chain and laid it over Quincy's shoulders. George whispered, "Nearly done, Captain."

George shook hands with Quincy and smiled. "My greatest thanks for your bravery, Quincy. Now let's go and let the nation say thank you."

Quincy let out a breath, smiled, and then bowed. "Thank you, ma'am."

❖

After a service of thanksgiving, the royal family and Quincy descended the steps of St. George's chapel. They were greeted by their friends, and Cammy shook her hand and pulled her into a brief hug.

"Congratulations, Garter Knight."

"Thank you. Just a few weeks and you'll be back here yourself for your wedding," Quincy said smiling.

Cammy turned and winked at Lali. "Can't wait."

Neither could Quincy, because just a few months after Cammy and Lali's wedding, she and Holly would be getting married, and it couldn't come quick enough for her.

Quincy and Holly were led by the Queen and her consort down into the carriages. Quincy and Holly were given the honour of riding with Queen Georgina and Queen Beatrice.

The crowds were cheering, waving flags, and holding up signs of thanks.

Holly was so proud of Quincy. She was the last person who would ask for this, and that was what made Captain Quincy special, and a true hero. The carriage set off along the route, and Holly took Quincy's hand.

"Remember to smile, baby," Holly said.

"And wave," Bea added.

Holly gave her a nudge and she started to wave.

"This is all for you, Quincy," George said.

Quincy squeezed Holly's hand. "It's all a bit overwhelming, but at least I'll have something interesting to talk to people about when I meet them. I think this is the most exciting thing about me."

"Exciting is overrated." Holly looked over at her friend Bea. "A wise woman once told me, that sometimes the most quiet, unassuming people are the ones who will love you the fiercest." Quincy kissed her and the crowd cheered. "I love you, Stompy."

"And I love you."

About the Author

Jenny Frame is from the small town of Motherwell in Scotland, where she lives with her partner, Lou, and their well-loved and very spoiled dog.

She has a diverse range of qualifications, including a BA in public management and a diploma in acting and performance. Nowadays, she likes to put her creative energies into writing rather than treading the boards.

When not writing or reading, Jenny loves cheering on her local football team, cooking, and spending time with her family.

Jenny can be contacted at www.jennyframe.com.

Books Available from Bold Strokes Books

Emily's Art and Soul by Joy Argento. When Emily meets Andi Marino she thinks she's found a new best friend but Emily doesn't know that Andi is fast falling in love with her. Caught up in exploring her sexuality, will Emily see the only woman she needs is right in front of her? (978-1-63555-355-0)

Escape to Pleasure: Lesbian Travel Erotica edited by Sandy Lowe and Victoria Villasenor. Join these award-winning authors as they explore the sensual side of erotic lesbian travel. (978-1-63555-339-0)

Music City Dreamers by Robyn Nyx. Music can bring lovers together. In Music City, it can tear them apart. (978-1-63555-207-2)

Ordinary is Perfect by D. Jackson Leigh. Atlanta marketing superstar Autumn Swan's life derails when she inherits a country home, a child, and a very interesting neighbor. (978-1-63555-280-5)

Royal Court by Jenny Frame. When royal dresser Holly Weaver's passionate personality begins to melt Royal Marine Captain Quincy's icy heart, will Holly be ready for what she exposes beneath? (978-1-63555-290-4)

Strings Attached by Holly Stratimore. Success. Riches. Music. Passion. It's a life most can only dream of, but stardom comes at a cost. (978-1-63555-347-5)

The Ashford Place by Jean Copeland. When Isabelle Ashford inherits an old house in small-town Connecticut, family secrets, a shocking discovery, and an unexpected romance complicate her plan for a fast profit and a temporary stay. (978-1-63555-316-1)

Treason by Gun Brooke. Zoem Malderyn's existence is a deadly threat to everyone on Gemocon and Commander Neenja KahSandra must find a way to save the woman she loves from having to commit the ultimate sacrifice. (978-1-63555-244-7)

A Wish Upon a Star by Jeannie Levig. Erica Cooper has learned to depend on only herself, but when her new neighbor, Leslie Raymond, befriends Erica's special needs daughter, the walls protecting her heart threaten to crumble. (978-1-63555-274-4)

Answering the Call by Ali Vali. Detective Sept Savoie returns to the streets of New Orleans, as do the dead bodies from ritualistic killings, and she does everything in her power to bring them to justice while trying to keep her partner, Keegan Blanchard, safe. (978-1-63555-050-4)

Breaking Down Her Walls by Erin Zak. Could a love worth staying for be the key to breaking down Julia Finch's walls? (978-1-63555-369-7)

Exit Plans for Teenage Freaks by 'Nathan Burgoine. Cole always has a plan—especially for escaping his small-town reputation as "that kid who was kidnapped when he was four"—but when he teleports to a museum, it's time to face facts: it's possible he's a total freak after all. (978-1-63555-098-6)

Friends Without Benefits by Dena Blake. When Dex Putman gets the woman she thought she always wanted, she soon wonders if it's really love after all. (978-1-63555-349-9)

Invalid Evidence by Stevie Mikayne. Private Investigator Jil Kidd is called away to investigate a possible killer whale, just when her partner Jess needs her most. (978-1-63555-307-9)

Pursuit of Happiness by Carsen Taite. When attorney Stevie Palmer's client reveals a scandal that could derail Senator Meredith Mitchell's presidential bid, their chance at love may be collateral damage. (978-1-63555-044-3)

Seascape by Karis Walsh. Marine biologist Tess Hansen returns to Washington's isolated northern coast where she struggles to adjust to small-town living while courting an endowment for her orca research center from Brittany James. (978-1-63555-079-5)

Second in Command by VK Powell. Jazz Perry's life is disrupted and her career jeopardized when she becomes personally involved with the case of an abandoned child and the child's competent but strict social worker, Emory Blake. (978-1-63555-185-3)

Taking Chances by Erin McKenzie. When Valerie Cruz and Paige Wellington clash over what's in the best interest of the children in Valerie's care, the children may be the ones who teach them it's worth taking chances for love. (978-1-63555-209-6)

All of Me by Emily Smith. When chief surgical resident Galen Burgess meets her new intern, Rowan Duncan, she may finally discover that doing what you've always done will only give you what you've always had. (978-1-63555-321-5)

As the Crow Flies by Karen F. Williams. Romance seems to be blooming all around, but problems arise when a restless ghost emerges from the ether to roam the dark corners of this haunting tale. (978-1-63555-285-0)

Both Ways by Ileandra Young. SPEAR agent Danika Karson races to protect the city from a supernatural threat and must rely on the woman she's trained to despise: Rayne, an achingly beautiful vampire. (978-1-63555-298-0)

Calendar Girl by Georgia Beers. Forced to work together, Addison Fairchild and Kate Cooper discover that opposites really do attract. (978-1-63555-333-8)

Lovebirds by Lisa Moreau. Two women from different worlds collide in a small California mountain town, each with a mission that doesn't include falling in love. (978-1-63555-213-3)

Media Darling by Fiona Riley. Can Hollywood bad girl Emerson and reluctant celebrity gossip reporter Hayley work together to make each other's dreams come true? Or will Emerson's secrets ruin not one career, but two? (978-1-63555-278-2)

Stroke of Fate by Renee Roman. Can Sean Moore live up to her reputation and save Jade Rivers from the stalker determined to end Jade's career and, ultimately, her life? (978-1-63555-62-4)

The Rise of the Resistance by Jackie D. The soul of America has been lost for almost a century. A few people may be the difference between a phoenix rising to save the masses or permanent destruction. (978-1-63555-259-1)

The Sex Therapist Next Door by Meghan O'Brien. At the intersection of sex and intimacy, anything is possible. Even love. (978-1-63555-296-6)

Unexpected Lightning by Cass Sellars. Lightning strikes once more when Sydney and Parker fight a dangerous stranger who threatens the peace they both desperately want. (978-1-63555-276-8)

Unforgettable by Elle Spencer. When one night changes a lifetime… Two romance novellas from best-selling author Elle Spencer. (978-1-63555-429-8)

Against All Odds by Kris Bryant, Maggie Cummings, M. Ullrich. Peyton and Tory escaped death once, but will they survive when Bradley's determined to make his kill rate one hundred percent? (978-1-63555-193-8)

Autumn's Light by Aurora Rey. Casual hookups aren't supposed to include romantic dinners and meeting the family. Can Mat Pero see beyond the heartbreak that led her to keep her worlds so separate, and will Graham Connor be waiting if she does? (978-1-63555-272-0)

Breaking the Rules by Larkin Rose. When Virginia and Carmen are thrown together by an embarrassing mistake they find out their stubborn determination isn't so heroic after all. (978-1-63555-261-4)

Broad Awakening by Mickey Brent. In the sequel to *Underwater Vibes*, Hélène and Sylvie find ruts in their road to eternal bliss. (978-1-63555-270-6)

Broken Vows by MJ Williamz. Sister Mary Margaret must reconcile her divided heart or risk losing a love that just might be heaven sent. (978-1-63555-022-1)

Flesh and Gold by Ann Aptaker. Havana, 1952, where art thief and smuggler Cantor Gold dodges gangland bullets and mobsters' schemes while she searches Havana' s steamy Red Light district for her kidnapped love. (978-1-63555-153-2)

Isle of Broken Years by Jane Fletcher. Spanish noblewoman Catalina de Valasco is in peril, even before the pirates holding her for ransom sail into seas destined to become known as the Bermuda Triangle. (978-1-63555-175-4)

Love Like This by Melissa Brayden. Hadley Cooper and Spencer Adair set out to take the fashion world by storm. If only they knew their hearts were about to be taken. (978-1-63555-018-4)

Secrets On the Clock by Nicole Disney. Jenna and Danielle love their jobs helping endangered children, but that might not be enough to stop them from breaking the rules by falling in love. (978-1-63555-292-8)

Unexpected Partners by Michelle Larkin. Dr. Chloe Maddox tries desperately to deny her attraction for Detective Dana Blake as they flee from a serial killer who's hunting them both. (978-1-63555-203-4)

A Fighting Chance by T. L. Hayes. Will Lou be able to come to terms with her past to give love a fighting chance? (978-1-63555-257-7)

Chosen by Brey Willows. When the choice is adapt or die, can love save us all? (978-1-63555-110-5)

Death Checks In by David S. Pederson. Despite Heath's promises to Alan to not get involved, Heath can't resist investigating a shopkeeper's murder in Chicago, which dashes their plans for a romantic weekend getaway. (978-1-63555-329-1)

Gnarled Hollow by Charlotte Greene. After they are invited to study a secluded nineteenth-century estate, a former English professor and a group of historians discover that they will have to fight against the unknown if they have any hope of staying alive. (978-1-63555-235-5)

Jacob's Grace by C.P. Rowlands. Captain Tag Becket wants to keep her head down and her past behind her, but her feelings for AJ's second-in-command, Grace Fields, makes keeping secrets next to impossible. (978-1-63555-187-7)

On the Fly by PJ Trebelhorn. Hockey player Courtney Abbott is content with her solitary life until visiting concert violinist Lana Caruso makes her second-guess everything she always thought she wanted. (978-1-63555-255-3)

Passionate Rivals by Radclyffe. Professional rivalry and long-simmering passions create a combustible combination when Emmett McCabe and Sydney Stevens are forced to work together, especially when past attractions won't stay buried. (978-1-63555-231-7)

Proxima Five by Missouri Vaun. When geologist Leah Warren crash-lands on a preindustrial planet and is claimed by its tyrant, Tiago, will clan warrior Keegan's love for Leah give her the strength to defeat him? (978-1-63555-122-8)

Racing Hearts by Dena Blake. When you cross a hot-tempered race car mechanic with a reckless cop, the result can only be spontaneous combustion. (978-1-63555-251-5)

Shadowboxer by Jessica L. Webb. Jordan McAddie is prepared to keep her street kids safe from a dangerous underground protest group, but she isn't prepared for her first love to walk back into her life. (978-1-63555-267-6)

The Tattered Lands by Barbara Ann Wright. As Vandra and Lilani strive to make peace, they slowly fall in love. With mistrust and murder surrounding them, only their faith in each other can keep their plan to save the world from falling apart. (978-1-63555-108-2)